Mys.
DRU

Drummond, John Keith.

'Tis the season to be dying

$16.95

DATE			

100931

HOPKINSVILLE - CHRISTIAN COUNTY PUBLIC LIBRARY
1101 BETHEL STREET
HOPKINSVILLE, KY 42240

JE 88   © THE BAKER & TAYLOR CO.

'TIS THE SEASON TO BE DYING

Also by John Keith Drummond:

Thy Sting Oh Death

'TIS THE SEASON TO BE DYING

JOHN KEITH DRUMMOND

ST. MARTIN'S PRESS
NEW YORK

'TIS THE SEASON TO BE DYING. Copyright © 1988 by John Keith Drummond. All rights reserved. Printed in the United States of America. No part of this book may be used or reproduced in any manner whatsoever without written permission except in the case of brief quotations embodied in critical articles or reviews. For information, address St. Martin's Press, 175 Fifth Avenue, New York, N.Y. 10010.

Design by Judy Stagnitto.

Library of Congress Cataloging in Publication Data

Drummond, John Keith.
   'Tis the season to be dying.
  "A Thomas Dunne Book."
  I. Title.
PS3554.R75T57 1988   813'.54   88-1007
ISBN 0-312-01901-7
First Edition

10 9 8 7 6 5 4 3 2 1

For
My Mother and My Father
Thank You

CAST OF CHARACTERS
(In Order of Appearance)

MISS MATILDA WORTHING—a pleasant, mild-mannered retired lady for whom the enormities of humankind hold few surprises.

MISS MARTHA SHAW—housemate and general factotum to Miss Worthing; a large, rather florid woman whose dithery manner covers a very practical mind.

REX DECASTRE, M.D.—he knows that something is going on, but he's a good enough friend to leave it to Miss Worthing.

JESSICA WU, R.N.—the General's nurse and a friend of the family's—she knows something's going on, too, but she's more concerned about the General.

SIBYL ANDERSON—the well-known writer of books on the spiritual life, and doyen of a troubled family.

EULALIA LADY FAIRGRIEF—Miss Worthing's redoubtable aunt, nearly a hundred, but with a mind at least as sharp as her tongue.

BILLY MCCLURE—a young would-be opera singer and acting "butler" to Lady Fairgrief.

LARRY WORTHING—Miss Worthing's nephew, author of spy thrillers and longtime friend of Benjamin Anderson.

BENJAMIN ANDERSON—the fat, eccentric, facetious, and famous character actor.

GENERAL HENRY ANDERSON, U.S. ARMY (RET.)—husband of Sibyl Anderson, father of Benjamin, Helen, and Cyrus, he enlivened his retirement by making pots of money and was then disgruntled to find that suddenly everybody wanted some.

CYRUS ANDERSON—a late flower in General and Mrs. Anderson's garden, strikingly handsome, an accomplished pianist, and difficult.

BOB E. TAYLOR—the Anderson's fleshy, dynamic, and bumptious son-in-law, a self-made man and rather too proud of it.

HELEN ANDERSON TAYLOR—middle child of the Andersons' and wife to Bob E. Taylor. Prickly, lazy, and selfish, she is yet a devoted wife and mother—if hardly the ideal daughter and sister.

MARY ELIZABETH TAYLOR—Helen and Bob E.'s adopted infant daughter and apparently the only one who could not possibly have committed murder.

ARLETTA TAYLOR—Bob E.'s mother, a boozy and blowsy, rather stupid person.

BETTE WANDA TAYLOR—Bob E.'s sister, angular, angry, and aggressively upwardly mobile.

'TIS THE SEASON TO BE DYING

PROLOGUE

i

Afterward, whenever Miss Worthing had occasion to recall the murder which pretty effectively blighted her Christmas that year, she would almost invariably preface her remarks with some rather feckless observation to the effect that, really, she should have been expecting something unpleasant.

"And all I simply mean by that," she would explain to anyone who might have arched a somewhat skeptical brow, "is that, all day long, things had been going just a mite *too* beautifully. And if that isn't always a sure sign that something truly nasty is heading down the pike, then I don't know what is."

It is, of course, true in point of fact that "something really nasty" was hurtling down said pike. Nevertheless, in spite of her profession of this hoary superstition, as Christmas Day faded into Christmas Night, all that Miss Matilda Worthing and Miss Martha Shaw—her housemate, general factotum, sometime business partner, and boon companion—were actually feeling was a rather dazed euphoria compounded of about equal parts of exhaustion and exultation.

The exhaustion was a perfectly natural concomitant of the fact that from twelve noon until a scant quarter hour before, the two women had run themselves thoroughly ragged hosting their annual Christmas Open House. The exultation was an equally natural result of the fact that, once again, it had been an unqualified triumph.

At least half the population of the Jolliston Valley had dutifully trooped through that slightly absurd Victorian pile on Jasmine Avenue in Jolliston proper, and there they had been plied with good food and better drink, been made to feel very merry indeed, then sent again upon their ways rejoicing, to leave behind them their hostesses with a house in appalling disarray, the aforementioned sense of benumbed triumph, and an immense distaste for Christmas carols and dirty glasses.

Oh yes. And the lingerers. The lingerers, who—like the poor—are with us always. It matters not a whit that the invitations may have read quite distinctly that from such-and-such an hour till thus-and-so, the following festivities will proceed . . . These irredeemable souls, by some intelligence privy solely to themselves and to the angels, simply know that such temporal restrictions could surely not have been intended for *them*!

Well, the invitations had read—and quite distinctly, too— from twelve until five, and, like well-brought-up little boys and girls, the vast preponderance of those forgathered that afternoon had long since hied themselves homeward to whatever delights the bosoms of their sundry families might afford.

Not so, alas, the lingerers.

At twenty minutes past the stated hour, a small knot of enduring conviviality was still tightly clustered about the piano in the living room caroling away in a chorus of voices the tunelessness of which was matched only by their boozy lugubriousness.

Miss Worthing was actively reminding herself that it was, after all, the birthday of the Prince of Peace and that charity and loving kindness in all things really ought to be the watchwords of the day, when a particularly piercing soprano voice leapt upward, like unto the shrill-engorged lark, into positively empyrean reaches in pursuit of a high B-flat—which had no difficulty whatever in eluding the pursuit.

A moment of awe-stricken silence ensued before the woman's fellow *dévots* erupted into a frenzy of applause, in response to which our diva dropped a rather wobbling curtsy, blushed a becomingly modest smile, and wondered aloud of the long-suffering pianist if she happened to know "O Holy Night" in the key of Z-sharp major?

At which point, across the room, Miss Worthing—who had been standing together with Miss Shaw eyeing the lot of them with something of the uncertain expression of a pair of poodles contemplating the rout of a wolf pack—took heart of grace, fixed her own formidable features into a most determined expression and, muttering a clipped "I think not!" marched directly toward the piano, having reached the conclusion that any further charity that Christmas was going to be of a firmish sort. Not only had that truly awesome note probably disintegrated every glass in the room to microscopic flinders—and most of them had been rented—but Miss Worthing was by no means prepared to stand by and listen to Adolphe Adam's masterpiece being savaged by these vocal villains. And never mind that M. Adam had himself been thoroughly sozzled in some Paris *boîte* the night he wrote the thing.

Miss Shaw, meanwhile, only muttered a fervent "Thank God," and, leaving Miss Worthing to her chore, turned her own attention to the melancholy business of surveying the wreckage . . .

It is a tribute to Miss Worthing's general abilities with people—as well as a measure of the thickness of her lingering guests' genial hides—that it was but a matter of minutes before they were all bundled up, out the front door, and trotting obediently down the path to the front gate, all still o'erflowing with the cheerful goodwill brought on by an overflow of good cheer.

Calling out one final Christmas greeting, and a very resolute "Good night, everyone," Miss Worthing closed the front door, bolted it, and—with a sharp little gesture—turned off the outside lights lest any chance passerby be suddenly struck with the notion that it only wanted his or her presence to round off Miss Shaw's or Miss Worthing's own holiday to a dazzling perfection.

And then, giving a sigh of the profoundest relief, she turned and leaned against the door, acutely disinclined ever to move again.

She was not a tall woman—the top of her head barely came even with the bottom of the small window let in the door—

but people, even those taller than she, frequently thought of her as tall. Partly it was because of her really admirable posture, that ramrod-straight carriage of one raised very much under the old book-on-the-head school of deportment. But it was also probably a bit due to the fact that all her life she had been a slender woman and, in spite of the intervening years, had retained something of the tranquil grace of a well-bred lady of the early-Georgian era wherein she had had her beginnings. It was true that in recent years there had been a perhaps inevitable tendency to spread a bit, but it was a tendency she had vowed an eternal vow to fight. And furthermore, she didn't think it was funny.

She was closer to eighty than seventy, but anyone mad enough to inquire after particulars was liable to find himself transfixed upon the spot with the sulfurous and mortal glare of the basilisk. Her eyes, of that dark China-blue found on classic willowware, were really quite hopeless and, as a consequence, she was compelled to wear spectacles the lenses of which were the thickness of the bottom of a bottle and which magnified her eyes into enormous and baleful orbs.

Her hair, though generously streaked throughout with iron-gray, was still largely and miraculously auburn, having gone the white one might expect at her age only over the temples. She had been, for a number of years, fully prepared to resent anyone's assuming that she "did something" to her hair, thus to have preserved its color. Then Miss Shaw had, rather carefully, one day pointed out that any such resentment was, on the whole, quite silly, since no one in her right mind would deliberately do to her hair what had happened to the hair of Matilda Worthing. For, with the years, it had gone wiry and, generally speaking, totally unmanageable, and no matter how she might wrangle a hairbrush through it, it still always seemed to wind up a regular mare's nest of sprung and willful curls.

But worst of all—at least to Miss Worthing's mind—far, far worse than that sheepdog fringe or even those goggle eyes, was her face. It was a face which, once upon a time in a transport of honesty, even she had been heard to describe as that of a dyspeptic Gorgon.

In her youth, she had been something of a comely lass. But

time, her profession, and, alas, genetics had all conspired, and the evanescent beauty of youth had definitely evanesced. She looked every one of her years and more.

She had spent forty years of her life as a professional court stenographer, a profession which requires, above all else, an ability to concentrate rather ferociously. But four decades and more of single-pointed concentration had not been kind, had left her, in fact, with a habitual expression—particularly in repose—which instantly called to mind wrathful teaching nuns, disinheriting maiden aunts, soured civil servants, and other viragoes of similar kidney. Of course there were, she candidly admitted, occasions when it was actually very useful to have a face which frightened dogs and little children. Nevertheless, those who knew her came very soon to see that behind that bulldog countenance was a quite mild-mannered, pleasant, and rather old-fashioned sort of a *lady*—who just happened also to have a mind like the proverbial steel trap and a clear-sighted, dispassionate, and rather exuberant appreciation for even the most outré manifestations of fallen human nature.

Presently—as she reclined there against the front door savoring both the glorious renewal of silence and a rather grim sense of accomplishment—she became aware of a soft noise emanating from the living room, the faint, melodious, and irregular clink of glass upon glass.

"Martha!" she called out. "What are you doing?"

"Nothing!" came the patently mendacious reply.

"Nothing, my foot!" muttered Miss Worthing and, summoning a spurt of energy from some forgotten depth, she pushed against the door, struggled to an upright position, stalked into the living room and came to halt just inside the doorway, arms akimbo. "I thought as much!" she said in sour satisfaction.

Miss Shaw—a round beer tray wholly inadequate to the task in hand—was wandering in a kind of shocked stupor amid the carnage of the living room, picking up the occasional dirty glass here and there.

"May I inquire as to what you are doing?" asked Miss Worthing in suspiciously honeyed tones as she advanced across the wasteland toward Miss Shaw.

"It's so awful," said Miss Shaw, pausing in her aimless wanderings like Israel at the foot of Sinai. "I just thought I'd clear a little."

The expression that flitted across Miss Worthing's face would have done justice to the feelings of Aaron when besought to fashion the calf of gold. What followed, however, was rather more like Moses laying down the law.

"You will do no such thing," she said succinctly and, relieving Miss Shaw of the tray, placed it—and none too gently either—on an occasional table. "We agreed that we've both gotten just too old to deal with this horror anymore. Which is, I would remind you, why we've paid that astronomical sum to the professional cleaners to come in tomorrow and do it all up for us. And I suggest that, considering what said astronomical sum is, they can bloody well start where the last glass landed. Right? Dear?"

Miss Shaw, in turn, chuckled richly. The worried expression vanished from her face and—quite visibly—she relaxed.

"All right, Mattie; all right," she said, still chuckling. "There's no need to take on so. If you can live with the place looking like a battlefield, so can I." And hoisting up her skirts, she kicked off a pair of high-heeled shoes and subsided with a small grunt of satisfaction to the restored full use of her feet. "Oh Lord, that feels good!"

"I really don't know how you can go about all day up on point like that," observed Miss Worthing.

It was certainly true that the two women were almost a classic study in contrasts.

Miss Worthing had, quite typically, gotten herself up for the party in a severely tailored navy suit, an ecru silk blouse, and good, solid, and sensible Cuban-heeled slippers, with her only jewel a chaste little circle pin in diamonds and white gold affixed to the left lapel of her suit.

Miss Shaw, on the other hand, had arrayed herself—and it is the only adequate word for it—in a vast concoction she had made herself in crimson velvet, which partook partly of a muumuu and partly of a tent, and which covered her from collarbone to the floor and from shoulder to the elbow. Like many large women—and Miss Shaw was very definitely large, a head and a half taller than Miss Worthing and ever, *ever,* so much bigger—she had a rather perverse taste for the tiniest of jewels, of which she had, nevertheless, managed to get quite a bit on—a choker of seed pearls, and earrings, bracelets, rings, all confected of infinitesimal fragments of rubies, garnets, and diamonds.

Her baby-fine hair was a perpetually billowing cloud of the snowiest lawn, and ironically—an irony, incidentally, completely lost on Miss Worthing—although Miss Worthing's senior, she yet managed to look appreciably her junior.

Miss Shaw had also been an excellent court reporter in her day. For her, however, the end result of all that concentration had been a round, smooth, and rather blank expression. Her skin was still quite remarkably free of wrinkles and lines—which had as much to do with her amplitude as anything else—and it still had all the luminous clarity of a very ripe Babcock peach. Her eyes, the light blue of a summer sky, were large, prominent, and really rather startling, which, combined with that round and placid countenance, contrived to lend her a look of almost blithering idiocy.

She was, however, no one's fool. Though by no means an intellectual woman, she was yet possessed of a clear and practical intelligence which, like Miss Worthing's, encompassed no illusions whatever about people.

"I like the view up there," she responded crushingly to Miss Worthing's somewhat snide remark about her shoes and, turning about, began to waddle toward a low credenza. "How 'bout a drink?" she called back over her shoulder.

In reply to which Miss Worthing herself rather unexpectedly giggled and literally dropped into a favorite easy chair. "Oh, Martha!" she said fervently. "The true answer to a maiden's prayer!"

Presently, Miss Shaw ambled back with two large and fizzing tumblers of a suspiciously dense color, one of which she handed to Miss Worthing, saying as she did so, "Next year—now that we're going to have the whole thing catered—I intend to forget all about our rule about no drinking while on duty and get thoroughly squiffy as early as I decently can." She, too, collapsed onto a large sofa, spilling not a drop. "I don't even think I've got the energy left to get upstairs to bed."

"Me either," averred Miss Worthing and, leaning back, took

a sip of her drink. At once she choked, swallowed, and drew a gasping breath. "Martha, what on earth did you put in this?"

Miss Shaw merely chuckled and sipped at her own brimming tumbler. "Now that's good!" she muttered, and then admonished Miss Worthing, "Just think of it as medicinal, dear; it'll ward off the cold."

"Ward off the cold!" said Miss Worthing. "This could melt the polar ice pack."

Miss Shaw chuckled again, set her drink on the coffee table in front of her, swung her feet up onto the couch and suddenly and cavernously yawned while simultaneously stretching her arms and legs.

"Don't do that, Martha!" said Miss Worthing, yawning in helpless reply.

"Sorry, Mattie," said Miss Shaw. "Can't help it." She yawned again, shook her head to clear it, and picked up her drink and took a good healthy slug. "Anything on TV?"

"Christmas programming!" replied Miss Worthing with a singularly venomous inflection.

"No, thanks!" said Miss Shaw in matching tones.

Just then, however, the grandfather clock quietly bonged six times.

"Oh!" said Miss Worthing. "It's five to six; the news will be on."

She began looking around for the remote control for the television.

"Better than nothing," said Miss Shaw. "And what are you doing?"

"Looking for the remote."

"It's on the TV," said Miss Shaw. "Where it belongs."

"I was so hoping not to have to get up again," muttered Miss Worthing.

Nevertheless, she hauled herself upright, stalked to the TV, turned it on, retrieved the remote and subsided gratefully into her chair, vowing not to get up again. Although, as she sipped her drink and began to enjoy it very much indeed, she did admit that—when it was done and Martha, too, was ready for another—it would, after all, be only the right thing to do to get up and fix them both another . . .

ii

Meanwhile—at virtually the same moment that Miss Shaw had so thankfully kicked off her shoes—on the other side of Jolliston, in the upstairs corridor of another large Victorian house, a door at the top of the front stairs opened, allowing light to spill out into the passage. Through it, his face grimly set, stalked a rather weary-looking man. His light-brown tweed suit had a distinctly rumpled look, and he bore in his right hand a large black leather bag. He looked to be about sixty, and the expression of his eyes was not a happy one.

Coming behind him and pulling the door to was a middle-aged Oriental woman of medium height. She was dressed in the uniform of a hospital nurse, and indeed her whole being breathed that placid strength one associates with the best members of that profession. Her own expression yielded nothing to scrutiny, but her eyes carefully watched those of the man as she waited for him to speak.

"I don't like it. I don't like it one bit," he finally bit out in a low, intense voice.

"It . . . it just doesn't sound right," admitted the nurse, and then, after hesitating a moment, asked, "and shouldn't he be in the hospital?"

"Course he should," the doctor barked.

Her eyebrows jerked upward the smallest fraction of an inch.

"Sorry, Jessica," he said immediately and frowned, shaking his head. "I'm just so damned . . ." He left it unfinished.

"Puzzled?" supplied the nurse.

"That'll do as well as anything." He shook his head and took a long, deep breath. "Well, there's no help for it," he said. "Of course he should be in the hospital. But we both know that the most that could be done would be to postpone the inevitable for maybe a day or two. And Henry . . ." He shrugged. "Henry says he wants to die at home."

"It's certain then?"

"It's certain."

For a short interval, neither said anything. There was nothing left to say.

"I'd better get back inside," said the nurse.

The doctor nodded.

"You'll be all right?" he asked.

"It's not the first time I've kept deathwatch, Doctor," she replied calmly, and ignored the momentary irritation that flashed across his face. She knew perfectly well it was nothing more than the reflexive fury of any good doctor finding himself helpless before his ancient enemy. "Sibyl showed me where everything is if I need coffee or a sandwich in the night."

"I'll send a relief in the morning."

"That's not necessary."

He frowned.

"Sibyl and Henry Anderson were very kind to me once," she explained, "when a fresh-off-the-boat Chinese desperately needed a little kindness. This is the least I can do for him now."

"He's a good man," said the doctor.

And the nurse, not trusting herself to reply, merely nodded, turned, and reentered the room.

For a moment longer, the doctor, lost in thought, lingered outside the door. Then, finally, with a little snort, he nodded his head as though he had come to some kind of a decision, and, turning about, went down the stairs.

As he rounded the corner on the landing, he saw below—as he had expected to—a woman seated rigidly upright in one of the small, gold-leafed, and intensely uncomfortable-looking chairs which flanked the front door.

She was a small woman, elegant and exquisitely finished, and she sat, to all outward appearances, composed and collected. Her only movement was the rapid tumbling of the beads of a small jet-and-silver rosary between her fingers.

She looked up and, as always, he found himself shaken by the depth of those black eyes which—nowadays—contrasted so sharply with her snow-white hair.

With a smooth economy of movement, she got to her feet, at the same time slipping the rosary into the pocket of her tweed skirt. She waited patiently until he had reached the fifth or sixth step from the bottom, then asked, "Well, Rex?"

He could find no word with which to reply. Instead, he

merely shook his head and said, as gently as he could say it, "I'm sorry, Sibyl."

"Thank you," she said formally and lapsed into silence. Nevertheless, he sustained the distinct impression that she was actually waiting to find out what, if anything, further he might have to say.

"Sibyl, I don't . . . that is, I mean, is there anything . . ." he stammered, suddenly feeling an awkward fool. He was, however, still rather taken aback when, almost immediately, she interrupted.

"No," she said. "There isn't. Thank you."

There was something in the way she said it, too, which caused him then to look rather more intelligently at her than he had. Almost at once, he realized that this woman was not only not bowled over by the debilitating grief one might reasonably expect in one who—in a mere day or so—was going to be a widow, she was actually in the grip of the worst rage he had seen her in in years. And this unexpected and unwelcome fury served only to deepen the puzzle and worry the growing shadows at the corners of his mind.

"Sibyl!" he said quite sharply.

And he began to get some idea of the tension which held her as her head actually jerked back as though she had been physically shaken.

"Yes?"

He came the rest of the way down the stairs, set his bag on a small half-table which stood against the wall beneath the mirror there in the foyer, snapped it open and withdrew from its depths a small vial of clear plastic that revealed a number of tiny yellow pills within. He handed it toward her. She did not, however, take it.

"What's that for?" she asked.

"For you."

"I don't need anything," she said, with a small shake of her head. "I'll be all right."

"Are you?"

"Just what is that supposed to mean, Rex?"

"It simply means, Sibyl, that I haven't seen you this—" He brought himself up very short. Then, after a barely perceptible pause, he finished, "—this upset in years."

"You mean angry, don't you?"

His head bowed momentarily in acknowledgment.

"I know," she said softly. "But I think—" She, too, caught herself up and then actually tossed her head defiantly. "Anger is not exactly unreasonable, is it?"

By way of reply, he merely gestured with the pills.

She sighed and nodded. "Very well," she said and took the bottle. "What are they?" she asked, holding it up to peer at the pills within.

"Valium."

A look of rather bleak amusement crossed her face and was gone.

"Then perhaps I'd better wait a bit."

"Why?"

"Because I've still got entirely too much alcohol in my system."

She slipped the vial into the same pocket where she had put her rosary.

"You look okay to me."

At that, she actually managed a rather mirthless chuckle. "That's only because I've got enough adrenaline in me to last till the Judgment Day. But I do assure you, I've had a lot to drink. But I thank you, Rex. These"—she patted the pocket—"will come in handy, no doubt, when it all really does hit me."

He frowned, puzzled, yet again, by the turn of phrase she had used. He turned back to his bag and snapped it shut as a kind of lull seemed to settle over the conversation which, in any case, had possessed an elliptical quality that both as a friend and as a physician he detested. Furthermore, it had made it that much more difficult to come right out and ask the questions which, in duty both to his profession and the ethics thereof, he was bound to ask.

"Sibyl . . ." he began, just as she, behind him, said, "Rex, I . . ."

He turned around and found himself once more staring into the black, oracular depths of her eyes.

"Ladies first." He smiled wanly.

Instead, however, of saying whatever it was that she had been about to say, she cast her eyes downward, shook her head and then, in a very soft voice, said, "No. Never mind." She looked back up at him. "Thank you."

It was, clearly, a dismissal. But before he could in good conscience go and leave this unhappy family to its grief—and rage—there was something he had to ask.

"Sibyl, I'm sorry to have to bother you at such a time . . ."

"Yes?" She looked up. "Oh yes. I imagine there are—you do have a few questions you want—need to ask."

"I do," he said. "Primarily, of course, is the obvious one: Sibyl, how in the name of all that's holy did Henry manage to get that drunk?"

"I don't know," she said, again shaking her head, and it was plain she was just as puzzled as was he. "But I do have to admit that there's been an awful lot of drinking going on in this family these last few days."

"More than usual?"

"A lot more than usual. People have been—well, let's just say difficult."

"Family troubles?" he asked.

She gave a little shrug, her face expressive of extreme distaste.

"That still doesn't explain—"

"I know." Again she interrupted. "All I can think of is that maybe a glass got knocked over into the orange juice, or even more likely, Henry just picked up someone's glass by mistake. Did you ask him?"

He could have sworn that there was ever so slight a note of apprehension in her voice.

"No," he said, "he isn't conscious, and I don't want him being bothered with questions like that."

She nodded.

"Were people other than Henry drinking orange juice?" he asked.

"Practically everyone."

He paused then a moment and looked at her while she just as candidly stared back at him.

Presently, "An accident?" he said.

"I think so. I don't know whose drink it might have been—" Clearly, she leaned toward the second theory she had suggested. "—and I wouldn't want anyone to feel that it was their fault . . ."

"Y-e-e-s," he agreed carefully, "it would be a nasty thing to have on one's conscience. If it was an accident."

"Rex." She looked up.

"Sibyl, I have to ask," he said. "I'm going to have to sign a certificate, you know."

She flinched at that. "I know," she said in a small voice.

For a moment longer, he seemed unsure. Finally, however, he sighed and took his coat from the coat tree near the door.

"Rex," she asked, "how long will it be?"

"Possibly a day or two."

"Will he—can I see him?"

He sighed and clamped on his hat. "He'll be conscious a good bit of the time. I've left something for pain; it isn't much; his liver's too . . ."

She put out a hand. "Thank you, Rex. For coming. I'm sorry if we ruined your Christmas."

He took her hand and leaned over her and gently kissed her cheek.

"I'm glad I could come," he said. "I just wish it had been for happier reasons."

He went.

iii

For a long moment after the door had closed behind the departing doctor, Sibyl stood silent and motionless, facing the blankness of the door. Her face was as expressionless and enigmatic as that of her ancient namesake. Then, visibly, her jaw set and her shoulders straightened and she marched across the passage to the double doors guarding the entry to the living room. With an almost theatrical gesture, she thrust them open so forcefully that they rebounded several inches along the well-oiled grooves in the recesses of the wall.

Before crossing the threshold, her eyes swept the room within. Then she took a step forward, turned back and, with another flourish, pulled the doors so that they slammed together with a report as sharp—in the silence that had greeted her entrance—as a gunshot.

There were, all told, ten people in the room—five male and five female, ranging in age from a six months' infant asleep in its mother's arms to an ancient crone of unguessable age crouched at the back of the room in that old-fashioned kind of wood-and-wicker wheelchair which once upon a time was called a bath chair.

With the exception of the sleeping babe, all eyes in the room were intently focused on Sibyl Anderson as, having shut the doors, she turned and once more let her eyes move slowly from one to another of the people present until it seemed she had accounted for each one of them.

Then, "He's dying." she announced in a flat, almost emotionless voice.

In response to her announcement, not a soul in the room so much as moved a muscle or even, for that matter, blinked an eyelid. Only the eyes of the old woman in the bath chair glittered brightly as—like those of Sibyl Anderson—they darted swiftly round the room as though to gauge the reactions of everyone present. As she did so, her eyebrows began slowly to rise, as though she found the total lack of response to be, all things considered, rather queer.

Certainly Mrs. Anderson was astounded. But astonishment was consumed in the fiercer emotion of rage.

"Didn't you hear me?" she demanded. "I said he's dying."

"We heard you, Mother," said a tall and quite remarkably fat man who stood smoking a cigarette by the fireplace.

"Good!" said Mrs. Anderson, her voice heavy with irony. She was, by now, making no effort to disguise her anger. "Because there's something else everyone had better hear, and hear well."

"And what's that, Mother?" asked the woman holding the child.

"It means that one of you in this room is a murderer."

Again—and this time the old woman was clearly shocked—there was virtually no reaction to this other than an utterly intangible one, when, as the ancient Saxon word was spoken aloud, everyone seemed to come to a new peak of alertness.

15

"I thought so," finally said a young man standing on the other side of the fireplace from the fat man.

"Why is that?" demanded Mrs. Anderson.

"Because"—he tossed a cigarette butt into the fire—"it's all a little bit too pat for an accident."

"I'll want your thoughts on that, Larry," said Mrs. Anderson.

"I'm not sure that would be proper," he said.

Before Mrs. Anderson could respond to that, however, a large well-fleshed and rather buxom woman on the couch left off strangling her handkerchief and spoke. "But what if it *was* an accident, Sibyl?"

The fat man, snubbing the woman on the couch as thoroughly as did his mother, then asked, "What *did* you tell the doctor?"

"I fobbed him off with a handful of accident scenarios," replied Mrs. Anderson, "and let him think I was leaning to the theory that your father drank out of someone else's glass."

"Not good, Mother," said the fat man. "Didn't it occur to him that Dad would have tasted something?"

"Don't you worry about the doctor. I can deal with him. Just as," she addressed the room more generally, "I'm going to deal with all of you."

"What do you mean?" asked the mother of the babe.

"None of you is going to leave this house or even this room until we've got to the bottom of this." She took a step forward and jabbed a finger angrily at each of them in turn. "One of you has murdered my husband, and I swear by the throne of Almighty God that I'm going to find out which one of you did it."

"What are you going to do, Mother?" asked the mother of the child sarcastically. "Keep us prisoner here till one of us confesses?"

"If that's the only way of it, yes," said Mrs. Anderson implacably.

A young woman sitting in the window embrasure and dressed somewhat incongruously in a biscuit-colored business suit managed to squeak, "But that's illegal," into the rather stunned silence that followed Mrs. Anderson's statement, before rockets of protest shot up and conversation became general and very loud.

Under cover of the ensuing fracas, the old woman in the wheelchair frowned malignantly and abruptly reached up to pluck at the sleeve of the very tall and almost cadaverously thin young man standing protectively beside her chair.

"Billy!" she whispered fiercely.

"Yes, my lady?" He bent at the waist toward her.

"Wheel me into the kitchen. Now."

A look of alarm swept over his face. He glanced apprehensively toward the storm at the other end of the living room.

"Mrs. Anderson won't like it," he ventured.

"Of course she won't," snapped the old woman. "But don't worry about her. She's just being hysterical. Take me into the kitchen."

Incapable of suppressing a sigh, and expecting at any second to hear an angry voice call out to stop them, Billy moved behind the chair and pushed it first through the archway into the dining room, past the dining table still littered with the detritus of a large meal, through the service area, and on into the kitchen.

"Over there," commanded the old woman; "by the telephone."

"Anything else?" he asked when he had complied.

"Yes, please. Now reach me down the telephone. These damned wall phones are never very conveniently placed for infirm people, are they? Thank you. And now would you please dial the following number?"

He dialed.

iv

Miss Worthing, meanwhile, was finding herself astonished—and not for the first time—at the twaddle passing for news on television. Of course, in a way, it was hardly the fault of the grinning cretins whose business it was to stare into the eye of the camera and read the stuff, Christmas being a notoriously "slow news day." Indeed, all the stories seemed to consist of the human-interest variety: a shot of the papal blessing; a story on a collection of certifiable lunatics plunging into San Francisco Bay; another of some family's pet pig with a cannibalistic passion for smoked ham . . .

But tranquillity blessedly reigned. Silence—but for the fretful squawk of the television—had been restored, even if order had not, and both ladies were enjoying a very pleasant buzz and happy thoughts of approaching bedtime.

Whereupon—loud, demanding, and incredibly startling—the telephone rang.

Miss Worthing was jarred from mesmerized contemplation of the stupefying banality of the national football highlights while Miss Shaw, who had actually dozed off, came to in an eruption of those noises not uncommon to those waking in unfamiliar circumstances: "What? Where am—? Who?" and began the varied heavings required to haul herself from her recumbent position on the couch.

Miss Worthing, however, took charge. At once. Slamming her empty tumbler down onto the table beside her with considerable force, she struggled from the embraces of her own chair and stood up.

"Lie still," she commanded. "I'll deal with this." And she marched to the phone.

Every year it happened. Some dolt who could not read plain English called up—deep in his cups, as likely as not—to say, "Shay, Mattie, I jusht thought I could shtop over and have a few with ya . . ."

"Well, not this year, kiddo," she muttered and quite literally snatching up the phone, barked into it, "Who is it!"

Whereupon in her ear sounded a quite unmistakable voice saying, "Precisely what the innkeeper said to Joseph! And poor Mary already laboring to bring forth the infant Jesus."

Miss Shaw, who had begun rather ponderously to laugh at the hardly very welcoming way her friend had answered the telephone, watched as, almost immediately, Miss Worthing pulled the phone a foot or so away from her ear and the receiver squawked into the quiet room. She herself could not hear the words, but she certainly recognized the voice.

"All right, Aunt Eulalia," said Miss Worthing, confirming

Miss Shaw's suspicions, "slow down. What's got you all in a dither?"

Miss Shaw, casting her eyes toward the heavens, hauled her bulk upright and, picking up Miss Worthing's glass, trundled toward the drinks cabinet to refill it and her own. Eulalia Lady Fairgrief, Miss Worthing's ancient, venerable (and, in Miss Shaw's opinion, slightly potty) aunt was not given to short telephone conversations. Dear Mattie would no doubt need a refill by the time she finished. And on this, of all days.

When she had replenished the two glasses, she turned to hand one to Miss Worthing and came to a complete stop.

Miss Worthing had all but collapsed, standing with her head against the wall as she listened to whatever it was that her aunt was shouting at her. She looked as though every tendon in her body had suddenly gone limp.

She raised her eyes and looked first at Miss Shaw and then to the two drinks in her hand and then back at Miss Shaw and twice shook her head.

Miss Shaw frowned.

"Very well, Aunt Eulalia," Miss Worthing finally said. "Try to keep them from flaying one another. We'll do what we can." And, to Miss Shaw's surprise, she hung up the phone in what must surely have been record time for any telephone conversation with her mad ladyship.

Miss Shaw did not, however, like the look on Miss Worthing's face. Not at all.

"Mattie, what's wrong?"

Miss Worthing sighed, shook her head and essayed a weak little laugh. "It never fails. Always when we're the most tired."

"Mattie, what are you talking about?" Miss Shaw was now definitely worried.

"Oh, Martha, I hate to tell you this, but you'd better go put the kettle on and brew us up a quick cup of very strong tea. And then, I think, we'd both better go change."

"Kettle? Tea? Change? Why?"

"Because, my dear, that was Aunt Eulalia . . ."

"I know!"

19

"... she was having Christmas dinner with the Anderson clan today."

Again, Miss Shaw snapped out an irritated little "I know!"

"Well, Martha—it seems that someone contrived to put alcohol, and rather a lot of it, too, into General Anderson's orange juice."

Miss Shaw uttered a horrified little gasp. "On purpose?"

"Sibyl—and Aunt Eulalia—seem to think so. She also said that Sibyl has some crazy idea about holding them all there till one of them confesses, so Aunt Eulalia thought it would probably be better if you and I . . ." She gestured eloquently.

Suddenly, Miss Shaw realized that she was still holding the two tumblers of whiskey and soda. She looked down at them, frowning as though she could not quite remember whence they had come. Deliberately she set them down on the cabinet.

"Okay, Mattie. No need to explain. Of course, we'll do it. You go take a quick shower," she said kindly, "while I get the kettle on. Although I do expect that we'd best get cracking. If I know anything about that family, they'll be tearing each other into itsy-bitsy pieces before poor Henry is cold in his coffin. But oh, I do wish people wouldn't go about murdering each other. At least," she added as she waddled toward the kitchen, "not on Christmas!"

CHAPTER 1

i

With something of a flourish, Eulalia Lady Fairgrief handed the telephone back up to the hovering Billy McClure. Billy took it obediently enough and cradled it, but then, unable to contain himself, burst out, "You do realize, don't you, that as soon as Mrs. Anderson gets wind of this, she's going to have herself a first-class fit?"

Her ladyship chuckled mirthlessly and observed, "It does seem at least moderately likely."

"Are you quite sure you know what you're doing?"

"Oh, quite. Sibyl may have some harebrained idea she can get away with this—this charade. But I know perfectly well that she cannot."

"I don't see why not," said Billy.

At that her ladyship suddenly and rather unexpectedly smiled as though enjoying a private joke. Billy frowned. "Is something funny?" he demanded.

"No, Billy. Nothing's funny. Except in the remotest meaning of the word. All I really meant was that Sibyl hasn't got a clue—no pun intended—about how to handle this. She may be a first-class theologian, but it is all too obvious that Sibyl's never tried to snuffle out a murderer before."

"Oh," said Billy. "And you have?"

"You needn't take quite such a high and mighty line with

me, young man," rejoined her ladyship, though she said it mildly enough. "It might surprise you to learn what I've managed to get done in a lifetime of nearly a hundred years. And though Sibyl appears to have forgotten or ignored a certain fact, I haven't, and neither will Matilda—who, I might warn you, is very experienced at this kind of thing."

"Okay, then, so what has Mrs. Anderson forgotten?"

"The simple fact that if Henry was, in fact, murdered, then she—as his wife—is inevitably a suspect, too."

"I don't believe she had a thing to do with it."

"Perhaps she didn't," acknowledged her ladyship. "But whatever else you may learn while you are working for me, Billy, you will discover that in affairs of this kind, words such as 'believe' have no place at all. We need to weasel out the facts, and—as I said—Sibyl has forgotten, or is choosing to ignore, a rather appreciable one and it is simply not to be borne."

"It isn't going to prevent her having a conniption. She is," he added with genuine awe in his voice, "a formidable woman."

"So she is, Billy. So she is. But let us not forget for a moment that so, dear boy, am I."

Which was, after all, only the truth.

All her life, Eulalia Lady Fairgrief—*née* Worthing—had been and was still, in the ninety-eighth year of her age, a remarkable phenomenon. Relict of the late Sir Arthur Fairgrief (late also of His Majesty's Diplomatic), and confined to a wheelchair for the past twenty years, there were still evident, amid the ruins, remnants of that extraordinary beauty that had led a California farm girl to become the feted darling of four continents in the dim but never to be forgotten years of the seventh Edward's reign.

It had been, to be sure, an appreciably different standard of beauty than that of the anorexic chorines foisted on a compliant public by sixty-odd years of Hollywood & Co. Her high-bridged, aristocratic nose was now a great beak wholly dominating her face—her nose and that determined nutcracker of a chin from which depended an astonishing assortment of folds and wattles and crepelike draperies of skin. But her mouth, though surrounded by a maze of lines, was straight and true, with not the least hint of that downturn at the corners which bespeaks one discontent with her lot. It was the mouth of one who had suffered much, to be sure, but one who had laughed much also.

Her hair was baby-fine, thinning somewhat and white as wind-driven powder, but it was dressed as beautifully as it ever had been and covering it was a veil of the finest and sheerest muslin which she wore tucked about her face in the timeless and infinitely flattering manner of a wimple. Her dress was of black silk cut in the perennial elegance of a lady's morning frock, though incongruously wrapped about her useless lower limbs was a coarse woolen blanket in vibrant aniline red-and-blue stripes.

She came of an era when beauty disdained makeup, and she had remained free ever since of any kind of maquillage whatever. Which had probably on the whole been a very good thing. Her skin, though all overwritten with the myriad fine lines that come to the truly old, still had something of the freshness of a woman much, much younger. And if her hands toying in her lap with a tortoiseshell-and-gold lorgnon were gnarled and twisted arthritic claws, her eyes yet managed completely to belie her age. Snapping with wit, humor, wisdom, and not a little innocent malice, and dark as deep water at midnight, they were simply two of the most wicked eyes ever to shine upon unhappy middle earth.

"Indeed you are, my lady," said Billy with a grin. "So what happens now?"

"We get out there and take control."

"I'm yours to command."

"Very well"—she waved an imperious hand—"propel me!"

At once Billy's face blanked of all expression as he snapped back into his well-nigh perfect—if perhaps rather theatrical—imitation of the perfect upper servant of yore.

He was, to say the least, an unlikely-looking attendant upon her ladyship. He was, first of all, dressed in the most bewildering array of garments—a pink polo shirt, rather tatty blue jeans, running shoes ditto, while over the whole ensemble he wore an old-fashioned cutaway coat so old it was green and practically iridescent with age. As has already been mentioned, he was exceedingly tall and exceedingly thin, with a very long and very mournful face, and he had to crouch a bit to grasp the handles of his employer's chair, all of which made him look rather like an ungainly cross between a crane and a Houdan rooster. Nor was his resemblance to the latter untidy bird one whit mitigated by the fact that his hair was a flyaway bush of ash-blond ringlets that seemed in their sheer exuberance so at variance with the mournfulness of his habitual expression. And of his voice. It was really quite a beautiful voice, a rich, deep, resonant basso profundo. Unfortunately, as is so often the case with basses, it had yet a note of ineluctable melancholy. Surprisingly, and contrary perhaps to all expectation, he was actually quite a young man, no more than twenty-one or twenty-two.

It was immediately obvious as they passed once more from the dining room to the living room that the fracas had spent itself. The several parties had repaired, as it were, to their corners to recruit themselves, which had the unfortunate effect of leaving Mrs. Anderson's attention to focus sharply on the returning pair.

"Where have you been?" She advanced toward them.

"I beg your pardon, Sibyl," said her ladyship, bringing her lorgnette to bear. "I'm not sure that you have any right to question—"

"I have every right. Where have you been?" The woman's eyes were actually narrowed, her mouth a thin, intense line.

"Well," said her ladyship expansively, "I suppose I could tell you that I had Billy take me to the cloakroom . . ."

And she had her reward as a wash of pink suffused Mrs. Anderson's white cheeks. Then the peculiar way in which Lady Fairgrief had spoken penetrated through the woman's shell of anger.

"What are you saying?" she demanded. "What did you do?"

"I had Billy wheel me into the kitchen," said her ladyship. She then added deliberately, "To the telephone."

"Did you call the police?" It was almost a shriek.

"No, I did not," said Lady Fairgrief. "Although," she added the sour parenthesis, "it is hardly a bad idea."

"I don't—"

"Yes, Sibyl, I know," said her ladyship calmly. "That's the reason I called Matilda instead."

What happened next upon that announcement surprised everyone, not least Lady Fairgrief. Instead of the immediate explosion that might confidently and legitimately have been expected from the woman, she seemed almost to stagger backward a step or two until the back of her legs caught on the edge of a Sheraton chair and she sat down. Heavily.

"Mother, are you . . ." The fat man started forward.

She waved him away.

"I'm all right. Really, I'm all right." And then she actually uttered a weak little chuckle, almost, but not quite, a giggle. "I don't know why," she finally explained, "but it really never occurred to me to call Matilda. Silly of me." She shook her head. "And thank you, Eulalia."

Her face bland as cream, her ladyship caught Billy McClure's eyes. Billy briefly and ever so discreetly sketched that universal facial gesture which involves a deliberate lengthening of the face and which says as clear as any words, "I'm impressed."

But self-congratulation was definitely premature. There was, reflected her ladyship, rather a lot to be done if poor Matilda's labors were not going to be positively Sisyphean.

"Sibyl," she said, leaning forward in her chair and speaking quietly but urgently, "once thirty years ago you had occasion to trust me."

"Yes."

"Trust me now."

"But you . . ."

"No, Sibyl. Not me."

"What's going on here?" demanded a burly man seated on the arm of the chair of the woman holding the baby.

"Nothing that either of us would care to discuss with you, Mr. Taylor," said her ladyship crisply and returned her gaze to the troubled woman in front of her who, presently, took a deep breath, held it a moment as she hesitated, until finally letting the air out in an audible sigh, then nodded.

"Very well."

"Very wise, Sibyl," commented her ladyship and, indicating to Billy McClure that he was to turn her chair the better to face the assemblage, she waxed immediately practical. "Now listen here, everyone. This is what we're going to do."

ii

Twenty minutes later, Lady Fairgrief sat in solitary splendor in the library, wishing more than anything else that she could go to bed. She could not remember the last time she had been so weary and she knew all too well that before very long she would pay for this sustained effort in some excessively disagreeable fashion.

Nevertheless, Matilda and Martha would be with her presently and they would expect—as they had every right to—as clear a report from her as she could provide. And so, weary as she was, she ruthlessly disciplined the scattered dartings of her mind and began to order her thoughts.

It seemed to her ladyship that she had only begun when there was a rather unnecessarily loud knock on the library door, which quite startled her. She opened her eyes just as the door opened and Miss Worthing poked her head in, her enormously magnified eyes bulging in concern.

"Sibyl said you were in here alone."

"I am as you find me."

"Is that really a wise thing with a murderer running about the house?"

"Hardly running," said her ladyship. "Everyone's cooped up in the parlor, with Billy brooding over them, and other than them there's only Jessica Wu upstairs and poor Henry, who, I'm sorry to say, will never cause anyone any trouble again."

Miss Worthing came the rest of the way into the room. She had changed her navy suit for a suitably somber one in black wool and her blouse was white instead of ecru—but otherwise she looked much as she had earlier that day when Lady Fairgrief had seen her at her open house. It seemed a hundred years ago now.

"How are you feeling?" asked Miss Worthing.

"How do you think I'm feeling?" said her ladyship. "I'm exhausted, and I'm going to lose one of my dearest friends."

"I'm sorry, Aunt Eulalia. Martha will be with us in a minute. She's in the kitchen making us some tea."

The thought was instantly so very comforting that Lady Fairgrief could not help but utter a small laugh.

Miss Worthing arched an inquiring brow.

"I just couldn't help think that here we are, embroiled in yet another of these nasty little affairs, and neither one of us really wants to get the ball rolling till we've had a dish of boiled water and bitter herbs."

It was then that Miss Worthing realized that, in her own way, her aunt was taking this one especially hard.

"Aunt Eulalia," she said, "you know that if you are too tired, we can put this off till tomorrow. I can talk to Sibyl and Larry."

"You're going to have to do that in any event."

"That's true."

"Still," mused her ladyship, and considered it rationally. She was tired, far more so than was good for her. Were her dear old Maude with her now, that impregnable bastion of a nurse and companion would no doubt long since have tucked her into bed despite all protests. But Lady Fairgrief came of a generation and a conditioning to duty on the whole inconceivable to modern minds, and it can fairly be reported that, while the thought of retiring was indeed a powerful longing, she thrust it from her with hardly a second thought.

"I'll be just fine," she said. "It won't take that long anyway."

Miss Worthing looked dubious, but before she could say anything, there came the sound without in the passage of rattling crockery. A sharp rap on the door and Miss Shaw waddled in pushing a tea trolley.

Soon, restored somewhat, her ladyship deliberately set her cup and saucer down on the trolley.

"Thank you, Martha," she said. "That will keep me going till I've filled you in."

"Why did they leave it to you?" asked Miss Shaw. She had been, in fact, slightly scandalized that out of all the people there were in the party, her ladyship should have been the one elected to perform the rather difficult chore of gathering the necessary information.

"It's really very simple," said Lady Fairgrief, rather grimly. "Billy and I are the only people present who could not possibly have done this thing."

She looked expectantly at her niece, who caught the implication right away. "I see," she said equally grim and observed with ill-concealed distaste, "one of those!"

It took Miss Shaw a moment longer.

"Wait a minute," she said sharply. "Are you saying that Larry . . ."

"If the possibility exists," said Miss Worthing, "we have to examine it."

"Mattie," said the scandalized Miss Shaw, "he's your own nephew."

"And my grandnephew," said Lady Fairgrief. "But we can't allow for such considerations."

"Why not?" demanded Miss Shaw.

"Martha," said her ladyship quite sharply, "do you think I *like* being put into such an invidious position? One of my oldest friends in the world is upstairs dying and I can only conclude that he was murdered by his wife, one of his children, or my very own grandnephew."

"Martha," said Miss Worthing, "shut up."

Miss Shaw could not quite suppress a sniff but lapsed into an attentive silence as Miss Worthing said, "Very well, Aunt Eulalia, tell us what happened."

iii

"Billy and I arrived about one-thirty," began her ladyship. "Here at the Elms, I mean. Prior to that we had been, of course, at your and Martha's open house. But then, so had most everyone here, hadn't they?"

"Yes," said Miss Shaw. "The only ones here who hadn't been there are Arletta and Bette Wanda Taylor."

"Just so. And they, presumably," her ladyship went on, "were at home. It is something for you to check." She airily dismissed it. "Now I know for a fact that Sibyl, Henry, and Cy left your house about an hour before Billy and I did because Sibyl told me not to rush; dinner would not be until two-thirty at the earliest. Henry was chafing at the bit over something to do with a football game. And Cy was"—she shrugged—"being Cy. Bob E. Taylor and Helen and the baby,

28

on the other hand, left no more than ten minutes before I did, and Ben and Larry left about ten minutes before them."

"Is any of this relevant?"

"I'm sure I don't know," rejoined her ladyship. "It may be; it may not be. But what I am trying to say is that everyone was here when I arrived. What passed before I got here, you will, of course, have to get from the others. But I must say," observed her ladyship, grim again, "the breath of the glacier was strong on the land."

"What do you mean?"

"Everyone was being oh-so-very polite to one another. Everyone was full of positively Confucian little courtesies."

"So?"

"Matilda, don't be simple. You know this family as well as I. Better. You watched the children grow up. They were always bickering, making snide remarks, putting each other down, and after Helen married Bob E.—"

"All right, all right. I see your point."

"So, when I could finally get Sibyl alone, I asked her what had happened."

"And?"

"Oh, she tried to pull that 'My dear, what *are* you talking about' routine until I pointed out to her that it was, please to remember, I to whom she was speaking."

Miss Shaw and Miss Worthing both smiled appreciatively.

"And did she tell you?" asked Miss Shaw.

"Not really," replied her ladyship. "I gathered from what she said—"

"What did she say?" asked Miss Worthing.

"As near as I can remember, she said there was a big scene at Helen's house last night and everyone was trying, very carefully, to forget what they said to each other.

"Very well, thought I; I shall do my great hostess routine and put everyone at their ease. So I sent Sibyl on about her business—she and Cy were the ones who were actually cooking the meal—"

"Where was Larry?" Miss Shaw, who was, after all, devoted to her friend's nephew, could no longer contain herself.

"In the kitchen, too," replied Lady Fairgrief. "Apparently he'd volunteered to make a nog, which was good, to be sure, but was really rather much as a preface to a heavy Christmas dinner."

"Stick to the point, Aunt Eulalia," said Miss Worthing severely. "Where was Ben?"

"Ben was wandering about a good deal playing host and bartender."

"Oh, really?" said Miss Worthing. "Not Henry?"

"Not Henry," said Lady Fairgrief. "Definitely not Henry. Henry sat glued to the television the whole time before dinner, ignoring everyone in the house except Sibyl, Larry, Ben, and me."

"Good heavens! Was he angry?"

"Not at all. He was actually very pleasant to Billy and me. Asked him how he liked working for me. Asked me when Maude would be back from England."

"That's very interesting."

"Isn't it, though."

"And the Taylors?"

"Oh dear me, yes. Well, Helen, with Mary Elizabeth, took up rather a prominent position on one of the couches in the living room and proceeded to play with her daughter. Loudly."

"Oh dear."

"Henry was annoyed. I could tell that. And certainly by what he said later."

"What was that?"

"I'll tell you in the proper place."

"Fine. Bob E.?"

"Very much in the living room cheering the television."

"Poor Henry."

"Indeed," said Miss Worthing. "And what about Arletta and Bette Wanda?"

"They were," said her ladyship, "apparently rather singlemindedly getting sloshed in the kitchen."

"What!"

"But I don't *know* that," said Lady Fairgrief. "I only saw the evident results. I think you'd be better off talking to Sibyl or Larry about that. Or Cy. There had been some fuss at first. Something about a box of oranges. Again, you'll have to ask one of the others about it. That began when Henry rather querulously told Ben to get him some orange juice. And there was some flapdoodle that Helen was supposed to bring the box at her house and Bette Wanda offered to fetch it, but she was in no condition to drive, so Bob E. told Helen to go get it and so *they* got into it. Finally, Bob E. stormed out and was back in half an hour or so with it and returned immediately to his football game while, I gather, his mother and sister took on the merry chore of squeezing the oranges."

"Helen stayed put?"

"Very put."

"What do you mean?"

"She was furious about something, and while she played with Mary Elizabeth, what she was actually saying was an endless stream of the most vitriolic little observations about all and sundry. You know the kind of thing—no one was ever mentioned by name, but you'd have to have been simpleminded not to *hear* what she was saying."

"At whom were these little fountains of venom aimed?" asked Miss Worthing.

"Everyone came in for his or hers. But they did seem predominantly aimed at Henry and Bob E."

"Anything happen?"

"I thought Henry was getting very close to telling her to button up. But just then Sibyl came in and announced that dinner would be in ten minutes."

"And?"

"Henry got up and muttered something about compost and left the rest of us to begin a kind of Völkerwanderung into the dining room."

"No procession?" asked Miss Worthing with something of a twinkle.

"People haven't processed since Queen Mary died," sniffed her ladyship. "Anyway, Henry came back in rubbing his hands. I don't know why I remember that. But I could see that his hands were still wet from his no doubt hasty ablutions, and without a word he stalked to his chair at the head of the table. People had moved in a kind of casual way toward the table, and Helen appeared at Henry's elbow. That was when Henry barked at her, 'No—take your brat and sit by your mother!'

"He then put Larry on his right and Ben in starvation corner and in effect ignored everyone else. Sibyl, of course, took over and seated everyone else. Henry barked out a terse little verse of Bobbie Burns by way of a grace and hoisted his nog. He tasted it, complimented Larry on it, and sat down.

"So did we all, after which Sibyl and Cy got up and went to the kitchen and began bringing foodstuffs out."

"And the juice?"

"That was later. The first pitcher was already on the table."

"The *first* pitcher?"

"Yes. It was really quite extraordinary the way that business developed. There was—for everyone but the General, naturally—champagne. I began to realize that everyone was already more than a little tiddly—"

"Everyone?"

"Oh yes. And apparently everyone had decided that fresh orange juice was just what the doctor ordered."

"They all had the thirsties from the night before, I'll betcha," said Miss Shaw.

"No doubt," said her ladyship. "But actually it was I that decided that a mimosa or two would go down nicely—especially with a turkey dinner. So when Henry asked—rather grudgingly, I must say—if anyone else wanted juice, I spoke up and said that yes, I would.

"Well, I must certainly have struck a responsive chord in the assembled—before you know it, everyone at the table was drinking mimosas. And things were finally beginning to thaw out and get a bit festive. Sibyl was beginning to relax a little and even Henry—under Larry's and Ben's facetiousness—was starting to look a little less grumpy.

"Then, all of a sudden, Bette Wanda Taylor gave this great hiccup, announced in tones of sheerest wonderment that she was really seriously drunk. Whereupon, if you please, the poor girl passed out right in her mashed potatoes."

"My dear!" said Miss Worthing.

"Indeed," said her ladyship. "The next few minutes were, to put it mildly, rather painful. I don't believe I've ever seen Henry angrier. The Taylors, bless their hearts, were all of them mortified, as who wouldn't be, but—well, you know the kind of man Bob E. is. He just got hopping mad himself at Henry for getting mad at poor Bette Wanda."

"Arletta?"

"Arletta was sufficiently blitzed herself that all she could do was to keep muttering about 'my baby!'"

Miss Shaw could not help really snorting at that one.

"The poor girl was got to bed by Sibyl and Bob E., with Mrs. Taylor wringing her hands like some overblown Cassandra, and when—after a few minutes—they returned, the meal was resumed in the Byzantine silence I had originally feared. Even I was glad to get a fresh mimosa from the new pitcher."

"What new pitcher?"

"The pitcher of orange juice."

"But why a new one?"

"Because Bette Wanda had finished the second one just as she passed out."

"*Second* one?"

"Yes. We had three pitcherfuls altogether."

"Good Lord!" said Miss Worthing.

"Who got them?" asked Miss Shaw.

"Sibyl got the first one, Cy got the second, and Sibyl, I believe, got the third one."

"And everyone kept eating?"

"Well, it was really the only thing to do under the circumstances. I have to admit my own eyes were pretty firmly glued to my plate. I think," she said and then paused as though considering it, "I think we must all have been doing so."

"Why?"

"Because I don't recall anyone noticing when the General stopped eating. I don't think anyone noticed anything until Sibyl suddenly screamed his name and rose to her feet." Her ladyship raised troubled eyes to her niece. "And needless to say, with that kind of a thing, everyone's eyes immediately went to Sibyl. Not Henry. But we all turned. Just in time to see him try to rise out of his chair, his face absolutely white with pain as he clutched at his side. And then he just fell over and lay still.

"'Call the doctor!' Sibyl shrieked at me.

"'In the kitchen,' I told Billy. 'You do it. You're faster.'

"Ben and Larry made a bos'n's chair for Henry—after Larry

checked to see that he wasn't dead. Cy and Sibyl followed, leaving me, Helen, Mary Elizabeth, Bob E., and Arletta at the table.

"'Someone finally got the old bastard, didn't they,' said Arletta.

"'What do you mean, Mrs. Taylor?' I asked. The woman was very deep in her cups, but the way she said it meant that, drunk or not, she had no love for Henry Anderson."

"What happened then?"

"I'm still not certain I altogether believe it, but"—the old woman shrugged—"there was something hateful about Arletta's little question. I dumped the remains of my mimosa into my plate, swilled the wineglass out with water, and then poured orange juice into it from the pitcher."

"And?"

"I couldn't taste a thing! Not a thing! Other than orange juice. That and the touch of vanilla that Sibyl puts into it on red-letter days."

"Vanilla?"

Her ladyship shook her head violently. "No. It's not what you're thinking. It isn't commercial stuff; too much alcohol in it. It's some orange flower concoction Sibyl makes herself."

"And then?"

"That's what's so bizarre."

"Tell me."

"Helen was watching me. So, for that matter, was Bob E. I'm sure it was pretty obvious what I was doing. And then, cool as a cucumber, Helen said to her husband, 'Why, Bob E., there must be something in the OJ!' And before I could say Bob's your uncle,' Bob E. jumped to his feet, grabbed the pitcher, and all but ran into the kitchen.

"Billy had already told me he had finished on the telephone and was puzzling over something there in the kitchen when Bob E. rushed in and, before Billy even realized what was happening, Bob E. had dumped the rest of the pitcher of juice down the drain and sluiced out the pitcher at the tap."

iv

"He did *what*?"

Both Miss Worthing and Miss Shaw were slack-jawed in astonishment.

"Just that," said Lady Fairgrief. "And I daresay you'd better speak to Billy about the little scene which ensued."

"Don't worry," said Miss Worthing.

"Needless to say," said Lady Fairgrief, "this has quite a number of folks convinced that if there was any chicanery—and incidentally, not all of 'em are by any means convinced of it—it seems moderately likely that it was Bob E. who was responsible."

"Because of that?"

Her ladyship nodded. "I pointed out, however, that judging from what little I was aware of, Bob E. Taylor may have been the one person today who could not have added anything to Henry's orange juice."

"Why?"

"Want of opportunity. You, of course, will have to draw your own conclusions after you've delved somewhat more deeply than I was in any position to do."

"Did Bob E. say why he did such a very foolish thing?" asked Miss Shaw.

"To be sure," said Lady Fairgrief. "He said that there must have been something wrong with the juice and he didn't want anyone else to 'get it.'"

"Thin," said Miss Worthing. "Very thin."

Her ladyship shrugged. "I am merely reporting. And now, Matilda, please. I have got to get to bed. You won't be needing me anymore tonight."

"What? Oh, of course," said Miss Worthing, emerging from a brief abstraction. "Are you going home?"

"No. Sibyl's already made arrangements for me to sleep here."

"Very well; Martha, take her up, would you?"

"And then?" asked Miss Shaw.

"Come back for me here. I have a little thinking to do before we face the onslaught."

Miss Shaw nodded and, taking the handle of Lady Fairgrief's chair, wheeled it through the door Miss Worthing held open.

V

When they had gone, Miss Worthing stood still for a long, long moment and then, slowly at first and then more restlessly, began to pace up and down the room.

It was a pleasant place—a bit dark perhaps to be serving as a library, but the walls were lined with books, and several free-standing double-sided shelves broke the large room into smaller, comfortable bays at the back of which small, well-lit little tables invited to scholarly endeavor, while the well-used leather chairs grouped round the unlit fireplace spoke of many hours spent comfortably immersed in reading. Even the smells—old leather, neat's-foot oil, furniture polish, and that indefinable smell of slowly perishing paper which is part of any large congeries of books—were good and pleasing.

But Miss Worthing paid only the scantest attention to her surroundings. For one thing, she had been here too many times before to be other than minimally struck by the ambience of the room.

Instead, she was trying to clear her thoughts. To review, so to speak, what she knew of this wretched clan of Taylors and Andersons.

It was, by no means, an unusual story, and the bare bones of it were easily told. A young woman, well-bred, well-educated, rather strikingly beautiful, and for all intents and purposes rich, had married a man who was none of the above. In another, less democratic era, she would have been pointedly accused of having married beneath her, and he whom she had wed dismissed as a fortune hunter!

At the time of the nuptials, Miss Worthing had wondered at the wisdom of it. Not, to be sure, because of any twaddle about social or economic classes. But rather for the eminently practical reason that the bride and groom had been so inexorably alien one to the other.

But Helen Anderson had married Bob E. Taylor for Love Which Conquers All—and ever since, virtually everyone in both families had been miserable, including—Dame Rumor had it—the principals.

The problem was one that any third-rate sociologist would have recognized. The Andersons were rich, cultured, educated, liberal, Catholic, and well connected in all the right places. The Taylors had been poor, ill-educated, fundamentalist, narrow, and from among that population of drifters from ill-defined locations in Oklahoma and points south and east thereof which had simply blown away in the economic winds of the 1930s.

They had come wandering into the Valley in pursuit of the demand for unskilled labor, which was just about all they had the wits or training to perform.

And the sins of the fathers had been visited even unto the third generation. And though Bob E. Taylor was now reputed to be a very rich man himself, and in spite of the fact that both families had labored mightily, they remained as immiscible as oil and water. Sibyl Anderson once told Miss Worthing about taking Arletta Taylor—on her own asking—to a stately Anglo-Catholic High Mass at the Church of All Saints, which was the Anderson family parish. At the end of it, it seems that Arletta had wondered aloud when the invitation to baptism was to be issued! A minor incident, to be sure, but a *signum magnum* of the gulf that separated the families.

Miss Shaw opened the door and looked inquiringly at Miss Worthing. With a sign and a nod, she left off her depressing meditations and passed into the foyer and her job.

CHAPTER 2

In the passage, they found—as they had rather expected to—Mrs. Anderson waiting, still and inflexible in the open doorway to the living room.

"Go on in, Martha," Miss Worthing instructed quietly. "There's a few things I have to talk to Sibyl about."

"No notes?" asked Miss Shaw.

Miss Worthing shook her head. "I'll jot 'em down later myself if it should be necessary."

Miss Shaw shambled off into the living room as Mrs. Anderson looked inquiringly at Miss Worthing.

"Shut the doors, Sibyl," said Miss Worthing. "I want to talk to you."

Mrs. Anderson's brow furrowed, but she turned and pulled the doors to. Miss Worthing, meanwhile, sat down on one of the small gold-leafed chairs flanking the door, and when Mrs. Anderson turned around again, she gestured to the other. Mrs. Anderson sat.

"Yes, Matilda?"

"I have a few questions which I need to ask as a kind of preliminary."

"But didn't Eulalia . . ."

"My aunt's story was revealing. But the questions I have to ask right now are not about that."

"Very well," said Mrs. Anderson, placidly folding her hands

in her lap, a gesture that fooled Miss Worthing not in the least. Dim though the light was, it was adequate to see the line of tension along the woman's jaw.

"Sibyl, I have heard now from Aunt Eulalia and from you too that—whatever happened here—you don't want the police called in."

"That is correct."

"Why?"

Mrs. Anderson sighed and shook her head. "You have to realize, Matilda, that I personally would not so have objected. But as we were putting Henry into bed, he"—she raised her head and looked directly at Miss Worthing—"he pulled me close and whispered, 'No police, Sibyl. I won't have the police.'"

"Did he now?"

Mrs. Anderson nodded.

"So he thought, too . . ."

Again, the younger woman nodded. "He knew that someone had tried to murder him."

The change of verb from "think" to "know" was not lost on Miss Worthing.

"Very well," she said. "So no police. You do know, don't you, that it could have very serious repercussions?"

"Yes. But it's what Henry wants."

"I can't imagine why."

"Don't let it bother you too much, Matilda. You'll get a chance to ask him, you know."

"What!"

"He was awake a little bit ago. I told him you and Martha were here. He seemed pleased and said that he wants to see you."

Miss Worthing was instantly on her feet.

"But not now," said Mrs. Anderson. "He's gone out again."

"Is he—does he have much pain?"

"My God, the pain!" whispered Mrs. Anderson, as her hands clenched one another. She took a long and rather ragged breath and then, deliberately setting her shoulders, she too stood up, facing Miss Worthing. "Is there anything else?"

"I'm afraid so. I have been thinking rather a lot about what

Aunt Eulalia has told me. And while it may seem frivolous to you, Sibyl, believe me, it isn't. We're going in there now to tell them what the drill is going to be—tomorrow."

"Tomorrow!" The woman was outraged.

"Yes, Sibyl, tomorrow."

"But why not get started tonight?"

"For a number of reasons. For one, just how sober is everyone?"

"Sober enough."

And hung over, thought Miss Worthing, but decided for the moment to let it go. "And secondly, there's the fact that all I've got so far is Aunt Eulalia's narrative and the bald assertion that Henry's been poisoned with alcohol. I want—no, scratch that"—she waved a hand—"I need to talk to you, Ben, and Larry."

"But they're under suspicion as much as—"

"As much as you are, Sibyl!" Miss Worthing interrupted implacably.

For a moment, neither woman said a word. Then Mrs. Anderson cocked her head ever so slightly, as though she were listening to some faint and distant sound, whereupon a small half-smile lifted a corner of her mouth.

"I'm sorry, Matilda." She nodded slowly. "You're absolutely right. I leave it in your hands."

"Thank you," said Miss Worthing. "Now, as I said, all I have is the naked assertion that someone put alcohol into Henry's orange juice, and secondly that everyone has already tagged Bob E. with the credit. And that, my dear woman, is the sum total of what I have, what I know. I need to talk to you and Ben and Larry to find out what in blazes has been going on here."

"Nothing that hasn't gone on for the last eighteen months," said Mrs. Anderson bitterly.

"Sibyl," said Miss Worthing, "that's nonsense, and furthermore you know it."

Again the other woman sighed. "You're right," she said grudgingly after a moment. "No one's tried to commit murder before." And, turning away once more, she led them into the living room to confront the assemblage gathered there.

It was a large room, with the kind of odd shape to it one

might expect to find in such a house. There was a big, almost walk-in fireplace against the outer wall, with a massive brick chimney rising above the mantel. The room itself was a rather untidy jumble of rugs, books, and furniture, the latter of almost every imaginable period and style, all of it, however, sharing the virtues of comfort or great beauty or both, all of it, too, with that patina of shabbiness which bespeaks long and appreciative use. Only in the corner alcove—which was actually the tower room—was a note of austerity struck. There, on an uncarpeted floor, reposed a large concert Steinway grand piano, with the only piece of furniture sharing the room—other than a gruesomely uncomfortable-looking piano chair—a smallish cabinet filled to bursting with the yellow, chartreuse, and crimson folios of the various publishers of music. A small Christmas tree blinked dispiritedly in the corner near the archway leading into the foyer—about as far from the fireplace as it could be and still be in the same room—and the room had been trimmed up for Christmas, although clearly in that rather desultory manner typical of nests from which the chicks have largely flown.

Comfortable and indifferently festive the room might have been, the collection of people in it, however, were definitely neither comfortable nor festive. There were not all that many, really—twelve, all told, counting Mrs. Anderson and the two new arrivals. What was fascinating, though—at least to Miss Worthing's curious gaze as it swept the room—was the astounding disparity of emotions being silently broadcast by them: fear, impatience, fury, avid curiosity; only Billy McClure, standing sentry at the door to the dining room, was wearing a stony and inexpressive countenance as he continued his impression of the perfect upper servant.

Intercepting that summarizing glance, Larry Worthing, Miss Worthing's nephew, stood up from the easy chair opposite the fire where he had been sitting and came to kiss his aunt on the cheek.

"I think you'll find tumultuous rejoicing in the Incarnation in rather short supply, Aunt Matilda," he murmured as he did so.

"Larry!" she admonished severely, but returned the kiss and said softly, "We have to talk."

"I daresay," he muttered and returned to his place.

"Martha," Miss Worthing commanded, "sit there!" There was one of a pair of self-consciously medieval Pre-Raphaelite throne chairs flanking the archway to the foyer.

"That should help keep me awake," Miss Shaw groused, eyeing the high seat and uncompromisingly straight back of the chair.

Miss Worthing, acutely aware that all the eyes in the room followed her progression, moved to take up a position in front of the fire around which the furniture of the room was naturally grouped.

Mrs. Anderson followed too, until she paused to speak to Billy. "Anyone say anything while I was in the hall?"

"Only Mr. Benjamin Anderson suggesting that if I were tired, we could always switch on the video recorder."

Mrs. Anderson turned to eye her enormous elder son sitting in the corner nearest Larry on a sofa set perpendicular to the chair in which his friend was sitting.

"I think the remark was meant kindly, ma'am," Billy hastened to add.

"It certainly was," said Ben, squirming somewhat.

Mrs. Anderson explained this curious passage to Miss Worthing. "I asked Billy to take note of anything anyone said to anyone."

Miss Worthing's attention was once more wandering around the room. She did not, therefore, could not, have missed the assorted dirty looks this explanation garnered for Mrs. Anderson and for Billy. Privately she considered it to be more than a trifle melodramatic, even considering the circumstances. It was also, very likely, illegal. But as for *that* . . . oh well. She mentally shrugged her shoulders and got hold of herself. This whole business was illegal; what did one more little bit matter?

"Thank you, Sibyl," she said. "That was good thinking."

Mrs. Anderson subsided onto the hearth end of a couch at Miss Worthing's right, which stood at ninety degrees to the fire. At the farther end of the same couch, Helen Anderson Taylor brooded over her sleeping infant daughter. She had looked up only once, at which time she had leveled a glance at Miss Worthing of such compelling loathing that it considerably shook the older woman, who then watched, appalled, as the younger swept the room with much the same expression before returning her glance and her whole attention to the sleeping babe she rocked so gently in her enfolding arms.

At right angles to that couch was another easy chair, crouched in which was Helen's mother-in-law, Arletta Taylor, her eyes rapt on her granddaughter, twisting her hands and looking as if she would transpire of sheer terror at any moment.

Somehow, Miss Worthing thought, we are going to have to address that poor woman's fear. It was as much a practical thought as a charitable one. Mrs. Taylor would be useless unless they could somehow still her fear. The woman was furthermore looking haggard and older than Miss Worthing had ever before seen her.

Hangovers! suddenly Miss Worthing thought to herself. That's what it is. They *are* all hung over. "Sibyl," she said, "do you have any cold beer in the house?"

"Of course."

"Splendid! Billy!" she commanded. "Fetch beer. For anyone who wants it. Two. For everyone."

"For you and Miss Shaw?" he asked.

"No," said Miss Shaw and Miss Worthing almost simultaneously.

"Nor for me, Billy," said Mrs. Anderson, clearly not best pleased.

Everyone else, though, cheered up considerably at the thought of a cold beer. And seeing it, Miss Worthing was somewhat cheered herself.

Good, she thought. Now I'll have them with me. At least, she added more realistically, at first.

Under the subdued murmur of the business of beer, she continued her survey.

The Andersons' youngest, Cyrus, sat in the window seat to the right of the fireplace, his fair and handsome face flushed, partly with the heat from the fire, but also, definitely, with emotion. In fact, he alone of the assembled looked to be actually awash with grief for his father.

Next to him, occasionally touching Cy's arm or brushing his hand with her own, was Arletta's daughter, Bette Wanda, looking particularly haggard, which—if she had only just been aroused from a drunken stupor—was hardly surprising. Her jaw was set and her dark eyes smoldered angrily as they darted from Miss Worthing to Mrs. Anderson and back again. The rage in them softened only when she spoke in an almost inaudible murmur to Cy or when they would briefly rest on the back of the head of the last person in the room to be counted, her brother, Bob E. Taylor.

Bob E. sat almost directly at Miss Worthing's left as she took up her position in front of the fire. He occupied the hearth end of the same couch as Benjamin Anderson. He sat, half-turned from the fire so that he was in profile to Miss Worthing, his eyes downcast, raising them only to take his beer and once again to cast a look of remarkable longing at his wife sitting in determined isolation across the room.

Well, Miss Worthing thought, time to get on with it. She began crisply, "Sorry to have kept you all waiting, but it could not be helped. Nor am I going to keep you very long tonight.

"I'm sure you're all very tired and would like to get to bed," she continued, ignoring the gasps which greeted that unexpected announcement. "But before you do, I think I'd better tell you precisely where we stand so that there is no possibility of a misunderstanding.

"The worst problem is that, at the moment, I know nothing. Nothing whatever. This means, I'm afraid, that I'm going to have to do some probing and—as I'm sure you're all aware—probing can sometimes be very uncomfortable. Now I've known some of you quite well over the years and others of you not so well. I want you all to know, first of all, that that acquaintanceship or lack of it means nothing at all."

"Bullshit!" interrupted Bette Wanda Taylor angrily.

Miss Worthing eyed that young woman mildly enough as she responded, "I didn't say I expected to be believed, you know. But it does happen to be the truth." She turned back to her address. "All I know at the moment is that Henry Anderson's upstairs dying. I am told—and at the moment I have no particular reason to think otherwise—that he is dying because someone—some one of you, here in this house, acting alone or in concert, contrived to put alcohol of some kind into the General's orange juice. That is, I repeat, all I know.

"I am, therefore, going to require the cooperation of each

one of you to help me find out the truth of the matter. And do let me assure you, people, we *are* going to find out the truth of it."

"But if it was one of us," Arletta Taylor interrupted, "he's gonna lie."

"He or she," Benjamin Anderson rumbled in.

"He or she," agreed Miss Worthing grimly, but then, still trying to calm the woman, explained, "Arletta, sometimes it is precisely by the presence of lies and half-truths and misdirections that one presently finds one's way to the truth."

The woman nodded, but it was plain she understood not at all.

"And then what?" Again it was Bette Wanda.

Really, thought Miss Worthing, what a very aggressive young person she is.

"I have no idea," she replied. "That, thank God, is not my province." She turned and looked at Mrs. Anderson, who shrugged and ventured, "I don't know either. Why don't we simply find out first and then, yes, then I think we should let Henry decide."

The response to this was sudden, loud, and violent. Bob E. shouted, "This is the craziest thing I ever heard in my life!"

It was very much like someone throwing a stone into a pond that had hitherto been still. The violence with which he spoke rippled around the room as everyone turned to regard the man—some, like his mother—with fear and worry transparent in their faces; or others—like Ben and Mrs. Anderson—with a regard that was cold, implacable, and totally hostile. Ben indeed swelled up even more than usual with wrath and no doubt would have most willingly blasted Bob E., had not the latter, lurching from his chair, rounded on Miss Worthing.

"And who are you?" he demanded. "Who the hell are you comin' in here and tellin' us what we're gonna and not gonna do? How can some old coot like you know what the hell you're doing?"

It was a point Miss Worthing was quite prepared to acknowledge. As it happened, however, it was unnecessary.

Ben, too, had hauled himself out of his chair, breathing heavily, his face purple, while his mother, her face a stern mask, had also risen. At that last speech of Bob E.'s, however—that query, an obviously honest if angry demand for Miss Worthing's credentials—Ben and his mother both stared almost openmouthed, not entirely certain that they had heard correctly.

It was, curiously enough, Arletta Taylor who responded. "Why, my goodness, Bob E.," she said, as she desisted from her handwringing and stared at her son. "I thought ever'body in Jolliston knew 'bout Miss Worthing."

She said it almost primly, rather like a schoolgirl reciting a lesson. Having said it, however, she turned her eyes toward Miss Worthing; once again the woman was literally atwitch with terror. "But I don't know," she said to Miss Worthing directly, "if she knows anything 'bout folks like us."

And speaking in that simple statement was a habitual hopelessness that, for a moment, Miss Worthing found quite wrenching.

"I do wish you would all calm down!" Miss Shaw suddenly spoke from her throne across the room. "Mattie and I knew that one or another of you was going to make some remark like that—"

"What's that supposed to mean?" challenged Bette Wanda.

"Just that," snapped Miss Shaw. "Some nonsensical remark—like Arletta's just now—about 'our kind of folks.'"

"Well?" Bette Wanda continued to insist on the issue. "It's got some point, you know."

"Perhaps it has," said Miss Shaw crossly, "but you're just going to have to trust us."

"Crap!" said Bob E. and took a step forward, which nearly resulted in his falling headlong. He caught himself in time, however, and began a loud and not altogether intelligible tirade.

Good heavens, thought Miss Worthing, the man is drunk as a lord. She sighed. This really had gone on quite long enough. It was late, there was a tremendous deal of spadework to be got through, and she was tired of politics.

"Mr. Taylor!" Her voice slashed right through his drunken posturings and brought him up short. "I very much regret that the only alternative to having Martha and me taking this business in hand is to call in the police."

Bob E., at the first sharp command in her voice, had halted his nonsense and stared, owlishly glaring at her.

"Why don'tcha?" he challenged. "Why don'tcha get the goddamn cops in here."

"I've told you already, Bob E., that Henry—"

"Sibyl!" snapped Miss Worthing. "I'm not altogether certain that is relevant."

"What isn't?"

"What Henry wants or doesn't want. Good Lord, as it stands now, every blasted one of us is an accessory after the fact just for not reporting it."

"I told you, Matilda; no police."

"That's right, Bob E.," Arletta added almost querulously. "Ain't nobody wants the cops, so you just hush now, y'hear?"

No, thought Miss Worthing, neither you—nor yours—*are* much likely to want the police after that bit of business last year, are they?

Aloud, she said, "All right, that's about enough. All of you, go to bed. All of you"—she smiled rather grimly—"but Billy, Martha, Sibyl, Ben, and Larry. And also, alas, yours truly."

Instantly, Bette Wanda was on the warpath again. "What are you gonna do?"

"Billy," replied Miss Worthing, "is going to patrol."

"Patrol?"

"Yes, dear, patrol. I do not know if there is any physical evidence of any kind still in situ here, but I'll be damned if I'm going to allow—well, shall we retire into an ancient convention and call him or her X?—I am not going to allow X an altogether free hand to possibly mess things up. So yes, my dear, patrol."

"But what about Ben and Larry?" Bette Wanda demanded. "And her?" She offensively pointed at Mrs. Anderson.

"I'm going to question them."

"About what?"

"I'm not certain that's any business of yours, young lady," Miss Worthing snapped, out of patience.

"What about what we have to say?"

That "we" was by no means lost on Miss Worthing. For the moment, however, she chose to ignore it.

47

"Let me be the first to assure you that I am definitely going to question all of you. But not tonight. Go to bed!"

And, though clearly dissatisfied, there they all had to rest content. It did not, however, prevent comments.

"Mother," said Helen, as she undulated toward the door, completely ignoring Miss Worthing, as she had during the entire tableau. "I must say that I think this is all very silly, you know. Mary Elizabeth should have been home and in bed hours—"

"Good night, Helen," said her mother through clenched teeth. "You're in your old room. I've put the rocking cradle in there for Mary Elizabeth."

"Oh, very well," said Helen with a sigh and left. Ben and Larry assisted the sodden Bob E. out. "We'll be back," said Larry.

"And we'll be in the kitchen," called Miss Worthing after him. "We've got to have some tea," she muttered half to herself.

"In the cabinet over the counter," said Mrs. Anderson, shepherding her involuntary guests ahead of her. "Kettle's on the stove."

Bette Wanda grabbed her mother by the hand and stormed out of the room.

Finally, at the door, Mrs. Anderson called back, "Cyrus!"

That young man was still seated in the window seat. Indeed, it was almost as though he were waking up when he responded to his mother's call.

"Oh, sorry," he said, springing up. "I didn't—"

Suddenly it occurred to Miss Worthing that—other than his older sister, Helen—Cy had been the only person in the room who had said not one word, just as he had been the only one who had been at all visibly grieving for his father. Which made it all the more shocking when—as he was heading out the door ahead of his mother—he turned and said, both to her and to Miss Worthing, "I'm sorry Dad is dying. I am. I really am. But I'll tell you something else: I'm still not certain that whoever did it just might not deserve a medal."

CHAPTER 3

Half an hour later, five people—Miss Worthing, Miss Shaw, Mrs. Anderson, Ben, and Larry—had taken their places around the scrubbed plain pine kitchen table. In the center of the table was a brown earthenware Chinese teapot of that tall cylindrical type manufactured in the Middle Kingdom for the average family of eighty or more. Steam spouted jauntily from the spout, and at each person's elbow stood a large steaming mug of tea brewed as dark as coffee.

That it was welcome, even necessary, was made clear by the way no one spoke—for anything other than the briefest request for milk or sugar or lemon—until the first cup had been drunk and the second nearly so.

"A friend of mine—who's a real tea maven," said Ben as he squeezed an eighth of a lemon into his second cup, to which he had already added four teaspoons of sugar, "told me that after the English had successfully managed to tweak some tea plants out of the Chinese and raced off to India to plant them, they discovered a subspecies of *Camellia sinensis* already growing in Assam that turned out to be far more to English tastes than had the Chinese."

"Consider the English palate," said Larry.

"Don't let Lady Fairgrief hear you say that."

"Don't let her fool you—she's just as American as you or I," said Larry. "Though, I do have to admit, she sure can put on the dog."

"If that's true," said Mrs. Anderson to her son, "what your friend said about the Assamese tea plants, it makes all that opium traffic the English perpetrated and the way they put down the so-called Boxer Rebellion even more immoral than ever, doesn't it?" She shook her head angrily. "The wicked things people do. And for what? A fistful of silver they fritter away as fast as they've acquired it." Something in her own words seemed to recall her to the present situation. Almost primly she said, "I thought India would be better to keep us all awake. But really, don't you think we should keep to the point?"

The two men—Larry to Miss Worthing's left and Ben across the table from her—were both practically chain-smoking. Between them, a sizable ashtray in green glass was rapidly filling.

Mrs. Anderson sat at the end of the table to Miss Worthing's right, while directly to Miss Worthing's left, on the same side of the table, sat Miss Shaw, patiently laying out a large stenographer's notebook, three fountain pens, a bottle of ink, and several of the rather tatty and discolored pen wipers Miss Shaw had laboriously crocheted years before.

Promptly ignoring her own admonition, Mrs. Anderson picked one of them up and turned it thoughtfully in her hands, a little smile on her face. "I'd forgotten about pen wipers."

"A curious custom," murmured Ben. "To expend all that energy on something to wipe excess ink from the point of a pen."

Miss Shaw chuckled. "I suppose it does seem like that now. But we all did it. Tissue paper was not to be wasted on pen points. Not then."

"I use a felt tip," said Larry.

"You write longhand?" asked Mrs. Anderson, surprised.

He nodded. "And you?"

She looked quite amused as she said, "I'm afraid I use a word processor.

And Ben laughed. "I love it. The up-to-date novelist writes longhand and the theological scholar uses a word processor. I like that a lot."

"Can't abide any of 'em myself," said Miss Shaw succinctly. "Felt tips. Word processors. And as for ballpoints!"

The others laughed at her evident disapproval of all modern innovations.

"I bet you'd use a quill if you could," said Larry banteringly.

"No," said Miss Shaw. "Too much work to keep 'em sharp."

Larry laughed. "There! I knew you would have at least tried them."

Miss Worthing had let the small talk ramble quite deliberately. Tea was, as ever, pepping her up, and as the business of refills and prattle about the China trade and Miss Shaw's impedimenta and writers' tools in general went on, she found her mind kicking blessedly into gear as she looked round the table considering them, each in turn.

First of all there was her nephew, Lawrence Allen Worthing, Larry to his friends and relations, L. A. Worthing to his readership. He was of medium height, fair of hair, with a short snubbed nose, a cupid-bow mouth, and a strongly cleft chin. Miss Shaw had once observed rather tartly that he was, "cute—and won't it be wonderful when he outgrows it!" And it was true that he had the rather vacant appearance of a superannuated preppie, a young banker perhaps or a junior partner in a prestigious law firm.

In fact, the man made a quite handsome living writing the most decadent thrillers Miss Worthing had ever read, full of streams of consciousness, existential despair, climates where it did nothing but drizzle, and lots and lots of sex. It was the latter elements which had caused "Hollywood"—that mythical entity with money to burn—to speak to Larry's agent in terms of such agreeable sums that he had forthwith caught the next plane to Los Angeles and put up at the Beverly-Wilshire to wallow in Sybaritic splendor for the duration of the film.

It was there, during a preliminary script conference, that Larry had had the pleasant surprise of renewing his old acquaintance with Benjamin Anderson. The two had known each other as boys when—for a period of ten years—Larry had come to the Jolliston Valley to spend each summer with his Aunt Matilda. They had passed from each other's ken in their late middle teens and it was an agreeable twist of fate that they should have fetched up working on the same film together, Larry as one of a whole committee of writers, and Ben cast as the villain of the piece. The heavy. Literally.

For Benjamin Anderson was, without question, one of the fattest people Miss Worthing had ever known. He had been a chubby baby, a fat little boy, a porcine adolescent, and was now a perfectly grotesque adult. However, it did seem likely that his condition was not entirely his own fault. Sibyl did tend rather to go on about glands and metabolisms whenever the subject of her elder son arose.

And arise the subject frequently did. Turning his size to singular advantage, after college Ben had removed himself to southern California. There he immersed himself in the cultural quiddities of lotusland until, by dint of sheer determination, coupled with an astonishing capacity for hard work, he had established himself as an accomplished and solid character actor, gradually endearing himself to audiences as a modern-day villain of the Sidney Greenstreet variety. Finally, the year before, his remarkable performance as the menacing Colonel von Gratz in *Operation: Limbo* had earned him an Academy Award, national recognition, and the freedom to be somewhat choosier about his material.

He was also a man with one of those quiet but persistent reputations for being in private life a very good man, generous both of himself and of his fortune. It was the kind of reputation a son of Sibyl Anderson might almost be expected to have. Still—as Miss Worthing and Ben now eyed each other expressionlessly across the width of the table—she reflected rather grimly that she was going to have to keep that reputation in mind as a not insignificant datum.

All the more so because she found herself harboring something of a suspicion about really fat people, particularly fat men of middle age. It did not quite descend to the depths of a prejudice, but she could never entirely shake the feeling that the obesity of such all too often signified an unrestrained appetence, an inability or even an unwillingness to curb their appetites and, a fortiori, their passions. A suspicion that, if thwarted, they could turn out so easily to be very dangerous men indeed.

Still, he was Sibyl Anderson's son.

Not, unfortunately, that that was not something of a double-edged sword, Miss Worthing reflected with a sigh.

For a moment—idly, irrelevantly—she wondered just how many people today remembered the Sibyl Anderson of forty years ago. Certainly, if anyone had had the temerity to thwart the woman in those days, coruscating pyrotechnics would have been a flat certainty.

Miss Worthing had actually not known her very well then. Deliberately. And the sole reason had been the truly abominable personality which had possessed the woman in those days. Miss Worthing, furthermore, was not herself living in the Valley then either and had been spared, for the most part, Sibyl's trying acquaintance. Moreover, after the war, the Andersons had had time to do little more than purchase their enormous manse in Jolliston before Captain Anderson (as he was then) had been posted to London, where they had remained throughout the chilliest days of the Cold War.

What Miss Worthing knew of the Andersons' life in London she had learned from her aunt, Lady Fairgrief. Her ladyship had met the couple at some function or other. She had been absolutely tickled to discover that they actually owned a house in her own home town and so set about cultivating what was to become an enduring friendship.

At that time, Mrs. Anderson had been a bewitching beauty. Unfortunately her really striking loveliness had been flawed by an operatic temperament of the worst possible kind. With utter disregard for the feelings of others, she had regularly created endless series of ugly scenes, putting family, friends, tradesmen, servants, and acquaintances through an agony of fury and embarrassment, which were all the more difficult to forgive because of her evident enjoyment of their discomfiting.

Then, one afternoon in 1954, Lady Fairgrief (who held old-fashioned ideas about the obligations of friendship) had pointed out, with glacial calm, that—haring down the path she was pursuing—Mrs. Anderson would very soon end up bereft of all family, all friends, and probably all hope in a place altogether indistinguishable from hell.

No one else had been present during the ensuing battle royal, and neither woman had ever felt it to be sufficiently anyone else's business to enlighten them as to what, precisely, had passed between them that afternoon. What everyone did see, however, was the beginning of a struggle which was to span the next two decades as Sibyl Anderson slowly wrestled her temperament under control.

Eventually, with grace and the firm guidance of a great spiritual director, the battle had been won, and she was a now a woman of almost radiant serenity, in her person to be sure, but in her writings as well. For Mrs. Anderson had gone on, at the behest of her director, to write a whole series of books about the intricacies of pursuing the dedicated life.

Her dark sloe eyes were like shimmering pools which regarded the world with an abundance both of charity and that light, ironic amusement at the way of things which seems to be one of the more outstanding earthly rewards of those who have worked to conquer themselves. No longer perhaps the alluring beauty of yore, she was still a remarkably handsome woman.

It's those splendid bones, thought Miss Worthing with almost reverence. In her sixties now, the woman's face was still virtually unlined, the smooth planes and high cheekbones miraculously unchanged. Her hair, once so black, was now the purest white, and Miss Worthing had never seen her other than immaculately coiffed. Her clothing tended toward the tweedy—a taste (or sensibility, rather) acquired during her sojourn in the English countryside, and she was in fact dressed now in a heavy brown tweed skirt, oxfords, and an eggshell silk blouse. A single strand of pearls lay about her throat while her hands, tightly clasped before her on the table, made small involuntary jerks which set the diamonds of her wedding-ring guard to sparkling and flashing in the light.

It was those twitchings that Miss Worthing found most unsettling. She put a hand out and covered Mrs. Anderson's to try and still them. She wondered—and knew somehow instinctively that it was a question that wanted answering: How much of that passionate temperament yet remained in the woman, repressed now beneath her control and will of iron?

"It's all right," she heard herself saying. "We'll get through this as fast as we can, Sibyl."

"I know," said Mrs. Anderson. "It's just . . ." She shook her head and drank tea.

Ben looked toward his mother with an absolutely unreadable face.

"I think I know why you wanted to take Ben and me first." It was Larry who picked the ball up and began to run with it.

"Yes, I daresay you do," said his aunt. "It's really quite simple. You are a writer, Larry, and Ben, you're an actor—two professions whose very lifeblood is observation." She sighed and explained. "I need background. So far I haven't a notion, half the time, of what you people are talking about."

"Okay," said Larry, "that's what I thought. But both Ben and I—" He broke off and tried again. "Well, I'm afraid that both of us will have to be under suspicion too, that is, if—"

"Oh?" queried Miss Worthing, interrupting.

Before Larry could reply, however, Ben burst out, "Larry, that's crap! How on earth—"

"Believe me, Ben," said Larry. "I know something about this process—I have to know, and that means—" Again he pulled himself up short and addressed his aunt. "Look! How much do you know?"

"I told you already, next to nothing. Other," she added delicately, "than something of the family's—history."

"How tactful," said Ben.

"Well, you have the advantage of me there," said Larry, darting a quick glance at Ben, who merely arched a somewhat defiant eyebrow.

"Perhaps," Mrs. Anderson interjected, "that's why it will be useful for you to supply some background to your aunt."

In response to that, however, Ben suddenly ground out his cigarette and leaned forward, thumping the table and speaking almost angrily. "Which I submit is nonsense. If am not mistaken, all we have to do is to find out who had the opportunity to put booze in my father's orange juice."

"And if—as my Aunt Eulalia tells me—most of you did?"

"Then look to the cui bono!"

"Ah yes," smiled Miss Worthing. "The motive. And—once again—if there are several of you with excellent motives?"

This time, Ben merely frowned.

"Which brings me back," said Miss Worthing, "to needing—"

"Phooey," said Ben rudely. "Talk to Bob E. and you'll find all you need of means, motive, and opportunity."

"So you are convinced it was Bob E. Aunt Eulalia said you were."

"Course I am."

"Fine," said Miss Worthing equably. "I want to know why."

"He did do some awfully strange things." Even Larry was looking rather grim.

"Like what?" said Miss Worthing. She too leaned forward and, as Ben had done, tapped the table for emphasis. "Don't you see? I can't just take your word that Bob E. did it. As soon as I did—even assuming I'd want to—Bette Wanda and Arletta would be all over me like a rash, and quite rightly too. And that means that there must be at least *some* reasonable doubt."

"It seems to me," said Ben, "that dumping that juice was as close to a smoking gun as you can get."

"It is odd," admitted Miss Worthing. "But," she reminded, "he would not by any means be the first to be found holding a smoking gun over a fresh corpse who was nevertheless not guilty."

"Then you're assuming . . ."

"I am trying not to assume anything. Why can't you see that? I refuse to hang my hat on a peg of ice, and the only thing which can prevent that is data. Facts. From the beginning, and from both of you. And that goes for you, too, Sibyl. How many times do I have to say it? What in blazes is going on here? What has been going on? Why—after living with this situation for so long, did it—finally—today, eventuate in murder?"

After this outburst, it was Ben who—meekly enough—said, "Okay, Miss Worthing. I'm sorry. You're right." And he began then to speak in a quiet, narrative voice, looking inward, allowing the reconstructive imagination to play.

"I guess," he said, "for me—and for Larry—it began really about three days ago. That was when I found that I really was going to be able to get home for Christmas. I talked to Mom and Dad several weeks before and told them that yet again it looked as though they shouldn't plan on me this year. Then—by some miracle—the film wrapped and I was free."

Larry then took up the narrative.

"That was when he asked me if I would like to spend the

holidays here in Jolliston. I did have plans," he said when his aunt lifted a brow, "but they were mostly to do with a—well, a business deal I had coming down. And then I realized how many years it had been since I had visited with the Andersons and then I began to picture what it would be like"—he grinned—"when I walked in on you and Martha and surprised the bejesus out of you on Christmas Day during your open house."

"Which you very effectively did," said Miss Worthing, as Miss Shaw too looked up from her pot hooks and squiggles and grinned back at him.

"And so," he resumed, "Ben and I came winging northward, with little me still thinking all was as in the halcyon days of yore."

"When did you begin to suspect it might be otherwise?" asked Miss Worthing.

"When we arrived in Jolliston," he replied, "turned off Main Street onto Fremont, and Ben drove right on past the Elms."

"I know," said Larry, after a moment of stunned silence, "you've been away so long, you've forgotten where your folks live."

In reply, Ben merely growled something utterly unintelligible.

"Say what?" needled Larry.

"I said I haven't forgotten."

"Then where are we going?"

"For a drive."

"And what, pray, have we been doing these past two hours and more?"

For a moment, Ben made no reply, merely focusing on the endless turnings and permutations of the streets in front of them. "Finally, he said, "I have to tell you something."

"Don't you think you could have told me on the plane, or during the drive up here?"

"Yes, but . . . Well, at first I decided that it would be best that you just—found out. Now I'm not so sure."

"Find out what?" Larry, justifiably suspicious, demanded.

They were still threading the windings of Jolliston's residential districts.

"You know," said Larry, "Jolliston is not exactly the kind of town you can drive around in aimlessly. Someone is sure to call the sheriff about a suspicious rent-a-car and we'll have Sam Marshall barreling down on us—he is still the sheriff, isn't he?"

Ben nodded but held his peace.

"Look, Ben," said Larry with some exasperation, "why don't you pull up at Winesville? We're practically at the Cut anyway. We can get some coffee—which, if you still insist on sitting in a car in this weather, will not be unwelcome. And you can"—he chuckled—"tell me All!"

"'Tain't funny, McGee," growled Ben, but he did turn left at the Cut and headed southeast toward the minuscule community of Winesville.

The Cut was one of those utterly unfathomable "agricultural" projects which abound in California and which—though always seeming of crucial import at the time they're built—afterward somehow completely lose their point.

In the case of the Cut, all anyone knew at this juncture was that it had originally been dug in order to slice a two-and-a-half-mile oxbow out of the Jolliston River. It had, however, proved thoroughly ineffective, and the canal was now nothing more than a very nice, rather picturesque, one-mile-long and geometrically precise swamp, the only real purpose of which was to provide local tables with a goodly summer supply of bullfrogs, catfish, and crayfish.

As they pulled up beside the Winesville General Store, which overlooked the upstream end of the canal, the Cut only looked greasy, muddy, and depressing, with the spating river sloshing fitfully over the sandbar in the gusting wind.

Above them, the heavily overcast late-afternoon sky had already darkened to deep pearl-gray while occasional bursts of rain began splashing on the roof of the car. Larry waited for the latest squall to die and dashed out of the car and up the warped stairboards into the murky depths of the Winesville General, leaving Ben brooding behind the wheel and staring sightlessly into the roiling waters of the river.

In a moment, Larry emerged onto the porch of the store and, after pausing till the next shower abated, sprinted back across the potholed tarmac to the car. Ben leaned over and snapped the door open and Larry slid in. He then put the large cardboard containers on the dash, removed a beautifully ironed linen handkerchief from his hip pocket, and used it to sop dry his really only marginally wet hair. After which operation, he extracted from the other hip pocket a narrow-toothed tortoiseshell comb and, hunching himself forward to peer into the rearview mirror, carefully combed every strand of hair back in place.

"You know," said Ben, watching this performance, "I've been observing this behavior of yours for some time now with all the enthralled fascination of Dr. Lorenz for his geese and I still can't figure it out. You're not an especially vain man, Larry, so what gives?"

Grinning, Larry handed him his coffee. "I do it, old son, precisely because I'm not vain. I'm not naturally neat like you are, you know, and during the—the rough years I'm afraid I got to be a really unbelievable slob. Unfortunately, you can't ever get anything done—not nothing—if you're fundamentally disorganized, so I promised myself, never again! And though I'm sure it seems a bit obsessive sometimes, I know, all too well, that if I don't stay on top of it, it overwhelms me every time."

He sipped coffee and then sagged visibly into the welcoming curve of the seat.

"Oh Lord!" he breathed with an upward glance. "We do give Thee most humble and hearty thanks that in a world of almost constant change, Mrs. Fanoff's coffee is just as awful as ever."

Ben chortled and tasted his own.

"Ah yes," he grimaced, "the true Winesville flavor—seven months of unwashed coffee oil in the urn with the added piquant delight of soggy cardboard."

"It's wonderful!" Larry sighed, enjoying the heat of the stuff if not the flavor. "The whole world has switched to using polyurethane cups for coffee-to-go and Mrs. Fanoff still uses these vanilla-cream jobbies."

"That, my boy, is quite easily explained," said Ben expansively. "She bought five million of them from Army surplus after the Second World War and just hasn't seen any reason to change till she's used them all up."

He chortled again and, gingerly sipping the scalding stuff, once more fell silent. Once more the only sounds were the tumble of the river, the wind in the naked branches or the rustle of the leaves in the live oaks, and the occasional spate of rain upon the roof.

"Ben?"

"Yeah. I know."

Finally, after yet another long moment, Ben turned his face to look out the car window on his side.

"Larry," he asked without turning around, "by any chance do you happen to remember a kid named Bob E. Taylor?"

"Bobby Taylor? No, I don't think so. No. Now, wait a minute. Yes, I think I do—black matte hair, skin liked a peeled mushroom, an accent out of a third-rate touring company of *Tobacco Road,* and no manners to speak of?"

"Jesus!" Ben muttered softly.

"Yeah, I remember him all right," Larry went on cheerfully. "I remember he was always trying to tag along with us and we weren't having any, thank you very much. My God!" he shook his head, suddenly feeling thoroughly ashamed of himself, "what a bunch of little snobs we were."

"Precisely the word I've heard used," murmured Ben.

"Huh?"

"Larry." Ben turned and looked directly at him. "Helen married him. Two years ago."

For quite an appreciable interval, Larry did nothing but stare at Ben, thoroughly and genuinely shocked.

Helen Anderson? Married to Bobby Taylor?

He had, it was true, never much liked her, not even as a child, and still less as a teenager. Even Ben had once characterized his sister as the "ice goddess," while the other children had been considerably less polite and had thought her a snooty and unapproachable bitch.

"Helen married Bobby Taylor?" he finally managed to gasp.

Ben was once more contemplating the tumbling Jolliston through his window and sipping the noisome coffee.

"How . . ." Larry began and then hesitated, sharply aware of how crude the question might sound.

"How did it happen?" Ben supplied for him. "None of us ever really knew."

"But how did she meet him? I mean, we certainly never would have brought him around, and she wasn't likely to meet him in any of her circles, was she? I mean . . ." And again Larry trailed off, his face suddenly flaming at the tight knowing smile on Ben's face as the large man again turned to look at him.

"You see," said Ben, "we still are snobs. However," he shrugged and went on, "as it happens, she went to work for him."

"But I thought she was working for some doctor over in Steuber. Didn't she take an RN?"

"She did and she was," replied Ben very dryly indeed. "But the man was politely requested to go back to Pakistan; do not pass go, do not collect two hundred dollars."

"What for?"

"He wrote a scrip for five thousand downers for an AMA investigator and gave him a fistful of disposable syringes besides."

"Oh dear," said Larry helplessly. "How unpleasant."

"I'm told it could have been a lot more unpleasant," Ben continued. "For Helen, I mean. She was, after all, working for the man. She always maintained that she had not known anything of what was going on. Unfortunately, there was a lot of inventory still missing—drugs, syringes, pills—so that when the fuss was finally over, no one would touch her. Mom and Dad wanted her to go spend some time in England for a year or two with friends who offered to have her, but she said it would look too much like she was running away."

"Good for her," said Larry.

"I suppose so," said Ben dubiously. "But anyway, that was when Bob E. suddenly popped up and was all sympathy and understanding and offered her the job of his 'Gal Friday.'"

"Dear God, what a loathsome expression!" said Larry. "I haven't even heard it in years."

"Yes, well, it's the kind of thing Bob E. says," said Ben and then added, "and incidentally, that's his name—Bob, space, *E*, period."

"What does the *E* stand for?" asked Larry rather nastily. "Elvis?"

Admittedly it was not exactly the most helpful remark to

have made. Nevertheless Larry was stunned by Ben's suddenly erupting into a stentorian bellow, quite deafening in the closed confines of the car. "Goddamn it, Larry! Do you have to make this any more difficult than it is already?" Then, seeing Larry's expression, he exhaled rather loudly, ran a hand over his face, and visibly regained control of himself. "I'm sorry," he apologized. "There really wasn't any reason for that. Besides," he added in a wry voice, "you happen to have hit the nail on the head. His middle name really is Elvis."

"You're joking," said Larry, secretly more than a little tickled by the revelation.

"No, I'm not," said Ben and then sighed. "You'll understand more clearly when you've met his charming mother."

And that was when it began to come clear to Larry what precisely he was getting himself into. Of *course* there would be family there! Wasn't that one of the things Christmas was all about? It was *not* going to be as he had so fondly imagined it would—a pleasant week bantering with Ben and being overfed by Mrs. Anderson and Aunt Matilda and laughing at the slightly malicious wisdom of Aunt Eulalia. There were also going to be unpleasant aspects of the affair—more specifically, he was going to have to deal with one or two or perhaps whole rafts of people of whom he was not likely to be fond at all.

"Look, Larry," said Ben, "if, well, now that you know about this—complication, would you rather I drove you over to your aunt's house and just say that's that?"

"Not really," said Larry more confidently now. "Why should I? I really am looking forward to seeing your folks, and why should I object to your sister marrying Bob E., unlikely though it may seem. Maybe we overlooked something in him."

And her, too, he added privately, as Ben sighed with obvious relief.

"Thank you," said Ben. "I knew I should have told you in LA, but I didn't know if you would come, knowing about the Taylor connection."

"God, Ben!" Larry declared almost irritably. "I'm not that much of a prig." And then added, more honestly, "I hope."

"I hope not, too," said Ben, "because I expect they're going to be in our pockets quite a bit. That," he chuckled, "was one of the reasons I wanted you along. Moral support, don'tcha know."

"What are they like, Ben?"

"Who? The Taylors?"

Larry nodded.

"Well, now," said Ben. He raised his eyebrows and exhaled slowly and noisily through pursed lips as he meditated briefly on how best to answer. "By and large," he finally said, "I think you would have to describe them as unabashed, dyed-in-the-wool, genuine, true-blue swamp trash."

"How kind," said Larry.

"Actually," said Ben, "the kid sister's not so bad."

"Ben," Larry snorted, "that sounds suspiciously like damning with faint praise. I gather, then, that you don't like Bob E."

"No, I don't," said Ben. "But then I really can't say I actively dislike him either. It would be obvious to a blind man that he really does carry quite a torch for Helen, and Mother tells me he's been wonderful with the baby."

"That was quick!" blurted Larry before he could stop himself.

"My word." Ben frowned censoriously. "What a lovely mind you do have on occasion. But I do know it wasn't anything like that. It's adopted. A girl. Bob E., apparently, can't. I don't know why not," he added hastily, "and furthermore I do not in the slightest degree care. All I know is Helen wanted a baby, so Bob E. went out and bought her one."

"I beg your pardon."

"You know the routine, surely—find some kid in trouble, pay all the medical expenses, plus a little bonus, and then take the brat home with you."

"Sounds a bit risky, doesn't it?"

Ben shrugged. "Depends on which side of the nurture/nature argument you're on."

And what, thought Larry, could one possibly say to that?

"Fascinating," he said ambiguously. "And tell me, how do your folks cope with all these—all these changes?"

"They cope," said Ben. "Although I know that Mom is tickled silly with the baby. At least," he explained dryly, "it seems to be her primary topic of conversation on the telephone or in letters."

"And—is it Cy? Your brother?"

Ben smiled reflectively. "Cy may be doing better than all of us in the long run and in his own way," he replied, before adding the rather gnomic observation, "after all, he's pretty much had to make his own rules."

For another long moment, neither man said anything as they finished the dregs of the coffee. Another squall of rain drubbed loudly on the roof of the car and proceeded down the Cut. They watched it as it went, roughing the surface of the murky gray waters.

"You know, Ben," said Larry very quietly, "when I was cooking on that oil rig out in the Gulf, I used to think about your family. A lot. I envied you your mother and father. I really did. In some ways I think I still do."

"I never met yours," said Ben. "I gather they didn't really approve of your aunt—"

Larry laughed. But it was not a happy laugh.

"Or me," he said. "But then they disapproved of everything. It was okay for Aunt Matilda to be stinking rich, but quite another for her to have had the bad taste to have made it herself—and she an orphaned maiden lady."

Ben said nothing.

"Well," Larry continued," they soured themselves into early and unnecessary graves—in which cramped quarters," he observed harshly, "they are no doubt finally at peace. But"—he shook his head vigorously to clear it of the ghosts, "your folks aren't like that. That's what I've been trying to say. There's nothing small about them, Ben."

Ben smiled enigmatically.

"No," he said, "I don't suppose there is. Not really." He leaned forward to turn the ignition key. "Come on, Larry. It's high time we were home."

CHAPTER 4

"So you came straight back to the Elms?" asked Miss Worthing.

There was a moment of silence. The two men paused, flicked a glance at each other, and then lit fresh cigarettes, their faces devoid of any expression soever.

"Yes," said Ben. "We came directly home."

"Which was when I made my suggestion," said Larry.

"What was that?" asked Miss Worthing.

"That the two of us stand ready to send in the clowns."

"What is that supposed to mean?"

Larry uttered a little snort that was not quite laughter and shook his head while pinching the bridge of his nose. "That both of us should keep on our toes, and when the signals read stormy weather ahead, to rush in with a little patter. You know, a buck and a wing and a song and a dance from that great vaudeville team of Anderson and Worthing?"

"Do you mean," said Mrs. Anderson, "that you two *planned* all that nonsense you were spouting over these last few days?"

"Not to put too fine a point on it, Mother," said Ben, "yes. And furthermore," he added, looking almost defiantly at Larry, "I still think it was a good idea."

"You don't agree?" asked Miss Worthing of Larry.

"Well, obviously," said Larry, "since I suggested it, I thought it was a good idea. At least at the time."

"It does, however," said Mrs. Anderson, though not unkindly, "strike one as rather an odd thing to suggest."

"Yes, I suppose it does," said Larry. "But there was Ben pregnant with apprehension, and, well—" He flushed slightly. "When we got back here, to the Elms, we were walking up the garden path when it suddenly struck me that both of us have something of a flair for facetiousness . . ."

"Which you never noticed until you were walking up our garden path?" asked Mrs. Anderson dryly.

Larry's face flushed even more deeply. "No, of course not. But as we were walking up the path, Ben went off on this farrago of nonsense . . ."

By the time Ben finally brought the car to a halt in front of the Elms, the sun had long since passed beyond the western rim of the Valley. Only a thin and diffuse kind of light still illumined the world, a combination of streetlights, automobile lights, the bleed from the business district a few blocks away, and overhead the meager light of a half-moon trying to break through the cloud cover.

Larry smiled to himself as they passed through the gate in the trim white picket fence around the yard. The paint on the fence, slick with moisture, gleamed immaculately even in the gloom. The great elms from which the house derived its name were completely barren of leaves, yet not a trace of fallen leaf littered the neatly manicured lawn, the edges of which—along the neatly flagged pathway—were trimmed with almost mathematical precision.

"You know," said Larry, observing these things with a delighted smile, "I bet you that even if I did not know that your father was a military man, I could guess it just by looking at this yard."

"No bet," said Ben, looking about with an amused expression. "It truly is remarkable what will happen when the military itch for tidiness gets linked up to a passion for gardening. And you wouldn't believe how many of 'em wind up going to seed amid the roses." He chuckled reminiscently. "You should hear them when they get together—they will prattle on in the most serious voices about compost, nematodes, the best times to manure vegetable plots, and other delightful topics. Put me off asparagus for years! But, of course, you always missed the good part every year."

"What was that?"

"If all the leaves had not fallen by October the fifteenth, he made poor Helen and me climb up and pick the rest of them off."

Larry eyed Ben very much askance. "You're joking."

"Not at all. People came from miles around to watch. One year it even got into the *San Francisco Chronicle*. Dad would stand below shouting out directions whilst Helen and I clambered about like monkeys snatching at moribund elm leaves with our pudgy infant paws. Mother would hover about below making anxious noises while the neighbors either climbed up to help, thinking it was all great fun, or stood about shouting encouragement. A grand time was had by all."

"You have got to be putting me on!"

Ben sighed. "I only wish I were. It stopped for me when I finally tipped the scales at two hundred pounds and Mother rather firmly put her foot down. After that, Helen had to carry on by herself—at least until Cy was old enough to help." A curious expression crossed his face. "She hated it like poison too. She never had much of a head for heights."

"And so," said Larry, "that was when I suggested our little routine. With a capacity for twaddle like that—"

He broke off. Mrs. Anderson and Miss Worthing were looking at each other with an almost embarrassed air while Ben's subterranean chuckle rumbled through the kitchen like a subway train.

"You're joking!" said Larry, repeating himself. "It's true?"

"I told you," said Ben and clasped Larry's shoulder with rather a patronizing air. "But never mind. Your idea was still a good one."

"Larry?" said his aunt, again trying to read her nephew's expression."

"He's right," said Larry. "For the most part, I think I'd have to agree. There were times over the next few days when it did help to lighten things. But I have to admit also that there were times I felt like a perfect fool."

"Why?" asked Ben.

"Because," said Larry angrily, "there I was, prattling away, a perfect performing seal, and by then"—he turned back to his aunt—"I had seen the General."

"Oh," said Ben.

"Yeah," said Larry. "Oh!"

"I suppose I should have warned you about that, too," Ben admitted, "but, honestly, I've just been so used to it that it never really occurred to me . . ."

"Horsepuckey, Ben!" Larry snapped. "If that were true, why did you kick up such a fuss?"

"Fuss?" immediately asked Miss Worthing, but Ben was already saying, "I told you at the time, I just didn't like him being reminded."

"Christ, Ben. I only offered to fix him a drink."

The offer, moreover, had been made with some diffidence—it would have been obvious to a wanting child that there was something quite seriously wrong with General Anderson. Once you got a look at him, that is.

Their welcome had been all they could have wished for.

"Okay," agreed Ben, after considering a moment. "It's a good idea. I'll do the pukka Colonel and you can do your egregious-preppie-brat number. Which should come naturally to you anyway," he added with a regal sniff.

"That's the ticket," said Larry.

And as both of them laughed, they climbed the stairs to the veranda.

For a moment it almost seemed that there was no one at home. No light shone in the fanlight above the door, and the windows were all dark and blank. Only in one window—in the tower—was there a dull-yellow line of light where the edges of the draperies did not quite meet. There in the deep gloom of the veranda, it all seemed to be somehow uninviting, dampening to the spirit. They felt as though they were scrutinizing a house in a ghost town for signs of habitation.

Then they heard it, the stripped-down sound of a piano being played at breakneck speed, muted by the massiveness of those Victorian walls.

"That's Hanon," said Larry, identifying what was being played.

"That's Cy," said Ben at virtually the same moment, identifying the player.

They stood and listened, even though it sounded as though it were coming from a vast distance. It was a dazzling exhibition of technique. Larry, whose own childish fingers had been regularly subjected to those same tortuous exercises being played within with such panache, was delighted.

"He's good!" he said.

Ben nodded and muttered, "He is, isn't he?" almost as though he had not been sure till then.

But the night was growing colder. A chill wind had sprung up, gusting around the corners and whistling through the gingerbread of the house. Ben turned back to address himself to the door.

"I've been visualizing this moment for a week now," he said and gave a thunderous knock.

The sound of the piano halted abruptly. A second later, light suddenly bloomed in the fanlight, the door opened a crack, and a soft, polite voice said, "Yes?"

Then—without perceptible pause—the door was flung open and a bellow that would have done justice to Ben himself echoed in the confines of the veranda. "Ben! You came home!" And one of the most extraordinarily handsome young men Larry had ever seen literally catapulted himself into Ben's willing and waiting arms.

Larry had withdrawn into the gloom beyond the light spilling from the open door as he watched this affecting scene. As a result, he was so positioned to see—and hear—as down the hall within, a door opened and revealed a backlit figure. Then he heard that voice. It was a sound which he had been all unconsciously eagerly anticipating all day, even all week, since Ben had asked him to come with him to the Valley.

"Cy," she said, "who is—" And then she too was running down the hall toward the door, pausing only to call back into the room from which she had come, "Henry! He's come. Ben's home."

And as she ran down the hall to greet her son, after her came the General, his handsome old face alight with pleasure and happiness.

Before the General was even close, however, Cy had spotted

Larry lurking in the gloom. He was clearly puzzled as to who this person might be with his brother, but with the ingenuous and indefatigable politeness of the tribe, he stuck out a hand. "Hello. I'm Cy Anderson."

Which had the effect of bringing Ben to his senses.

"Mother," he said when he had released her from one of his characteristic bear hugs, "look who I brought with me."

She peered into the murk, which was when Larry realized that he had been holding himself back. The surprise he and Ben had cooked up between them suddenly seemed not only childish but downright rude. He stepped forward and was half embarrassed and half delighted when Sibyl Anderson's face lit up. "Larry? Is it really little Larry Worthing?" And he found himself being embraced and made much of, just as the General reached the door and was also swept into Ben's promiscuous embrace.

It had, indeed, been very pleasant. And rather more affecting than Larry had thought it would be. Afterward, he had no clear idea of how long all the handwringing, kissing, and hugging had gone on.

It was the General, however, who brought things back to earth.

"Now, Sibyl," he said with a laugh, "I do think we have all been quite fatted-calf enough. Surely we can move this indoors where it is warm and"—he peered over the half-glasses he wore half down his nose—"get these boys a drink?"

Thereafter, the next few minutes were taken up with those purely domestic details of which so much of life seems to consist: Who would go into what bedrooms? "Cy, fetch the luggage!" Sorry, but there was just no room in the garage for another car; it was a half converted stable anyway. Could theirs stay on the street? Would they excuse Cy and Mrs. Anderson while they made up the rooms? They'd see them again at supper. The General would take them into the living room and pour them drinks . . .

Finally, Larry and Ben were seated side by side in the engulfing depths of one of the sofas in the living room, slurping at very large and very strong whiskeys and soda, gratefully inhaling cigarettes and generally feeling happy and relaxed.

Except that it was so dreadfully obvious that the General

was seriously ill. The light in the living room, even with the chandelier turned down low, was sufficient to see that by, though not perhaps very clearly. In fact, Larry was more than a little tempted to hoist himself out of the sofa, march across the room to the rheostat and turn it up full, just to get a really good look at the General. Of course, one cannot do such things. Besides which, he was quite sure he would see clearly enough when the right and proper time came.

It was not even as though you could point to any one thing and say, now *that* looks bad. In fact, General Anderson appeared much as he always had: lean, trim, not overly tall, impeccably groomed; his once corn-gold hair, now white, still severely crew-cut, and the crease of his trousers still as knife-sharp as ever. But the erect and graceful carriage of the professional soldier had been replaced by something rather more rigid and, Larry suspected, rather more costing, and instead of his former clean economy of movement, the man now shuffled.

The strong lines of his face had become, it seemed, merely wrinkles, and his skin, which had always been so tanned and glowing with health from the General's predilection for practically living outdoors, had now a distinctly yellowish cast to it, a hue visible also in the whites of his eyes and which clashed unpleasantly with the periwinkle-blue irises. Those eyes, too, had always been wise, calm, and observing. Now they seemed somehow vulnerable and hurt. And it was—again Larry realized it rather suddenly—because of an aggregation of crow's-feet in that unfailing mirror of pain at the center of the brow.

Larry had been able to pursue these observations without being too terribly obvious while Ben and his father made small talk of a purely local interest. Then the General made the simplest of remarks.

He had settled into a rather tatty leather lounging chair that stood at right angles to the sofa. Ben had just lighted a fresh cigarette and was somewhat taken aback when the General closed his eyes, sniffed at the air with appreciative gusto, and said, "Boy! Do you guys have any idea how good those cigarettes smell right now?"

Ben promptly pulled his pack out of his breast pocket and made to hand it to his father. "Do you want one, Dad?"

But the General only waved his hand.

"Nah," he said roughly, "you know I could never really stand those things. Just missing my pipe, I guess," he finished with a sigh.

Larry's reaction to this was a curious combination of social apprehension, self-directed worry, and satisfied curiosity. For a number of minutes now he had not been able to put his finger on what was so different about the General. As soon as General Anderson spoke, however, he realized what it was. The man's hands were fidgeting and had been ever since they sat down. In former years, the General had always had one pipe or another in his hands. Now, without that focus, they seemed to move hither and yon to no real purpose or effect.

Rather more immediate, however, was the fact that apparently the General could not smoke anymore because of—well, because of whatever it was. And here Larry had brought the old boy a really beautiful bit of briar for Christmas.

". . . only one pipeful after meals now," the General was saying, "that's all the old quack allows me."

Whew! thought Larry and drained his drink. So *that* was all right.

"How 'bout a refill?" asked the General, beginning the struggle to get to his feet.

Quickly, Larry jumped up and moved toward the drinks cabinet. "Please, General Anderson, I can manage," he said and was aware of Ben regarding him with a measured approval.

Larry turned away and busied himself with ice and siphon and rapidly made up his mind that he was tired of pussyfooting about. "Can I get you something, General?" he asked in a studiedly casual voice and turned around.

He had not really expected to fool Ben. Nor had he. The man was far too adroit an actor not to know when someone else was mumming.

General Anderson caught the expression on his son's face and chuckled appreciatively. "My God, Ben, how many folks do you intimidate with that look?"

"Lots," said Larry, deliberately pointing toward the drinks again.

Ben growled meaningfully.

Again the General chortled and answered Larry's unspoken question. "No, thanks, son," he sighed. "I'm afraid this old soldier's drinking days are gone forever."

"As if he couldn't tell," muttered Ben.

Larry sauntered to the couch and admitted, "You're right. I could tell that something was wrong. But no booze? No tobacco? Good God, General, what happened to you?"

"Larry!" Ben bellowed it. "Are you trying my patience on purpose?"

The General eyed his son with genuine admiration. "Wish I had been able to bellow like that on the parade ground," he said, and then, almost immediately, his expression sobered and with all his authority he ordered, "But it's time to knock it off, Ben. There's no harm in Larry asking. If he's going to be staying with us, he has every right to know what happened."

"I don't like to see you reminded," said his son.

It was plain that Ben's response rather touched the General. Almost as much as it amused him. "Thank you, Ben," he began soberly enough. But the absurdity of it got to him and his smile broadened. "Ben," he said, thoroughly amused, "everybody in Jolliston knows by now. If I was going to be touchy about it, I'd be in a rage every day of the week."

He turned back to Larry. "It was my own fault," he explained. "I just wouldn't accept that my soldiering days were done. It wasn't even as though I was bored or had nothing to do . . ."

Both men smiled at the exceedingly dry tone with which he had said the last. After the General's retirement from the Army, he had developed something of a flair for finance. Actually, it had been the rather more dicey business of playing the markets rather freely, which, however, he had done with consummate skill and quite astonishing success, so much so that he had transformed an already handsome family fortune into quite fabulous wealth.

"Then, when that business got out of hand in Vietnam"—the General waved a hand vaguely in the direction of Southeast Asia—"I figured that—well, I was a combat officer in Korea and I was getting bored as hell sitting around making money, so I volunteered.

"I thought I'd be back in action again," he continued,

"doing—well . . ." He brought himself up short and grinned over his glasses at the two younger men. "Doing the things combat officers do, which I don't suppose either of you knows a damn thing about." He chuckled softly. "Probably just as well," he observed half to himself and shrugged. "But for me"—his voice grew stronger—"for me it was what I figured I did best. Hell, I'm West Point, aren't I? I was a young man in the Second World War and a good field officer in Korea. But you know, I spent most of my career sitting in a goddamn office somewhere pushing papers around a lousy desk."

He twisted his neck around to look toward the drinks cabinet. "Ben, if there's any soda water left, would you pour me a little?"

Ben, still sprawled voluptuously in the depths of the sofa, looked imploringly at Larry, who stood up to fetch the General his drink.

When the old man had swallowed, he cleared his throat and continued. "Anyway, son, that's what they set me to doing in Vietnam. I sat behind a desk and counted shoes and trousers and decided if there was enough booze in the officers' clubs."

Larry frowned and seemed about to say something.

"Now don't get me wrong, Larry," the General went on before he could speak. "I did it well. I volunteered and I did what I was told even though it sure as hell wasn't what I expected. But I'll betcha I'm the only two-star general in the entire history of the goddamn—" Again he broke off to fight down his rising choler. "I shouldn't say that. It's a hell of an important job." He said it as though he were trying to convince himself. "And I did get around the countryside a bit, checking depots and that kind of thing. That," he said fervently, "was fun. But I'm afraid it was the thing that got me, too. I was down in the Mekong Delta and got caught in the middle of the goddamn monsoon. The river rose and got into the water supply and—" He shrugged. "A week later I was back in San Francisco in Letterman Hospital with some kind of hepatitis no one in a civilized country ever knew existed." He paused to swallow soda water. "Matter of fact," he continued after a moment, "I haven't got much of a liver left.

"And so," he sighed and summed it all up. "No more booze, no more coffee, no tea, no eggs, no cream, no fats.

And, you know, son"—his trembling hands gestured helplessly—"I think I could live with all that. But the worst of it is that now even good tobacco tastes like nothing so much as dirty iron filings."

"My God, sir," whispered Larry, "I'm so sorry."

"Well, don't fret yourself too much," General Anderson answered gruffly after a moment, apparently somewhat embarrassed at the grim shadow he had cast over the holiday homecoming. "I'm getting used to it, and orange juice is supposed to be good for you. Come on, Ben"—he grinned down at his son, who was staring moodily into his highball glass—"drink up. Your mother will be calling us soon for supper."

As though on cue, Cy appeared in the doorway leading to the dining room to inform them that dinner was, in fact, served.

"Which was when," said Larry, "you might say that I became aware of something—rather strange."

"What?" asked Miss Worthing.

Larry's glance flicked first at Ben and thence to Mrs. Anderson as he said, "Cy's relationship with his father," and watched both of their faces go instantly closed and stony.

Cyrus Anderson's parting shot in the living room earlier had hardly gone unnoticed by Miss Worthing. Comment, however, at the time, would have been distinctly premature. So too, now, she waited, observing, as did Larry, the wary alertness of the two Andersons.

"I mean," pursued Larry, "it is not exactly unheard of for a father to dislike his son." He made an insouciant gesture. "My own, you may recall, was none too fond of me."

"My dear departed younger brother, your father," said Miss Worthing, "was a jerk . . ."

"Which the General is not," Larry finished the sentence for her. "Furthermore, I remember him—" He made a very Italianate gesture, waving his right hand over his right shoulder.

"And what is that supposed to mean?" asked Ben sarcastically.

"It means," said Larry, "that I remember your father was a very good father to you and Helen, taking time with you, teaching you—and the rest of us kids, for that matter—all

75

kinds of things. So of course I knew that something was wrong."

Miss Worthing looked at Ben and Mrs. Anderson, both of whom were doing a marvelous imitation of a statue.

"This is crazy," said Larry. "It has to come out."

"What an unfortunate choice of words," growled Ben.

"Isn't it?" said Larry.

"What *are* you two talking about?" demanded Miss Worthing.

Supper had been a singularly frugal meal, one obviously designed for the appetite and restrictions of an invalid diet—the leanest of ham, parsleyed potatoes, peas. Not that it was unpleasant. Far from it. And certainly the California Riesling which had been provided, cold and crisp and semi-still, helped considerably.

It was, for all that, rather an unlikely meal to have had in that house where Larry could remember sitting to any number of meals which had always seemed to consist of mountains of pasta or spaetzle, alps of mashed potatoes or candied yams, rice puddings, Yorkshire puddings, steak and kidney puddings, haunches of rare beef, crackling pork, seared lamb, and all dished up with overdone vegetables and fruit stewed in sugar and water to a fibrous indeterminacy. A festive and hearty American board which—never mind his "glands"—had clearly not done Ben a bit of good, and had done heaven only knew what to the General's system, so that, when put to the test in Asia, it had proved utterly wanting. Would those two men's lives have been different had their diet been a bit more intelligent? It was, of course, the most useless kind of speculation.

What was not speculation was that the General had changed, not only physically, but morally as well.

In former times, it had been Mrs. Anderson who would sometimes go off like a rocket and make everyone more than a little uncomfortable, while the General had presided over the groaning board—unflappable, gracious, tolerant, and amusing.

Now their roles had suffered some strange reversal. Mrs. Anderson presided, all grace, poise, and tranquillity, over the meal, eliciting stories from Ben and Larry, laughing happily, pouring wine, refilling plates.

And it was very good. It was clearly from his mother that Ben derived his considerable histrionic abilities. For that was what it was—a performance. And one that would very likely have succeeded admirably with anyone less fascinated with the peculiarities of human behavior than was Larry.

The General, on the other hand, was crotchety—and there was really no other word for it. He groused about his ham—too much fat on it. He complained about the potatoes—too soft, not enough parsley. At his right stood a large crystal pitcher of freshly squeezed orange juice. They weren't good oranges. Where had Mrs. Anderson got them? Don't ever buy them there again. Or that kind, either.

It was in his interaction with Cy, however, that the old man's behavior seemed to reach its nadir. As, for that matter, did Cy's. When passing a serving dish of potatoes to his younger son sitting to his left, the sole communication between them had been an irritated growl of inquiry answered by a surly grunt of acceptance.

Cy contributed now and then to the general conversation, but for the most part he kept his eyes to his plate as he worked his way through his food.

And Larry was flat out itching with curiosity. But he felt Ben's eyes on him now and again and so contented himself with surreptitious observations as the meal and conversation progressed.

First of all, there was the simple fact that Cy was remarkably young. Eighteen years had passed since Larry had ceased to come to the Valley regularly, but he recalled that curious summer twenty years gone by when he had arrived to stay with his aunt and renew his acquaintance with the other adolescent savages of Jolliston.

And there had been Mrs. Anderson with a brand-new babe. An enigma (though by no means a silent one) which seemed positively to enthrall his aunt, and every other woman in the Valley, and not a few of the menfolk, all of whom had couched their speculations, surmises, and observations in expressions of positively Victorian delicacy.

Now, of course, he knew why. Ben was thirty-seven and Helen therefore must be just on thirty-four. Accordingly, Mrs. Anderson must have been a woman in her late forties when Cy was born. And, to be sure, the lad had to a degree that self-assurance which seems to be the peculiar portion of an only child or a late arrival to middle-aged parents.

Earlier, when first they had come in, he had thought Cy to be one of the most handsome people he had ever seen. As he observed him now, however, he realized that that effect of beauty had less perhaps to do with form than with the fact of youth itself coupled with a burning vitality which, for whatever reasons, the young man was keeping firmly in check.

He was only five feet seven or eight, with a breadth that made him appear shorter and stockier still. He was abstemious with food. Larry had already noticed that he had taken one plateful of food and rejected other services; which, if he had anything at all of Ben's tendency to obesity, was probably as well. His hair was almost a strawberry blond, though it would grow more and more straw-colored as the years passed, and he had inherited the strongly defined brow and chin of the General as well as his deep-blue periwinkle-colored eyes. Over all, his features were regular, and he looked like nothing so much as a well-scrubbed, well-dressed upperclassman at a military academy—except perhaps for that occasional glint of sharp, intellectual appreciation for his brother's sallies of wit as Ben described his life in Los Angeles.

Then, of course, there were Cy's hands. Thick, strong, with broad, spatulate fingers, the nails of which had been immaculately and beautifully manicured. It was an extraordinary bit of vanity, which seemed—even for an accomplished pianist—strangely out of place . . .

"Is all of this really necessary?" demanded Ben angrily. "What difference could it possibly make . . ."

"It makes a difference," said Larry wearily.

Miss Worthing said nothing. Far better to keep out of this—and any other—squabble, whatever it might be about, and try to learn from it.

Mrs. Anderson still had not appreciably relaxed from her sphinxlike rigidity. At Ben's sudden interruption, however, she had frowned and now spoke sharply, "Ben, hush!"

"But, Mother—"

"I know, son, but we can't be keeping things to ourselves. Not anymore."

"Very sensible of you, Sibyl," said Miss Worthing.

"But Cy couldn't possibly . . ." began Ben.

"How do you know?" snapped his mother and then, again, visibly took control of herself. She nodded to Miss Worthing. "Matilda?"

"Larry," prompted Miss Worthing, "what happened?"

"It was when the salad course arrived," said Larry rather grimly.

That in itself was a surprise, and Larry could see that Ben was more than a little taken aback, too.

"No dessert, Mother?" he asked.

For a moment, Mrs. Anderson almost looked surprised and then, quite naturally, she laughed.

"Oh, my dear Ben, I'm sorry!" she said. "I'd forgotten that of course you wouldn't know that we've adopted the European custom of salad after."

"It's my fault," said the General, cheerfully enough, and then, "Now, Sibyl, hold on there." He eyed the nest of salad she was heaping onto his plate with no favor whatsoever. "Christ," he said, shaking his head, "I'd sell my soul for a chocolate cream pie."

And considering that the lettuce, tomatoes, radishes, and carrot curls all being borne to the man's mouth had not a trace of oil or vinegar on them, Larry could hardly blame him for feeling that way.

And that was when Cy chose to speak up. "It's a lot better than the way we used to eat when I was a kid," he observed and asked, "Larry, could you hand me the cruets?"

It was, all things considered, a fairly innocuous comment. Unfortunately, coming hard on the heels of the General's own remark, it somehow managed to have the effect of a full-scale nose tweak.

The General's brow contracted into a thunderous expression. He put his salad fork down with deliberation, wiped his mouth on his napkin, which he threw on the table, and, for the first time that evening looking his younger son squarely in the eye, he said, "You would." His voice was cold with contempt. "You would like this—this rabbit food, wouldn't you?"

Cy's face flushed furiously red. But gamely he responded to his father, "Yes, I do. I've told you before, I do." And Larry wished that the boy's voice had not sounded quite so sullen in the saying of it; it would have made it a lot more impressive when he speared a wedge of tomato from his father's plate, adding, "It's what healthy people eat," and popped it into his mouth.

Which brought the General literally rising out of his chair in sheer access of fury. "What the hell would you know about healthy?" he shouted. "You wouldn't know what to do with a good meal. Any more than you or your kind know what to do with your—"

"Henry!" Mrs. Anderson almost shrieked.

"Father!" bellowed Ben simultaneously.

Cy had gone from bright-red to bone-white, his nostrils pinched in anger, which had the ironic effect of making him look more like his father than ever before. "You were saying, Father?" he said through clenched teeth.

But the General, brought to a halt by his wife and elder son, merely flashed the boy another look of unfathomable contempt and turned to Larry, to whom he said, his voice as controlled as a courtier's, "I'm sorry, Larry; there really wasn't any excuse for that."

Larry murmured the appropriate nothings, feeling—as always—how dreadfully inadequate they are at such times.

"Henry," said Mrs. Anderson sharply, "finish your salad."

"I don't want my salad," said the General evenly but firmly. "What I want is my pipe."

He pushed his chair back and turned toward the hall door of the dining room, where he paused and looked back. Again that look of disdain rested briefly on the head of his younger son before he addressed Ben and Larry, "When you two—*men*—are finished, come to my study. I've got some old brandy you'll like."

On which mild yet incalculably venomous note, the old man left.

And how do we get back to where we were from here? thought Larry.

"Cy," said Mrs. Anderson crisply, injecting a welcome note of normalcy into the air, "have you finished your practicing?"

Cy shook his head.

"Then do it now, please," she went on. "Before the news comes on."

Cy departed into the living room and soon the sound of coruscating scales came once again. Mrs. Anderson went and closed the double doors into the living room and then stood a minute, her back turned to Larry and Ben still seated at the table. Presently they heard her sigh and she turned back to them, social and poised as ever.

"Now, let's see," she said, resuming her place, "is there any of that wine left? I rather think I'd like a drop."

She was very good. No question about it. Nevertheless, as Ben poured the wine into her glass, she suddenly let go of the glass, which fell to the table, spilling the wine into a spreading puddle as Mrs. Anderson swiftly lifted her napkin to cover her face.

Wordlessly, Ben mopped up the spilled wine, fetched another bottle from the sideboard, uncorked it, poured wine into his mother's glass and handed it to her.

"Mother," he said, "drink this."

She had not moved a muscle. Now she lowered the napkin, pausing only to dab at the corners of her eyes and uttering a shaky little laugh, accepted the wine and drank deeply and gratefully.

"I'm sorry, Larry," she said very softly after a moment.

"I am too, Mrs. Anderson," he murmured.

"What's that supposed to mean?" muttered Ben.

Larry shrugged, far too weary of roiling emotions to care any more what Ben might think. "Just what I said. I'm sorry that there seems to be trouble in paradise."

"Paradise?" said Mrs. Anderson again with that shaky laugh.

"That's what the Elms always seemed to me as a kid," said Larry. "I was telling Ben that this afternoon."

Mrs. Anderson smiled—rather more successfully—at that as Ben leaned forward and poured himself some more wine. When he had done so he leaned back and said to his mother, "I gather, from all this, that he didn't take it well."

"Of course he didn't!" Mrs. Anderson immediately snapped

at him. "How do you think he took it. I wonder sometimes that Cy has the nerve to go on living here . . ."

"Don't put it all on Cy," said Ben.

"Oh, Ben, I don't, I really don't, but when the two of them . . ."

"Look, folks," said Larry, "I realize that it's probably none of my business, but I really don't have the foggiest notion what you two are talking about."

Which was not—in the strictest sense—true; a very clear suspicion had already formulated itself in his mind, but it would simply not do to make that kind of assumption without corroboration.

Ben and his mother exchanged a wary glance. Finally, with a little sigh, she nodded and turned her attention on the wine in her glass before her on the table.

"Larry, if you ever breathe a word of this," Ben began by threat posturing.

"Ben, dry up and tell me," said Larry.

Ben snorted, looking grim. "I suppose we should all get used to this kind of thing happening, but somehow I can't—" He cut off his scatty reflections and went on, "Anyway, a few months ago, just after he got back from college, Cy—my little baby brother—made a decision to come, as they say, out of the closet."

Larry's first impulse was to say that he had thought as much but realized almost as quickly as the thought had formed that it would never do to say it. Instead he poured wine and lit himself another cigarette.

"I thought the General was being a bit unfair," he finally said, "though I do have to admit I can understand why he might be."

Mrs. Anderson looked up, her expression unreadable.

For Larry's part, for the moment he was rather completely at a loss for words—not because he did not know what to say; he did; but he was sufficiently an old wordsmith to know that, if ever a situation required *le mot juste*, this was it.

Presently, he said carefully, "You've mentioned how the General took the news. How did you, Mrs. Anderson?"

A small half-smile lifted the corner of the woman's mouth. "As a theologian, I am appalled—moderately appalled, to be sure, but appalled nevertheless. As a mother?" she lifted her shoulders and dropped them. "I'm disappointed, of course. But"—she looked up—"he's still my son and I love him, and I want him to be as happy as he can possibly be."

A small grunt of satisfaction escaped Ben, and as they pursued each his own thoughts, another brief silence descended upon them, with only the muted sounds of the School of Velocity to accompany it.

It was Ben who broke up this momentary tableau. "I had no idea things had gotten so bad, Mother," he said thoughtfully.

Mrs. Anderson frowned. "What do you mean?"

"I mean with Dad."

"Ben," said his mother rather severely, "this business of Cy goes against everything your father has ever stood for—"

"Including honesty and forthrightness?"

"That's not fair."

"I think it is. And furthermore, I think Dad would once have thought so too if he hadn't been so sick when—" He gestured and left the sentence unfinished.

Mrs. Anderson said nothing. Instead it was Larry who asked, "Excuse me, Mrs. Anderson. I know it isn't really any of my business, but you said something about Cy continuing to stay here. Well, why does he?"

Both Ben and Mrs. Anderson regarded him for a moment with that quizzical expression of people who are not altogether certain whether they ought to be offended.

"What I mean," Larry hastily explained, "is that he is, after all, wasting himself here in Jolliston, isn't he? Surely with his talent he should be in New York, or London or Munich, shouldn't he?"

Mrs. Anderson's shoulders visibly dropped as she took a ragged breath. "You're right," she said, her voice strained and tight. "And he knows it too and he wants to go."

"Well then, why doesn't he?" asked Ben.

"Money," said Mrs. Anderson succinctly. "Cy doesn't have any, and your father apparently isn't about to give him any."

"But he set up—" Ben clearly was genuinely shocked.

"I know, but he won't do it for Cy. Not now."

"Won't do *what*?" asked Larry.

"When both Helen and I turned twenty-one," Ben explained, "Dad set up trusts for each one of us. And now you're telling me"—he turned his attention back to his mother, his demeanor one of righteous indignation—"that he won't do it for Cy?"

"I'm afraid not," said Mrs. Anderson dejectedly. "He was going to, was, in fact, all set up to do it when Cy sprung the news on us." She made a helpless little gesture with her hand. "And Henry just never went ahead with the preparations. I— I've tried to encourage him to go ahead and give Cy the money, but . . . You've seen what he's become, Ben. He won't even let me bring the subject up now."

"How does Cy feel?" asked Ben.

"How do you expect?" his mother almost snapped back. "He's angry and he's bitter, and while I may not be any too happy with him at the moment, I for one cannot blame him."

For a moment there was silence. Then, purposefully, Ben stood up.

"You'll forgive us, Mother, if we don't help clear," he said. "But Dad did ask us to his study for brandy, and for brandy to his study we shall go."

"Ben!" his mother started up anxiously.

He turned. "Yes?"

"Don't, please. Not tonight."

"Why not?"

"He's got his dander up already. Don't make it any worse."

Ben paused and frowned. "Okay, Mother. As you say. Not tonight."

"I'll try talking to him again," she said doubtfully. "I promise."

Somehow, as they left, Larry sustained the impression that something had yet been left out, something Mrs. Anderson could not quite make up her mind whether or not to tell them. He mulled it over for a moment, as he and Ben went wordlessly down the hall toward the door of the General's study, and then he let it go. If it was important, he would find out soon enough. He had, after all, learned already altogether more than he had actually wanted to know.

"And did you find out?" asked Miss Worthing.

"Oh yes," said Larry and for a moment it looked as though

he were going to leave it at that bald affirmative. "It was the next evening—Christmas Eve—last night," he said and frowned as though he could not quite believe it had been only that small amount of time before.

"Does it fit into the narrative?"

"Of course," said Larry.

"Then perhaps . . ."

"Oh, for goodness' sake, Matilda," said Mrs. Anderson. "All I was going to tell them—all I did tell them was about the way Bob E. and Helen had taken the news."

"How did they?"

"It was, I think you would have to say, a conventional reaction."

Miss Worthing seemed actually to find this rather amusing. Nor did that fact escape Mrs. Anderson's attention.

"Yes, Matilda?" she asked rather coldly.

"I'm sorry, Sibyl," said Miss Worthing, "but one could hardly call your and Henry's reaction unconventional."

Mrs. Anderson ceded the point. "That may be so; but at our worst, neither Henry nor I were ever—"

"Were ever what?"

"Hateful."

"What do you mean?"

"Bob E., when he found out—Helen must have told him—he immediately told his sister, Bette Wanda, who was already half in love with poor Cy, that Cy had a crush on her."

"What a singularly unkind thing to do," said Miss Worthing.

"Even Henry was disgusted. Although he was never overly fond of Bob E., at the best of times," Mrs. Anderson added in a very dry tone of voice. "Fortunately, Cy and Bette Wanda were able to work it out between them."

"Interesting." Miss Worthing frowned. She turned to Miss Shaw. "Martha, may I?" She took the steno book from Miss Shaw, flipped through a page or two, nodding the while. "What did you two do then?" she asked almost absently.

"When?"

"After you'd had brandy with the General?"

"Went to bed," said Larry.

"What did you talk about with the General before you went to bed?"

"Nothing much," said Ben. "A bit of football. A little politics. I think," he chuckled, "we spent most of the time invoking the juju to crush the minions of OPEC."

Larry laughed at that. "You would not believe the money one spends driving around LA. Lord, to go to a movie and dinner, you can drive a hundred miles."

"And so," continued Ben, "we reminisced about the cheap price of gasoline of yesteryear and went off to bed."

Still Miss Worthing said nothing, continuing only to turn the pages of Miss Shaw's notebook.

"We were very tired," said Larry rather lamely.

Miss Worthing looked up. "Yes, I expect you were," she said mildly enough, handing the notebook back to Miss Shaw, who resumed her note-taking.

She had said it mildly enough, to be sure, but immediately Larry frowned and looked rather sharply at his aunt. So did Mrs. Anderson. Even Miss Shaw peered quizzically at Miss Worthing.

"Was he, Cy, I mean," asked Miss Worthing, "one of the people who had access to the General's orange juice?"

Mrs. Anderson gasped.

"Surely you cannot believe—"

"Why ever not?" asked Miss Worthing. "If the possibility exists . . ." She shrugged and left the corollary unspoken.

"He did," said Larry bluntly. And then added, as Ben's glance immediately darted at him, "You want maybe I should lie?" He turned back to his aunt. "Do you want it now or in its proper place?"

"I think we'd better get back to things in their proper places," said Miss Worthing with a grimace. "If we start cutting and chopping now—"

"But this is simply ludicrous," thundered Ben. "I know that Cy's had a rough time lately," he conceded, and was interrupted by Miss Worthing.

"And so far, Ben, I'm afraid he's the only one I know of that—if I am to believe you two—had access to the means and a damn good motive."

"What about Bob E.?" demanded Ben.

"Frankly, Ben, the only reason anyone has been able to adduce for suspecting Bob E. is that he poured out that juice."

Ben gaped at Miss Worthing. As did Larry and Mrs. Anderson.

"But he—"

"Don't!" commanded Miss Worthing. "Don't give me isolated details. Tell me what happened, damn it. So far"—she looked over Miss Shaw's shoulder—"no one but Cy—" She interrupted herself and turned to Mrs. Anderson. "Sibyl, tell me. In light of this—development about Cy, did Henry make any more of it, like to cut Cy out of his will?"

"No, there was never any question about that. At least as far as I know."

Whereupon Ben's fist crashed into the table. "If you want to know about who was going to be cut out of the will . . ."

"I do," said Miss Worthing. "But I want to know it at the proper place in the narrative."

"Good God, we'll be here all night."

"Then we'll be here all night," said Miss Worthing angrily. "Do you think—can you possibly think that I'm enjoying this, sorting through your family's dirty linen?"

In response to which Larry suddenly snorted, earning thereby a sullen glare from Ben and a rather pained one from Mrs. Anderson.

"This isn't funny," said Miss Worthing.

"Alas, I know," said Larry. "But I was just remembering the next bit—"

"Do you mean Christmas Eve?" asked Ben, interrupting. "At Helen's house?"

"Good heavens, no," said Larry. "I was thinking about what happened in the afternoon."

"Oh that," said Ben, and for the first time that evening both men grinned and visibly relaxed a bit.

"What are you two talking about? What happened yesterday?" asked Miss Worthing.

"We went to see Aunt Eulalia," said Larry.

"And?"

"What you said about dirty linen rather reminded me. As I was going to say, the next bit that came my way was there at

Aunt Eulalia's. I certainly learned some interesting things about the Anderson-Taylor connection."

"So, I must admit," conceded Ben, "did I."

Mrs. Anderson looked wary, but Larry ignored her as he continued, "But more importantly—at least to me," he said almost wistfully, "was that it was a really pleasant kind of day—the sort you ought to have on a vacation. Unfortunately, from then on, things seemed to head downhill at a pretty rapid clip."

CHAPTER 5

i

The next day—Christmas Eve—Larry woke up ridiculously early and for a moment could not for the life of him think of a single good reason ever to get up again. A glance through the curtains told him it was going to be another ghastly day of wind and the sundry unpleasant things the wind carries with it. He had a dull, thudding headache and, though the General's brandy was as excellent as it was old, he knew perfectly well he had not drunk that much the night before. All he wanted to do was to turn over and go right back to sleep.

Which made it all the more disgusting when Ben burst in. "Rise and shine," he bellowed offensively, "there's daylight in the swamp." And, seizing the draperies over the window, he slung them vigorously back, setting the rings to chiming melodiously and allowing the daylight, such as it was, murkily to illumine the large and comfortable bedroom.

"Christ, Ben!" Larry moaned and tried to pull the covers over his head, "I feel like I've committed every mortal sin in the world."

"Knowing you," said Ben agreeably, stripping the bedclothes back, "you probably have, and only feel the agony now that you're hedged about by Mother's appalling sanctity.

Come on." He swatted Larry briskly on the butt. "Get up."

"What for?" groaned Larry, struggling upright and peering blearily at Ben, who gurgled offensively.

"You look like a split infinitive," said Ben judiciously and fielded the pillow thrown at him. "Get up."

"I repeat, you bastard, what for?" said Larry and chuckled. "Who's whining?" he asked no one in particular and flopped down again.

"For one thing," Ben explained, opening drawers and setting out Larry's clothes, "you promised to take me to see Lady Fairgrief. And for another, I still have some shopping to do, and so do you."

Larry opened one eye.

"I do?" he asked and then opened both eyes. "I can't wear that shirt with those pants."

"Yes, you do," Ben answered the question and put an even redder pair of socks with the green shirt and blue sweater already on the chair.

He threw Larry's dressing gown at his head. "Here, cover your shameless nudity lest Cy sees you and compromises your virtue before breakfast."

"You're disgusting, Benjamin Anderson."

"I know," said Ben placidly, "it's how I make a living. But do get up. You and I are going to drive over to the North Valley Mall armed with checkbooks and credit cards, where we are going to mingle with the vulgar herd and spend some of that revolting glut of gold we make."

"I've already bought things for everyone," Larry protested. "And some of us have to live on the money we make," he pointed out indignantly, "and so will you for at least a year."

"Picky, picky, picky." Ben waved it all aside with the impatience of a very rich man. "Did you get anything for the baby?" he asked.

That brought Larry up in a hurry. "Oh, Lord, no, I didn't," he said quickly. "And I have to get something for your new relatives, too."

Ben nodded massively. "It's nice to see a proper spirit, because, old man, I'm afraid we're going to their house after Mass tonight."

"Oh, Ben!" said Larry with a sinking feeling.

"It was all planned weeks ago," Ben said with a shrug. "Of course, no one thinks to write to Los Angeles and tell *me*. Try to make the best of it, won't you? It's just your incurable shyness," he said offensively.

Larry snorted.

"Besides," Ben continued musingly, "it will be such fun to see the technique of the literary master, so disgustingly successful heretofore with thundering hosts of starlets, at work on the susceptibilities of the female Okie . . ."

"Will you go away," Larry growled. "I'll be down in ten minutes."

The rest of the morning passed in an agreeable whirl—elbowing into shops to pick over much-picked-over merchandise, listening to badly arranged Christmas carols blaring tinnily from ineffectual speakers. And, like any right-thinking people on a money-spending spree, there was always, it seemed, one more thing to be bought. It was true, however, that Ben lost interest much, much earlier than Larry.

"Larry," he finally barked at his friend, who was pirouetting in front of a clothier's mirror, "my inner timetable is being severely put upon."

Engulfed in his own and Larry's purchases, he was seated in a wholly inadequate chair.

At that point, one of the salesmen happened by and glanced down at the floor beside the chair, as a look of ever so discreet surprise lifted the man's brow.

"Excuse me," he excused himself in that unctuous voice peculiar to clothiers, undertakers, and the more exalted hierarchs of Holy Church. "Is this yours?"

He bent over and extracted from between the chair and the wall a toy monkey wearing a clown hat, on the face of which was fixed a smile of the most consummate idiocy.

"Yes, it is," growled Ben and murmured an exceedingly ungracious "thank you," when the man—his face bland as ever—courteously placed the toy precisely on top of the already huge pile in Ben's lap.

"O ye gods, I am avenged," chanted Larry as he leaned against the wall and gave himself up to mirth.

"If you're quite through," muttered Ben, "perhaps we could do something constructive with the day?"

"Come on, Ben" was all Larry said, taking his share of the parcels. "I've just been killing time."

"What? Do you mean . . ."

"Oh, dry up," chortled Larry, leading the way to the parking lot for their car. "I called Aunt Eulalia and she said to come over for lunch."

"Lunch!" exclaimed Ben. "It's almost suppertime."

It was, in fact, a little after one.

"I know. You see, I asked her to hold lunch till one-thirty so that you'd really have an appetite. I told her you'd been off your feed lately . . ."

The sight of two grown men laden with parcels running through a crowded parking lot, the one grinning shamelessly, and the other puffing out the direst threats imaginable, was a sight to delight any onlooker—all the more so when Ben was recognized and hailed.

Larry leaned against the car, winded with running and laughing simultaneously, while Ben's wheezing might have been truly alarming had he not shut it off obviously at will.

"Haven't run like that since I was a boy," said Ben, as he dumped the parcels in the trunk. "And I am looking forward to seeing your great-aunt."

ii

"Lord, it's been a long time since I was here," said Ben as they crawled at a dignified ten miles an hour up the broad circular drive.

It was a magnificent and well-maintained antebellum-style house, with a classical portico over the front door, from the ceiling of which depended a large wrought-iron lantern.

"I always thought it looked like a smaller version of the White House, myself," said Larry.

"Old Rudy Bessermann did a really beautiful job with it," said Ben as they paused to admire the house and the really exquisite landscaping around it. "I'm glad Lady Fairgrief is keeping it up."

The whole estate seemed wrapped in a silence so thick as to seem almost tangible, silence broken only by the distant scolding of a jay.

"There was a fund set up for maintenance," explained Larry. "I'm glad of that, too; Aunt Eulalia always says that Rudy's landscape work was as good as any that Capability Brown might have . . ."

A woman's frenzied screaming within the house abruptly shattered the silence.

Ben and Larry charged headlong up the broad steps onto the portico and flung themselves against the massive front door, which opened easily (and rather unexpectedly), catapulting them into a group of six extremely scruffy males, one of whom was poised over a buxom young woman who cowered beneath him as he wielded a very wicked-looking hunting knife.

Without further thought, Ben launched his bulk at the knife wielder while Larry's right fist connected most satisfactorily with a large dissolute individual who appeared to block his way. Then, quickly, he bent to grasp the arm of the cowering woman to help her to her feet, while Ben twisted the arm of the knife-wielding recreant behind him and wrested the evil implement from him.

Whereupon, at the top of her lungs, the rescued damsel demanded, "What the hell are you two goons doing?"

"Huh?" asked Larry articulately.

Meanwhile, the individual whom he had decked so beautifully was already trying to sit up, shaking his head and sputtering in a singularly picturesque manner as the other members of the putative gang also managed to find their voices and began to use them to very good effect.

The man whose arm Ben was still holding twisted behind him wrested it from the massive arm lock with a withering "Do you mind?"

From the sidelines, as it were, of the angry group stalked forth an immensely tall, youngish individual, his ash-blond hair an astonishing bush of dusty-looking ringlets. He gestured the others to silence and advanced on Larry and Ben, an expression of disdain on his angular features.

"May I inquire," he asked in a lugubrious bass voice, "what you—what you *gentlemen* are doing?"

Larry risked a glance at Ben and very quickly decided that perhaps that was not such a good idea. He turned back to this scarecrow apparition, who was dressed with bizarre incongruity in jeans, tennis shoes, and a polo shirt, over which an ancient and threadbare swallowtail coat had been thrown. Could this possibly, as unlikely as it seemed, be one of the servants? In any case, it was obvious that the best course was to bluster.

"I'm sorry," Larry barked, sending his interlocutor back a pace or two, "but when we pulled up outside, we heard that person shrieking like a banshee"—he gestured sharply at the erstwhile damsel in distress, who promptly swelled with indignation at his characterization—"so you can hardly blame us for thinking things amiss."

"You still haven't told me," this untidy footman persisted, "what you two are doing here in the first place."

"We might ask the same of you," Ben interjected, taking the cue for his behavior from Larry.

"I," the fellow announced loftily, "am Lady Fairgrief's butler."

"Oh," said Ben, somewhat taken aback, but he recovered himself quickly enough. "Well, we came out here to have a quiet luncheon with Lady Fairgrief, who is this gentleman's aunt," he informed the man equally glacially, "and instead, we find the premises invaded by a gaggle of delinquent hippies."

The recovering victim of Larry's fist began to gobble not unlike a turkey, as the butler turned a sallow red.

"You have interrupted, sir," he informed them, his nostrils quivering with indignation, "a rehearsal of the Jolliston Opera Company of the last scene of Puccini's *Il Tabarro*. I shall announce you to her ladyship at once."

Names were coldly requested and as coldly provided and the butler withdrew to distant reaches of the house.

Ben's name had immediately penetrated the minds of the assembled crew, and even the bruised degenerate whom Larry had KO'd began to be extremely agreeable, he turning out to be the opera's director.

Both Ben and Larry unbent to be polite, but it was all too clear to each that the other wanted only to fall on the floor and roll about helplessly with mirth.

"So!" an unmistakable voice called out, "it seems I can't even have people to my house without them being harassed by uncultured Hollywood riffraff."

Ben and Larry swung around to confront Lady Fairgrief, who was glaring at them through a tortoiseshell lorgnette. The scruffy butler was pushing her wheelchair from out of the murky depths of a cavernous corridor which led away to some distant wing of the house.

"Well, Aunt Eulalia," said Larry rather slyly, "how were we to know that something awful wasn't happening when blood-curdling shrieks pierce the winter night?"

"You might have read my letters," replied her ladyship, and caught sight of the soprano, once more glaring daggers. "And now you've offended our star soprano's feelings. Please, dear Lucia," said her ladyship with all graciousness, "do forgive my scapegrace nephew—he writes sordid thrillers for a living and naturally always expects the very worst of people."

"Aw, it's okay, Lady Fairgrief." The offended woman suddenly grinned and relaxed, placated by her ladyship's charm. "It's just I spent three lessons getting that scream just right."

"And what a scream it was, too," said her ladyship in a very dry voice. She turned next to the director, who was prancing about impatiently. "And now, dear Gregory—it's past one-thirty and I've promised to give these ruffians their lunch, so why don't you and the company have yours? Larry, take me in, and Billy," she addressed her unlikely butler, "see our guests out before you bring in lunch."

With a regal gesture, she waved to the company as Larry pushed her, at her direction, into the dining room, where luncheon plates had already been laid. Larry parked her at the head of her table and, as commanded, went to the tray of bottles on the sideboard to mix them all a cocktail, while Ben turned, closed the dining room doors behind them, and promptly fell against them, helplessly laughing.

iii

In fact, when Lady Fairgrief heard what had happened, she spent a goodish amount of time herself snickering into her sherry.

"Delicious," she agreed, but then added rather more acidly, "but still, my boy, don't you think you could have read my letters?"

"I'm sorry, Aunt Eulalia," said Larry, looking not in the least contrite. "I do remember something about the opera company rehearsing here; I'm afraid I'd completely forgotten about it."

"And you have to admit it *was* quite a shriek," said Ben, still burbling. "'I spent three lessons getting that scream just right,'" he quoted with ruthless fidelity.

Unfortunately, at that very juncture, the young, peculiarly dressed butler appeared with a deep dish pie. He glared once at Ben and Larry, served up the food with frigid correctitude, and stalked back through the service room, leaving their plates heaped and their spirits subdued.

"Oh dear, I'm afraid Billy's offended too," said her ladyship.

"Who is he?" asked Ben, hoisting his fork.

"I meant to ask, too," said Larry, pouring wine. "And why haven't I seen dear old Maude's smiling face?"

Lady Fairgrief made a sound suspiciously like a snort and pushed her wineglass across the gleaming walnut expanse toward Larry.

"Half a glass, dear; thank you." She sipped and sighed. "Maude and this chap cooked it up between 'em: He would come to work for me as cook and man-of-all-work so he could get a reference from me when he goes to New York next fall. Apparently, he hasn't any great hopes of getting a job singing right away, and as folks are always looking for servants high and low, he thinks a reference from an old witch like me will help him."

"Probably will," said Ben. "We Americans adore a title." He smiled. "Sounds like a sensible fellow to be prepared for less than stellar success."

"He's learning," said her ladyship enigmatically and again sipped wine. "Anyway, the two of them decided that with him here in the house and Matilda across the Valley and a nurse to come in twice a day to put me to bed in the evening and get me up in the morning, it would be the perfect time for Maude to go home to England for what the woman actually had the nerve to call, to my face, a desperately needed holiday." She cackled wickedly. "I pretended to be just horribly offended and then gave her a round-trip ticket." She sighed then and picked up her fork. "But I do miss my Maude."

"When will she be back?" asked Larry.

"After the New Year."

"That's not so bad, then," he observed rather callously.

"Not really," her ladyship admitted. "I actually did try to get her to take longer, but I'm afraid the woman assumes that I shall fall apart without her. Then, of course," she added to Ben, "there's your mother."

Ben looked up blankly from his plate of corn pie. "My mother?"

"Yes, my dear, your mother. She comes over several times a week—more than a little, I suspect, to keep an eye on me, bless her heart. But we chitchat about old times and old friends and she brings serenity to the house that even they"—she nodded in the direction of the living room—"can't quite manage to shatter."

"Why do you let them?" asked Ben.

"Poor old Rudy Besserman wanted it so, though I had no idea," she added dryly, "it could ever get quite so lively."

Larry sought solitude in his wineglass.

"My goodness," she said gleefully, "I should dearly love to have seen you give a thorough drubbing to Gregory. You probably made the poor thing's day."

"Aunt Eulalia!"

"Oh, tush!" she said. "I'm sure it was most eminently satisfying."

As they finished the bottle of wine, Larry looked first at Ben and thence to his ancient relative.

"You didn't say anything to Aunt Matilda about my coming, did you?"

"I was going to," she admitted candidly. "But Sibyl was here when you called this morning and so I said I wouldn't. I look forward to being there when you walk in; dearest Matilda will be so tickled."

"I do wonder how Mother finds the time," muttered Ben.

"I don't know either," said Lady Fairgrief, "but she just goes on and on with that old saw about busy people having all the time. Besides, I rather think she's working on a new book."

"What's that got to do with you?" asked Larry.

"I realize I am not the person one would expect to be interviewed by a writer of books on Christian spirituality, but this time it's different. I think she's finally decided to write the biography."

"Of Lord Freddy?" asked Ben.

Her ladyship nodded.

"Who's he?" asked Larry.

"Mother's—I guess you would have to say—spiritual director."

"Is he dead?"

"Oh my, yes," said Lady Fairgrief. "A good twenty years ago. But I knew him in the dear old decadent days of Edward the Seventh. In fact, it was Arthur who told him that if he wished to pursue a career as a theologian, the only thing standing in his way was his own determination." She paused a moment and chuckled. "And, of course, the duchess."

"Who?"

"His mother. One of those dotty old ladies that dear old Saki was always scarifying. So, while Arthur bolstered Freddy's failing nerve, I set out for Northumbria to quell her antic grace."

"Speaking of quelling people," said Ben, "did you really tell the King not to smoke so much?"

And so, for the next half hour, they sat enthralled as she entertained them with tales of that fabulous and vanished era and ended: "So, you see, it wasn't exactly that I told him not to smoke, but that we all loved him so much, it would be better if he cut right down."

"How tactful," said Larry.

"I was in those days," said her ladyship smugly, and all three of them laughed.

"Well, I'm glad Mother's got something new going."

"Frankly, I am too," admitted Lady Fairgrief. "She was inclined to be a bit broody about your father, and then, too, she was beginning to get quite besotted with that child."

"What child?" cried both men in unison.

"Why, Helen's, of course."

"Oh, that one," said Ben. "What's-her-name."

"What's-her-name, indeed," said Lady Fairgrief. "Your own niece and you don't know her name."

Ben said nothing.

"I see," said Lady Fairgrief after a moment. "Well, my dear Benjamin, her name is Mary Elizabeth, though, I'm afraid," she added on a note of austere distaste, "her father's already taken to calling her Lizzy May."

Larry snorted and stood up to fetch port.

"But what's wrong with Mother getting entranced with the child?" asked Ben. "She's their first and so far only grandchild, and aren't grandparents ordained of heaven to spoil their grandchildren?"

"Very true," said her ladyship, but her mouth pursed angrily. "But I gather that your sister hinted rather broadly that daily visits would no longer be encouraged."

Ben's expression was sour as he said, almost to himself, "I really don't understand about Helen sometimes."

"There's a number of people in the Valley feel that way," observed Lady Fairgrief.

"But why?"

"That business with the doctor? It wasn't pretty."

"But what did that have to do with Helen?" asked Ben.

"That's what rather a lot of people wondered. Helen simply kept maintaining that she hadn't seen or heard a thing."

"And?"

"A number of people—physicians, pharmacists—had a rougher time of it during the ensuing investigation than they might have had."

"Didn't it occur to them that she might be telling the truth?" asked Ben harshly.

"It did to me," replied her ladyship calmly. "Your sister—if you'll pardon my saying it—is lazy to the point of inanition. But most people in the Valley think she was lying, perhaps even hiding evidence, and that it was only the General's money and position that saved her."

"No wonder he offered to send her abroad," said Larry.

"I never knew," said Ben.

"No, your mother probably wouldn't have wanted to write

to you about it," said Lady Fairgrief. "Still, you have to admit, your sister has managed to pull quite a rabbit out of the hat."

Ben merely looked blankly at her.

"Her marriage," explained her ladyship.

"Bob E.?" said Ben.

"Yes, Bob E.," retorted her ladyship tartly. "He's a good man for her in spite—" She hesitated. "Well, in spite of other things."

"Do you like him, Aunt Eulalia?" asked Larry.

For a moment, the old woman paused to consider. Then she gestured to a bowl of apples and walnuts. "Ben, peel me an apple and crack precisely six walnuts." She turned her head back to Larry and scowled. "No, I can't say that I do like him. But then I'm a disgusting old relic of a considerably less democratic age than this one. But I will tell you something. I do respect him. A great deal indeed. He's done what he's done with no help from anyone—in fact," she added dryly, "quite the reverse. And a large number of people here in the Valley feel much the same as I do. When his father was shot to death last year . . ."

"What?" cried Larry.

"'struth," said her ladyship. "You know what a drunken sot he was?"

"Actually, I didn't," murmured Larry.

"Well, apparently he was out swilling his way through his Social Security when a quarrel erupted and some other dipsomaniac pulled out a .357 Magnum and put an end to old Jimmy Bob's partying forever."

Larry looked a long level look across the table at Ben, who was sedulously not meeting that glance.

"It was all terribly sordid," her ladyship went on. "But do you know that in the Valley people sent flowers and came to the funeral solely because of their respect for Bob E.?"

"I'm glad," said Ben fervently. He looked up and caught and held Larry's eye for a moment before adding, "And I'm glad for Helen, too."

"Good," said Lady Fairgrief, "then I've accomplished something. He may be a perfect boor, but this is America, for goodness' sake, and such things aren't supposed to matter."

"Perhaps so," said Larry, considering, "but things like the wrong accent, the wrong manners . . ."

"Why can't you just say the wrong class and be done with it?" interrupted Lady Fairgrief.

"Okay, class," said Larry. "But I think there's a lot more to it than just to say simply class. But never mind that. The fact remains that it does count. A helluva a lot."

"Yes, I know," replied her ladyship, "and though it may be silly, there it is. But there is something here, you know, that is considerably different from the Old World: You can be as well-bred as can be, but unless you've got something else, you're still a nobody, and don't ever forget that."

"What's that?" asked Ben.

"Why, money, you goose," said her ladyship. "The lolly, the loot, the green stuff. And your brother-in-law's rolling in it."

"How lucky for Helen," said Larry.

"Indeed," agreed Ben. "A rich Old Guard father and now a brash parvenu husband."

"Dear God, what snobs you two have turned out," said Lady Fairgrief as she rang the small silver bell near her hand. "But I think it's time you two were on your way. The company will be back soon and I'm afraid I want my nap."

iv

On the whole, they were rather subdued on the drive back to the Elms; conversation lagged as both recovered from Lady Fairgrief's solid fare and excellent port. The sun, moreover, had briefly emerged, and there was a kind of golden haze hanging over the Valley as the shadows began to lengthen toward the Vigil of Christmas.

Presently, Larry observed quietly, "Fascinating day."

"Do you mean the information your aunt imparted," asked Ben, "or our misplaced heroics?"

Larry chortled happily. "Well, it was fun."

"Nevertheless," said Ben severely, "you should have remembered that the opera company rehearsed there."

"I know," said Larry, still laughing, "but he really did go down so beautifully."

Ben merely snorted.

"How much of that did you know?" asked Larry when a few more moments had passed.

"About Helen?"

"Yes, and about Bob E.'s father."

"I didn't know about the other doctors."

"And Bob E.?"

"Yes, I knew it. But personally, I don't see what difference it makes. As I said, I don't dislike the man, and I know for a fact that he really does love Helen. Although . . ." His voice drew the word out before halting.

"Yes?"

"I have to confess that there's a question in my mind right now that is both uncharitable and speculative."

"It wouldn't be the first time," observed Larry.

"Sharp but true," sighed Ben. "I was just struck by something your aunt said which has put things into a different perspective."

Larry said nothing.

"I'm just wondering whether Bob E.'s money and respected position might not have been the reason Helen said yes to him."

"No," said Larry, "it's not kind. But is Helen the sort to use a man like that?"

Ben looked utterly astonished. "I'm sorry," he said after a moment; "I keep forgetting you never really knew her. She's one of the most selfish people I've ever known in my life," he said and, without further ado, snapped the door open and stood up.

"What's the drill for this evening?" asked Larry as together they sauntered leisurely up the front path. "You said something this morning about going somewhere."

"I expect it will be after church," said Ben. "You know, champagne and some gloppy dessert in the wee smalls while everyone opens one of their gifts and exclaims how it was *'just what I've always wanted . . .'*"

"You're rehearsing for unpleasantness," said Larry.

Ben sighed. "I know. I'm letting your aunt's grim little tales get to me. But at least we have time for a nap," he added with a cavernous yawn as he led the way indoors.

"Oh, there you are," they heard from the end of the corridor. "I was beginning to get worried."

Mrs. Anderson came down the hall toward them, a rather harried expression on her face.

"I'm sorry, Mother." Ben kissed her brow. "I should have called. We had a late lunch with Lady Fairgrief and she got to talking."

"She does, doesn't she," said Mrs. Anderson. "I was just wondering if you'd get home in time to go with us."

"But it's hours yet," said Ben.

"Oh dear," said she with an apologetic little smile. "I guess no one told you. We won't be going to church this evening."

"What?" Ben was obviously astonished but sharply controlled himself to ask with studied politeness, "Why ever not?"

"Bob E. wanted us to have Christmas Eve with Mary Elizabeth, so we decided we could all go to Mass tomorrow morning instead of this evening."

"What time are we going?"

"We should leave in about an hour. Do you think you can be ready?"

"Of course, Mother."

"Oh, good," she said and went back down the hall toward the back of the house.

"So much for a nap," said Larry.

Ben had not moved. One hand still rested on the newel post, one foot raised on the first riser. His face was completely blank of expression.

"Ben?"

Abruptly coming to, Ben jerked his head toward the upper regions.

Presently, in Ben's room with the door shut, Ben delivered himself of rather a number of quite colorful remarks on the subject of the Taylor family in general and of Bob E. in particular.

"Ben," Larry protested, "lots of people have the ceremony of gifts on Christmas Eve. And I personally think it sheds rather a new light on Bob E. to want to have the baby included."

"Phooey," said Ben. "It's Helen's doing and she put Bob E. up to it because she knows perfectly well that Mother and Dad's Midnight Mass is special to them. Midnight Mass, cocoa, bed, and presents in the morning. That's the way it's always been and she knows it."

Larry snorted, and sat in an easy chair by the fire.

"What's so funny?" demanded Ben.

"You know what you're angry about?" said Larry.

"Pray enlighten me," said Ben sarcastically.

"You're just upset, Ben," said Larry, "because, while the schedule you just outlined may be special to the General and to your mother, it's even more special to you. Here you are," he explained, "having finally made it home for Christmas after who knows how many years, and very little is the way it used to be and you're ticked off because things aren't the way you want 'em to be."

He sat back and once more contemplated the fire, the protracted silence from Ben indicating that his dart had definitely found the bull's-eye.

Any further discussion, however, was precluded by a knock on the door.

"Ben!" It was Cy.

"Yes?" Ben opened the door.

"Dad asked me to load the car with everything we're taking over to Helen's. D'you think you could lend me a hand?"

"Sure," said Ben and looked a glare at Larry. "And you, for your sins, can also bend your back."

"That's no penance," said Larry rising. "I love packages."

He spoke, however, too soon, for there was a remarkable number, all neatly done up in festive paper and ribbons and bows.

After the second armload he had carried to the yawning tailgate of the Anderson family station wagon, Ben watched Cy stashing them into tidy piles and remarked to Larry that Christmas boxes had a depressing sameness to them, in reply to which Larry laughed and said that it was even more true than usual.

"I swear," he said, handing his own burdens to Cy, "that they're all marked 'Mary Elizabeth,' too."

"Dear, dear," said Ben archly. "I do believe that our novelist has been snooping."

"No need to," said Cy from within the car amid the stacks of presents. "I think they've been Christmas shopping since February." He jumped out and eyed his handiwork critically. "After all"—he put out a hand to test the stability of a pile—"she's probably the only grandchild they'll ever have."

He said it almost absently, clearly having given no thought whatever to the myriad assumptions that simple statement implied.

Larry glanced hastily at Ben, whose eyebrows were raised on high, taken aback and surprised at having had his own expectations of any future reproduction thus impugned so very insouciantly.

Whereupon, apparently, it dawned on Cy what he had said. He, too, looked almost startled as he flushed furiously and began to stammer, "Jesus, Ben, I didn't mean . . . I mean, I never meant . . . I'm sorry . . ."

Ben, however, recovered quickly and when he realized that he had become very much the center of concern, shrugged indifferently. "Forget it, Cy. Not to worry," he said and then added wryly, "especially since it's probably true."

It was fortunate that at that point they were all three of them diverted by the appearance of Mrs. Anderson on the veranda stairs struggling under the weight of a large box of oranges. Larry quickly ran up the path to relieve her of her burden, with Cy right behind him.

"I wondered about that," said Cy. "No, Larry, here. I'll take them. I have a place all ready for them."

"Thank you, Cy," said Mrs. Anderson rather breathlessly. "Larry, could you come in a moment?" she asked and then raised her voice. "Ben," she called, "come inside, will you?"

Larry frowned as he followed her up the stairs and into the house. She looked worried about something as well as rather more exercised than one would have expected from lugging a box of oranges.

When Ben joined them in the living room, she was standing at the fireplace warming her hands. She turned to face the two of them, her face clouded, her hands still toying nervously with each other.

"Mom, what's wrong?" asked Ben.

"It's your father, Ben."

"What do you mean?"

"He says he doesn't want to go tonight, that he doesn't feel well."

"Is there something—?"

"Yes, there is. I think both of you had better know that one of the reasons Henry dislikes Bob E. so much is because he twits him."

"Who twits whom?"

"Bob E. twits your father."

The idea of anyone twitting General Anderson was frankly opaque to Larry's imagination. "What do you mean, Mrs. Anderson?" he asked. "How?"

"He makes little digs. All the time. About how the boys in Vietnam were always doing drugs and drinking in the field. And Henry, I don't need to tell you, I'm sure, hates it like poison. And I think—Henry's implied—that when—when I'm not around, the jokes get even coarser, about *roistering* in Saigon and that kind of thing."

"That's disgusting," said Larry.

"I know, but what—" began Mrs. Anderson but she was interrupted by her son.

"And what, may I ask," Ben demanded with ominous calm, "does Helen have to say about these singularly ill-bred remarks?"

Mrs. Anderson muttered something Larry did not quite catch. Ben, however, did.

"What!" he bellowed.

Mrs. Anderson nodded. "She laughs," she repeated.

"God!" said Ben.

"I know," said Mrs. Anderson, and they watched as she closed her eyes as a spasm of some undetermined emotion swept over her. When, however, she opened her eyes again, they were blazing. "I think sometimes I'm ashamed I ever bore her."

What can one ever say that is really adequate to such a remark? Nevertheless, *some*thing had to be said.

"Is there anything we can do, Mrs. Anderson?" asked Larry.

"Yes," replied Mrs. Anderson. "As a matter of fact, there is. First of all, Ben, you can go to try and talk some sense into your father. Really, I'm afraid he just has to go tonight."

"I agree," said Ben. "I'll talk to him. Right away. Is there anything else?"

"Yes," she said. "You two are both of you fairly adroit socially. Help me tonight."

Ben and Larry exchanged a grin.

"I think we can manage that, Mother," said Ben.

"I hope so. You see, I . . ." She hesitated. "Your father's upset right now. With me."

"Whatever for?"

"Well, he's been—he was in fairly good spirits all day today, and just now I went to try to talk to him again about Cy's trust fund, and I'm afraid that all I accomplished"—she gestured helplessly—"is that now he's angry with me for bringing it up again and I don't know—"

"And Merry Christmas, Cy!" said a harsh voice in the doorway of the living room. The three whirled to see Cy standing in the archway, his face mottled, his nostrils pinched, his mouth a thin line. "Merry Christmas, Cy," he repeated, "and let's all play coddle the General while that little faggot Cy gets to linger about in Jolliston and rot."

He turned and fled.

"Oh, no!" cried Mrs. Anderson.

"I'll go to him," said Larry, hurrying toward the archway. "Ben, you see to the General."

"Got you," said Ben.

They moved.

By the time Larry finished hunting down Cy and chivying him back to some semblance of his usual humor, a scant half hour remained before their scheduled departure and he longed for a hot shower as the hart longeth for the water brooks.

When he had bathed and paused briefly to check out his ensemble in the mirror behind the door, he could hardly help dwelling upon the extraordinary situation in which he had fetched up.

All those years he had remembered his days of summer in the Valley with a peculiar nostalgia, all the more plangent for the reverent envy in which he had always held the Anderson clan. So much so that, as the years, the unpleasant years, had passed in a bleak and dreary sameness, they had come to represent to him the *beau ideal* of what an American family ought to be.

And now he was finding out that the idol had—if not feet of clay—soiled patches about the ankles. Nor was it solely the Taylor entanglement, though the Lord alone knew that that was fascinating and likely to be more so. It was amazing how cranky the General had gotten from his illness. And as for the added complication of Cy's being so talented and on the other hand so . . .

Oh, never mind, he told himself and all but yanked the door open. It could go on and on, couldn't it? Who under the vault of heaven was without problems? At least they were all alive, reasonably content, and ready to greet the eve of Christmas and its solemn remembrance of the birth of Hope to a weary and despondent world.

CHAPTER 6

"So you all went to the party," said Miss Worthing when the silence had gone on quite long enough.

Each of her three interlocutors had quietly retired within himself and was engaged in pursuing his own thoughts.

"I must say," she added, "that it doesn't exactly sound like a very festive crew."

Larry snorted while Ben uttered a short bark of a laugh and Mrs. Anderson clicked her tongue.

"Well," demanded Miss Worthing, "how am I to know unless you get on with it? And furthermore"—she leaned forward and looked intently at each of them in turn—"I don't want you leaving anything out. Not even the smallest detail if you can remember it."

"Why?" demanded Mrs. Anderson.

"I'm not altogether sure," admitted Miss Worthing, "but all of you—each of you—were in something of an emotional turmoil. And you were going to a full gathering of the clan. I don't know why, but something tells me that there had to be something, some nexus that finally led to—this afternoon."

"Of course there was," snapped Ben.

Again Miss Worthing leaned on him. "Is it something you saw or merely something which you think corroborates your conviction of Bob E.'s guilt?"

Ben tried to waffle. "Of course it's an observation, but just because it does corroborate—as you say—"

"Then we'll leave it for its proper place," Miss Worthing interrupted crisply. She picked up her mug of tea and leaned back and muttered, half to herself, "Something had to have happened."

"Oh, it did, Aunt Matilda."

"With all of you in such a pet over one thing or another, I can't say I'm surprised."

"Actually," said Mrs. Anderson, "if it comes to that, we weren't."

"Oh?"

"No. Actually by the time we arrived we were all very much a happy family. At least," she added dryly, "Larry had Henry and the boys laughing."

"I see," said Miss Worthing. "You two went into your routine, did you?"

"It was time," said Larry simply. "Although I know you weren't exactly happy with the turn it took," he said to Mrs. Anderson.

Mrs. Anderson nodded but said nothing.

"But I barely had set foot on the stairs," Larry went on, "when I knew it was time."

As Larry descended the stairs, he found them all, Cy, Ben, Mrs. Anderson, and the General, already coated, hatted, and gloved in the foyer, and it seemed that that was as far as anyone had gotten for some time. The General and Mrs. Anderson had reached the stage where it was clear that they were only repeating what had already been said and that neither was particularly interested in hearing what the other really had to say.

"I've told you for the last time, Sibyl, that I feel fine."

"But all afternoon—"

"All afternoon I was feeling punk. But I'm fine now and I will not be driven in my own car like an invalid when I am quite capable—"

"But what if you have an attack? People on the roads will have been drinking . . ."

"I can manage, Sibyl."

"But it's such a long way."

Equally clear was the fact that it could go on like this for quite some time if something weren't done. Below, only Ben had seen Larry's slight pause on the landing. Larry raised an inquiring brow and ever so slightly Ben nodded. Taking a deep breath and muttering a prayer for guidance in this, his new career as fool, he tripped down the stairs all specious prattle.

"Well, well, well, what's going on here? Something wrong? Or have we decided to keep the sacred festival here in the foyer of the Elms? It's big enough, I warrant. We could move the tree in here and use the table there as an altar and arrange the choir tastefully on the stairs. Cy would be stuck off in his alcove because the piano definitely won't fit . . ." Good, he thought, there's Cy grinning. "But he can thump loudly enough, no doubt, to accompany our giddy wassailing."

"Larry," said Ben, "shut up and get your coat."

"Did I say something wrong?" Larry inquired, all wide-eyed innocence.

"Larry, I—" began Mrs. Anderson.

"Now, Sibyl, just hush up. I'm going to drive," said the General, taking his opportunity.

"Was there some question?" asked Larry.

"Not really," said the General with a scowl. "But my wife here thinks I'm too *non compos corporis* to drive."

Larry recoiled in mock terror. "Oh my God," he said, "Mrs. Anderson, I beseech you, on bended knee"—he suited the action to the word—"let your husband drive." Mrs. Anderson was by no means amused, but Larry gave her no opportunity to interrupt. "Otherwise Ben will drive and we truly will be endangering our immortal souls as well as our bodies for the sin of presumption both upon the mercy of God and of our guardian angels."

Whereupon, to his delight, the General actually laughed, a rather sour cackle, to be sure, but for all that a laugh.

"For that," said Ben rotundly, "you shall walk back to San Francisco."

"On the whole," said Larry, "I'd rather."

"I think you are a very foolish young man," said Mrs. Anderson severely. "Get up off your knees."

"I am, I am," chirruped Larry, "but you know the General's liver isn't likely to shrivel away in the twenty minutes it will take to drive across town, whereas in twenty minutes with Ben driving . . ."

Cy was by now grinning broadly and said to his mother, "Come on, Mom, let's go. Dad's a good-enough driver to know if he couldn't handle it. And besides, we're going to be late."

The General's reaction to this was rather priceless. On the one hand he obviously resented being thus succored by this most difficult of his children, while, on the other hand, he was equally pleased that the boy had presented the most cogent reason for refraining from further dawdling and just go.

Reluctantly, Mrs. Anderson consented, and they all, heaving a collective sigh of relief, trooped out the front door and down the path to climb into the station wagon. The awkward moment was over, but it was all too plain that Mrs. Anderson had not left off worrying. In the back, Larry, squeezed between Ben and Cy on either side of him, concluded that she probably never would stop worrying, and so, to keep things as light as possible, began, in duet with Ben, a running commentary on the passing scene.

It was not, however, until they began to approach the outer excrescences of Steuber that the duet ended and Larry took off on an extended solo, egged on by the General.

"My God," he said as the car stole down the first street where home after home stood cheek by jowl, most of them with front yards barely ten feet deep, universally blanketed with patchy lawns in which crabgrass seedpods stood weary and depressing sentinel. "When did all this occur?"

"It was about twelve years ago," said the General. "Some guy from Salt Lake put them up."

"Put them up or threw them up? I'm sorry," he apologized. "I do try not to be vulgar, but did he have an architect? Excuse me, what a question. Of course he did. He had the same architect whose designs for supermarkets and suburban banks are all the rage. Rather like that." He pointed as they passed a large supermarket which, even at this hour on Christmas Eve, was doing a land-office business. "Concrete, glass, and no soul whatever."

"Oh, come," said the General. "What has the soul to do with supermarkets?"

"Nothing, judging from the one that I shop in," said Larry agreeably. "We may be neighbors, but I refuse to be friends. But the houses! Ye gods, the soul of a house is at least a casual nod to some canon of aesthetics, *n'est-ce pas*? Am I wrong?" he asked rhetorically, in reply to which Ben groaned theatrically and Cy and the General laughed aloud. Mrs. Anderson said nothing.

"Even in the squalid villages of southern Europe, or the Middle East, or Los Angeles," Larry continued wildly to expatiate, "where indeed, like here, all houses look alike, some principles of aesthetics are observed. Yet here, *here*," he emphasized, "in northern California, which I would have thought the last bastion of hope, here is our suburban equivalent. They're not even building in California Gothic anymore," he lamented.

"Form follows function," said Ben, "and all architects would agree."

"A principle which only excuses an utter want of imagination," rejoined Larry austerely and was rewarded with a real guffaw from the General.

Thus encouraged, he pointed ahead of them. "Behold the examples which rise to meet us," he lectured. "The only windows small, inadequate, and very likely modeled after those in the Lubyanka Prison. All, that is, but for the large picture window in the center of which reposes an enormous Christmas tree, thus effectively blocking any view whatever. Not, God knows, that there's much to see, considering that half of 'em don't even have their angular contours softened with grass. It is, therefore, as well. What, I ask you, possessed the first person who assumed that gravel and misshapen cacti were an adequate substitute for a neatly tended lawn?

"And then, look there! There, clearly, the itch for doing it yourself has possessed the owner of that concrete wonder like the veriest demon. What is that strange two-story structure so utterly unlike anything else on the street? What was the original intention of such . . ."

Whereupon, without any warning whatsoever, the General pulled into the driveway of the very house of which Larry had been making fun.

For quite a long time no one said anything. Then, in rather

an unexpectedly bitchy tone of voice, Cy announced gleefully, "We're there!" And all Larry could think of with any coherence for the next few seconds was that he was enormously grateful that it was as dark as it was there in the interior of the car. Judging from the successive waves of fiery heat he could feel passing over his face, he knew perfectly well he must be nearly beet-colored.

Miss Worthing—for the first time that night—found herself actually laughing in spite, it must be said, of her nephew's obvious discomfiture; his face was again deeply flushed in remembered and now renewed embarrassment.

"Aunt Matilda!" he remonstrated.

"I'm sorry," she said, "but really, it does my heart good to hear about you getting hoist a bit on your own petard."

Larry flushed again. This time, however, it was with anger. "Go ahead; laugh," he said. "But the fact remains that I was only doing what Ben and I had agreed to do, and even what you yourself"—he addressed Mrs. Anderson—"had asked us to do."

Mrs. Anderson remained eyes downcast, yet replied readily enough, "I know."

"Then why," demanded Larry, "did you get so offended?"

"I was worried about my husband."

"What happened?" asked Miss Worthing of Mrs. Anderson.

It was, however, Larry who replied. "After the General and Ben and Cy got out of the car, I—well, rather naturally, apologized for steamrolling her a bit. And she said . . ."

"Yes, you are rather a clever young man, aren't you?"

For a moment, Larry could think of absolutely nothing whatever to say, caught as he was between embarrassment and vexation—embarrassment because of the fact that, yet again, he had managed to get his foot inextricably planted in his mouth, and vexation that, in a situation in which he was apparently the only one who did not know the rules of the game, when he tried to play the part that was asked of him, all it seemed to earn him were patronizing remarks.

Muttering half-incoherently, he hauled himself out of the car to lend a hand in the transport of the mountain of presents in the back of the wagon. As he did so, a coachman's lantern standing beside the drive was switched on, illuminating the crushed rock, weeds, and assorted winter-blighted cacti which constituted the yard. At the same time, the front door opened to frame a squat and rather burly outline.

Each bearing an armload of gifts, Larry and Ben followed Cy, similarly burdened, along the pathway of none-too-stable flags which crossed the expanse of gravel to a minuscule front porch which was really little more than an awning propped up by two painted wrought-iron supports.

"Evenin', Cy, Ben," boomed a voice of the greatest possible bonhomie, "come on in. Come on in. Is the General—oh, there he is now. Evenin, General, how ya doing? Mama Anderson. Howdy, howdy. Helen's in the kitchen with Mary Beth." Bob E. Taylor stepped aside to allow them entry.

And five minutes later Larry found himself wondering what all the shouting had been about. To be sure, Bob E. was clearly of a type that might be difficult for a lot of folks to take with any degree of equanimity—he was loud, he was abrasively self-confident, he was crude and was patently wanting in any kind of taste. He had met them at the door wearing a pair of green leather carpet slippers, a pair of trousers in a plaid that would never be seen in the Highlands, and a T-shirt over which he wore a plush turquoise smoking jacket with very broad and very purple quilted satin lapels. In his right hand he hefted a brandy snifter which could easily have accommodated a half gallon of spirits, while his left hand held a positively phallic cigar. Nor did he make even a pretense of a move to assist in carrying the contents of the station wagon into the house.

He was not a tall man, and the bulk of his torso made him appear, if anything, even squatter. His head was rather larger than the accepted canons of proportion would have indicated, as were his hands and feet. His legs were short, however, as were his arms, and remembering the grinding poverty in which the man had been raised, Larry could only wonder what Bob E. might have been like had a diet of balloon bread, "greens," and black-eyed peas allowed him to reach his full genetic potential.

He was, for all that, however, a powerful presence, one of

those individuals whose sheer vitality is like a fist to the chest, and as the first inevitably awkward moments had passed, Larry found that, pace the Andersons, he rather liked Bob E. Taylor.

All the more so, when—somewhat to his discomfort—he found Bob E. not very covertly eyeing him.

"What's wrong with him?" Larry whispered furiously to Ben.

"Why, din'tchu know, honey-chile," Ben replied in a rather unnecessarily broad parody of Bob E.'s accent, "it jest wun't be may-anly for him to he'p us."

"I don't mean that," snapped Larry. "He keeps staring at me. Does he think I've come to steal the spoons or something?"

The two men had returned to the station wagon for one last load of gifts and the almost forgotten box of oranges.

"Out-of-date image, me boy," chortled Ben. "He's probably just remembering what a toad you were."

Any fit response to this monstrous allegation was prevented by the fact that they had once more entered the house. They trooped down the inner hall to the living room to find that Mrs. Anderson had vanished, presumably to the kitchen, and that the party still consisted of the General and Bob E., who were standing idle while Cy was busy trying his best to arrange things under the Christmas tree.

Upon Ben's and Larry's entrance Cy leapt to his feet and took Larry's armload and returned to his chore. Ben, meanwhile, rested his burden of oranges against the back of an easy chair, as Larry, with great determination, strode up to Bob E. and offered him a hand.

"There," he said. "Couldn't do that with all those presents in hand. How are you doing, Bob E.?"

"I'm just fine," boomed Bob E. He shook his head and stood back to give Larry, yet again, the once-over. "Boy, you sure have changed. Why, I remember—well," he chuckled, "maybe we better not talk 'bout it. You look like you done real good. I hear you even wrote a couple of books."

Which was a nice thing to say to an author whose books have several times headed the best-selling charts. Larry, fortunately, was anything but vain.

He laughed. "I did," he conceded, "but I hear you've done rather well for yourself, too."

"Yup," said Bob E. with obvious and happy pride. "I got me an auto-parts store and repair shop that's just about the best here in the Valley. I got folks come all the way from Sacramento to have my boys fix 'em up. You need fixin' or tires, or anything, you come see me, y'hear?"

It would, perhaps, have been pleasanter had he not so immediately and obviously peacocked himself up over it, but he was hardly the first self-made man who could not resist pointing out to all and sundry precisely how well he had managed from what had been, at best, unpromising beginnings.

For all that, Larry was charmed. He was not, however, unaware of the concerted blankness of expression on the Anderson faces as they watched this little interchange, nor the contempt in the eyes of the General when Bob E. proceeded to go on to, admittedly, rather a tedious degree about his business.

It was all very well and good for a man of the net worth of the General to disdain Bob E.'s perhaps modest temporal success. But the fact was, and Larry well knew it, that more than one millionaire had been made in these United States by supplying parts and repairs to those among us whose cars are their religion.

Furthermore, Larry—at this point largely unconsciously—was a little ticked off with the Andersons. Ever since his arrival in Jolliston they had been filling his only mildly interested ear with dire tales and warnings of the doings of the Taylor gens. It remained moderately obvious that Bob E. was unlikely to be quite the cup of tea of the staid and stolid Andersons and their friends. Now, instead of the monster of depravity he had been led to expect, he found a man, crude enough to be sure, who was expending his not inconsiderable charm to be welcoming and pleasant to people who manifestly despised him.

That—and the pronunciation of the name—might perhaps explain why, when Cy interrupted to ask with rather an edge to his voice, "Bob E., where's Bette Wanda?" it was Larry who responded, thinking only to save Bob E. any aggravation and, at the same time, wondering why on earth Cy would want to know such an obscure geographical fact at such a juncture, "Why, isn't that one of those emerging African nations?"

The responses to this were as varied as they were immediate. The General's eyebrows shot upward toward his hairline, while his eyes twinkled and he folded his hands across his belly, looking for all the world like a nodding Mandarin monk. Ben gave one great shout of laughter, while Cy literally fell back on the floor giggling loudly. Bob E. looked approximately as blank as Larry felt, whilst from behind him Larry heard a another laugh, silvery, infectious, and wholly feminine and attractive.

He turned, his face yet again a flaming red, to face an extremely beautiful woman advancing toward him, a six month-old child held in the crook of her right arm, hilarity and affection plain on her face.

"Larry, that was wonderful," said Helen Anderson Taylor and, pausing only to shift the babe to her left arm, offered him her hand. And as he took it, still mightily confused, she stood on her toes and kissed his cheek. She stood back and regarded him and, lifting her free hand to his cheek, she patted it and said, her eyes still twinkling with mirth, "But I think you should know that that's the name of my sister-in-law."

"I think you meant Botswana," said Ben, not unkindly.

"I can't wait to tell her," said Cy, recovering himself and then, being a not insensitive person, he added, "don't worry, Larry; she'll think it's a hoot."

Very little of this, quite frankly, registered with Larry during those first moments, for one very obvious reason. He had been immediately and quite literally entranced with Helen.

That she was beautiful has already been stated, but it would be difficult really to say exactly wherein the beauty lay. She was rather tall, even stately, and Larry could not help but notice that with maturity her figure had filled out in a most agreeable fashion. Her face was round, her lips rather full, and her nose a pleasant little retroussé affair. Her hair was perhaps the most ordinary thing about her, a pleasant-enough chestnut brown, glossy and well cared for but cut in a not very original or even very flattering page boy. It was, however, her eyes that raised her from the merely pretty to genuine beauty, a rich green hazel, slightly tilted at the corners, with long lashes and brows that tended ever so slightly to feather.

There was, however, something else, a vitality perhaps, a kind of bubbling happiness about her that was as appealing as it was rare. She moved with a kind of decisive energy and unself-conscious authority that was pure Anderson. Yet, in spite of the fact that one was—or at least Larry was—all too aware that one was very much in a Presence, she possessed in full measure that aristocratic ability to place you immediately at your ease so that you felt that her whole attention was focused upon you.

Furthermore, it was all too plain that Bob E. was like a circling planet to its mother star as far as Helen was concerned, and with nary a backward glance Larry immediately fell into the same besotted orbit about the woman. It was not Larry's usual habit to dance attendance to a married woman, nor had he entirely taken leave of his senses. But the abrasive and rather bitchy girl he had known as a teenager had been completely superseded by a singularly attractive, robust, and agreeable woman, and what male in his right mind could possibly object to having to spend an evening in the company of such an eminently decorative female?

Once more, as Helen swept into the living room, commanding, "Oh, Cy, yes, that's the general idea, but, oh dear, not like that!"—Larry, hovering around like everyone else, again found himself querying what had all the fuss been about. These people were delightful.

It was at this point that Ben—observing the effect Helen was having upon his friend—came forcefully forward.

"Bob E.," he thundered, pointing with a sweeping gesture to Mrs. Anderson and Helen and Cy, who were rearranging the truly enormous stack of presents under the tree, "while Santa's elves here do their part for this holiest of eves, you are going to fix me a drink, or I shall not be responsible for my actions, and holiness will have precious little part in it."

Bob E. chortled richly at this elaborate bit of piffle and led the General, Larry, and Ben into the dining room—an alcove off the living room with a serving hatch from the kitchen, and showed them the bar. "He'p yase'f, fellas," he said, and with more tact than Larry might have suspected of him added, "and there's a fresh pitcher of OJ for you, General. And Larry, they said you was a Scotch drinker." He hefted a bottle of Scotch rather dubiously, but Larry, seeing the maker and the age thereof, said rapidly, "That'll do very nicely indeed, Bob E., and thank you. Thank you very much."

"Cain't stand the stuff myself," muttered Bob E. and poured himself a very generous bourbon, which he then proceeded to mix with 7-Up.

Both Ben and Larry winced involuntarily, but Helen covered for them nicely. She had of course heard the request for drinks and suddenly looked up, all concern. "Mama, did you remember the oranges?"

"She did indeed," said Ben, more than willing to join Larry in the twenty-year-old Scotch Bob E. had provided. He pointed to the box still poised on the back of the easy chair. "There they are, right in front of your eyes, where this poor brother of yours dropped them after lugging them in through the ice and snow."

"Oh, Ben," said Helen but was clearly relieved.

"But why didn't you just go get some?" her brother said. "The Safeway was still open when we drove over here."

Helen clicked her tongue and shook her head, "Ben, come on, it's Christmas Eve."

"That, my wench, is a sorry excuse."

In reply to which his sister merely stuck out her tongue and returned her attention to the sorting of presents in appropriate piles.

"And thus are we answered," muttered Ben with a frown, not pleased, but Larry was not in any fit mood to hear any more vague criticism.

"Come on, Ben, she had to get dinner ready for a houseful of people."

"She could have sent that lout of a husband," Ben pointed out.

"He isn't a lout, Ben," said Larry very precisely. "And don't get prickly. Not at least until you've had rather more to drink in order to excuse it."

Upon which withering advice he rejoined the others in the living room, leaving Ben to eye him with slack-jawed astonishment from the archway to the dining room. He advanced to a position to the right of and slightly behind the Barcalounger wherein Bob E. wallowed, drink and cigar still in hand.

It was quite apparent that, for the moment at least, no one really knew what to say next. Larry had reported the latter bit of business equably enough, but it was rather painfully obvious that both Mrs. Anderson and Ben were more than a little abashed to hear it.

Larry eyed the two of them all but expressionlessly and then deliberately lit a fresh cigarette, inhaled deeply and, as he breathed smoke and shook the match to extinction, said, "You don't have to worry; I don't feel that way anymore."

"Why not?" Miss Worthing was on it like a shot.

He shrugged. "Developments," he said succinctly. Then, almost irritably, he added, "What the hell are you asking for? You must know her a lot better than I'm ever going to."

"Probably," conceded Miss Worthing, "but I wasn't there."

"Does it matter?"

Interestingly enough, it was Ben who snorted at that.

"Something amuse you, Ben?" asked Larry.

"Larry, I'm an actor," said Ben. "When you're working up a role, you need to know what the other characters think of your character; to a degree, it's almost irrelevant what the audience is going to think."

"Thank you, Ben," said Miss Worthing.

"Okay," said Larry. "So Bob E.'s an asshole and Helen is a shrew. Does that satisfy—"

"Of course it doesn't," snapped Miss Worthing.

"Larry," said Miss Shaw, looking up from her pothooks, "get back to the point. What happened? And in order!"

Larry and Ben exchanged a glance and a frown.

"I don't . . ." Ben began.

"I do," said Mrs. Anderson. "The tour."

"Oh," said Larry, blushing slightly. "Yes. That."

Helen finished her ministrations under the tree. Larry was still totally rapt in admiration for the woman. She had prepared Christmas supper for a dozen or so, decorated the house, and now had taken the time to arrange the piles of gifts 'neath the tree as though the editors of *Life* were about to descend on the house for photographs.

"There," she said, "that's more like it." She sat back on her heels and admired the effect of her handiwork and then, almost musically, laughed. "Even though I'll have to do it all over again as soon as Mother Taylor and Bette Wanda get here."

"Why all the fuss?" asked Ben.

His sister looked at him as though he had taken leave of her senses. "We're going to take pictures. You want them to look nice, don't you?"

Bob E., with a laugh, said, "She's been naggin' me for a week to get film for the camera."

"You did, didn't you?" said his wife and Larry distinctly saw Ben's eyebrows go up over the tone of voice with which she said it.

Bob E. chuckled and pointed to a camera on the mantelpiece. "Loaded for bear."

"Helen," said Cy, "where *are* Bette Wanda and Arletta? Shouldn't they be here by now?"

"They certainly should, and I hope they get here soon or the casserole will be overcooked. However"—Helen stood up with a lithe movement—"in the meantime, how about a tour? You've never seen my home, have you, Ben? Or you either, Larry."

By this point, Larry would have been willing to repair a plumbing failure had she suggested it. He acquiesced readily. Ben agreed a trifle less exuberantly. He was still acting more than a little subdued. Larry suspected—accurately, as it transpired—that he was still somewhat taken aback by Larry's earlier admonishment.

It was Cy who leapt to his feet and tugged at the older men. "Yeah, come on. It's a neat house."

Both men followed willingly enough. Who, after all, can resist a chance to explore another's territory? There was, moreover, the business of that curious extension to the house upon which Larry had so unfortunately remarked earlier. It was a splendid opportunity to kill two birds with one stone, so to speak, by spending some time trailing around the house with this very agreeable woman and satisfy his curiosity at the same time.

Mrs. Anderson, the General, and Bob E. demurred. "I already seen the house," said Bob E. good-humoredly, in response to which Helen said with mock severity, "Then you can mind your daughter."

Mrs. Anderson, who was still holding the somnolent Mary Elizabeth, said, "I'll manage, Helen."

"Are you sure you don't mind, Mother?"

"Are you serious?" said Mrs. Anderson, gazing fondly at the baby.

"Well, let's go," said Helen.

When all was said and done, the house was just a house. Larry did rather wonder at Cy's evident and continuing enthusiasm for it until he realized that, in all probability, that young man liked the place precisely because it was everything the Elms was not. Nothing, in fact, could have been further from the rather giddy Victorian mansion in which the Andersons lived. But neither Larry nor Ben were particularly impressed. Both of them, after all, had spent an appreciable amount of time in Los Angeles and environs where, generally speaking, any building more than ten years old is regarded as a major obstacle in the relentless march of civilization.

Indeed, to them, the comparison between the Taylors' villa and the Elms only made the older house seem much the more sensible dwelling. This place was—at least to Larry's mind—rather horrible. A utility room was right next to the master bedroom, a bathroom opened directly off the dining room, and the nursery was at the end of a blind corridor.

"What if there's a fire?" he whispered to Ben. "They'd never be able to get to the baby."

"Don't ask me," said Ben. "But Cy sure likes it. All the mod cons, no doubt. I wouldn't actually mind having a shower like that myself."

"I don't know; seven shower heads seems a bit decadent."

It was while they were in the nursery, however, that Ben frowned and whispered very sotto voce, "It's the green door."

"Huh?" said Larry, who was trying to pay attention to Helen's expatiation on the wonderful provisions which had been made for Mary Elizabeth.

"The green door in the corridor," repeated Ben. "That leads to that extension."

It rather amused Larry that his own curiosity about that addition to the house had touched a responsive chord in Ben. He had himself assumed that everyone knew what that bizarre structure was and confidently expected to be told. Now, it appeared, Ben had no idea what it was, and his expectation seemed doomed to disappointment.

At that point, Helen clicked her tongue and put a hand on her hip. "Really, you guys!" she said, and then laughed. "Look at you, bored silly, and I don't blame you for a minute. Cy, what's wrong with you? See a mouse?"

Her younger brother turned from inspecting something down the passage and blushed. "No. I just thought I heard Dad and Bob E. go into a room down there."

"Oh well," she said with a shrug and another laugh. "Let's go. I'm sorry about this," she said, taking both Ben and Larry by the arm. "I'm just so taken up with my new daughter, I forget that not everyone else is. Come on. Let me show you something really special."

And she led them, chatting amiably of agreeable trifles, back through the living room into the dining room and on into the garage, where she flipped on a light and both Larry and Ben gasped. In front of them, elevated on blocks and obviously in the process of a painstaking and loving restoration, was a saloon Daimler from the mid-1920s. Both men started eagerly forward, full of questions.

"Sorry, fellas," said Helen, laughing. "You're going to have to ask Bob E. about all that. But isn't she a beauty? I knew you'd like it."

"He's done a lot since I saw it last," said Cy.

In response to which Helen gave a rueful little snort. "And you wouldn't believe the money that it's eating either."

Suddenly, from within, came a loud "Yoo hoo! We're here!"

"It's about time!" called Helen and hurried back into the dining room.

"Hey, Bette Wanda!" yelled Cy.

And presently only Ben and Larry remained. Ben led the way out. "Come on," he said. "These two you got to meet."

"Ben, wait a minute," said Larry.

Ben paused, his hand on the light switch.

"I'm sorry I snapped at you earlier."

"It's okay," said Ben. "I understand."

"Do you?"

"Sure. You're seeing them"—he shrugged—"at their best."

"I like them. A lot."

"That's moderately obvious," said Ben. "Let's just hope that everything stays this pleasant. But come on. I like Bette Wanda, and Arletta is, shall we say, priceless."

The professions of actor and novelist are similar in that both have as their subject the endless permutations of human nature. As the two men entered the kitchen from the dining room, it was immediately apparent to Larry why Ben had used such an unlikely adjective with which to describe Mrs. Arletta Taylor, relict of the late, and apparently unlamented, Jimmy Bob.

She was, first of all, and obvious to everyone, already more than half drunk, and there was in the skin of her neck and bosom that suggestion of goose flesh which indicated the condition was not an unusual one. She was by no means an unattractive woman in a fleshy kind of way, with the exuberant bosom and broad hips of the Lillian Russell variety. Her hair had been dyed a chemical yellow, and she was attired in a dress with a full white muslin skirt and a scarlet-sequined bodice which would have been daringly cut for the theater in July.

Her features were small and all bunched together in the middle of a round and moonlike countenance, and she had obviously been in her youth pretty in a rather vapid kind of way. It was immediately evident that she was furthermore given to simpering in a meaningless fashion. In her, however, it was not irritating, at least not to Larry, in the way simpering so often can be, because—and it took him a moment to locate it—the expression of the woman's eyes. They were dark brown puppy eyes—like those of her son. But, more than that, they were the eyes of a woman who had been hurt unconscionably and had never understood the meaning of any of it.

He—Larry—felt a surge of genuine pity and the urge to move forward and take this strange woman in his arms and mutter, "There, there," like a comforting Victorian angel. And when he turned to exchange a glance with Ben, he could tell from the rueful half-smile on his friend's face that he too had read much the same thing in the woman's unhappy expression.

The daughter, on the other hand, could not have been more different.

Whereas her mother was all zaftig roundness and curves, Bette Wanda Taylor was tight—and uptight—angles, not so much, one suspected, because of any inherent boniness or awkwardness as because of a kind of psychically projected rigidity of character.

She was dressed in a distinctly dowdy business suit in Lincoln green of mid-calf length, and her light brown hair had been pulled back from her face in a French roll. She wore, in addition, a pair of well-broken-in running shoes and clutched, as for dear life, a rather cheap-looking black plastic attaché case. Unlike her mother, she wore next to no makeup; a rather pale lipstick and mascara seemed to be the extent of it.

The strange thing was that Larry had the distinct impression that he had met her somewhere before. He could not recall precisely where, but expected that—as these things happen—he would recall presently. The extraordinary part of it was that it struck him as rather odd that he, a novelist, would not have recalled anyone named Bette Wanda anything; the syllables were just too classically American—almost Dickensian—for him not to remember them.

She came in behind her mother accompanied by Cy, who flashed a glance across the kitchen to the doorway of the dining room as though, it seemed, to verify that Ben and Larry were, in fact, standing there. He was looking rather grim about something as he took Bette Wanda's elbow and guided her straight toward them, whereupon, as they drew close, it became obvious that the young woman was considerably rattled about something.

Ben stepped forward, offering his hand. "Bette Wanda! How nice to see you again. What's wrong?"

"Fix her a drink, Ben," said Cy.

"Please," said Bette Wanda, "I really need it."

"What happened?" asked Ben.

"The ride over here is what happened," she replied. "Mother met the bus and—well, you see how she is already. I wasn't sure if either one of us would get here alive."

Clucking sympathetically, Ben took the young woman's arm and guided her around the dining room table to the drinks tray, where he rapidly mixed the requested bourbon and ginger ale. Bette Wanda took it from him with a grateful glance and bolted half of it without once coming up for air.

Chuckling, Ben addressed the other two. "How 'bout a refill, Cy? Larry?"

"Okay," said Cy, "but I think I'll have a bourbon and ginger, too; sounds good."

Larry laughed at that. "They are good," he said, "but I always feel like a middle-aged alkie when I drink one. I'll have Scotch." He handed his glass to Ben.

"Your usual repellent English fashion?" asked Ben.

Larry nodded. As he did so he could not help but notice that Bette Wanda had gone completely still and rather pale as she turned to stare at him.

"Mr. Worthing?" she said.

So he had met her somewhere before. It was Cy, however, who leapt into the breach. "I'm sorry, Bette Wanda. Where are my manners? Bette Wanda Taylor, meet—"

"I know Mr. Worthing," the young woman interrupted without really taking her eyes off Larry. She seemed, in fact, rather confused.

"Funny," said Larry, "I've been thinking ever since you came in that I know you, but for the life of me . . ."

He broke off as a rather knowing, almost cynical look gradually suffused the young woman's face.

"No," she said. "No, I don't suppose you do." She turned to Ben and in a tight little voice said, "Thanks for the drink, Ben; but I'd better see if the *women* need any help in the *kitchen*."

Still holding her attaché case, she swept from the room.

"What was all that about?" asked Ben.

Larry shrugged eloquently and turned to the equally mystified Cy. "What does she do?" he asked.

"She works for some lawyer down in San Francisco. She's a—"

"She's his secretary!" said Larry. "Oh Christ!" he said, feeling very bad indeed.

"Figure it out?" asked Ben.

Larry nodded. "She's *my* lawyer's secretary."

Ben seemed actually more amused by the situation than anything else.

"Oh well," he said, "it *is* a depressing fact of life that no matter how good a secretary might be—and where would we be without them—no one ever really seems to notice them."

Cy nodded. "She hates it."

"Then why does she do it?" asked his brother.

"She's saving money to go to law school."

"Joining the opposition," said Ben.

"But I don't remember her being named Bette Wanda," protested Larry.

"You wouldn't," said Cy. "She uses Kate as a professional name."

"Nor, I notice, does she talk like either her mother or her brother," said Ben, clearly intrigued.

Cy shook his head. "No. She took speech lessons when she first went down to San Francisco. She told me she was tired of talking like a cracker because if you talk like that, that was how you got treated."

"An ambitious young person," said Ben.

"I have to apologize," said Larry, starting forward.

"No. Wait," said Cy. "Let her calm down first."

At that point, Mrs. Anderson came through the kitchen door making the usual incoherent noises at the baby, who was now awake and producing happy gurgling sounds back at its adoptive ancestress.

Mrs. Anderson paused in her progress toward the living room. "You boys should probably go into the living room. They're going to start laying the table in here. Don't drink too much, Cy," she admonished and continued on her way.

Before any of them could move, however, a singularly peeved-looking and -sounding Arletta heaved her way through the kitchen door, bouncing off the lintel.

"Goddamn it," she mouthed. "Who the hell does she think she is? Telling me I can't hold my very own granddaughter."

Bette Wanda's face appeared at her shoulder. "Come on, Mother; never mind about that. We need to help Helen set out the food."

Arletta was still muttering under her breath and casting malevolent glances toward Mrs. Anderson, who had taken up a position near the tree. The flashing lights seemed to tickle the baby enormously, and she was squealing with delight.

And Larry would have had to be blind not to see the Significant Glance that Ben and Cy exchanged.

"I'll see if I can lend a hand in there," said Cy, blushing slightly, and betook himself off to the kitchen.

Larry turned an eye on Ben. "Am I missing something?"

Ben regarded him a moment rather expressionlessly. "Do you have to know everything, Larry?"

"No," conceded Larry. "But since I seem to have fetched up in this reenactment of *God's Little Acre,* I would appreciate . . ."

"It's not that bad."

"Perhaps not. But I am beginning to feel that I'm reliving an old theatrical nightmare. You know the one—where you're on a stage and you don't even know what the lines are—or even what play you're in."

For a moment, the two men stared wordlessly at one another. Then, just as Ben opened his mouth to speak, Helen emerged from the kitchen bearing a large casserole while directly behind her came Arletta, Cy, and Bette Wanda, all bearing platters and serving dishes.

Ben frowned and jerked his head toward the living room and stalked to the far end thereof, where he picked up a *TV Guide* from the top of the television and, under cover of perusing it, said, "It's just a lively little bit of Jolliston folklore that makes most of us believe that, for the most part, Arletta is not exactly to be trusted around children."

"What!"

"She tried to drown Bob E. when he was about nine or ten."

"What!" repeated Larry with an entirely different inflection.

"Keep your voice down!" said Ben severely.

"Sorry," said Larry. "Are you joshing me?"

"Not at all," said Ben.

"But I thought she was such an Earth Mother type."

"She likes to give that impression," said Ben. "But I've heard folks say she hates her children like poison. Look at her," he said with emphasis. "Fifty going on fourteen. I would guess—judging from her character—that she hates anything that reminds her she's getting old."

"What happened?"

Ben shrugged. "Jimmy Bob apparently heard the struggle and waled the tar out of her. She hated him, too."

"Go on!"

"No, I mean it. Fact is"—Ben sighed loudly—"scuttlebutt has it that the fella that finally offed Jimmy Bob last year was Bette Wanda's real father."

"Jesus!" said Larry with utter revulsion.

"I know," said Ben. "Altogether too sordid." A half-smile lifted a corner of his mouth. "The really pleasant thing after that was Helen and Bob E.'s little bit."

"What do you mean?"

"Arletta and Jimmy Bob refused to come to the wedding. Bob E. then—very properly—took the attitude that they could both rot in hell. And then came Jim Bob's little 'accident' and—what do you know?—his insurance policy paid double indemnity. And here we all are, suddenly one big happy family again. Oh, shit!"

Larry had been standing with his back to the room while Ben rehearsed the squalid little tale, his eyes flickering about the room ready to stop on a dime should anyone approach, his voice—usually so rich and resonant—flat, unemphatic, and toneless. It was the voice actors use on stage to communicate one with another when they do not wish the audience to hear. The last expletive, however, had been, as it were, wrenched out of him.

Larry turned. The General, his face set in an angry scowl, was stalking into the living room from some back region of the house. Without a word to anyone, he marched to the fieldstone ledge in front of the fireplace, retrieved his tumbler of orange juice from the mantelpiece, and stood staring angrily into the fire, sipping juice and breathing heavily.

And right behind him had come Bob E., pale, his face set, the hand holding his cigar trembling with emotion. For a fraction of a second he eyed the General, his eyes blazing, before he turned sharply and, pushing past his wife and sister (or half-sister, as the case might be), seized a bottle of brandy and, upending it over his retrieved snifter, poured at least six fingers of liquor into the glass.

Mrs. Anderson had turned to watch her husband with a greatly troubled aspect as Helen did the same to Bob E. The two women then sharply glanced in each other's direction. Mrs. Anderson shook her head. Helen shrugged, and then, in a voice that was far too bright, announced, "Come on, everybody. Food's on!"

"And oh, what a meal it was," said Ben, shaking his head in reminiscent horror.

"That bad?" asked Miss Worthing.

"Worse," averred Ben.

She looked quickly at Mrs. Anderson and Larry, both of whom rather grimly nodded their agreement.

"What was wrong with it?" asked Miss Shaw.

"Far better to inquire what was right with it," said Ben.

"Very well," said Miss Worthing, "what was right with it?"

"Nothing."

"Larry?" said Miss Worthing angrily.

"One suspects," said Larry, "that Helen gets her cookery ideas out of the pages of the—shall we say—more idiotic women's magazines?"

"That is not very instructive!"

"I know," said Larry. "All I mean is that everything—everything—was either a canned, frozen, or pre-cooked something that had been gussied up in some crazy way to try and make it resemble food."

"Even the ham was canned," lamented Ben.

"It did have the taste and texture of something that owed a great deal more to plastics chemistry than animal husbandry," said Larry.

"That's all very amusing," said Mrs. Anderson suddenly, "but it does rather completely miss the point."

"Which is?" prompted Miss Worthing.

"No one ate very much," replied Mrs. Anderson. "And everyone was drinking a great deal. I suppose it's utterly feckless of me at this point, but I can't help but wonder how much of what happened would have had people had more food in their bellies to buffer the booze."

"Everyone was drinking?" asked Miss Worthing.

"Especially Bob E.," said Ben.

"So were you," said Larry. "Especially after the ceremony of the gifts began."

It was, at least in the beginning, almost the paradigm of the commercial Christmas. The happy extended family surrounds the tree and opens present after present, round-robin, round and around.

It might almost have been better if everyone had merely dived onto his or her pile, as it were, ripped the packages open, expressed general and particular thanks, and called it a night.

It was not, however, to be.

I hate Christmas like this, thought Larry, and was all too painfully aware of the fact that he was none too sober himself. He was, however, horrified and more than a little appalled at the change that had gradually overtaken Helen. The agreeable, mellow-voiced hostess of earlier had been replaced with something rather more like the girl he had known—and loathed—of old: brittle, sharp-voiced, peremptory. Not that—he recognized with mingled apprehension and disgust—she was entirely unjustified.

Bob E. had parked himself in his Barcalounger with the bottle of Courvoisier within easy reach at his side and sat sullen and uncommunicative except for an occasional and exceedingly ungracious "Thank you" upon the opening of this or that gift.

Her father, too, had retreated inward and sat on the fireplace ledge leafing through old copies of *National Geographic,* having given up even the pretense of joining in. Indeed, Mrs. Anderson had found it necessary to open his gifts for him. She, too, had grown increasingly edgy and overbright, shooting up little fountains of gush in a way that Larry would have hardly believed possible of her.

Arletta meanwhile had reached the sodden and somnolent stage of her rake's progress and her only contribution was an occasional incoherent mutter followed by a toothy grin that would have done credit to a shark, followed by her eyes shutting again, followed by a relapse into semiconsciousness.

The booze that *her* daughter was putting away was only, it appeared, making that uptight young woman even more so. Her bosom buddy, Cy, was being, to put it brutally, a snippy little queen, taking an unnecessary and unhelpful delight in feeding bitchery to his elder brother, who stood in no need of such encouragement.

For Ben was really, to Larry's mind, the worst of the lot. He had taken up a position on the hearthrug, knocking back Scotch and soda—with less and less soda as time passed—posturing with cigarettes and informing the whole proceeding with what he no doubt took for wit but which, as he grew more and more drunk, was nothing more than cheap shots.

In her playpen beneath the tree, Mary Elizabeth, utterly ignoring the piled-up goodies about her, had—with the abandoned perversity of childhood—found the fascination of her young life in a length of aquamarine silk ribbon and was unquestionably the only person in the whole room who was truly happy.

Later, Larry would admit that—disagreeable as things may have been at that point—it would have been just ducky if they could have remained right there. However, in a Heraclitean universe, movement is required; things have to get either better or worse.

In this case, they got much, much worse.

And it all began innocently enough—it always does, doesn't it?—when it was, yet again, time for Helen to open another present for her daughter.

She removed a box—rather a small box—from the still appreciable pile labeled "For Mary Elizabeth."

"Why don't you open three at a time for the dear infant," said Ben. "We'll never get through her pile of swag at this rate."

"Mummy's little darling wants to take her time, doesn't she?" said Helen with a felonious smile at her daughter, who promptly responded with a loud hiccup.

"An appropriate response," said Ben with a rather nasty chortle, but broke off. Helen was looking rather blankly at the box she held in her hand.

"What's the matter, Helen?" said Ben. "Recognize the wrapping?"

She frowned and looked up irritably at him. "Yes," she said, "I do." She lifted the tag up to the light and again frowned and cast a quick look at Arletta, who had momentarily come to and was engaged in the utterly unnecessary guzzling of more gin and tonic.

"For Mary Elizabeth," read out Helen, "from Grandma Taylor."

Grandma Taylor gave vent to a rather more basso hiccup than that which had escaped her granddaughter, lowered her glass, tried to focus on her daughter-in-law, closing one eye the more readily to do so, and erupted into a boozy grin which she turned on Mary Elizabeth, who—perceiving it—promptly scuttled to the farthest reach of her playpen and looked over her shoulder with lively apprehension.

Helen, meanwhile, began to unwrap the gift, slowly, and, it seemed, almost reluctantly, until finally a small jeweler's box in white, gold-embossed satin sat in her hand.

To Larry, standing as he was well out of the center of the scene, it was as though everyone in the room held his or her breath as, slowly and with a creak that was clearly audible in the suddenly silent room, Helen opened the box.

She gasped. Again her glance darted to Arletta and—worriedly—to her husband. Then, with hand almost trembling, she reached in, her fingers came together, and, her face rapt with the reverence anyone must feel for really good jewelry, she withdrew her hand. From it dangling on a finely wrought chain in white gold was a cross, also in white gold. But as fine as were the cross and chain, finer still were the five stones set upon the thing—faceted stones of a clear white purity that caught and refracted the light in an absolutely unmistakable way.

And a more unsuitable gift for a six-month-old child it would have been impossible to conceive.

Arletta, as alert as she was ever going to be that night, leaned forward. "They's five half-carat diamonds," she announced. "Ain't it pretty?"

At this point, Helen was looking almost frightened. For a moment, Larry could not imagine why, until he followed the direction of her glance.

Bob E.—his face suffused by so deep a maroon Larry

wondered if he wasn't going to have a stroke—had lurched to his feet, his mouth struggling with utterance but achieving no sound whatever. Then, overhand, as though pitching a baseball, he threw the brandy snifter to smash into the fireplace, causing a whoosh of blue flame to erupt up the chimney.

Before, however, Bob E. could rise above his momentary aphasia, his sister, who had similarly got to her feet, all but shrieked, "Mama!"

In response to which Arletta turned very slowly and faced her daughter before asking with quiet belligerence, "What?"

"What did you buy that with?" The younger woman sounded actually frightened about something.

"My money. So mind your business."

"What money?"

"You know what money."

"The money in the account?"

"Course."

"But that wasn't your money, Mama."

"The hell it wasn't."

"Oh, Jesus!" The younger woman looked as though she wanted to tear her mother's hair out and cry, both at that same time. "You didn't even have enough to lend Bob E. a goddamn nickle 'cause you spent it all and now you're spending—"

"Bette Wanda," snapped Helen. "Control yourself."

"I won't," she yelled. "I can't. That bank account didn't just have Daddy's insurance money in it. It had my money in it, too. My money for law school. And she's spending it. She's gonna spend us right back into that tar-paper shack she called home till Daddy died. Oh, Jesus, help me, Helen!"

"I see," said Helen, her lips thin with anger and distaste. She turned to Arletta. "If that's the case, Mother Taylor, I don't see how we can possibly accept—"

"Shut up!" Bob E., it seemed, had recovered. He stalked toward his wife and grabbed her hand and held it up, the chain still dangling therefrom as a gloating look spread over his drink-raddled features. "Shut up," he repeated and then addressed his mother with a smile that was more than half a snarl. "Course we'll accept it. And thank ya, *Mama!*"

"But she bought it with my money," Bette Wanda protested

again. "It was my money, I tell you. How much did you spend for that thing, Mama?"

"It was my money! And I'll damn well spend it however I please. And how dare you speak to me like that. After all I done for you."

"Done for me? Done for me!"

"Yeah, done for you. You and Bob E. I been good to both my kids . . ."

"What have you done for me? What the hell did you ever do for either one of us, you drunken bitch?"

The two women proceeded at length and loudly, in response to which, naturally enough, the babe, too, roused and added her own lusty yells to the fray.

"Very good, Bob E.," said Ben, projecting theatrically above these surging ebullitions. "*Very* good!" he went on relentlessly and unforgivably. "You should be able to hock it for quite a nice piece of change."

Bob E. rounded ferociously on his brother-in-law, his face suffused with choler. "Butt out of this, fat man."

"Ah, yes. Fat I am. Fat I concede. But thank God at least trash I am not."

"Who you calling trash?"

"Why, you, you dreary little vulgarian—and your monstrous regiment of women besides." He gestured toward Arletta and Bette Wanda.

"Trash, am I?" Bob E. snarled. "Then how come I was good enough for your sister, fat boy?"

"You watch your mouth, you jumped-up garage mechanic."

"Bob E.! Ben, stop! Bob E.!" Helen attempted to come between the by now circling men and tried to restrain her husband, hand on his arm.

Angrily, he shook her off and raised a hand as though about to hit her.

"You touch my sister and, by God, you'll be sorry you were ever born," snarled Ben menacingly.

"Your sister. Your sister," Bob E. sneered. "Your precious sister—that, don't forget, I took out of the gutter, you piss-ant pansy."

Whereupon, finally speechless in his rage, Ben threw his

only recently replenished tumbler of Scotch and soda full into Bob E.'s face.

It took Larry and Cy both to keep Bob E. restrained after that. The two Taylor women's yelling had been quickly subsumed in the outbreak of further hostilities, and for a minute both of them just watched, openmouthed, at Bob E. struggling and cursing in Cy's and Larry's arm lock.

"How dare you!" Helen, roused by now to shrill and shrewish anger, stopped in front of her husband and, as she repeated, "How dare you!" slapped his face. "Look at you. Look at all of you," she screamed. "How dare you ruin my Christmas?"

Bob E.'s struggles subsided in his sheer astonishment at what his wife had just done. Larry still kept a firm grip on him, but he was in truth nearly bowled over by the sheer sublime egomania of Helen's remark.

Mrs. Anderson, meanwhile, had picked up the baby and was trying to comfort her squalling. The child, however, was quite rudely snatched from her by a still-raging Helen who, shaking with emotion, shouted, "Now sit *down*! Everybody!"

Later, Larry would remember how totally unsurprised he was when, in the lull that greeted Helen's furious command, came one little word.

"No," said the General.

He was standing in the same spot where he had sat all night and now, as all eyes turned to him, he turned and very deliberately set his half-empty tumbler of orange juice on the mantelpiece and then repeated, "No. I've had enough."

"Father!" said Helen through gritted teeth and narrowed eyes.

"Don't threaten me, Helen," he said. "I don't have to put up with your nonsense. Just as," he added, "I'm not going to put up with any more of these antics. Sibyl, get your coat. Cy, Ben, Larry. We're leaving."

He began to walk to the door.

Bob E. shrugged off Larry's and Cy's hands. "Go on, then. Get out!"

"Shut up, Bob E.," snapped Helen and marched toward the General. "Father!" she commanded.

With a sigh, he turned. "What could you possibly have to say to me?" he asked wearily.

"All right, then, if that's the way you feel, *go* home. But you can at least kiss your granddaughter good night." She held the squirming infant toward him.

For a long moment, he neither said nor did anything other than look at his daughter and blink mildly once or twice. Finally, in a very soft but very firm voice, he said, "Helen, she is not my granddaughter. She's some stranger's brat that, for whatever strange ambitions of your own, Helen, you have chosen to rear. But she is not mine, and I think that you had better get it quite clear right now that she has not nor ever will have any claim on me. Do you understand?" His voice had risen marginally and he stepped forward and the clarity of his anger was such that, involuntarily, Helen took a corresponding step backward.

"No one has any claim on me," he said. "Not a one of you. And Christmas Eve notwithstanding, I'll tell you all plain that I'm tired of seeing your grubby little hands thrust out at me and hearing nothing but gimme, gimme, gimme. And furthermore, as soon as Christmas is over, I'm going to call my lawyer and make sure of it. So you can all stuff that in your Christmas stockings and walk to hell on it for all I care."

He turned and, without looking back, went down the passage and out the door. After a moment of stunned silence, Cy uttered one great sob and ran after him. Larry wrestled Ben—who was standing as though poleaxed and muttering malevolently under his breath—toward the front door. As he did so, he heard Mrs. Anderson say to Helen, "I'll talk to him and call you in the morning."

She kissed her daughter's cheek, but the woman might as well have been carved out of stone, the babe fretting unnoticed in the crook of her left arm.

Mrs. Anderson passed Larry and Ben and snapped, "Ben! Come along and don't dawdle," in a way that seemed to rouse her son as she passed down the hall before them.

They were on the front porch when Larry turned to pull the door to and found Bob E. there instead, his face alight with malignant hate.

"Don't bother," he said, and slammed the door behind them.

And suddenly Ben bellowed, "Merry Christmas! Ho! Ho! Ho!"—to reverberate up and down the quiet suburban street.

"Ben," said Larry. "Come on."

And to his intense irritation, Ben began singing, *"Minuit, Chrétiens, c'est l'heure solennelle, ou l'homme dieu descendit jusqu'à nous."*

"Ben!"

"Pour effacer la tache originelle . . ."

"Ben!"

"*La tache originelle!* Why, that means 'original sin.' Now what do you suppose could possibly be an original sin? I must ask Mother sometime. I mean, all of our sins always seem so dreadfully common. Don't they?"

CHAPTER 7

i

For quite a lengthy interval after the tale had reached its depressing conclusion, no one said a thing, not even when the clock in the passage bonged out once and again and they knew it to be two o'clock in the morning.

"And tell me, Sibyl," said Miss Worthing, "just how *did* you get them all back together again today? After all that?"

"I phoned Helen next morning and told her that Henry had been persuaded that it was a result of everyone's drinking too much."

"And was Henry persuaded?"

"Grudgingly, but I thought so. Until today, of course. Helen said later that she told Bob E.—and his mother and sister—that she would personally skin 'em alive if they didn't behave."

"And she could do it," muttered Ben.

Larry gave a mirthless chuckle. "So she could. But you know, Aunt Matilda, they did."

"Did what?"

"Behave. Bob E. was certainly okay at your open house today."

"Oh?"

Ben nodded massively. "He even offered us a snort from his flask."

"Flask?" asked Miss Shaw. "But we had our wine."

"I know," said Larry with a smile, "but Bob E. was a mite hung over and he said he wasn't overfond of herbal wine at the best of times. So he brought some Jack Daniels to take up the slack."

"Which we finished," said Ben.

"And what about our rule about no drinking for the bartenders?" said Miss Worthing.

"Well, when you pressed us into service, I thought that just meant the wine," said Ben.

"You should have been a Jesuit, Benjamin Anderson," said Miss Worthing severely.

But that, as they say, was that. Briefly she entertained the notion of getting them all to go over the incidents of the day immediately past, but decided against it.

First, of course, there was the simple and unavoidable physical fact that everyone was already half gaga with fatigue.

Second, and a point of equal sharpness, was the fact that all she would get would be another joint narrative from which, in all likelihood, much would be left out or, at the very least, go unremarked. It had been only too obvious that there had been various points, here and there in the narrative, over which one or another of the narrators had blithely skipped for whatever painful, embarrassing, or merely uncomfortable reason.

Which, finally, led to the third reason for letting them all go to bed: She knew now that, like it or not, she was going to have to speak to each of them again. Separately. And she was just too damned weary to contemplate such a thankless exercise until she had had at least a few hours' sleep.

"Okay, folks," she said, leaning forward and placing both hands flat on the table. "That's it for now. Go to bed!"

Under other circumstances, the response might have been funny. In spite of their manifest fatigue, all three witnesses actually looked quite shocked by this sudden dismissal.

"Really?" said Ben rather blankly.

"Really," said Miss Worthing.

And astonishment rapidly gave way to sheer giddy relief

writ large on their faces as they realized that, for the moment, the flogging had ended.

Ben hoisted himself to his feet by hunching forward and pressing down on the table. He then bent to kiss his mother's cheek, murmured a yawning "Good night, everyone," and, sketching a gesture of farewell, lumbered out into the corridor without so much as a backward glance.

Larry, too, struggled to his feet, bussed the proffered cheeks of Miss Shaw and Miss Worthing respectively, muttered good night to Mrs. Anderson, shambled to the door into the passage, paused for the briefest of moments, and was gone.

Miss Shaw patiently and methodically shut up shop, handed the notebook in which she had been writing to Miss Worthing, and also took her departure, after cocking an inquiring eyebrow at Miss Worthing, who nodded but said nothing.

Finally, Mrs. Anderson too rose from her place. Though obviously weary, she yet rinsed out the teapot, tossing the dead leaves into a separate garbage bin with an embossed blue plastic strip on it with raised white letters, which—peering more closely—Miss Worthing finally realized spelled out "Compost."

For a moment, it made her feel singularly bleak. As the younger woman moved about her kitchen, she had not unnaturally done what she always had and so added the tea leaves to the other organic detritus to be mixed into the composter. Except that the avid gardener who had inspired this by now unconscious habit lay upstairs dying of someone's runaway malice.

Miss Worthing watched wordlessly as Mrs. Anderson rinsed out the tea basket, dried it, and measured tea into it from the canister and then replaced the basket into the pot.

"Doesn't it lose flavor sitting out overnight?" asked Miss Worthing.

"Not enough to notice and it saves a few moments in the morning."

"You're an efficient housekeeper, Sibyl."

"I've rather had to be," said Mrs. Anderson, "to take care of this old house, fix meals, raise a family—and on top of it, write my books. That's why I moved to a word processor as soon as they evolved into something a human being could use."

"Why didn't you just hire a few servants? Or a couple? Henry could afford it."

Mrs. Anderson laughed at that.

"Matilda, first of all, have you ever tried to use any of the local people who are willing to take the job on?"

Miss Worthing nodded, a number of unfortunate incidents crowding in upon her.

"Then you know perfectly well that to train them is at least as difficult a chore as doing it all yourself."

"But you could have hired someone—or several some-ones—from San Francisco or Sacramento, surely."

"Probably," conceded Mrs. Anderson. "But as rich as Henry became in recent years, he would have balked at that kind of outlay for work he and I were perfectly capable of doing ourselves. And I wouldn't have let him even if he had been willing. I found my peace in being a wife and a mother. It may not be the most enviable or envied vocation for a woman anymore, and," she added dryly, "I may not have been all that successful as either, but it was my vocation. My books are nothing but the fruit of pursuing that vocation a little more self-consciously perhaps than most."

She said it all simply enough, placidly going about the business of tidying the kitchen. The woman had always taken such a modest view of her own works, and to this day, Miss Worthing still did not know whether to hoot derisively or murmur appreciatively. Her own admiration for Mrs. Anderson's books was, frankly, enormous. They were clearly thought out and founded on irrefragable logic and a great fund of common sense and *(mirabile dictu)* lucid as sunlight. She had once heard a certain famous cleric refer to Mrs. Anderson as a "garden-variety theologian," and had felt, angrily, at the time that the man's own works and sermons would have been substantially improved by spending some time in the very same garden. . . .

ii

"Would you like some more tea, Matilda?" Mrs. Anderson's voice shook her awake. To her surprise, the woman had actually placed the kettle once more on the stove to boil.

"No, Sibyl," said Miss Worthing tartly. "I want to go to bed."

"And so, Matilda, do I."

"So why don't you?"

"Because we have to talk. And tomorrow, I suspect, is going to be far too busy for either of us."

"I wouldn't bet on that, Sibyl."

"What *do* you mean?"

"Oh, now don't play coy with me, Sibyl. You know perfectly well what I'm thinking."

"Oh?"

"Oh, dear Gussie!" breathed Miss Worthing. "Sibyl, earlier tonight you were all quivering eagerness to be listed among the suspects. Why are you playing games with me now?"

"Am I a suspect?" asked Mrs. Anderson.

"You'd better believe it," replied Miss Worthing.

It did not escape Miss Worthing's attention, either, that Mrs. Anderson seemed rather more pleased than annoyed with the answer.

"Why?" Mrs. Anderson demanded.

"My dear—" began Miss Worthing, but Mrs. Anderson quickly intervened, "You needn't toy with me, Matilda; both of us have been trained in logic."

"Very well," said Miss Worthing grimly, and began ticking points off on her fingers: "*(a)* you are an extraordinary mother; *(b)* you are not likely ever to have another grandchild; *(c)* you are—were—as out of patience with Henry as anyone else; *(d)* you have better access to the means of murder than anyone by virtue of (1) the orange-flower water; and (2) the first and third pitchers of orange juice. I would have liked," Miss Worthing said sarcastically, "to have put all this in a nice scholastic syllogism, but frankly, I didn't have time."

Mrs. Anderson's brows were furrowed. Presently she said thoughtfully, "Never mind the Thomist method. That's very good."

"There's only one question, well, actually two, that I would like to ask you."

"Did I do it?"

"Well, did you?"

"I have to admit," said Mrs. Anderson, "that had I thought

of it—bumping Henry off, that is—there have been several occasions these last few months when the idea would not have been either wanting appeal or difficult of execution. But first of all, Matilda, and I don't know whether you'll believe me, it never did occur to me. Nor would it have. And secondly, I would never have chosen such a horrible method."

"Why?" asked Miss Worthing and was not exactly surprised when the answer came.

"Because, Matilda, strange as it might seem, I love my husband very much, still and in spite of all. In fact, I cannot even begin to imagine what my life is going to be like without him . . ." She stopped and visibly sought to regain her composure.

For Miss Worthing's part, it was interesting, completely credible, and entirely irrelevant. Far too many people have done truly appalling things to their loved ones for her to be taken in by any such heartfelt protestations.

"Nevertheless," said Miss Worthing, "that was not the question I wanted to ask."

"Then what was it?"

"What were you drinking? During the preparations for the dinner."

For a moment, Mrs. Anderson looked genuinely startled. "But why—"

"Never mind why," said Miss Worthing. "What were you drinking?"

"A beer. One. I don't like to drink much when I'm engaged in something like that."

"Nothing else at all?"

"I had wine with my meal, of course. And everyone was drinking mimosas as well," said Mrs. Anderson.

But Miss Worthing was no longer really paying attention. Instead she was leafing through the notebook, looking more than a little sour. "Blast it!" she muttered.

"Is something wrong?"

Miss Worthing looked up. "Wrong? Not at all. Not wrong. Okay, Sibyl, one more thing and you can go to bed. What did you put in the orange-flower water?"

Mrs. Anderson smiled. "Orange-flower water."

"Are you being coy with me again, Sibyl?"

"Not in the least. That's really all there is. Commercial orange-flower water, a chopped-up bit of vanilla bean, and the merest sliver of cinnamon bark. You see," she explained, "I can't use commercial vanilla extract; it's usually forty percent alcohol—that's eighty proof. And ground cinnamon was just too irritating to Henry in this weakened state."

"Does anyone know you made it?"

"Cy. Henry."

"Anyone else?"

"I don't really know. I doubt it. It's one of those little domestic chores one hardly goes around talking about."

"Where was it kept?"

"In the pantry."

"What kind of bottle?"

"A rubber-sealed mason jar."

"Not vacuum-packed."

"There was no need. It never needs refrigeration and I put the vanilla bean in—what?—five days ago."

"Was anyone with you when you bought the bean?"

"No. I got it at Gennaro's Market—as I'm sure you're aware, it's the only place in Jolliston you can get them."

"So 'tis," said Miss Worthing, frowning and pursing her lips thoughtfully. A thought had suddenly occurred to her, and hastily she made a note to inquire if Tony Gennaro had mentioned the bean to anyone. When she was through, she sat a moment trying to think if there was anything . . .

Mrs. Anderson yawned. "Matilda, is there anything else?"

Suddenly, it came to Miss Worthing what it was she was forgetting. "Good Lord, yes, Sibyl, there is."

Mrs. Anderson smiled wearily. "Somehow I knew this was going to happen."

"Sorry, Sibyl, I did say only two more questions. But I do have a third."

"What's that?"

A curious smile lifted Miss Worthing's mouth as she asked, "Just how good a housekeeper are you, Sibyl?"

"I beg your pardon."

"I'm sorry, Sibyl," said Miss Worthing with a laugh. "What a way to ask the question. What I meant was, do you keep a cellar book?"

"Oh," said Mrs. Anderson. "Well, yes, actually I do. Sort of." Whereupon she chuckled. "But I'm afraid it's rather like keeping a journal. Unless one is fastidious to an uncommon degree, it's usually just a question of the best intentions . . ." She stopped. Miss Worthing was not laughing. "Is it important, Matilda?"

"I don't know," replied Miss Worthing. "It could be."

Mrs. Anderson rose from the table and beckoned Miss Worthing to follow. "Than let's go take a look both at the cellar book and the cellar."

She led the way out into the hallway, turned right, and opened a door beyond which all that could be seen was stairs descending into unrelieved blackness, down which Mrs. Anderson proceeded.

"Sibyl, turn on the light," said Miss Worthing, in reply to which Mrs. Anderson laughed and looked over her shoulder. "I'm afraid that, quite in keeping with this crazy old house, the lights are at the bottom of the stairs. Wait there till I get them, Matilda."

The figure of Mrs. Anderson receded into the darkness, the sound of her footsteps on the stairs loud and hollow as they too receded downward.

"Good Lord, Sibyl," said Miss Worthing, calling downward, "how deep is this cellar?"

"Quite deep," came the voice of Mrs. Anderson. "I just thank God we've never had a really major quake here in Jolliston. We've gotten through all of 'em so far with no damage at all to speak of." She switched on the lights.

The stairs, ancient gray unfinished wood, led downward, broken only by a landing and a turn about five steps down. Thereafter they led downward a full twenty feet below.

"I had no idea," said Miss Worthing as she descended the stairs and looked about. The place was a cavern spreading out the entire width and length of the house above, with support columns and pillars of masonry holding up the house, an arrangement upon which Miss Worthing looked with singular and acute disfavor.

"If there ever is a major quake, Sibyl, this will collapse like a house of cards. Why ever haven't you had it shored up properly and had the house bolted to the foundation?"

"That's what everyone says," agreed Mrs. Anderson, "and really, we always were intending to get around to it. But"—she shrugged—"nothing's really shaken it so far, and if it withstood 1906. . ." She left the sentence unfinished and turned and led the way through the accumulated detritus that will accumulate in the basement of any house which has been lived in for a quarter century. Discarded and neglected toys, rusting bicycles, shelf upon shelf of books and preserves, seedy-looking cabinets holding their secrets, and a great workbench along one wall, above which the tools had all been hung with the obsessive tidiness of the General. In another corner a washer-dryer combination gleamed next to a pair of deep freezes, whilst in the middle of it all, squat and many-armed as an Indian god, was the enormous and rather ancient furnace which, as they passed by it, clicked on loudly, followed by a great whoosh as the gas caught fire, and quite startling Miss Worthing.

Presently they came to a door of a small lath-and-timber structure tucked into a back corner of the cellar. Within, the darkness seemed even deeper and more impenetrable than in the other corners of the cellar. Nor was the impression greatly alleviated when Mrs. Anderson walked in, reached above her and pulled a string for which she had to grope blindly a time or two before she was able to grasp it.

A tiny fifteen-watt bulb came on to illumine a small wine cellar, the shelves of which were for the most part barren now, with only a single bottle here and there to remind of vanished glories.

From one of the uprights a small three-ring notebook bound in black shiny cloth dangled on a string. This Mrs. Anderson lifted, pausing briefly to blow dust from it and make the wry observation, "You see. I said it was only a good intention."

She sighed and let it fall. "Not a bit of good. We entered them often enough, but all too frequently the removal of things was accomplished by a mad dash down here and a quick grab of whatever was wanted and a firm intention to remember to enter it in the book someday. Is there something in particular?"

Miss Worthing shrugged almost irritably. "I suppose it

really doesn't matter, but frankly I was concerned more about spirits than wine, Sibyl."

"Spirits are over there." Mrs. Anderson pointed toward yet farther depths of the wine cellar. "They have a separate book, too, although—" She retreated into the gloom and reaching up, pulled yet another string to turn on another weak and ineffectual naked bulb. A smaller spiral notebook had been tied to a string to dangle in front of three shelves which, to Miss Worthing's eyes, looked as if they contained several bottles of every kind of liquor ever distilled on earth. Mrs. Anderson was already looking into this notebook with much the same dubious expression as she had the previous one. "I can't say that this is any better," she finally said, and dropped the notebook with a little shrug and turned to Miss Worthing. "Perhaps, Matilda, if I knew what you were looking for?"

Miss Worthing merely looked sour. It would have been useful had the cellar books—particularly the latter—been kept up. She sighed, and presently nodded. "Do you have any idea about liquor consumption in your house?"

Mrs. Anderson considered. "Pretty much so," she answered. "It's not that there's a tremendous amount of drinking done hereabouts anymore. It was different before—in the old days," she amended and then stopped abruptly. "Now Cy likes a cocktail before dinner now and again. So, for that matter, do I." Again she shrugged. "That's about it."

"So you keep track of what you've got down here?"

"More or less."

"How more, how less?"

"If I think of it when I'm down here, I'll look in to see if I need to pick anything up—if we're low on anything."

"Ah," said Miss Worthing, "so you probably would see if something were missing."

"Probably."

"Well, then." Miss Worthing gestured toward the shelves.

"Anything in particular?"

"Actually yes. I think we should concentrate on the white liquors—vodka, light rum, that kind of thing, or anything that could have been masked by the taste of the orange juice or the orange-flower water."

"Okay," said Mrs. Anderson. She turned her attention to the shelves and began shifting bottles, all the while muttering to herself. There were gin, vodka, and arrack, white rum, white brandy, kümmel; plus kirschwasser, Eau de Danzig, Cointreau, triple sec, and that curious orange liqueur made in Italy.

"Rather a lot of those, aren't there," said Miss Worthing.

"Well, I'm afraid that back at the beginning of Henry's illness," said Mrs. Anderson, "I made rather a thing about frugality and was determined to use all the orange peels as well as the juice. I grated hundreds of 'em and put them—and Cointreau or triple sec or this stuff into cookies, cakes, pound cakes, even pies. My family," she added dryly, "told me after rather a short time that they had had quite enough orange flavoring in everything to last a lifetime. After which the orange peels were consigned to heaven, and these"—she gestured at the shelves—"to oblivion. No"—she considered the shelves again—"the only thing that's missing is a two-liter jug of vodka, but I seem to recall that Ben came to get that yesterday." She hesitated and then looked faintly puzzled as she added, "Earlier today. Funny, it seems so much longer. And other than that"—again she glanced at the shelves—"there isn't a single thing missing that I can . . ." She stopped speaking very abruptly.

"What is it, Sibyl?"

"Nothing," said Mrs. Anderson a little shakily after a moment. "I just thought for a minute that something was missing."

"What?"

"A bottle of arrack. But I remember now I gave it to that little Orthodox church in Steuber for one of those pan-Orthodox food festivals they always seem to be having. The Arab section seemed to think I should be translated to heaven straightaway for providing it."

"It is expensive," murmured Miss Worthing as she followed Mrs. Anderson out of the cellar . . .

. . . And ten minutes later was back, having safely delivered Mrs. Anderson into the care and custody of Billy McClure at the top of the main stairs.

It had been a rather interesting performance. Miss Worthing was by no means certain that she herself—with decades of experience in dissembling behind her—could have managed as well. Larry was certainly right, it was indeed obvious from whom Ben derived his skill as an actor. And as for that farrago of nonsense about a bottle of arrack going to the Orthodox church . . .

Well now, wait a minute. Actually—Miss Worthing suddenly realized—that part was probably true. Sibyl was much too clever to be caught in an outright lie. She probably had given a bottle to enliven the festivities at one of St. Hermann's little parties. They were, after all, fun things, and lots of people in and around Jolliston contributed to them.

But . . .

First of all, it was highly unlikely that arrack had been used in the General's orange juice or anywhere else this Christmas Day. And secondly, if the good parishioners of St. Hermann of Alaska had indeed made such a fuss over Sibyl's offering, was it likely that she would have been so very startled when she found it missing?

Miss Worthing pulled on the naked light bulbs—after a good deal more groping about than Sibyl had required to effect the same purpose—and lifted up the small spiral-bound notebook. Not that she expected any significant insight to be gained thereby. If Sibyl had been right, the secret of what was missing from this little storeroom was probably locked firmly in her own head.

She peered at the entries, most of them in Sibyl's flowing and generous script, but a number, too, in Henry's crabbed scratchings. Entries certainly outnumbered deletions. She especially liked one entry by Henry. "Brandy," it said. No date, no price, no brand name, no stars, no description, no deletion date. Just "Brandy." It was all well and good to note that Henry was of a generation that considered matters of domestic food and drink to be women's work and more than a little infra dig to a man, but really!

Actually, thought Miss Worthing as she turned the pages looking for the end of the entries, they kept this up until very recently. For some reason that surprised her, although upon reflection, it really should not have. It would be the kind of futile domestic gesture that Sibyl would maintain. And never mind her protestations to the contrary. What deletions there were in the notebook had almost universally been made in Sibyl's handwriting.

Then she saw it—and afterward would sometimes wonder if she would have seen it had it not been in a handwriting completely different from either that of Henry or Sibyl.

"Hmm," she muttered half aloud to herself and looked up from the book to peruse the shelves. It did not take very long to see that it was not there. Not that that would necessarily mean anything. If Sibyl was right—and damn it, didn't she keep coming back to that? Nevertheless—she lifted the book and once more studied the entry to try to memorize the handwriting—she would dearly love to know who had removed from these shelves, less than a week before, a single fifth of Everclear—190 proof grain alcohol. And, at least as importantly, why.

iii

Once more, having returned to the kitchen, for a moment she hesitated. Should she brew just one more cup of tea? It would be pleasant to have to hand during what she was almost certain was about to happen. But the really considerable amounts of caffeine she had already put away was coursing in a not very agreeable manner through her veins, and the dismal fact was that she had to get some sleep, even if it would amount to little more than a brief nap. What she should have really was a hot brandy, but it just would not do to go about disturbing the liquor supply until she had had a chance thoroughly, and in daylight, to examine it. Who knew what might yet be found amid the bottles?

Then she remembered that Ben and Larry had mentioned that the General kept a good old brandy in his study. Quickly she rinsed out her cup, set the kettle on to boil, and nipped across the hall.

She found the liquor caddy without any difficulty and poured a generous tot into her cup. It was wonderful stuff, whatever it was—the fumes rising from the cup as she bustled back into the kitchen were distinctly heady. It rather went to her heart to be pouring boiling water into it. And wasn't it typical of the General that, though he himself was unable to drink, yet he would provide such a marvelous tipple for such friends as happened by.

And, as sometimes happens in these things, a sudden wave of tenderness and sorrow swept over her. Soon—within a matter of days—the General would be no more with them and for no other reason than sheer unalloyed greed. Though to find his murderer could not, to be sure, restore the General to them, there would yet be a measure of satisfaction that the perpetrator would enjoy no fruit of his deed.

And she would find out, had, in fact, a glimmering already, but she held up her cup and silently pledged to the General a successful outcome of the venture and then drank deeply of that excellent and ancient brandy.

"Miss Worthing?" came a voice, tentative and soft in the door to the hallway.

"Yes, Billy?"

"It's Larry, your nephew. He told me to come and ask if he could see you. Privately?"

"Of course, Billy. Bring him down."

Billy melted once more into the gloom. While she waited, Miss Worthing rinsed out another cup, retraced her steps to the study, and emerged to find both Billy and Larry coming noiselessly up the hall.

"Thank you, Billy," she said. "I'll bring him back up myself. You'd better get back up there."

"Yes, ma'am," murmured that young man and retreated back down the hall.

Larry sniffed the air. "Is that what I think it is?" he asked.

"Brandy? Yes. I thought you could use a hot brandy."

"You knew I'd be back down?" he said, as he followed his aunt once more into the kitchen. He resumed his place at the table and murmured gratefully as she set the mug in front of him and then filled it with hot water.

"It seemed likely," she said. "You were all but sending semaphore signals that you were leaving something out."

"Lord, that's good," he said, sipping the brandy. "I wonder if Ben noticed."

"Probably," said Miss Worthing. "He's a noticing kind of person."

"That's true," said Larry with a curious inflection.

"You don't agree?"

"Well, yes, I do. Fundamentally. But sometimes I don't think he pays very close attention."

"I don't think you have to worry about that while all this mess is going on," said Miss Worthing.

"No, I'm sure you're right about that, but sometimes . . ." His voice trailed off.

"Larry, what did you leave out earlier this evening?"

"The fact that Ben owes me twenty-five thousand dollars."

Miss Worthing's eyes widened. "Isn't that rather a lot of money to lend someone?"

"It is and it isn't," said Larry simply. "First of all, Ben's probably my best friend in the world right about now, so when he said he needed it—"

"Pardon me, but isn't Ben rather a rich man?"

"He is indeed. Quite rich. Unfortunately, at the moment, it's almost all of it on paper."

"What do you mean?"

"He sunk an enormous, even, one might say, a frivolous amount of his money into the Elephantic Gold Trust."

"Oh, ye pigs and little fishes of the Lord!" said Miss Worthing with feeling.

"And so, he is not," said Larry dryly, "what you would call liquid at the moment—and won't be until God and the Treasury Department alone know when. Any questions, Aunt Matilda?"

"Several," replied his aunt, although really her mind was in something of a whirl. She had seen clearly enough that Ben and Larry had been hiding something, yes. But this? "You, however, just happened to have twenty-five thousand dollars lying around?"

Larry nodded, looking quite uncomfortable. "Well, I had—I was going to, I mean there is this, uhm," he floundered.

"Yes?"

"I was going to make a down payment on a house in San Francisco," he blurted.

"And you put it off?"

Again Larry nodded. "I called the man who owns the house

and asked if he could possibly put the closing back a month. He wasn't happy but he did it."

"Do you have any real expectation of getting the money back in a month?"

"Again, that depends."

"On what?"

"Ben had a movie released last month. If it does well . . ."

"And if it doesn't?"

"Then he—and I—will have to look elsewhere."

Saying which, he looked rather uncomfortable. Both of them knew all too well to whom he would have to apply.

"But I know—at least he told me he did—that he asked the General to help him out a bit."

"Oh, brother!"

"I know. It didn't seem like a very likely thing—not after he finished telling everyone where to get off Christmas Eve."

"Did Ben tell you what he needed the money for?"

"Oh yes. Living expenses."

"Living . . . twenty-five thousand dollars' worth of *living* expenses?"

"He had some other debts to pay off. He called it consolidating."

"Good God, Larry, how much money did he lose in that gold scam?"

"Lots."

A rather uncomfortable sort of silence fell between them as each pursued his own thoughts. Presently, however, Larry ventured, "I bet I can guess what you're thinking about, Aunt Matilda."

"Oh?"

"Yes, indeed. That all of the above gave me a pretty powerful motive to make certain that Ben came into his inheritance as quickly as possible."

"Well . . ." temporized Miss Worthing. "It would also demonstrate a touching and rather pretty faith in the celerity of the probate courts and lawyers to have your money back by next month. Still . . ." She sighed. "Did you?"

"Did I what?"

"Did you put—whatever—into the eggnog, or slip something into the orange juice?"

"I could have," admitted Larry. "Fairly easily. But no, Aunt Matilda"—he looked up at her—"I didn't do it."

Again Miss Worthing sighed. "And, for the moment, I believe you. Not that that makes a particle's worth of difference. I am going to have to continue to regard you as a suspect. You're quite right, you know; that's a dilly of a motive."

"I would have guessed that," said Larry. "And, in fact," he added, "I would prefer to be suspected. I really wouldn't want to be treated any different than anyone else." Suddenly he shivered. "God, it all sounds so awful—*allowing* oneself to be suspected of committing a murder. But I know I didn't do it, and I trust you, Aunt Matilda, to find who did."

"Thank you," said Miss Worthing, "and I'm beginning to think that I'm really quite proud of you. This—these last few days can't have been easy on you."

"Oh, it hasn't been all that bad. Rather grim on occasion, frequently rather embarrassing, but"—he shrugged—"I've certainly learned my lesson about creating people in my own image."

"Don't let it sour you, Larry," she admonished. "They're really not bad people. People seldom are, you know."

"One of 'em is a murderer."

"That's true. But don't you think it would be far too easy to paint everyone with a black brush?"

Suddenly she yawned and almost immediately as she did so, Larry followed suit.

"Oh Lord," he said, "I've got to get some sleep." She nodded wearily. "That makes two of us." They stood up.

"Are you sure you didn't notice anything?" she asked. "Someone pouring alcohol into the nog or the juice?"

"No." Larry shook his head. "I wish I had, but—nothing."

"Not Arletta or Bette Wanda. They were both drinking gin, weren't they?"

"Which goes nicely in eggnog or in orange juice. Yes, but the simple fact is that I've drunk enough Ramos fizzes in my time to know what it would taste like in the nog, and I've put away a good many orange blossoms: ditto. At least," he conceded, "it doesn't seem likely I could have missed it."

"What were you drinking? No, wait." She flipped pages in the notebook. "Okay. Never mind. Here it is. Whiskey. Bourbon?"

"Scotch."

"'Repellent English fashion.' Soda, no ice?" He nodded as, half to herself, she muttered, "What *was* it?"

iv

Miss Worthing walked Larry to the bottom of the front stairs. Above them, barely outlined by dim light, was the silhouette of Billy, sitting in a chair at the top of the stairs.

"Billy!" she called softly. Even in the dim light they could see him start up and look about in a confused manner.

"This will never do," muttered Miss Worthing and, shooing Larry on up the stairs, she turned back into the library, peered round the shelves till she found what she wanted. Taking two of the volumes, she let herself back into the corridor and scooted up the stairs in time to meet Billy just back from delivering Larry safely to his room. The chair was positioned against the balustrade at the top of the stairs.

"Billy," she commanded, "move that over here." She gestured at a spot directly beneath one of the dim hurricane wall lamps which lit the upper corridor.

"Why?"

"Because you really mustn't fall asleep, and I've brought you a sovereign cure for sleepiness."

"What's that?"

She handed him the two books. "Dick Francis," she replied. "Thrillers. Get into one and I guarantee you won't put it down till you've finished it—hopefully after breakfast tomorrow."

He laughed more than a little ruefully. "I guess I was nodding out a bit."

"That's okay," she said. "But you can't just sit here waiting for something to happen, hour after hour. 'Tain't natural."

"Okay," he said cheerfully enough, examining the books. "Horses?"

"There's always horses in Mr. Francis's books," she said and once more yawned mightily. When she had done, she laughed and said, "Excuse me!" and then added firmly, "but I have *got* to get some sleep."

"Is there any time you'd like to be called?" asked Billy.

"Let me see," she said and peered rather blurrily at her wristwatch. Even as she did so the sound of the clock rose from below in the silence of the great house as it chimed musically three times.

"Three o'clock," Miss Worthing muttered, half to herself. "Let me sleep at least till eight. That is, unless"—she glanced at the door behind which the nurse still kept vigil with the General.

"Yes?"

"The General left word that he wished to speak to me. If—when he awakens—get me immediately. Oh, and if the nurse comes out, and wants some coffee or something like that, a sandwich or what have you, would you go get it for her?"

"Of course."

"Does she know what's going on here?"

"I doubt it. Mrs. Anderson did an awfully good job of stonewalling both her and the doctor."

"It's all rather crazy, isn't it, Billy?" said Miss Worthing wryly.

"I suppose so," said Billy, who then surprised her by adding, "but it's better this way."

"What do you mean?"

"What good would it do to get the cops in?" he demanded. "They'd spend precisely four and a quarter seconds talking to everyone at once, swoop down on whoever's face they don't like—and five'll get you ten it would be Cy for no other reason than that—" He halted abruptly, but Miss Worthing waved him on. "It's okay; I know about Cy."

"And then—even if Cy were the guilty one, he'd probably wind up in front of a judge who'd take one look at how much money the Andersons are worth and toss the whole thing out on some specious legal technicality."

What made this furious indictment even more intense was that never once did the young man forget where he was and raise his voice.

"You don't seem to have much respect for the system," observed Miss Worthing.

"On the contrary," said Billy, "I have the greatest respect for the system. What I have no respect for are the shabby little souls that have weaseled themselves into the system from the bottom on up to the highest office in the land—police, lawyers, judges, and, God help us all, politicians whose only interests are their own, and once that's been seen to, well, then it's chuck you, Farley."

"These aren't easy times to be an artist, are they?" said Miss Worthing sympathetically, trying to get to the root of this young man's terrible bitterness.

But he laughed at that, a genuine and friendly laugh. "People are always saying that," he said with a smile. "But the fact is, no time is any easier than any other. Not really. Except"—he frowned—"I don't know. There is something to be said about pursuing a career nowadays."

"How so?"

"You *can* make an adequate living fairly easily these days in the theater, or opera, or TV or movies, if you've got a modicum of training, aren't too greedy, and are content to do the job for the love of the job."

A light began to dawn in Miss Worthing's mind. "This touches you somehow, too, doesn't it?" she asked.

"I guess so. There is—there was—a member of the company. He's a pretty good singer and a dynamite actor. But he's married and now there's a baby on the way. So yesterday he shows up to tell us he's got to quit; he's going to law school. His wife's family finally managed to persuade him. I knew they were trying because he told me. Hell, yes, he'll make more money as a lawyer. A lot more. But what kind of a lawyer will he be? I wouldn't bet a plug nickel on his integrity. Not when he can't even be true to himself. And the 'system,' I need hardly remind you, is full of others just like him." He broke off and shook his head, uttering a little half-embarrassed laugh. "Sorry. End of sermon. It's just that now all this and . . ." He paused and took a deep breath. "I'm glad you and her ladyship are going to solve this one. Because when you really solve it, we'll know for sure who could do such a really rotten thing to another human being."

"Thank you, Billy," she said, strangely touched by the faith of this peculiar young man. "Enjoy the books, and good night."

She went and Billy resumed his place. His sudden eruption of anger at the stupidity and futility of all casual and callous wasting of human life, whether by murder or by attrition fettered to an office stool, had sent a goodly amount of adrenaline into his system. Now the reaction was setting in and what remained of the night stretched endlessly before him.

With a sigh he picked up the books and looked at them critically. He seemed to recall having heard something of the author before. Life in the theater being very much a hurry-up-and-wait kind of thing, theater folk tend to read rather a lot in the interstices between frenzied activity. That kind of on-again off-again schedule, however, is hardly conducive to the leisured and intelligent absorption of great literature. Something you can readily pick up and plunge into or put down with equal swiftness distinctly recommends itself. As a result, people in the theater tend to be either whodunit or science-fiction fans.

It is perhaps unfortunate that Billy was definitely of the latter camp. Had Miss Worthing selected a book wherein teeming hordes of intellectual slugs were kept at bay by the sword of some hulking inarticulate brute of a man with thunderous muscles and inadequate clothing, or one in which the evil and rancid empire was tweaked by an earnest and outrageously outnumbered gang of ever-so-pure-hearted and stalwart rebels, then Billy would probably have sat there till the crack of doom—or at least of dawn.

As it was, he found, through no fault of Mr. Francis, the characters humdrum, and their endless fascination with horses utterly unfathomable.

But he persisted gamely. His eyes focused sharply on the page. He had to read it several times and even then was not sure he could recall what it had said. His head nodded, his chin rested on his chest, his eyelids grew heavier.

Then—sharply and clearly—he heard the click of a door being opened.

He looked up. The nurse, Miss—Miss—now what was her name?—was saying something to him. And didn't Miss Worthing want him to do something for the nurse? But what was it? He couldn't quite put his finger on it. But that was all right because she was gone now and he really ought to finish this page he was on, but he couldn't quite recall what was on the previous page. Maybe he should turn back, but, dear Lord, it was all too much of an effort. And now there was the sound of another door opening. Briefly he wondered who it could be this time. But before the question was even fully formulated, he slept.

Mrs. Wu descended the stairs rather more amused than annoyed. No doubt Lady Fairgrief's "butler" had been left there in the hallway to lend a hand, were such needed, but it would have been unkind to have awakened him. And unnecessary.

The General was still in a deep slumber bordering on a coma. She would, of course, have to return as quickly as possible, but she knew also that she needed a cup of coffee and a cookie, and really it took no time at all to boil a cup of water, stir in some instant coffee. No need to awaken that young man.

Besides, she really did not feel like having any conversation. With anybody. The General was clearly dying, and Mrs. Wu, who had loved the Andersons for two decades and more, was distressed.

The water came to a boil and Mrs. Wu made her a cup of coffee and covered it with a saucer; she could drink it upstairs when it had cooled a bit. It was, moreover, high time she got back to the patient. With characteristic methodicality she glanced at her watch; it was just on four o'clock. It would begin to get light in another three or four hours, and for herself, the coming of the dawn would be welcome after this long and tedious night as she watched a patient, a dear friend, visibly deteriorating while she could just stand by and watch, doing nothing.

Picking up the cup and saucer and carrying it with the ease of long practice, she went to the doorway of the kitchen leading onto the hall and switched off the light.

An unexpected sound behind her caused her almost to upset her coffee. A board had creaked loudly in the passageway leading to the back stairs.

For a moment, it occurred to her that perhaps she should investigate. Then, of course, she laughed—a rich and wise laugh. The house was quite cold by now. It was nothing more than a board in this ancient house snapping back into its place. She turned and went back down the corridor and climbed the stairs.

Billy was by now sound asleep, crouched in his chair, the book still held loosely in his grip. Mrs. Wu chuckled again and tenderly slid the book from his hands, and, reaching up above the young man, switched off the lamp above him. She slipped back into the General's room and shut the door behind her.

And the house was completely wrapped in sleep. Only once was the enveloping silence disturbed. A figure, hugging itself to the deepest shadows, cautiously crept up the back stairs, paused at the top landing only long enough to peruse the lay of the land, and, seeing Billy still soundly asleep, nipped down the hall, opened a door with but a whisper of sound, and slipped in. And all was as still as a tomb but for the occasional groan of a board contracting in the chill, or the measured chiming of the clock below sounding the quarter, half, and full hours again and again and again . . .

CHAPTER 8

i

"Miss Worthing! Miss Worthing! Wake up! Please, wake up! Oh, my God! Oh, Jesus! Miss Worthing!"

In spite of these anguished calls from without and the onslaught of frantic knocking at the bedroom door, it still took Miss Worthing an appreciable time to realize that something other than an especially unpleasant dream was tripping through her mind.

"All right," she muttered irritably, as the pounding on the door continued. "I hear you!"

With a groan of the greatest possible reluctance she sat up and groped about on the night table for her glasses.

"Miss Worthing!"

"All right!" she barked. Good God! Who in the world could possibly be calling her out of a sound sleep? And in the middle of the night? And what on earth . . .

Whereupon the sunlight penetrating into the room from behind the pulled draperies suddenly penetrated her conscious mind and, as is the way of these things, the whole ghastly business came flooding back into her awareness. She shot a hand out to the night table again, this time seizing her wristwatch. It was nearly nine o'clock.

Momentarily, in the hall outside Miss Worthing's door,

Billy McClure took an involuntary step backward as that door was wrenched open, and he was confronted with a singularly daunting specter: Her hair a crown of corkscrews and hornlets sticking straight out from her head and swathed from neck to floor in a tent of white flannel, her eyes ablaze, Miss Worthing all but shrieked at him, "Why did you let me sleep so long?"

"I'm sorry," mumbled the wretched Billy; "I fell asleep."

"Oh, Billy!"

"I'm sorry. I *was* reading that book you gave me, but I guess I was more tired than I thought, and after a while I just couldn't keep my eyes open."

"Oh, Billy!" she repeated. "Well, let's just hope that it really doesn't matter," said Miss Worthing, though with a distinct note of dubiety. "Is anyone else up yet?"

"No. They're all still asleep," said Billy and then, more honestly, added, "I think."

"Well, that's a mercy. You'd better go get everyone up. Tell them—"

"Miss Worthing?"

"What is it?"

"It was Mrs. Wu who woke me up."

Miss Worthing's head snapped toward him. "Yes?"

"She said—"

"Never mind! I know what she said," Miss Worthing cut him off, and, pausing only to throw a blue terry-cloth bathrobe about her person, she pulled the door to and padded along down the passage to the room at the head of the stairs.

"Get them up," she instructed Billy as he trotted along beside her. "Tell them all to assemble in the living room. Then, I guess, you had better get on down to the kitchen and make some coffee and toast. Everyone's likely to be ravenous this morning, but I suspect they'll settle for that."

"But who will keep an eye on them while I'm in the kitchen?"

"Bless my soul!" She came to a stop and stared at him. "I'd forgotten that," she confessed, squelching a perfectly natural impulse to point out that continued surveillance was probably futile at that point. And yet, who was to say? Perhaps it really made no difference that Billy had not remained bright-eyed and alert all night. "Very well. Call Miss Shaw and have her get Aunt Eulalia up. See to it that they're installed in the living room before you get anyone else up. And then get Larry and, yes, I think, Mrs. Anderson, up first."

Even as she spoke, however, the door of the General's room was opened from within to frame Mrs. Anderson.

"Did I hear my name?"

"You did," said Miss Worthing.

"Matilda, he wants to speak to you."

"So I have been informed," said Miss Worthing, while at the same time, from behind her, Billy blurted, "Mrs. Anderson, when did you go in there?"

"Several hours ago," said Mrs. Anderson. "I came along to keep watch with Jessica. You were sound asleep. Jessica said you had dozed off last night and she turned the light off above you." She lowered her voice, and ignoring Billy's sotto-voce mutterings, said to Miss Worthing, "She thinks Billy was stationed out there to help her if she needed it."

"I suppose that's what you want her to think," said Miss Worthing. "Isn't it?"

"Yes," said Mrs. Anderson coolly. "What's the drill today, Matilda?"

Briefly, Miss Worthing explained the plan she had already outlined to Billy.

"Of course I'll help," said Mrs. Anderson; "but there's coffee and tea already made, and there's also muffins already split and ready to go under the electric broiler. But do come along, Matilda; he's awake and, thank God, not in so much pain."

Once again, Miss Worthing was visited by an all-too-familiar suspicion that, unless she took charge immediately, she was going to lose control of the situation.

"No, Sibyl," she said firmly. "I have to talk to Henry alone."

Mrs. Anderson's brow shot upward.

"Don't, Sibyl!"

Mrs. Anderson sighed. "Oh, very well. But what about Jessica?"

"Leave her to me."

Mrs. Anderson and Billy turned up the corridor to their appointed tasks as Miss Worthing knocked gently on the door and then went in. Mrs. Wu turned from some arcane medical pursuit at the bureau, nodded and smiled. "Hello, Matilda," she said in a low, clear voice. "He's been asking for you."

"Matilda!" came a soft croak from the bed. The figure lying there so very still made the briefest sketch of a gesture indicating she come closer.

"Hello, Henry," said Miss Worthing, taking the questing hand into her own.

The man's eyes—the whites of which were a deep, almost saffron, yellow, so that the blue of them looked, in spite of the dim light in the sickroom, even bluer—flicked toward the nurse, and then closed again.

Discreetly, Miss Worthing nodded. "Jessica," she said aloud and settled back with the man's hand held firmly in her lap. "I'll sit with Henry awhile now, if you'd like to go and get yourself some breakfast."

"That's sweet of you, Matilda. But I'm not really hungry."

And so what do I do now? thought Miss Worthing to herself; just tell her—go away, we need to talk?

Any such necessity was averted, however, as Mrs. Wu went on, "But if you really don't mind staying, I'd love to go take a shower and freshen up—and waken up—a bit."

"Of course," said Miss Worthing.

The nurse slipped quietly from the room. It was only when the door clicked shut behind her that the man's eyes opened again.

"Thank you," he whispered.

"Sibyl said you wanted to see me."

His eyelids closed as though to signify a yes.

There followed a long moment during which she wondered if he had fallen asleep again. Finally, however, almost imperceptibly, he sighed. And once more those pain-filled eyes opened to regard her.

"Yes and no," he whispered.

Miss Worthing said nothing, merely waiting.

"I expect you'll find—may have already found—that I—well, that I haven't been behaving too well lately." He frowned. "I haven't been feeling well and I let my irritability get the better of me—" He broke it off. "So," he sighed again, "here I am. But why would anybody want to do *this* to me?"

he asked, gazing at her with a genuinely puzzled look on his face.

"You are sure that someone 'did' it?" said Miss Worthing.

"It couldn't have been an accident."

"Why?"

"Matilda"—his head turned on the pillow the better to look at her—"I would have tasted something."

"Henry." She leaned forward as she asked, rather urgently, "Can you be sure of that?"

"I'm sorry?" he said.

"Henry, you've been very ill. For years now. Can you be so sure that your palate. . ." She left the rest of the question unasked for the simple reason that the General actually seemed to find the suggestion amusing.

"Mattie," he said dryly, "while it is true that I've been sick, what it's meant is that I haven't been able to drink coffee, booze, or even smoke very much." He essayed a weak smile. "Do you have any idea how much of a cleansing effect that will have on a palate after a while?"

"I suppose," assented Miss Worthing, not at all convinced.

"Believe me, Matilda; it's true."

"Okay, then. But, Henry, don't you see that, if you are right, it makes the whole thing all that much more implausible. You tasted nothing?"

"Nothing. And," he said after a short pause, "I really don't know"—he was looking very puzzled indeed—"but the more I think about it, the only thing I had that could have held much alcohol in it was the orange juice."

"We had more or less reached the same conclusion."

"But what was it?" It was clear that he was not so much querying her as the existential fact itself. She did, however, reply, "There are a number of possibilities, Henry."

And some, she reflected, from your own cellar. Later, she would regret that she had not spoken the thought aloud.

"That I wouldn't be able to taste?" asked General Anderson.

"Vodka. Curaçao. Grand Marnier."

"Not vodka. I'd have known vodka."

"What about the others?"

"I don't know," he said, a note of querulousness creeping into his voice. "That's what you're going to have to find out."

"Very well, Henry," said Miss Worthing, suppressing a sigh of exasperation. A few minutes passed in silence, then, as each of them pursued his own thoughts—Miss Worthing marshaling her line of inquiry; the General, God alone knew. "Are you feeling up to some more questions?" she asked.

"I guess so," he said. But it was already plain to see that in the few minutes that had passed, he was already slipping away.

"Oh, Henry, please don't fall asleep now."

"Sorry, Mattie. So sleepy. What you want?"

"Why don't you want the police, Henry? Why did you not want us to call the police?"

"No police. You find out."

"I'll try, Henry. But why not the police?"

"Make a fuss over me. Force me into hospital. Won't let me have my revenge."

"Your revenge?"

"They did this for money, Mattie. They did this for my money."

"I know."

Suddenly his eyes opened, blazing with some strong and potent emotion. So potent was it that his hand actually clawed out and seized the fabric of her sleeve and twisted it.

"Find out who it was." His voice was raucous as he tried not very successfully to shout at her. "Find out and tell me. Soon. Before I die. It's not too late to change my will. You can take it from me in dictation. You or Martha. And then I'll have the sweetest revenge of all on whatever son of a bitch killed me. That's why you've got to hurry, Mattie. Hurry!"

"Henry, stop exciting yourself. Here, now, let go my sleeve. Henry, I still have some questions I want to ask."

But that upsurge of bile had been too much for him. The interval of lucidity had passed, and he was once again lost in a pain so vast Miss Worthing had not the least idea in the world what to do about it.

Fortunately, not too many more moments passed before Mrs. Wu returned to her post and, assessing the situation in a single summing glance, was at the bureau holding an ampule in one hand while filling a syringe with the other. "I think you'd better go now, Matilda. He'll be going to sleep again."

Sleep, thought Miss Worthing to herself, as she stepped out into the corridor, feeling more than a little thwarted. Sleep, indeed. It was, she supposed, better than letting the man writhe in the unspeakable pain he was no doubt feeling; but what kind of dignity was it that a man should meet his end drugged to the eyeballs and uncertain of his very name.

Nevertheless, she was disturbed. That last demand for the wherewithal of revenge. It had not been pleasant. And now, more than ever, her misgivings swarmed around her.

She turned to head down the corridor toward the bedroom she had occupied when she heard a voice behind her. "Thank God! There you are, Mattie!"

She turned to confront a rather agitated Miss Shaw, stamping breathlessly up the stairs.

"Indeed I am, Martha. What's got you all atwitter?"

"I don't know. He wouldn't say." She turned about on the stairs to head downward again, gesturing for Miss Worthing to follow.

"Who wouldn't say? What? Martha, what are you talking about?"

"Cy. In the dining room. Something odd. Wouldn't say what," she reported in a breathless, telegraphic style. "Said we should get you."

"Where are the others?"

"Cooped up in the living room. Absorbing coffee and muffins."

"Well, make sure they stay there," said Miss Worthing, turning once again to hurry back up the passage. "Then join me in the dining room. I have to get dressed. Then let's go see what amazing discovery Cyrus has made."

ii

A scant ten minutes later, Miss Worthing scuttled down the back stairs, passed the empty kitchen, and came to a halt outside the closed corridor door to the dining room. Farther down the hall, toward the front of the house, the double door of the living room was open and from within came the muffled sound of desultory conversation mingled with a clinking of china.

Good, she thought. They seem adequately occupied. Now let's see what on earth this is all about. And she let herself into the dining room.

Standing together on the other side of the dining table, clustered in front of a rather imposing combination cabinet/étagère, were Miss Shaw, Mrs. Anderson, and Cy.

"Matilda," said Mrs. Anderson. "Thank God."

"What's all the fuss about?"

"Cy thinks he may have found something."

"How on earth could he tell?" asked Miss Worthing, taking a swift look around the room.

It was in a state of wholesale disarray. The table still bore all the detritus of the so disastrously interrupted holiday feast, most of it with a distinctly dried-out look about it, while a plate of cheeses sitting on the sideboard was quietly and effectively wafting ripe effluvia into the air.

"Very funny!" said Mrs. Anderson severely. "I would have been delighted to clear, but Eulalia said we should leave it."

"So you should," rejoined Miss Worthing. "What do you think you've got, Cy?"

"It was when I was getting the breakfast plates out," explained Cy none too coherently.

"So much for not disturbing things," muttered Miss Shaw.

"What else could I do?" asked Cy. "This is where we keep them."

"Of course. Of course," said Miss Worthing. "Never mind. What happened?"

"I heard something fall."

"In the cabinet?"

"No, behind it."

"Did anyone else hear it?"

"Well, it was really more like feeling it than hearing it. I doubt anyone else heard it; there wasn't anyone else in here."

"What!"

"Oh well, Billy was here," Cy hastened to explain. "He was

taking things—plates and silver—into the living room after I got them out."

"Okay," said Miss Worthing, "so what have we got here?"

"I don't know," said Cy. "I tried to look, but the space back there is too small; all I could see was something gleaming. Anyway, I think I should pull the étagère out from the wall far enough for me to reach it."

"Why don't we pull the étagère out and take a *look* at what we've got first," suggested Miss Worthing.

Accordingly, Miss Shaw and Cy placed themselves on either side of the cabinet. Its elderly casters, however, seemed staunchly disinclined to roll until, all at once, and with a squeal that could have etched glass, they yielded and the étagère came out from the wall with an ominous rattle of china from within. Mrs. Anderson protested sharply, earning thereby a glance of some irritation from both Miss Shaw and Miss Worthing.

"It's okay," said Cy, peering behind. "There's enough room for me to reach now."

"Just a moment, young man," said Miss Worthing.

She stepped to one of the curtained windows of the dining room and pulled back the draperies so that light from without, such as it was, might illumine the room somewhat better. Then, gesturing Cy aside, and with a great deal of muttering and discomfort, she got down on hands and knees and peered behind the looming fumed-oak cabinet.

"Very curious," said she after a minute, and sat back on her heels to address the others. "Sibyl, do you happen to have a knitting needle handy?"

"Why, yes. Of course. Cy, run across . . ." She caught Miss Worthing's eye.

"Martha?" said Miss Worthing.

Miss Shaw sighed. "Where are they, Sibyl?"

"Well, you should find several in the library. I sometimes like to knit in there while I'm reading."

In a trice, Miss Shaw returned, bearing aloft a number 7 knitting needle.

"This do, Mattie?" she asked.

"I think so," said Miss Worthing, who then addressed Cy. "Now, I rather think you would be better at this than me. I want you to get down and peer in there. It looks like a bottle of some kind. See if you can maneuver it round so you can stick the needle into the opening and bring it out that way. But be very careful not to touch it. Okay?"

"Okay," agreed Cy and got down into the place Miss Worthing had vacated. He, in turn, peered behind the cabinet and, after a moment, grunted. "Yes. I see it. Give me the knitting needle."

Miss Worthing handed it to him while indicating Mrs. Anderson should bring forward a plate.

Rather gingerly, Cy's hand went into the darkness behind the cabinet and he blindly worked the needle back and forth. After a minute or two he grunted again in such a way as to indicate that he had finally succeeded. That grunt of satisfaction, however, was immediately followed by an exclamation: "Oh, yuck!"

"What's wrong?" asked Miss Worthing.

"Something's running out of it onto my hand!"

Presently, Cy brought the object out of its hiding place. He swiftly transferred it to the plate Miss Worthing held out to him and stood up, vigorously wiping his hand on his trousers.

"What the hell is that?" he demanded, looking at it with profound distaste.

Miss Worthing gently lifted the plate toward her nose and gave a great sniff. She frowned and dipped a little finger into the effluent and ever so cautiously touched it to her tongue.

Finally, she replied, "Well, unless I miss my guess, it's vodka."

"Oh, wow!" said Cy.

"The question, however, remains," said Miss Worthing, "what is this thing?"

"I think I can tell you," said Mrs. Anderson.

"So can I," volunteered Cy. "It's Bob E.'s hip flask."

iii

"Really?" said Miss Worthing. "Why, how very intriguing."

She stepped to the window and held the silver flask up to the light. A pleasant little thing, thin and elegantly made, of a plain and simple design with only a modest bit of chasing around the shoulder. It held perhaps half a pint.

"Now this *is* interesting." She turned to Mrs. Anderson. "Sibyl, do you have any face powder?"

"Face powder?" said Mrs. Anderson rather blankly.

"Yes, face powder."

"Why, yes. Of course."

"Good. It's at times like this that I'm so glad you're an old-fashioned sort of a lady," said Miss Worthing.

"What are you going to use face powder for?"

"What do you think?"

"You're not seriously going to use face powder to try to lift fingerprints, are you?"

"Why ever not? I suppose I could try cornstarch. Or cake flour. All of them will do it, you know. But none of them work quite as well as a good old-fashioned face powder. The kind," she added with a peculiar note in her voice, "sold only in the best shops for gentlewomen."

"Am I really going to get to see fingerprints taken?" asked Cy, effectively covering the snort of derision his mother made.

"That remains very much to be seen," said Miss Worthing dryly. "Martha, go fetch it."

"This is turning into a real bore," said Miss Shaw. "All right, Sibyl; where do you keep it?"

"In my bedroom. On the dressing table. It's a large purple box."

As they waited for Miss Shaw to return, Miss Worthing turned to Cy and said, "Young man, there are a number of questions I'm going to have to ask you when this particular little adventure is over." She gestured toward the silver flask.

Cy just looked at her without saying anything. Then, after a moment, he nodded once. "Is there anything I can do in the meantime?" he asked.

"Yes, there is. Would you please take a piece of paper—one of those napkins will do—and write on it, 'flask.'"

The young man obeyed and presently handed it to her.

"I'm sorry. All I had was a fountain pen." He gestured at the breast pocket of his shirt whence a silver-capped pen stuck up.

In fact, the scrawled letters had feathered appreciably. Nevertheless, Miss Worthing felt a momentary glow as she looked at the single word on the damasked paper. "Thank you," she said, with rather more cordiality than was entirely called for; "that will do splendidly."

"Matilda," said Mrs. Anderson, "why don't you ask your questions now? I'm rather intrigued by what you're going to ask."

"I dare say you are, Sibyl. But it isn't going to work that way."

"Why not?"

"For one simple reason."

"Because I'm a suspect, too?"

Cy turned sharply to look at his mother.

"That is a good reason," said Miss Worthing. "But that's not the one I was thinking of."

"Oh?" said Mrs. Anderson.

"Sibyl," said Miss Worthing with considerable feeling, "do you know that, without a doubt, there are times when you are the most irritating woman in Christendom?"

"So I've been told," said Mrs. Anderson equably. "But you still haven't answered my question."

"Very well, I'll tell you why I'm not going to have you around when I question anyone: There were rather a number of things—important things, incidentally—which were left out of that conversation you, Larry, and Ben and I had last night. And they were things left out for no other reason than that you were there."

"Oh, really? What?"

"Sibyl, don't be simple. Do you really think I'm going to tell you?"

"Actually, I rather think you'd better."

"No," said Miss Worthing. "I'm not going to do it. My job in all this foofaraw, in case you've forgotten, is to discover facts."

"Am I standing in the way of facts?"

"Sibyl," said Miss Worthing with a patient air, "one of the facts with which we have to deal is that you are a very powerful personality, a much beloved mother, and, shall we say, a force to be reckoned with. I will not—I repeat—I will *not* try to interview people and elicit from them relevant and valid data with you sitting there dripping disapproval."

"I've done nothing of the kind!"

"I know you haven't," said Miss Worthing with a sigh. "Not directly. And I shouldn't have put it that way. But how can you expect people to be forthright with me when you are there, knowing every foible there is to them? It does rather tend to spoil the effect, you know."

"What effect is that?"

"The simple, though admittedly rather piquant, fact that people are frequently more honest with perfect strangers, or even relative strangers, than they are with immediate kin. But never mind that, here's Martha."

Miss Shaw, puffing rather, came in bearing a largish purple satin box.

"My goodness," said Miss Worthing, arching a brow, "you do yourself well, don't you?"

"It's one of the few luxuries I allow myself," said Mrs. Anderson, apparently believing her own words.

Miss Worthing and Miss Shaw exchanged a shrewd glance between them before mutually deciding that, all things considered, it would be better by far just to get on with the task at hand.

"Here, Martha," said Miss Worthing. "Hold this." She handed the flask on its plate to Miss Shaw.

Miss Shaw obediently took it as she transferred the powder to Miss Worthing, who opened the box and from within withdrew a very large and rather flyaway powder puff.

"Swansdown!" once again Miss Worthing remarked rather archly. "My, my, my."

"Matilda," snapped Mrs. Anderson with a vexed little frown, "would you please get on with it."

Cy, meanwhile, grinning at the exchange, asked, "Is there anything I can do?"

"Yes," said Miss Worthing with a little chuckle, "I think you had better open the windows."

The young man obeyed as Miss Worthing began very generously to sprinkle the flask with the powder. A cloud of lavender-scented dust rose through the air before the eddy from the windows began tugging it into the outdoors.

"Do you really have to get quite so carried away?" asked

Mrs. Anderson with some asperity. "It is rather expensive, you know."

Miss Worthing merely chuckled as she finally put the swansdown back into the powder box, closed it, and set it on the dining room table.

"Sorry, just wanting to be thorough," she said and, bending down, began very cautiously to blow away the layer of powder which had settled on the flask. Cy and Mrs. Anderson both came closer, fascinated by the procedure. Then, retrieving the knitting needle from Miss Shaw's pudgy paw, Miss Worthing stalked once more to the window and held the flask up to the light. She frowned.

"Turn that light on," she commanded.

Miss Shaw scuttled around the dining table to turn the overhead on and dialed the rheostat up to full as Miss Worthing went to the middle of the room, holding the flask up to the brighter artificial light, scrutinizing, it seemed, every square millimeter of it.

"Well?" said Mrs. Anderson.

"Look for yourselves," said Miss Worthing. She held it toward mother and son who, together, glanced over it.

"I don't see anything," said Cy.

"Neither do I," said Mrs. Anderson.

"It didn't work," said Cy, obviously disappointed.

"Oh yes, it did," said Miss Worthing.

"But there aren't any fingerprints on it," said Cy.

"Exactly so," said Miss Worthing. "Exactly so."

And without, apparently, any intention of further enlightening anyone, she deposited the flask into the labeled napkin and handed it to Miss Shaw. "Here, Martha. Take charge of this, and get on over to the library. And you," she addressed Mrs. Anderson, "will please go into the living room and join the rest of them. We'll be back presently. Cy, you come with me."

"Matilda . . ."

"No, Sibyl. We will now be doing this my way. Not yours."

"Oh, very well," said Mrs. Anderson. "But when this is over, I want a full report."

"But whatever for?" asked Miss Worthing. "Isn't who killed

Henry the only thing we really need to know?" There was no answer. "Well?" she demanded. "Isn't it?"

It took a moment, but presently Mrs. Anderson nodded. "I suppose you're right." She sighed. "Is there anything I can do in the meantime?"

"No," said Miss Worthing. "Well, I suppose you can clear this room up." Then, abruptly, she caught herself. "Well, no, actually you'd better not. You never know what we're likely to uncover at this point."

"Very funny," said Mrs. Anderson. Then, seeing Miss Worthing's expression, she asked, "Or are you serious?"

"Of course I'm serious, insofar as I do not know anything. Nothing."

"And as for you, young man," Miss Worthing said to Cy, "you come along with me to the library. There are rather a number of things I want to talk about with you."

CHAPTER 9

i

In the library, they found Miss Shaw in an easy chair, steno pad held before her, and fountain pen already poised. Miss Worthing took in the sight with one approving nod and ushered Cy inside.

"You'd better sit down," said Miss Worthing. "This may take some time."

"What is this all about?" demanded Cy, remaining on his feet.

Miss Worthing chuckled a bit, as did Miss Shaw. "Didn't you know that it's de rigueur to interview everyone who might be involved in one of these affairs?"

"No, I didn't," said the young man, and then added with hauteur, "I don't read mystery stories."

"Oh, it's not just the amateur detective who does this, you know," Miss Worthing explained cheerfully. "And if you are ever so unfortunate as to have to deal with the real police, you'll discover they do it, too—and with a lot less concern for the interviewee. However," she continued equanimously, "to answer your question specifically: There are a number of things."

"Do you think I killed my father?"

"Well, did you?"

"No."

"Nevertheless, we would be extremely remiss in our job if we did not consider the possibility, wouldn't we?"

"How dare you!"

"Oh, please!" said Miss Worthing, turning away and settling herself into an easy chair. She indicated for Cy do the same, but he remained standing. "This is going to be unpleasant enough," she continued, "without you—or anyone else—getting all touchy about personal—twiddles. Besides, though I was hardly in a position to say anything about it last night, don't you think what you said while leaving the living room was just a bit much?"

The tone of voice in which she asked the question was severe. Perhaps, in fact, too severe. The young man suddenly collapsed into a chair and put his face into his hands.

Presently, he looked up, his expression miserable.

"I didn't mean it to come out the way it did."

"Perhaps not. But you do have to admit that it is a bit thick for someone to suggest that the murderer of his father ought to receive a medal for it. Don't you?"

"He put me through such hell," said Cy with quiet and savage bitterness.

"So I've heard. But now someone has done the very same thing to him."

"Do you think I did it?"

"Isn't that what I'm supposed to be here to find out? Never mind. The question is rhetorical. But let's get on with it, shall we?

"Now, before I get into specifics, I have a few general questions I would like to ask. Please be honest. Please be forthright. If you can't remember something, tell me you can't remember it. Don't, whatever you do, make anything up."

The young man's expression changed. He frowned and then, almost defiantly, tossed his head in a not very attractive way. "But what if I did do it?"

Miss Worthing smiled. "That's precisely why I shall be talking to everyone. Alone and separately. And why Billy is on guard in the living room. You—or anyone else—might think you can get away with deception, here and now with me. But overall, anything you tell that is not right is going to come out. It will," she emphasized grimly, "come out."

Cy sat back in his chair, his eyes falling to the floor as he nodded. "Yes. I guess I can see how that would happen. Okay," he said with something of a sigh, "what do you want to ask?"

"First of all, I would like to know what precisely you were doing during the preparations for dinner yesterday. I'm told," she frowned slightly as she tried to recollect what Lady Fairgrief had told her, "that you arrived here with your mother and father."

He nodded. "Yes. Mom and I went right to the kitchen."

"To do?"

"Mostly odds and ends at that point."

"What were they?"

"Well, let's see. First of all, the turkey had not been basted since we left to go to church—that was before your open house. I tended to that while Mom drained the vegetables."

"Drained the vegetables?"

"Yes. We had cut them up before we left for church and left them sitting in ice water."

Miss Worthing looked a question at Miss Shaw.

"Yes," said the latter. "It's the proper thing to do."

"What else were you involved in, Cy?"

"I decided to make some hollandaise for the broccoli."

"Did you make a lot?"

"Quite a lot."

"Did you use vinegar, lemon juice, or sherry?"

"Vinegar? Sherry?" asked Cy, genuinely curious.

Miss Worthing smiled. "Some people do prefer it with one or the other."

"I used lemon juice. Never heard of using those other things."

"Was the juice bottled or fresh?"

"Fresh. I squeezed the lemons."

"This was before Arletta and Bette Wanda were doing the oranges?"

"Oh, yeah. Before they even got there."

"Very well. Now, can you tell me what your mother was doing? Surely she wasn't just fiddling with vegetables the whole time."

"No," said Cy, "she was putting together the relish plate.

You know, celery stalks, scallions, olives, pickles, that kind of thing. Oh yes, and stuffing dates."

"How long did all this take?"

Cy shrugged. "I don't really know. You don't really think about the time it takes. You know what little chores are left to be done and the only thing you're really thinking of is to make sure that everything gets on the table at the same time."

"Yes, but it's those little chores I want to know about."

"Okay. Well, let's see. I filled the ice bucket."

"Where was the drinks tray?"

"In the kitchen."

"Where it is now?"

"Yes. It never moved through the whole meal. And then, after I finished making the hollandaise and set it aside in the *bain-marie,* I decided to take over finishing the vegetables and mash the potatoes. That sort of thing."

"Okay. When did Arletta and Bette Wanda come in?"

"I'm not really sure. They wandered in sometime after Ben and Larry had already arrived."

"Really?"

"Yes. Larry was already busy making that eggnog when they arrived."

"Ah yes, the nog. How did that come about?"

"Why don't you ask him?"

"Don't worry; I will."

"Well, Mom sort of got this gleam in her eye." He smiled at the memory. "I think she was getting a bit peeved that everyone was collecting in the kitchen. So when Ben said that Larry made a really fabulous eggnog, Mom just got out the ingredients—without a word—cleared a counter space, and then told him to stay there and not move."

"And your brother?"

"He began mixing drinks."

"What were you drinking?"

"I had a kir."

"Black-currant brandy and white wine?"

"Yes. It's weak enough. I didn't want to get too much under my belt because—well, frankly, because I was still slightly hung over from the night before. Also, I just don't like to drink too much if I've got something complicated going."

"Okay. And when Arletta and Bette Wanda got there?"

Cy snorted. "At first, all they did was make general nuisances of themselves. Matter of fact, at one point Arletta was poking around the pots on the stove and I had to get pretty fierce with her."

"Had she been drinking already?"

"Not that I could see. She just seemed sort of subdued. She is when she's sober, you know."

"When did they start squeezing the orange juice?"

"You know about that." He smiled.

Miss Worthing nodded.

"They began right after Bob E. got back with the box of oranges."

"I gather that there had been some little contretemps about that, too."

"Not really. Bette Wanda volunteered to go, but she had already had a few drinks, and was not feeling any pain. We decided it wouldn't do to let her drive. Ben was busy being bartender. When I asked Helen if she'd go," he said with a sour expression, "she just ignored the question . . ."

"Why did you need the box at Helen's house?"

"Helen called us yesterday to bring them over and then we found that it was the last box we had on hand."

"Very well. So, in the end, Bob E. went to fetch them."

"That's right."

"And Arletta and Bette Wanda squeezed them."

"Yeah. We have an electric reamer and apparently neither one of 'em had ever worked one before. They seemed to think it was a marvel."

"What happened then?"

"Ben asked Bette Wanda if she wanted a refill. And Arletta made some remark about how good the juice smelled and could she have an orange blossom."

"Gin and orange juice."

"Right," agreed Cy and added ruefully, "and there went the first squeezing of oranges."

"I see. And then?"

"I really wasn't paying all that close attention."

"Okay. Can you remember anything else?"

"As far as I could tell, the two of them went on squeezing and squeezing and drinking and drinking."

"They drank rather a lot of the juice, then?"

"A lot? They must have put away nearly the whole of the first pitcher they squeezed. I know because Mom made some rather cutting remark to the two of them about the fact that there was, please to remember, only one box of oranges and it was Christmas Day and where would we get any more?"

"And?"

"I waded in and persuaded them—not easily—to do at least one whole pitcher so Dad would have some for his dinner. Both of them had reached the giggle point, and they agreed without *too* much persuasion. Unfortunately, their coordination, by that point, was none too good. I rescued the Waterford jug from them and took it to the dining room."

"Good. Very good. And what did you do there?"

"I stopped in the service room to get the saucer for the jug. It's kept in the cabinet there, and then I went into the dining room."

"And?"

"I guess I made some remark about the situation to Bob E."

"Bob E. was in the dining room?"

"Yes."

"Alone?"

"Yes. He was standing at the window by the half-table pigging out on the stuffed dates."

"Oh, really? How had they got to the dining room?"

"I assume Mom brought them in. Or maybe it was Ben on one of his drinks rounds."

"What did you do then?"

"I stopped and had a few of them myself. I figured if I left them to Bob E., I'd never get any."

"You spoke?"

"Just something about not eating too much and spoiling his appetite for dinner. He said there wasn't any chance of that. I think he was a little tight already. He gets that way when he's had a belt or two."

"What way?" asked Miss Worthing.

"You know, full of that god-awful redneck bonhomie. Back-slapping cheerfulness." He made a face of disgust.

"Then?"

"I went back to the kitchen and a little while later dinner was served. And I led Bette Wanda into the dining room. She was already pretty shit-faced, if you'll pardon the expression."

"What about Ben and Larry?"

"Ben and Larry were getting a bit flown. Ben was being rather expansive—you know the way he can be. Larry was arguing about something in a script that Ben didn't like and Larry kept saying it had to be that way. But, as I said, it wasn't too much later that we assembled in the dining room."

"What about your father during all of this?"

Again, the young man snorted. "He spent his time watching the goddamn TV—football. I don't think he was particularly interested in talking to anyone. He certainly didn't want to talk to me," he added the rather venomous coda.

"Did he come to the kitchen at all?"

"No. Not except to get the orange peels and vegetable pickings to toss into the composter. That was the only time he came out to the kitchen. That I can guarantee. And, as far as I know, it was also the only time he went out all day after we got back."

"My aunt tells me you were banished to the other end of the table during dinner."

"I was. It wasn't anything new. I can't even say that, at that point, I cared very much."

"What did you drink during the meal?"

"After Lady Fairgrief said she wanted a mimosa, I thought it sounded so good, I said I'd have one too. So did most everyone."

"Were Bette Wanda and Arletta drinking mimosas, too?"

"Everyone was. Except Dad, of course. Oh, yeah. And Mom."

"She wasn't drinking mimosas?"

"No. I got the impression that she wasn't pleased that everyone else was, either."

"Why not?"

"Because there was just the one box of oranges, as I said. In fact, after the third pitcher—she got that one—she told us there wasn't going to be any more; there was just enough for Dad for the rest of the day."

"She was drinking?"

"Riesling, I would guess. It's her favorite."

"What was the general reaction when Bette Wanda collapsed?"

"Well, 'surprised' would hardly be an adequate word for it," said Cy. "She is, after all, one of the most uptight people I know. Ordinarily, she'll go miles out of her way to make sure she does the proper thing."

"Okay. But let's get back to the incident. What happened when she did collapse?"

"I can't say that I'm the one to ask. Dad collapsed not long after, and I spent probably most of the afternoon upstairs looking after him till the doctor came. And, I'm afraid, I was feeling pretty sozzled myself."

"You were?"

"Yes, I was, and frankly, I'm still not entirely sure how I got that way. It was probably just the fact that, all in all, it was a pretty stressful day. And," he admitted with a shrug, "I was still pretty badly pissed off with Dad. Maybe the adrenaline and all didn't mix with champagne. Anyway, that's about all I can tell you. I really don't know anything else." He looked up then to see Miss Worthing regarding him with a rather provocatively speculative look in her eye. "It's true," he averred. "I haven't told you anything other than the way I remember it."

"When you took the pitcher into the dining room, you didn't perhaps . . ."

"No, I didn't."

"Okay. I'll take your word for it. For now. However, Cy, there is one thing—one datum, if you will—about which I have to ask."

"What's that?"

"Why did you take a bottle of Everclear from the cellar last week?"

The young man hesitated the merest fraction of a second, swallowed, and said, "What are you talking about?"

"It's really very simple. There's a bottle of Everclear entered in the cellar book. It has an entry date, in your mother's handwriting, for June of this year when, I presume, you brought it home from New Mexico with you, since, as I'm quite sure you're aware, it's not available in California."

"Yes."

"Well, I just thought that perhaps you could explain—or, if you've forgotten, I should like to know that, too—why there is next to it a delete date in your handwriting for December twenty-first of this year. Last Friday."

"I don't know what you're talking about."

"Cy, you happened to write the word 'flask' on that table napkin a little earlier. I've looked in the cellar book, and the delete date and the entry is in your handwriting. Now, I'm asking you, what did you do with that bottle of Everclear?"

"I . . ."

"Yes?"

The young man's face went closed and completely still.

"I don't have to answer that," said he.

"No, you don't," said Miss Worthing with a sigh. "But it might make this easier if you would."

"I . . ." he began again and then, abruptly, stood up. "I'm not going to tell you," he announced almost as though he were surprised to hear himself saying it. "But I sure as hell didn't give it to my father. Now if that will be all?"

"Very well," said Miss Worthing with a scowl. "But you should know that in a situation like this we really must know everything. And unfortunately, Cy, I think you ought to know that, right now, you've got not only the clearest motive, but also, it appears, access to the means and a particular open opportunity."

"I didn't do it."

"Then tell me what happened to the Everclear."

His mouth moved as though he were trying to speak. His eyes closed as he struggled with utterance. No sound, however, emerged.

"I—can't!" he finally burst out.

"Oh, very well," said Miss Worthing, out of patience. "Take him back to the living room, Martha. And let's hope we get more out of the others."

"Who's next?" asked Miss Shaw.

Miss Worthing looked as though she'd bitten into a lemon and said, "I guess I'd better have it out with Ben."

"But you spent all night talking to him," said Cy.

"And precisely what business is that of yours?" asked Miss Worthing coldly.

"Sorry," said Cy. He turned and left the room, followed closely by Miss Shaw . . .

ii

. . . who returned in a few short moments with a very surprised-looking Ben. "Martha said you wished to see me?"

"So I do," said Miss Worthing. "Do come in and sit down."

"I would have thought anything I could contribute would have been adequately covered last night."

"Not quite," said Miss Worthing dryly, and waited till Ben had seated himself and Miss Shaw had resumed her note-taking pose, before asking, "Ben, I would rather like to know what happened when you approached your father about a loan."

For rather a long moment, the man's face registered nothing whatsoever. Then, very levelly, he said, "I suppose Larry had to tell you, didn't he?"

"Well, it does rather put a different complexion on things, now, doesn't it?"

"I'm sure," said Ben.

"Are you very broke?"

He snorted at that. "Isn't that like asking if someone is very dead or very pregnant?" When, however, Miss Worthing said nothing, he sighed and said, "Actually, I'm not broke at all. At least on paper. But I suppose Larry told you that, too."

"He did."

"Nevertheless, the fact remains that I don't exactly have what you would call liquidity at the moment. I tried to tell Dad that it was just a temporary state of affairs and that it would be, in fact, just a loan."

"Larry said something about a film?"

The man shrugged massively. "One should never really count on that kind of thing. On the other hand," he sighed, "one always does."

"Did you tell your father that?"

"Yes."

"And did it do any good?"

"No."

For a moment, Miss Worthing wondered whether any elaboration of that bald negative would be forthcoming. When, however, none seemed to be in immediate evidence, she asked, "What happened, Ben?"

"Nothing that wouldn't be expected under the circs. He told me to go stuff myself."

"Did you tell him about your loan from Larry?"

"No. I figured that it would be infinitely more appealing to let him think his little boy was starving."

"So the long and short of it is you got your ears pinned back like everyone else."

"Oh yes."

"Tell me, Ben," said Miss Worthing, leaning forward, "do you have any idea what your share of the estate is going to be when it's probated?"

"A pretty good idea, yes," admitted Ben coolly. "Dad was never especially secretive about his financial condition—at least with his children."

"Okay. Thank you."

He made to rise.

"A few more questions, Ben."

He resumed his seat.

"Yes?"

"You were bartending yesterday."

"I was."

"And what were you drinking?"

"Gibsons."

"Vodka or gin?"

"Gin."

"How many?"

"I don't remember the precise number. By the time dinner was served, however, I was doing very nicely, thank you."

"Gibsons?"

"Gibsons."

"Drat!" muttered Miss Worthing half to herself.

"Something wrong?"

"No, not really. In fact, not at all. Damn it all."

Ben seemed to find her irritation rather amusing, which amused her not at all.

"Tell me, Ben," she said. "Larry told me that he had loaned you that rather enormous sum of money for living expenses. You'll pardon my saying it, but isn't twenty-five thousand dollars rather excessive living expenses? For what could be—what?—two or three months before you have some substantive return from that film?"

"*If* I have a return?" corrected Ben.

"Very well, if. But if it does well—and judging from the reports and reviews I've heard, it is opening to rather loud huzzahs."

"It is modestly to be hoped for," said Ben. "However, to answer your question, I have certain responsibilities both in Los Angeles and in San Francisco that I've never particularly objected to because I make a lot of money. *When* I make it." He smiled. "But while it will be a temporary hardship for me to be without liquid funds, for the—well, let's just call them 'projects' that I have, it would be a very real hardship. And I would just as soon avoid that at all costs."

"At all costs?"

"Oh, come now, Miss Worthing," said Ben with a frown, "I know how that sounds, but it strikes me that it would be, to say the least, karmically difficult to justify killing my father in order to continue my projects."

"Probably," agreed Miss Worthing. "Well then, where are we? I guess there's not much more to ask. Except perhaps: You were in the kitchen quite a bit yesterday, weren't you?"

"I was."

"Bartending."

He nodded.

"Your mother said something about you fetching a jug of vodka from the cellar."

"I did. We seemed to be out of it upstairs and I thought it would be needed. As it happened, however," he added, "no one wanted any."

"Oh?"

"No. No one called for vodka drinks at all yesterday. It just never seemed to enter anyone's mind. Which was kind of surprising since it's usually the first thing that gets asked for. But for all I know, the jug is still sitting there on the tray in the kitchen unopened."

"Very well. But if you were so busy with all of that, when did you manage to have an interview with your father?"

"It was, in fact, when I brought him his orange juice."

"Oh, really."

"I didn't put anything into it, you know."

"A naked assertion I'll take for what it's worth."

"I can't prove it."

"Yes, it is rather difficult to prove a negative, isn't it?"

"Quite," said Ben shortly.

Once again, a kind of considering silence seemed to fall on the pair of them. As he had done last night, as Miss Worthing had begun to anticipate any one of them doing at any given moment, he seemed to have retired inward in pursuit of his own thoughts—whatever they might have been.

Presently, however, Miss Worthing said, "Ben, I know this may seem difficult, but I would really like to take you over the incidents of yesterday, as you remember them, leading up to your father's collapse."

"I rather expected you would want to do that. I was more than a little surprised—although grateful—that you didn't do it last night."

"I was just too tired. And so, I might add, were you. And there was the fact which I had already figured out but which Larry merely underscored, that you and he were not being entirely candid with me."

The great head nodded. "Very well. Where would you like me to begin?"

iii

Meanwhile—as Miss Worthing once again began putting Ben through his paces, pursuing the tedious but necessary routine—in the living room, those foregathered eyed Cy Anderson covertly and very much askance as he entered their midst.

That young man had returned from his interview with Miss Worthing his head held high and walking with unfaltering step in front of Miss Shaw. But his had been the first of the formal interviews promised or, rather more accurately, threatened by Miss Worthing the evening before. Accordingly, it escaped no one's notice that the young man's variable complexion had gone white as a ghost. Neither did the fact that after Miss Shaw had departed with Ben and Bette Wanda sidled up to him, he turned irritably away and went to the window in the far corner of the living room, where he stood communing with his own thoughts and the gloomy winter day without.

And Mrs. Anderson, looking at him, longed for nothing so much as to be able to go to him and put her arms around this, her youngest child, and comfort him in whatever the difficulty was with which he was clearly struggling.

She also knew that it was just not possible.

She was—it should be fairly obvious—hardly a stupid woman. Nevertheless, the motivation that had led her to attempt to hide from Miss Worthing the truth about the bottle of Everclear was still somewhat opaque to her. But she had seen the full implications. The simple fact remained, however, that Cy *was* her youngest, and that fact, paramount over all others, effectively prevented her from any serious credence that he might perhaps have very well poured a quantity of that extraordinarily potent liquor into his father's orange juice.

Larry, on the other hand, being nowhere near as emotionally involved, had no such prejudice. He eyed the obviously shaken youth and found himself speculating, idly enough, whether all the sound and fury over the General's impending death did, in fact, signify nothing whatever and that all this was just a sordid little patricide committed for nothing more than the usual squalid suburban preoccupation with money.

Lady Fairgrief, too, esconced as she was in her bath chair in a position where, dutiful to the charge Miss Worthing had laid upon her, she could keep an eye on everyone and, at least as importantly, keep an ear on everyone as well—even she regarded the lad's brooding back with speculations rather more accurate than one might perhaps have anticipated in one of her age and generation.

Neither was she any kind of a fool and had, after all, a broad experience of people of all sorts and conditions, an experience which had left her little room for surprise. She did not know precisely what it was that was troubling Cy. At least in the particulars. But in the larger, more general sense, she had made up her mind, quite literally, years before. Like the wise friend she was, however, she had held her tongue. The old saw about not doing it in the streets and frightening the horses was less a standard of behavior to her than a moral imperative.

Nevertheless, she could not help but wonder what was going through the boy's head when, suddenly, at the window, Cy seemed to stand up straighter, square his shoulders and, taking a deep breath, turn round. He surveyed the room, his glance passing quickly from one to another of those present.

For a moment, his eyes lingered on her own, seeming almost to bore into her, before they moved on, finally coming to rest on Billy McClure.

"Billy," he called out.

Her ladyship felt Billy, standing beside her, stiffen as Cy gestured to him to come closer.

Billy quickly looked to his employer, who nodded.

"Of course," she said. "Go on."

Piqued now, she watched Billy shamble across the room to Cy and enter into conversation with him. The two of them seemed somehow to stand apart, separate, as it were, from everyone else in the room. Their conversation was certainly inaudible—a fact that did not escape the others' attention as they glanced almost angrily at Lady Fairgrief.

Finally, after a moment, Billy nodded and turned back, leaving Cy to turn himself and stare once again out the window as Billy approached her ladyship.

"My lady," he murmured very softly, "apparently there is something Cy wishes to discuss with me."

"About?"

Billy shrugged expressively and then, looking across the room, seemed more than a little taken aback to see that, except for Cy, everyone else was staring at him with the utmost avidity.

"I think," he said, his voice muted and subdued, "that I should probably talk to him somewhere else, though."

"Well, then, I'm afraid it will have to wait."

"He did say it's important."

"It is also rather important that there be one or the other of us, and preferably both, here and on duty at all times."

"Is it really all that necessary?"

Lady Fairgrief fetched a sigh and said, "Billy, I really don't know how to explain this to you except to say that we must not lose sight of the fact that it is by no means unheard of for a murder to have been perpetrated by a conspiracy."

"I'll have to take your word for it," said Billy with an unintentional dryness. "Nevertheless, I'm afraid there is something which—"

"Is it relevant?"

Billy frowned. "I'm not sure, of course. But I don't think Cy would have bothered me with it at this juncture if it weren't."

Her ladyship regarded her unusual retainer very much *plein d'oeil*. "I had no idea you and Cy were such good buddies."

"There's rather a great deal you don't know about me, my lady," said Billy.

"Very well," said her ladyship after a momentary impulse to snort had passed. "I'll keep watch in here. You take Cy to the other end of the dining room"—she gestured toward the open doors—"and interview your young friend there."

She watched, intrigued and not a little expectant, as Billy went back to Cy, touched him on the shoulder, and then gestured with his woolly head. He then turned and moved away without waiting and went to the absolute farthest end of the dining room, Cy following after wordlessly.

"Where they going?" demanded Bette Wanda sharply.

"There is, I am informed, something they wish to discuss," said Lady Fairgrief equanimously.

"Why couldn't they talk about it in here?"

"I'm sure I don't know. So why don't you do what the rest of us have to do."

"What's that?"

"Possess your soul in patience until we find out."

And indeed the two young men returned after only a few moments, both of them wearing somewhat sheepish expressions.

"Well!" said her ladyship as Billy once more resumed his place beside her.

"I would rather," said he, looking about the room and again very much aware of the eyes of all waiting upon him and of ears generally flapping in his direction, "—much rather wait till we can have a moment of privacy."

"Very well," said Lady Fairgrief, "we'll wait till Martha comes back in to fetch the next victim. Although I suppose I could leave Larry on duty," she said musingly, but then she settled her face into a scowl. "But then everyone else in the room—and probably Matilda, too—would have a hissy fit."

They settled down to wait.

CHAPTER 10

i

Ben stood up.

"Will there be anything else?"

"Not really."

"Shall I go?"

"Yes, indeed. Martha, take him back across the hall, would you? And I guess that it's time I talked to Helen."

"I don't envy you that little chore," said Ben. "She's being the bitch that ate La Jolla today."

"So I imagined," said Miss Worthing. "That's why I want to get her out of the way."

"You're dismissing her?"

"Of course not," replied Miss Worthing. "However, judging from what everyone has been telling me, she's one of the few people who didn't even so much as approach the kitchen yesterday."

"Oh, she approached it," said Ben. "She came floating in like an iceberg and like an iceberg floated out again, completely ignoring everything in its path."

"Oh?" prompted Miss Worthing.

"Yeah. When she and Bob E. arrived, she came flouncing down the hall like Miss God A'mighty. She wouldn't even acknowledge Larry or me. Course, I have to admit I can hardly blame her for not seeing me," he confessed ruefully. "I was a real bastard the night before." He shrugged. "But you knew that. But she seemed to like Larry. And God knows," he added dryly, "Larry liked her."

"What did she do?"

"Yesterday?"

Miss Worthing nodded.

"She came oozing down the corridor to the kitchen door and said, 'I'll be in the living room with Mary Elizabeth if anyone wants me,' turned around and walked away with Mary Elizabeth and then sat in the living room making these vicious little remarks into the air about all and sundry."

"Yes, I did hear about that."

He nodded. "It's the kind of thing that would get Lady Fairgrief's dander up, I would imagine. That good woman had to sit there and listen to it."

"And Helen did nothing to help?"

"Not a thing. Just sat there, dandling her brat and irritating the hell out of everyone."

"Was she drinking?"

"Not she. Not Miss Puritas Ipsissima. I did offer to fix her something and she just looked right through me."

"Fascinating," said Miss Worthing. "Well, Martha," she said to Miss Shaw, "let's have the creature in."

In the living room, Ben, like Cy before him, looked distinctly subdued, as he followed Miss Shaw back in.

With a casual air, which required a great deal of his particular art, he sauntered back to his usual place on the other side of the fireplace from Larry. He lit a cigarette, took a great drag on it, exhaled and observed, "What an unlikely pair of caryatids we are, holding up the mantelpiece."

"Bad?" asked Larry.

"You should know," said Ben.

"Come on, Ben. I had to tell."

"Yes, I suppose you did. It doesn't make it any easier, though."

Meanwhile, at the doorway of the living room, Miss Shaw said, "Helen? Mattie would like to see you now."

And although it was quite clear that, for a brief moment, Helen seriously considered rebellion, presently, with great reluctance, she rose.

Before she could join Miss Shaw, however, Lady Fairgrief interrupted. "Martha! Wait a moment. I want you to take over a minute. Billy and I have to go—" She gestured eloquently.

"Of course," said Miss Shaw.

ii

Once again in the kitchen, her ladyship looked at her butler and said, "*Now* will you tell me what this is all about?"

"Well, it is rather embarrassing," Billy immediately began to temporize.

"Balderdash," said Lady Fairgrief. "In a murder investigation, my dear boy, nothing can be allowed to be so bashful-making that you cannot tell it. Out with it. Now!"

"There's a bottle missing."

"Aha!" exclaimed her ladyship. "Now we're getting somewhere."

"And I'm afraid that Cy is responsible for it."

"So?"

"Well, you see, my lady, Cy wouldn't tell Miss Worthing how it came to be missing."

"Not good," observed her ladyship.

"To be sure," said Billy. "However, since, well, since I happened to be with him when he had the bottle . . ."

"Yes?"

Billy sighed rather distractedly. "Unfortunately, I'm afraid I really don't remember a great deal of that evening."

Rather struggling to maintain her gravity, Lady Fairgrief contented herself by asking, "But do you remember him having a bottle?"

"Yes. That I do. Quite clearly. It was, after all, before the—festivities got started."

"Was it the bottle in question?"

"I believe so. I don't altogether remember what it was, but, judging both from what I do remember, and what Cy has told me, I'm morally certain it was, in fact, a bottle of Everclear."

"And what, may I ask," said her ladyship, "might Everclear be?"

"I'm not altogether sure myself," said Billy. "But I do know that there's—well, someone who probably would remember."

"A disinterested witness!" exclaimed her ladyship. "How wonderful. And who might that be?"

"He lives in San Francisco."

"Can I telephone?"

"I think it would be better for everyone if you did."

"You do have," said her ladyship, "the number?"

"I do," said Billy composedly, and withdrawing his wallet, handed the old woman a slip of paper on which a 415 number had been hastily scrawled.

Presently, her ladyship was handed the telephone by Billy, with the number already ringing.

And it went on ringing for quite an inordinate amount of time. Lady Fairgrief was just on the verge of deciding that the whole exercise was useless when a very sleepy and a very gruff masculine voice answered. "'Lo?"

And her ladyship, her eyes flicking from the paper in her hand to Billy's immutable countenance, said, very dryly indeed, "Hello? May I please speak to—*Bubbles*?"

In response to which that extremely deep bass voice replied, "Speaking."

"Good heavens!" Lady Fairgrief could not prevent herself from exclaiming.

"Listen, lady!" said the voice with scarce-concealed impatience. "I don't know who you are, but for Chrissakes, it's only eleven o'clock on the day after Christmas. I got a hangover. Everybody that's normal's got a hangover. Didn't your mother ever teach you not to call folks before noon the days after holidays?"

It occurred, though admittedly only briefly, to her ladyship to inform this—person that her mother never had a telephone. Instead, she said, "I'm really frightfully sorry to bother you, young man, but I'm afraid I have rather an important question to ask you."

"And whassat?"

"Do you know Cyrus Anderson? Of Jolliston?"

"Cyrus Anderson?" the voice asked, punctuated with an audible yawn. "I don't think so. Cyrus Anderson? No, I don't know anybody named . . . No, wait. Wait just a minute.

Maybe I do. Kind of short? Stocky? Cute as hell and butch as they come?"

"Ahem!" her ladyship cleared her throat raucously. Nevertheless, while she was a trifle nonplussed by the description, she did have to concede its essential accuracy. "That sounds about right," she said dryly. "Did he come to a party at your house? Last Friday night?"

"Good God, yes. My dear, he was the hit of the evening."

"How nice for Cyrus!" said Lady Fairgrief, who found herself rather more pleased than otherwise that Cy had had such an enthusiastic reception—and then was quite shocked at herself for being so pleased. "Now, please, think clearly." She took herself in hand. "I have to ask you a question."

"You just did."

"So I did. But this is the question of importance: Did he bring a bottle of anything with him to your party?"

"Oh my Jesus, mercy," said the voice, stifling a giggle. "Did he! Let me tell you, honey, I was *days* getting over that hangover."

"How horrible for you! Do you remember what it was?"

"Grain alcohol. And I mean pure grain alcohol. One hundred and ninety proof—that's ninety-five percent pure booze! I don't even think it's legal in California. But that little son of a bitch said he thought it might liven things up a bit. Well, all I can say is I don't know how lively it made things. Everyone was sure drunk as hell. That tall droopy number he came with had to be carried out of here."

Her ladyship turned and eyed Billy as she repeated, "Tall *droopy number?*" with a vocal emphasis that would have done Queen Victoria proud as Billy quietly turned a very brilliant shade of mauve.

"And do you happen to remember what his name was?" asked Lady Fairgrief.

"Billy," responded the other promptly. "Looks like a cross between John Carradine and a Japanese crane?"

"That will do," said her ladyship. "And thank you. You've been most helpful. Oh, yes. One more thing. Would you be willing to sign a declaration about what you've just told me?"

"Jesus!" her interlocutor swore yet again. "What's he done?"

"Nothing. I hope," said her Lady Fairgrief, and without further ado, said "Thank you" very cheerfully into the receiver and handed the telephone back to the still wildly flushing Billy.

"Very interesting," said her ladyship not without a twinkle. "However, I'm still not altogether certain this solves Cy's problem."

"Why not?" asked Billy. "I would have thought it would clear it up completely. You have proof now about his taking the bottle somewhere and what he did with it. Don't you?"

"Yes, but only up to a point." Then, seeing Billy's perplexity was verging on anger, she asked, rather more gently, "Were you conscious on the ride back to Jolliston?"

"No."

"Then can you be certain that Cy didn't bring the bottle back with him—with whatever was left in it?"

"You could have asked Bubbles that."

"Yes, I suppose I could."

"And frankly, Lady Fairgrief, I can't imagine Cy being so ill-bred as to take back a bottle he's brought to a party."

"A point of good manners? Well, it may very well be a good point. But was Bubbles any more compos mentis at the end of this—ebullition than were you?"

"I tend to doubt it," said Billy. "Knowing him."

"Then can't you see that the whole thing could have been—and, mind you, I'm only saying *could* have been—nothing more than a sham to allow Cy to possess himself of a supply of exceedingly potent alcohol in preparation of administering it, somehow, to his father? He did drive you back, didn't he? And you dead drunk."

"I think you're making things complicated for the sake of their complexity. That's what I think."

"Very likely I am," conceded her ladyship. "But you still don't see, do you, that this is the way we must look at things. We have to try to work out all—and let me underscore that—all the possible scenarios. However," she relented, "be assured that I will tell Matilda this latest development. But you'd better be prepared for the possibility that she will do nothing but take note of it and rack it up like any other datum. Of no greater—and no lesser—value than that. And what can all that incredible ruckus be about?"

200

iii

What the ruckus was about was really very simple. In the living room, after Lady Fairgrief and Billy had left, Miss Shaw had chafed a bit, mildly at first and then with a fiery itch. Her ladyship and Billy were taking an unusually long time. Of course, as far as Miss Shaw knew, nothing more significant was happening than that Billy had taken his employer to—well, to tend to those things which must be tended to. But Matilda in the library would be wondering where she was and why she had not yet returned with Helen. Really, it was most vexing—and worrisome—of Lady Fairgrief to be gone so long. Finally, she could stand it no longer.

"Larry," she instructed without thinking, "go across and tell your aunt that things have been held up a bit."

Larry looked quite surprised but was agreeable enough. He pushed himself upright from his slouch against the mantelpiece and began to saunter toward the door into the passage.

"Actually, I don't think that's a very good idea," said Mrs. Anderson.

"I don't either," said Bette Wanda.

"That's right," put in Arletta. "You won't let none of us wander around. How come you gonna let him go when he coulda poisoned the old man just as much as anybody?"

And Ben's face began immediately to darken. He eyed Arletta in a not very pleasant way. Larry, in turn, eyed him and wondered what was going to happen. For his own part, he hardly cared. Of course suspicion rested upon him. As much as upon anyone else in that wretched household.

"Why, he coulda done it, just the same as one of us," Arletta repeated.

Whereupon, as Larry had feared might happen, Ben bellowed, "Goddamn it! I am sick to death of this nonsense. Nonsense, do you hear? And everyone in this room bloody well knows it's nonsense. Once and for all, you cretinous fools, Larry had nothing to do with this."

"Can you prove it ain't his fault?" sniffed Arletta.

"As Miss Worthing has so recently pointed out to me, no, I

can't; there are few things in this world more difficult to prove than a negative."

"The orange juice wasn't the only thing we all drank. We had to drink that goddamn eggnog, too. Like to make me puke with all that raw egg in it. I only drank it 'cause I knew you'd make a fuss if I didn't, you're all so damn high and mighty. He coulda put something in that."

Larry put a hand on Ben's arm.

"Ben, she's right. There is a possibility."

"Bull," said Ben. "But for once I think I can prove a negative. I can prove you didn't put anything in that eggnog."

"You can?" Larry was clearly taken aback.

"Of course I can."

"How you gonna go 'bout doing that?" asked Bob E., also suddenly interested and intrigued.

"You just come to the kitchen with me and I'll show you." He began to march into the dining room.

"Just a minute!" expostulated Miss Shaw. "I'm not sure I can allow this."

"Neither can I," said Mrs. Anderson.

"All right," said Ben through clenched teeth, "if Miss Worthing is in charge, then in charge she will be." And he marched to the door of the living room and bellowed in that voice which had rung the rafters in many a theater and thrilled many a moviegoer, "Miss Worthing! Get over here!"

It had been this bellow by which Lady Fairgrief and Billy in the kitchen were so startled, that bellow, followed by the murmuring of voices like the murmuring of many waters, as, in a closely collected group like a football scrimmage, the lot of them came through the dining room door into the kitchen, with Ben definitely carrying the ball.

Whereupon, from the doorway into the corridor, came a voice, loud and commanding. "All right, that will be just about enough."

They came to a halt clustered about Ben while Billy and Lady Fairgrief could only stare in amazement at this wholly unexpected tableau.

"May I inquire," said Miss Worthing, furious in the doorway, "what this is all about? Can't any of you obey a simple directive and stay put in the living room until we can bring some order to this chaos?"

"Stuff!" said Ben, very much on his mettle.

"Explain yourself," said Miss Worthing severely.

"I will be delighted to," said Ben, "if you can manage to hold your tongue a minute."

Miss Worthing glared angrily at Ben, once more irritated beyond endurance by the facility with which these Andersons seemed capable of escaping control.

Ben, however, had begun to lecture:

"Simply put, I have had quite enough of this circus. Whatever else the truth of this might be, Mother"—he looked levelly at Mrs. Anderson—"we have been asked to take altogether too much of this on faith."

"Think I'm not doing likewise?" asked his mother.

"Hmph," Ben snorted. "Well, I'm just going to make it all a little easier."

"What do you mean?" demanded Miss Worthing.

"I'm going to clear Larry once and for all from this. I had no idea until just now what kind of fatuous nonsense could be spoken in this house."

If anything, Larry was acutely embarrassed by all this. "Ben, I—"

"No!" said Ben angrily. "This is outrageous." Nor did he miss it when, across the breadth of the kitchen, Larry and Miss Worthing exchanged what has often been referred to as a Significant Glance.

"You needn't duck your eyes so guiltily, my boy," said Ben to Larry with a pointed tone. "Your aunt knows because you told her, and I know because she told me. And you know because I told you that I know that she knows. And you'll pardon me if I say that all in all I think it's a pretty piss-poor idea of a motive for anything, much less murder."

"What are you talking about, Ben?" demanded Helen.

"And as for you, puss-puss," Ben addressed his sister, "why the hell don't you just belt up and try out your snot-nosed posturings on someone who might possibly be impressed with them? And now," he addressed the crowd the more generally and literally wrenched open the refrigerator door, "to demonstrate conclusively that this ill-favored of fate"—he gestured at Larry—"could not and did not put alcohol in the eggnog of which we have heard so much!"

Larry suddenly began to look very frightened. "Ben, what are you doing?"

But in the doorway, his aunt—who had watched these proceedings with a certain grim expression of satisfaction—rather violently shushed him.

"What do you propose to do, Ben?" she asked.

"I should have thought that would be obvious." And from the refrigerator, he withdrew one of those all-purpose crockery bowls, over the top of which thin cellophane was stretched and secured with a bright-red rubber band. This he set down deliberately next to the stove, while from the cabinet above, he removed a small stainless-steel saucepan. The latter he slapped down upon one of the front burners, ripped the cellophane off the bowl and, hefting it up, poured a generous measure of the rather wan-looking fluid into the saucepan. With the methodicalness characteristic of the man, he covered the bowl again, before, with a sharp little twist of the knob, he turned the gas on under the saucepan and put the flame as high as it would go.

"You'll burn it!" protested Miss Shaw.

"Precisely the point," said Miss Worthing, as her eyes flickered around the room. The others seemed content merely to watch the playing out of this little drama, their faces for the most part expressionless. Only Larry and Helen seemed to have some idea of what was being done.

From the pocket of his jacket, Ben withdrew his cigarette lighter. Snapping it open, he flicked it into flame, and when the fluid in the saucepan began to curl and sizzle around the sides, releasing a very unpleasant odor into the kitchen as it did so, Ben said triumphantly, "Now will I prove once and for all there is no alcohol in this eggnog."

And gently and carefully, he lowered the flame of the lighter to the surface of the bubbling nog, moving the body of the lighter back and up in order to allow the flame itself closer access to the surface.

Everyone watched entranced. Nor was any word spoken, until—suddenly—Ben exclaimed, "Oh, my God!" as, from the flame of his lighter, a flickering blue flame suddenly caught and played gently back and forth across the surface of the boiling nog. "Oh, my God!" Ben repeated and looked at Larry, whose face had gone completely blank and whose complexion was literally white with shock.

"Well, Larry," said Helen with considerable relish, "and how do you explain this?"

"I . . . I . . ." He tried several times to begin as he looked from face to face. "I didn't!" he finally managed. "I did not put alcohol in it. The only time anyone got close to it was when this—when Arletta tried to pour rum into it."

"Don't you try to pin this on me!" Arletta fairly shrieked at him.

"Don't try to pin anything on anybody," said Bob E. with distinct menace.

It was Miss Worthing who defused the unpleasant scene.

"Is there any way we could find out what's in the nog?"

"I suppose there is enough left so we could taste it," said Ben, somewhat dubiously looking though the cellophane into the bowl. Then he snorted and looked up at Larry. "I don't know what to make of this, Larry," he averred, "but I don't believe for one minute you did this."

"What do you mean?" demanded Bette Wanda.

"I think it was tampered with," said Ben.

"I would say," said Billy suddenly, "that that is very likely to be true. And furthermore," he went on as all heads swiveled toward him, "I dare say you'll find that it was vodka."

"Why do you say that?" asked Lady Fairgrief.

"Because of that." He gestured toward the drinks tray still reposing upon the counter.

"What's so unusual about that?" demanded Bob E.

"The jug of vodka," said Billy.

Ben's face suddenly lighted up.

"It was unopened yesterday," Billy concluded.

"So it was," said Ben.

Billy nodded. "After the General's attack, I came in here to call the doctor, and I distinctly remember that the seal on that bottle had not been broken."

The jug in question, a half gallon of excellent vodka, had

now definitely been opened and a pint or so was missing from it.

"Anyone else remember anything?" asked Miss Worthing.

"Yes," said Miss Shaw. "It was still unopened when I went to bed last night."

"How do you know?"

"Because when we finished in here, I thought about asking for a vodka tonic before bed. But when I saw the jug was still unopened, I decided not to. It seemed impolite somehow."

"Thank you," said Miss Worthing and then looked over the assemblage. "Well, anyone for trying the nog to see what's in it?"

"I will," said Ben. "I know the taste of vodka and eggs together with cream. And since I'm the cause of Larry standing here condemned, I should be the one to try."

"I will, too," said Mrs. Anderson. "It would be better if several of us did."

And so, with a kind of solemn, almost ritualistic air, glasses were fetched, nog was poured, and Ben, Mrs. Anderson, and Miss Worthing each tasted and then delicately spat the contents into the sink. The three of them exchanged a glance and nodded almost simultaneously.

"It's vodka," said Ben.

"I agree," said Mrs. Anderson.

"Me too," said Miss Worthing. "Blast!"

"Aunt Matilda," protested Larry.

"You don't understand, Larry," said his aunt. "All this, and all it's done is to bring us right back to square one."

iv

It was a bit later that it occurred to Miss Worthing that this was not necessarily so. In the meantime, however, she and Miss Shaw were once more seated in the library. This time with Helen.

Irritatingly enough, the woman had brought her child with her.

"You know, Helen, I would have preferred," said Miss

Worthing coldly, "that you leave Mary Elizabeth in the other room."

"Why?" demanded Helen. "Who could possibly take care of her as well as I can? Martha said you wanted to speak to me. Although what about, I can't possibly imagine."

"Helen, do try not to make this any more difficult than it already is. You know perfectly well I have to ask you some questions."

"Questions! Why are you asking questions, anyway? You would think the way everyone is carrying on that someone tried deliberately to kill Father."

"It does begin to look as though that is precisely what happened," snapped Miss Worthing, piqued by the woman's transcendent arrogance.

"Bull," said Helen. "He probably poured some booze into his own orange juice, thinking that just for the holiday it wouldn't hurt. The pigheaded old bastard would try something like that on."

"Something tells me you don't much like your father."

The younger woman's eyes narrowed to slits as she sat down, rather abruptly, transferred the babe to her left arm, and began rocking it gently. Her motions were completely at variance with the expression of her eyes.

Finally, she said—half as though she were actually talking to herself, "I loved him, you know. He was the best thing that could have happened to a girl. He treated me like a princess."

"Yes. I know," said Miss Worthing, and forbore to opine that it would probably have been infinitely better if she had been swatted now and again for the good of her immortal soul.

"But then he changed." Helen looked up, her face hard. "He's been so horrible since he got sick."

Which, being translated, Miss Worthing had no doubt whatever, meant that he no longer made such a fuss over Helen Anderson Taylor.

She did not, of course, say it. Instead, she contented herself with saying rather severely, "Helen, he's dying. People do go through changes when facing their own mortality, you know."

"Yes, he is dying, isn't he? And God knows he's been a long time about it. And I'll never forgive him. Never!"

"For what?" asked Miss Worthing. "D'you mean that business of Mary Elizabeth having no possible claim on him?"

That caught the younger woman by surprise.

"How did you know about that?"

"It's rather my business to know about these things, isn't it?" asked Miss Worthing.

"I don't think it's any business of yours at all."

"Let me get this straight, Helen," said Miss Worthing. "What you're trying to tell me is that you don't believe anyone tried to murder your father, but that this was all an accident or even deliberate disobedience on your father's part of medical orders."

"I am a nurse," said Helen. "People do disobey the doctor."

"Helen, you can't be serious!"

"Why not?"

"I'll tell you why not. Because someone fiddled with that eggnog is why not. What other reason could anyone have to monkey about with it, if it weren't to create a red herring to throw us off the scent?"

"Do you know for certain that it was fiddled with?" demanded Helen.

"No," said Miss Worthing after a minute, honesty fighting with a perfectly natural desire to contradict anything this irritating woman had to say. "All right. Let's concede the point for a moment. I suppose the possibility exists," said Miss Worthing. "However, I think you should know that it's not only your mother who thinks there was some chicanery here. Your father does, too."

"You've talked to him?"

"I have."

"What did he say?"

"Not much."

"What *did* he say?"

"Now, Helen, you don't really think that I'm going to tell you, do you?"

Helen clicked her tongue and tossed her head. "What the hell do you want from me?"

"I have to ask questions."

Again, the click of the tongue. "Well, ask them and be quick about it."

"Very well. You didn't drink anything yesterday. Not till dinner. Why?"

"I didn't feel like it. Besides, I think that enough damage had been caused by alcohol the night before. Don't you?"

"I wasn't there."

"No, but you certainly seem to know a great deal about it."

Miss Worthing let it go. "Helen, you weren't especially occupied yesterday . . ."

"The hell I wasn't. I was busy with my daughter."

"Very well. So you were. And several people have mentioned that, too. You were apparently very much busy entertaining, if not your daughter, then yourself, with rather an endless series of snide remarks. About everyone. Which means, in turn, that you must have been at least somewhat aware of them."

Helen made no reply, merely looking aggravated.

"Didn't you notice anything?" asked Miss Worthing. "Didn't you see anything? Weren't you aware of anything?"

"I was aware of my father," said Helen. "And I was very aware of him when he called my baby a brat."

"So you did nothing yourself yesterday?"

"Why should I have? I didn't even want to be here."

"Then why did you come?"

"Because Mother practically forced us to."

"I see," murmured Miss Worthing and stood up. "Well, I guess that will be all. I won't say thank you because there's nothing to thank you for. You've been unhelpful. You've been ungracious. In fact, you've been downright unpleasant. Miss Shaw will see you back to the living room."

"I can find my own way."

"Of course you can," said Miss Worthing, "but you're not going to."

"Who now?" asked Miss Shaw laconically, as she stepped toward the door and the impatient and scowling Helen.

There was, however, no immediate response.

"Mattie!" she said more sharply.

"I'm sorry, Martha," said Miss Worthing, abruptly coming to. "What was that? I'm afraid I wasn't listening."

"I just want to know who next?"

"Who next? Yes, indeed. Who next?" Miss Worthing

seemed once more about to drift off into yet another brown study.

"Mattie," again prompted Miss Shaw.

"What! Oh. Yes. Oh, never mind, Martha." Miss Worthing gestured her rather irritably away. "No one at the moment."

Miss Shaw shrugged and, turning, gestured to Helen that she could now leave. Trundling after the mother and child, she closed the door behind her.

CHAPTER 11

i

A number of points had slowly begun to gain ground in the forefront of Miss Worthing's mind—the vast preponderance of them distinctly unpleasant, to be sure. And yet, already she had the sense of a pattern lurking just out of perception amid an abundance of seemingly unrelated and even contradictory data. And not for the first time in one of these explorations of human foolishness, she had the feeling that if only she could put her finger on the one single important *thing*—whatever it happened to be—the rest of the nonsense would begin to come to order coherently around it like sugar crystals growing in an oversaturated syrup.

She still had three people yet to talk to. Not, of course, counting the General. Was he going to remain lucid long enough for her to ask the question she still had to ask him? Of course, she did not really need him to answer it. Indeed, had this whole investigation been conducted in a rather more conventional setting, she would not have had the peculiar, well, *luxury* of interviewing the victim. Yet—and it was something upon which she reflected with sour disgust—Henry Anderson was probably the only person in the house who could or would answer that question with honesty.

And the day was growing apace. Those people in the living

room were going to get restive very soon. And who, in fact, would blame them?

Martha reentered and resumed her seat.

She said nothing, but then Miss Worthing had known her far too long not to be able to see that something was worrying her.

"Okay, Martha," she said, "what's eating you?"

Miss Shaw retrieved her notebook and began to flip back pages as she looked for something. Evidently she found it, for she grunted and, holding the book up to the light, read, "'MW: What other reason could anyone have to monkey about with it [the eggnog], if it weren't to create a red herring . . . ? HT: Do you know for certain that it was fiddled with?'

"Helen's a pretty sharp cookie," observed Miss Shaw, putting down the notebook, "for all that she's a disagreeable wench."

Miss Worthing chuckled mirthlessly. "Don't despair, Martha; I haven't lost my marbles quite yet. That was one of the things which have been bothering me. It's too easy for us just to say that the nog was interfered with. We don't have any real proof of any such thing. In fact, the only hard evidence we've got is that there was, is, vodka in it; and other than that, the only thing we've got is Larry's bald assertion that he wasn't the one who put it there. That and the direct testimony of Ben, Billy, and you that the bottle had not been opened yesterday."

"And then there's the flask."

"Oh yes, that flask. But you know there is something really screwy about that."

"What is?"

Miss Worthing told her.

"That does make an interesting difference, doesn't it?" said Miss Shaw.

"But I still don't like it, Martha."

"Why not?"

"Everything's getting muddled. Why? Why should things be so damnably complicated over a sordid little domestic murder?"

"Conspiracy," suggested Miss Shaw. "It is why we're keeping everyone closeted together."

"It's a possibility, of course," conceded Miss Worthing. "Although," she added dryly, "can you really see any two of these people conspiring together to do anything? They all hate each other too much."

"Except Ben and Larry," said Miss Shaw.

"Just so," admitted Miss Worthing, and the two women sighed in tandem.

"And," continued Miss Worthing after a moment, "another rather depressing possibility has occurred to me."

Miss Shaw said nothing.

"Oh well, I guess we'd best examine it," said Miss Worthing. "Martha, go over and get Billy to come to me. Then you might as well stay there with Aunt Eulalia. This won't take long."

A few minutes later, Billy McClure entered the library and stood at reverent attention just inside the door.

"All right, Billy," said Miss Worthing, "you can knock it off. I'm not the Edwardian relic you seem to think I am. Besides," she chuckled, as the young man approached and took a seat facing her, "if you're going to pull this gig off successfully in New York, you're going to have to stop doing such a perfect Arthur Treacher imitation."

Billy chuckled too and relaxed. "I don't see why I should," he said; "it seems to be what everyone expects a butler to be like these days."

"Except the ones used to the genuine article," she said and then frowned. "But never mind all that now. I need you to do something with me."

"What?"

"Come on," she said and stalked to the door of the library and, cautiously opening it, stuck her head out into the hall.

A murmur of voices emerged from the living room across the hall through the open doorway.

"Damn." She pulled her head back in.

"What's wrong?"

"The doors of the living room are open."

He smiled a superior smile. "No problem." And he shambled into the passage to the open doors, seized one in each hand and, announcing in a loud voice, "These are to remain shut till further notice," slammed them together.

"Thanks," said Miss Worthing as she joined him in the passage, and led the way down the corridor once more into the kitchen, where for a few seconds she stood examining the appalling detritus strewn about.

"You're quite sure that the vodka jug was not opened yesterday."

"Quite. At least not till after the General was taken ill."

"Was there any other vodka on the tray?"

"No."

"You're sure."

"I'm sure. I engaged to memorize the contents of the tray when the General was stricken. That's what I was doing when Bob E. Taylor came in and dumped the orange juice."

"Why?"

He looked rather blankly at her. "I don't know why he dumped it. You'll have to ask him."

"I don't mean that. I mean why did you 'engage' to memorize the tray?"

"Well, I knew about the General's—debility. Her ladyship had spoken of it to me. Then, when he clutched the general area of his liver and went down, my first thought was that he must have been drinking. After that I wondered what he'd had. And," he added with a rueful nod, "I have to admit I wondered why he'd been drinking, if what I had been told was true."

Miss Worthing eyed the young man with a certain new respect. "Very good," she murmured, and then asked yet again, "So you are certain there was no open bottle of vodka on the tray."

"Quite sure."

"Okay," she said and then crossed the kitchen to the countertop whereon the drinks tray sat.

Beside it, on the same countertop, was a large steel ice bucket with a firmly fitted lid. She cast her eyes round and pointed to a roll of paper towels above the sink. "Billy, bring me one of those."

She took it from him and, using it to cover the projecting knob, lifted the lid of the ice bucket. She had to tug at it, for moisture and the ambient air pressure had formed a seal around the rim of the lid. It was evidently a good and expensive member of the species, the ice bucket; though nearly twenty-four hours had passed since Cy had filled it, there was yet ice floating about in the quart or so of melt at the bottom.

She turned her head away and, flaring her nostrils, took several deep breaths through her nose. Then she bent over and sniffed deeply, practically putting her face into the bucket.

"Drat," she said, standing up. Drawing another number of breaths through her nose, she repeated the process.

"I can't tell," she said, frowning. "The air in the bucket is too cold; cold air just doesn't bear scents well."

"Would you like me to try?" asked Billy, tapping his own appreciable nasal apparatus.

She stood aside to give him access. He imitated her antics and, like her, thrust his entire face into the bucket. For a brief moment, she was all too absurdly reminded of a bird dog on point, a resemblance that became even more like when, abruptly, he stiffened. He stood straight up and looked gravely at her. "There's something in there. I'd swear to it. Someone put some booze in the ice bucket! Vodka, too, I'll betcha."

"No bet," said Miss Worthing.

She turned aside to the sink and picked up the tea mug from which she had been drinking the night before. She rinsed it out under the tap and then lowered it into the ice melt at the bottom of the ice bucket. She then raised it to her lips and, with great caution and an immense reluctance, sipped. She spat into the sink as had she, Ben, and Mrs. Anderson earlier with the eggnog, and finished by once again rinsing out the cup, filling it from the tap and, very vigorously indeed, rinsing out her mouth.

"Vodka," she said succinctly when she had done. "But from where?"

"From the jug, obviously," said Billy. "But it was not opened yesterday."

"I know."

Regardless of appearances, Billy was hardly an unintelligent man.

"Someone poured vodka into the ice bucket. And the eggnog," he said. "It would make—well, who?—look guilty as hell. Larry. Ben. Cy." He then flushed mightily. "And I wouldn't mind betting that it was done while I was asleep last night."

"No bet," said Miss Worthing again, though she said it gently and with a smile. "You will, I hope, keep this development under your hair."

"Don't worry," he said and then exclaimed, "boy! What a really scuzzy thing to do!"

"So it is," said Miss Worthing. "So it is. Okay, Billy"—she

waxed efficient—"get on back in there and tell Martha to meet me in the library again. Would you?"

Billy hustled.

Miss Worthing lingered for a moment, as much to ponder the implications of what had happened as to fume at the someone who had tried such a truly nasty trick. And it was a trick. All of it.

And yet, the lurking pattern seemed, precisely because of this, to be somewhat clearer—though still so faint that to grab at it would be to scare it off and leave her still floundering amid the data. And she had had far too much experience of her own mind not to know that if she just let it be, presently and in all good time, the whole would be revealed to her.

Meanwhile, she turned and, passing out of the kitchen, headed back down the passage toward the library.

She was halfway there when a truly horrible thought occurred to her and brought her to a sudden and unscheduled halt in front of the door to the General's study. And the whole of the carefully building substructure in her mind shook like Jell-O in an earthquake.

"Oh, dear God!" she prayed quite aloud. Oh, please, no! She licked her lips, which had gone suddenly very dry. Then, squaring her shoulders, she turned the knob of the door and let herself into the study and crossed the room to the cabinet whereupon reposed the General's liquor rack.

It was a pretty thing of crystal and silver, and round the necks of the several decanters were little labels of silver suspended by minute links of silver chain. Upon the plaques, in fine Spencerian chasing, were inscribed the names of the various spirits proper to each decanter. They all sat there, in muted splendor. Brandy—that she knew. Scotch—the palest of pale golds. Bourbon—of a rich and deep amber. Gin—clear as water but full of light refracting from the plenitude of oils swirling within in random Brownian movement. And on the end, next to the gin, vodka. Four of the bottles were full or at least two-thirds so. Only the decanter of vodka stood completely empty.

Miss Worthing's shoulders sagged. Idly, she picked up the decanter and examined it, willing it to surrender some intelligence to make some sense of all this mess. But it remained only mute crystal, yielding nothing to scrutiny, not even the faint and unsightly smudges that might have provided fingerprints—even supposing she were prepared to repeat the faintly ludicrous experiment she had conducted in the dining room upon the silver flask.

Whereupon, like a bolt of lightning, it occurred to it her that this too, rather like the flask—ludicrous though the business therewith may have been—yet had something to tell her.

ii

A few moments later, she let herself back into the library.

"Well!" said an odiously familiar voice. "She deigns to rejoin us."

"Hello, Aunt Eulalia. What a delightful surprise."

"Don't worry," said the old woman. "Billy's perfectly capable of remaining in charge over there."

"I don't doubt it," said Miss Worthing. "Nevertheless, I can't help but wonder what's brought you hither."

"I need to talk to you."

"Someone say something relevant?" asked Miss Worthing, jerking her head in the direction of the living room.

"After a manner of speaking," said her ladyship.

"I do so love it when you're being cryptic," said Miss Worthing.

"Matilda, hush! Do listen to what I have to say."

And without much more ado, Lady Fairgrief proceeded to narrate the events leading up to and the contents of her phone call to the distant Bubbles. Nor could she entirely resist making a few quite colorful observations of her own about the incident.

"You're right," said Miss Worthing, not overly pleased. "What we are left with is that Cy definitely had access to some particularly virulent booze, and only the word of some highly impeachable witnesses that it was used up at that gathering last week. Blast it all!"

"Mattie," said Miss Shaw, "what's wrong?"

"What's wrong is that nothing is making sense."

She shared with the two of them the fruits of her most recent researches.

"Awkward," commented her ladyship when her niece was finished.

"And the really strange thing is that I think I'm beginning to see some faint glimmer of light." She said it half to herself, almost as though she were not altogether aware that she had said it aloud. Until, that is, she came to, so to speak, and realized the other two women were looking at her in a most expectant manner.

"No," she said, "I'm not about to stick my neck out yet. I still have several people to talk to."

"Who?" demanded Lady Fairgrief ungrammatically.

Miss Worthing ticked them off on her fingers: Bette Wanda, Arletta, and Bob E. Oh yes, and, of course, the General.

"I thought you had spoken with Henry already," said Lady Fairgrief.

"I did."

"And?"

"Nothing useful."

"Then why do you want to talk to him again?"

"Because he has the answer to a question which is rather important."

"Well then," said her ladyship, "I have a suggestion."

"What's that?"

"Why don't you go up and sit with Henry. Jessica is surely more than due for a nap, don't you think, and Martha and I will attack Bette Wanda and Arletta while you are doing so."

Miss Worthing's eyes suddenly twinkled. "Not Bob E., Aunt Eulalia?"

"No," said Lady Fairgrief, "not Bob E. It's been obvious to everyone for at least the last two hours that, for whatever devious reasons of your own, you're saving that one for last."

Miss Worthing's expression turned sour. "I haven't been saving him, Aunt Eulalia. Not deliberately. I've just been trying to think what on earth I am going to say to him."

"I'm sure you'll think of something when the time comes," said her ladyship, managing to sound both practical and soothing in the same breath. "However," she went on, with a certain waspish note in her voice, "if you are going to leave Bette Wanda and Arletta to Martha and me (and have you ruled them out as possibilities?), then you'd better tell us something of what's been going on."

"No," said Miss Worthing, answering the parenthesis rather than the demand, "of course I haven't ruled them out. In fact, I think it's fairly obvious how *they* could have done it. Either alone or in concert."

"Well then, Matilda, tell us!" said her aunt. "You haven't exactly kept me au courant with your work this morning. And I do not wish unnecessarily to go over what has already proven to be barren ground. So *give!*" she ended on a note of incalculable malignance.

Miss Worthing gave . . .

iii

. . . and twenty minutes later was once more perched somewhat less than comfortably on the cane-bottomed bentwood chair beside the slumbering form of the General.

Although "slumber" was probably not the word for it. No healthy sleep had ever been so deep or so endlessly disturbed by sighings and moanings and whistlings of air from laboring lungs as often as not, then followed by a complete if momentary cessation of breath altogether. The latter frightened Miss Worthing rather thoroughly until she finally realized that it was naught but the pain-racked body of the man—even as he lay unconscious—seeking to still all activity that was painful to it. It did not perhaps have the dramatic violence of Cheyne-Stokes breathing—that explosive and stertorous rasping which tells that life has truly reached its final moments, but it was certainly sufficiently unpleasant to hear.

And seated there, Miss Worthing was slowly reaching a peak of anger she had not known she was capable of as she contemplated the revolting facts that: (1) this poor, dear friend of hers was dying in pain so great even breathing was a bitter agony to him; (2) it had been done for the most scurrilous of all motives—money; and (3) by one who was kin or (perhaps) kith to him.

So rapt in her meditations was she that when the chuckle sounded from the bed, it nearly startled her out of her skin.

"And what, may I ask, is so funny?" she asked, though she smiled as she said it.

By some curious chance he looked nearly normal. Well, no, perhaps not quite normal. His eyes were even more lackluster than they had been several hours before, and the texture of his skin—now almost a greenish yellow—was more waxy—corpselike. Surely the man could not last much longer!

And yet his expression was one of great peace, and the cranky restlessness with which he had plucked at the covers and his fate that morning had been replaced, it seemed, with something incalculably more accepting.

"How are you feeling?" she asked.

Again, to her puzzled joy, came that enigmatic but obviously happy chuckle.

"Since," he said, "I am quite sure you mean that in an existential and not an immediately physical sense, I can answer quite truthfully that I feel marvelous."

"I'm very glad, Henry."

"So am I," he answered, although in truth it seemed more as though he were footnoting his own remarks himself. Then, more strongly, he said, gesturing to the telephone beside the bed, "Matilda, call Father Reggie for me, would you. Ask him to come see me." He sighed. "It's time."

It was a simple-enough request; indeed, from a dying man, an eminently sensible one. But she knew also that General Anderson had steadfastly refused to admit that the time had been drawing nigh when thought should be given the Last Things. Accordingly, she practically ran to the telephone and dialed the number of the Church of All Saints.

Presently, she hung up the phone. "Sibyl will be pleased," she said.

"I'm rather hoping that she's not the only One," said the General dryly.

She resumed her place beside the bed.

"Henry, before the priest gets here, or before—" She broke off in some confusion.

He waved embarrassment aside, however, with a small flick

of a hand on the counterpane. "Or before I go off again," he finished her sentence for her.

"Just so, Henry," she said. "There are some questions I must ask you."

"Questions?" said General Anderson with a puzzled frown. Then his expression cleared and again came that little dry chuckle. "You know, I'd forgotten all about that."

"What?"

"Well, Mattie, I have been thinking about other things."

"Well, of course, you have, Henry, but . . ." She found herself suddenly at rather a loss for words. Finally she blurted, "Do you still want me to find out who's responsible for this?"

The man looked away in a thoughtful silence that seemed to stretch on and on for an unbearable length of time.

"Henry?"

"I don't know, Matilda," he finally said. "Probably. Yes. Well, no. I don't know." He looked up at her. "How close are you?"

"I'm not sure," she admitted. "It seemed so straightforward at first. Now . . ." She shrugged and looked helplessly at him.

His response was an interesting one. He was not—had never been—anyone's fool. A look of great hurt crossed his face, as though he had bitten down on a very bitter pill.

"There's more than one?" he asked, his voice full of unhappy surprise.

She nodded.

"Who?"

She hesitated.

"Who, Matilda?" he demanded.

"All," she answered in a small voice.

"All of them?" he all but shouted it at her. "*All* of them?" he repeated and tried to raise himself on one elbow and only collapsed again onto his back, glaring at her.

"Don't be angry with me, Henry."

"Why not?" he demanded. "It can't possibly be all that complicated . . ."

"It's complicated, Henry."

". . . or that Sibyl or Helen or Ben or Cy or Bob E. or Arletta or Larry or Bette Wanda—no!"

"But, Henry, one of them did. And I'm sorry to have to report it, but from what we've uncovered so far, each of 'em had a motive, means, and a whole lot of opportunity." Whereupon, perforce, her basic honesty forced her to add, "Although I do have to admit that—at the same time—none of them had the opportunity. Not really. Not if I've got the chronology right."

"Matilda, you're not making any sense."

"I know."

"Maybe you'd better tell me."

"Are you sure it wouldn't . . ."

"Matilda, in half an hour a priest is going to be here hearing my last confession. I think I deserve to know what's happening."

So she told him—sketching it loosely, to be sure—but she told him.

When she had finished, he said, "There are a few points. First of all, there was no vodka in the eggnog or in the orange juice."

"You're sure."

"I am. Folks can say what they like about the tastelessness of vodka, but it is not tasteless, and the mixing varieties—which I presume this was . . ."

She told him the brand name.

"Very well, it has—as do they all—a very strong flavor and a very characteristic nose as well."

"Then what was it, Henry?"

"You're quite sure it wasn't Curaçao or Grand Marnier or some such?"

"They're all present and accounted for by the cellar book. There was—has been—some confusion about a bottle of Everclear that Cy brought back from New Mexico with him . . . Henry, what's wrong?"

She had broken off and asked the question as the most amazing sequence of emotions began to play in rapid succession across the man's face: First, it was as though a great light had broken before his gape-mouthed gaze, to be followed immediately by an expression of sheer malignant rage which, in turn, was transformed into a look of near unbearable anguish. He looked away and covered his face with a hand.

"Henry?"

Moments passed during which the only sounds were the

General's ragged irregular breathing and the loud ticking of a mechanical alarm clock on the table beside the bed. Presently, however, he seemed to grow calmer until finally, after no small struggle, he once more seemed to relax and recover somewhat of the equanimity he had possessed earlier.

"I'm all right," he finally said. "Now."

"*Do* you wish me to pursue?"

"I don't care anymore, Matilda," he replied. "Although, I suspect, Sibyl will want you to go forward."

"Yes."

For a long time he said nothing. Then: "Mattie, I'd like to be alone now."

"I'm not supposed to leave you till Jessica gets back."

"So how am I supposed to prepare for confession with a lot of gabbling women about?"

"Henry!"

"All right, all right."

"And, Henry, please. I do have a question for you."

"Only one, Matilda?"

"My," said she, "aren't you feeling scrappy."

"Last time for everything, I guess."

And there was absolutely nothing she could find to respond in any way adequately to that.

Instead, she leaned forward. "Henry, two nights ago—Christmas Eve—you had a falling out with Bob E."

"Nothing new in that."

"Nevertheless, it was pretty serious."

"Yes," ceded the General, "it was."

"How serious?"

This time he hesitated somewhat before replying.

"Very, very serious," he said eventually.

"What was it about?"

"Money, Matilda," came the instantaneous reply.

"Henry, don't you dare play games with me. Not now."

"Why shouldn't I, Mattie? What've I got left to lose?"

"Henry, of *course* it was about money. We knew that. But, for God's sake, Henry, *how* about money?"

"And, Mattie," said General Anderson with all the patience of Job himself, "it is precisely for God's sake that I don't think that . . ."

223

A soft knock fell on the door of the bedroom, and before the General could finish his sentence, Mrs. Anderson opened the door and came rushing in. Miss Worthing, it hardly wants saying, was ready to scream aloud with frustration. Wherefore, instead of leaving—as by all decent lights she should have during the ensuing conversation—she sat adamant in the chair, chafing with impatience.

Sibyl Anderson seemed almost transported with excitement. "Henry!" she said. "Father Reggie is here. He said you sent for him!"

Her husband beckoned her closer and, still in the way of his newfound peace, took her hand when she approached and kissed it. "I did," he said and added simply, "it's time."

"Oh, Henry," said his wife and leaned down and kissed him. "I'll show him right up."

She left.

When she was gone, General Anderson eyed the infuriated Miss Worthing and blandly announced to her, "I think you'd better go now, Mattie."

Miss Worthing was out of her chair like a shot.

"Very well, Henry, I will. But will you tell me what I am to do if I do get to the bottom of this?"

"Bring it to me."

"But you won't help."

"Oh, I don't know. Bring your notes when you're through. We'll compare 'em."

The man seemed, incredibly, to be actually rather jaunty with it.

Any further discussion, however, was precluded by the ringing without in the corridor of the sacring bell. Given her present emotional state, Miss Worthing was not entirely certain she would not be struck by lightning if she remained in the presence of the sacred elements. The door opened and Cy, ringing the sacring bell, entered, looking both frightened and solemn. Behind him came the priest in cassock, surplice, and stole, followed in turn by Ben, Sibyl, and Helen. Miss Worthing stood aside and, when they were safely in, beat her own retreat, stomping down the stairs in a state that can only be described as high dudgeon.

CHAPTER 12

i

Though, naturally, there was no way she could possibly have known it, at the very moment Miss Worthing's interview with the General was proceeding to such a very unsatisfactory conclusion, there were others in that unhappy house experiencing much the same sense of frustration.

And, in large measure, it was due to the fact that hardly a minute had passed after Miss Worthing had gone upstairs, ostensibly to spell Jessica Wu, when Miss Shaw and Lady Fairgrief put their heads together over the interviews entrusted unto them and cheerfully exceeded their authority with an insoucient élan that was perhaps only to be expected of them.

"Martha?" said her ladyship with a conspiratorial air. "I have an excellent idea."

"Oh?" said the very properly suspicious Miss Shaw.

"You needn't take that tone with me, young woman."

Now to be called "young woman" when one is over eighty is an agreeable thing, to be sure. Miss Shaw, however, had far too much good sense to be waylaid by blandishments of that sort.

"What have you got up your sleeve?" she said.

"It's really very simple," replied her ladyship. "I've been in *there*"—she jabbed a finger in the direction of the living room—"all morning and there are two things I can tell you: Arletta Taylor, for whatever reason, is badly frightened. Badly. And Bette Wanda Taylor knows it and is, in consequence, a smoldering and poorly banked fire."

"So?" said Miss Shaw.

"I suggest we use both Arletta's fear and Bette Wanda's temperament to our advantage."

Miss Shaw was frowning.

"Yes, Martha?"

"Why do you suppose Arletta is so frightened?"

Her ladyship gestured dismissively. "Who's to say? It could be any number of things. Of course, if she did, in fact, commit murder," she added dryly, "then no doubt she is entitled to feel a bit apprehensive. And now, while it may be rather unkind of me—no, scrub that; I *know* it's unkind, downright hateful, in fact—it may be useful to bring them in here together and see what erupts out of the volcano."

For a moment, Miss Shaw said nothing as she considered the incendiary plot. Soon, however, she stirred and said, "You're quite right. It's mean. But I think you're also right that it may well be useful."

ii

Sometime later, Miss Shaw ushered a lowering Bette Wanda into the library whilst propping up a near-collapsing Arletta.

"It took you long enough," observed Lady Fairgrief.

"There was a small amount of difficulty," said Miss Shaw, earning thereby a glance of unutterable venom from Bette Wanda.

It was, after all, something of an understatement.

The atmosphere in the living room had become more than a little electric as Miss Shaw entered to fetch the Taylor women.

Mrs. Anderson sat still, unmoving, elegant and implacable in her Sheraton chair, telling her beads over and over, speaking to no one. As to the others, with the varied revelations of the morning, it had become clearer and clearer to them that they were, in fact, caught up in an investigation into a murder, and that each of them was at risk and any protestations of innocence would be accorded their right and proper value—which is to say, none at all.

The night before, Mrs. Anderson's coldly furious announcement that her husband had been deliberately assaulted had been greeted with much, if silent, skepticism or even dismissed out of hand as the ravings of a distracted widow-to-be. And if Bob E.'s peculiar actions the evening before had led the Andersons unanimously to suspect him of some complicity at the very least, now none of them—not Ben, not Larry, not Cy, not even Sibyl—was sure. Nor was the possessed and silent Sibyl by any means certain that in invoking the questing mind of Miss Worthing to penetrate the tangle, she might not have called down the fire of heaven—fire that could yet, she so painfully perceived now, burn them all.

What no one, however, had noticed—with the possible exception of Lady Fairgrief—was that the way in which the investigation had of its nature proceeded had had an unintended and rather cruel effect: None of the Taylors had been interviewed or even, for that matter, been much spoken to. Helen, of course, had been, but Helen was as much Anderson as Taylor. More so, for she alone in the room seemed utterly without concern.

Not so the Taylors. Of the three of them, Bette Wanda, with her legal training, had the closest thing to a logical mind. But even she was not without a generous measure of neurotic imagination. And—though her fury mounted hourly as she watched her mother being slowly reduced to a cowering jelly under the lashings of her own imaginings, and even her big stalwart brother, whom she had always admired and loved, was turning to white-faced stone under his—even she could not banish the suspicion that the Andersons and their friends (for so to her disordered imagination Miss Worthing and Miss Shaw appeared) were gradually herding them—the Taylors—into some kind of a trap. She was not unaware, however, that such a trap would not be entirely of Anderson contriving—the question stood out in her own mind as much as in anyone's: Why had Bob E. emptied that pitcher of orange juice with such unseemly alacrity?

Whereupon—adding totally unnecessary fuel to the fire—

Miss Shaw was in the doorway announcing that Arletta and Bette Wanda were to come with her.

And Arletta quite simply dissolved in terror, and it took all of Bette Wanda's and Bob E.'s combined soothing to calm the woman enough for her to be able to follow Miss Shaw. Even then she practically had to be bodily supported by her daughter and Miss Shaw.

Then, even before the two Taylor women were through the door and properly seated, Lady Fairgrief was admonishing, "Why on earth are you taking on so, Mrs. Taylor? Good Lord, the way you're acting, you would think we were planning to shove bamboo splints under your fingernails or burn your eyelids with lighted cigarettes. What do you have to fuss about? Unless, of course, you killed the General. Did you?"

The reaction to this was, unfortunately, twofold. First of all, as could have been hardly a surprise to her antic ladyship, Arletta very nearly swooned in redoubled surfeit of terror. Which, no doubt, was the idea. Lady Fairgrief came of an age when such tactics were considered to be of the essence in eliciting information from the cringing masses. Times, however, have rather definitely, thank God, changed, and in a trice Bette Wanda was effectively transformed from a sullen presence into a screaming tornado.

"What the hell do you think you're doing?" she rounded on the old woman. "Why don't you leave her alone? Why don't you leave us alone!"

"Oh, do shut up, child," said her ladyship. "I haven't done a blessed thing other than to ask if she had done it. And I was right to have done so," she added indignantly. "I have to ask each of you the same question, don't I?"

"What do you mean?"

"Well, did *you* do it, perchance?"

"What the hell are you asking for?"

"I told you," said her ladyship, looking the picture of antique ferocity. "I want to know if you killed the General."

"He isn't even dead yet!"

"No, but he's going to be soon enough, and someone in this house did him in."

Now really, thought Miss Shaw, this has gone quite far

enough. She stepped between the combatants and assisted the wilting Arletta to a chair.

"Lady Fairgrief"—she glared angrily at the older woman—"I think you'd better let me handle this."

"Nonsense, Martha. I've had years of experi—"

"I know you have," interrupted Miss Shaw equanimously. "But really I do think that in this case, with these particular people"—she gestured toward the Taylors—"it would be far better if you let me handle this."

"Handle what?" demanded Bette Wanda.

"Bette Wanda," said Miss Shaw, turning to face her, "we told you last night that we were going to have to do some probing. We need to ask questions."

"Then why didn't you ask them before now?" The young woman's voice was almost pleading. "Why did you hold us up to the last, sitting in there, scared half to death, wondering what kind of bullshit you've been hatching out to frame us?"

"Bette Wanda," said Miss Shaw severely, "that is not what's been going on."

"You expect me to believe that?"

Miss Shaw shrugged massively. "Actually, it's a matter of complete indifference to me whether or not you believe what I have to say."

"Any more," Lady Fairgrief thrust her oar, "than we are necessarily going to believe anything *you* have to say."

"Lady Fairgrief!"

"I'm sure I'm sorry, Martha. Dear."

"No one has been plotting against you," said Miss Shaw to Bette Wanda. "Or yours," she added as something of an afterthought. "What we have been trying to discover is what the sequence of events has been."

"What?" asked Bette Wanda.

"How things hung together. Whether this person or that person did a certain thing. That's what we've been doing."

"And you couldn't have consulted with me? Or with my mother? Or," she added meaningfully, "my brother?"

"My goodness, Bette Wanda. These things aren't done like they are on TV. They take time and sometimes—most times," she added sourly, "reconstruction is a dreary, painstaking, and time-consuming business."

"So do you have any idea what's been going on?" In a weak, but surprisingly steady, voice, it was Arletta asking.

"I'm sorry, Arletta," said Miss Shaw kindly, "but I am afraid we can't tell you."

"Can't or won't?" interposed Bette Wanda.

"Bette Wanda, now you just stop it," said Arletta with a frown.

"But, Mama, they're going to try to pin this on you. Or me. Or, most of all, Bob E. Do you think they're really interested in the truth?"

"Oh, will you please shut up!" her ladyship snapped in vexation. "Stupid child! Do you really think we've nothing better to do than to stretch the feeble wits of silly little geese like you? Hmmph! In spite of what you seem to be imagining in whatever passes for a mind rattling about in that resonating chamber of your head, we are not trying to 'frame' anyone. We are searching out the truth in the only way God gave to humans to do it. And if those two functioning neurons you've got left betwixt your ears cannot somehow be got to switch on, you can at least do us the favor of just shutting your mouth and letting the adults in the room get on with it."

It seemed rather more than likely that all this would do was to send the young woman into yet another round of shrieking fury. In the event, however, it was immediately obvious that never in the whole of her life had anyone spoken to her in quite such a manner before. And she was struck, momentarily but absolutely, speechless.

"And now, if you're quite through . . ." Lady Fairgrief glared malevolently. When no response whatever was forthcoming, her ladyship turned and nodded, the soul of graciousness, to Miss Shaw. "Martha, you may proceed."

iii

"Thank you," said Miss Shaw faintly, trying, not entirely successfully, to maintain a grave countenance and rather wondering how, after all that, to begin. Finally, however, she just took a deep breath and plunged in: "Do either of you know what it was the General and Bob E. were angry about on Christmas Eve?"

"Huh?" asked Bette Wanda. Arletta, on the other hand, merely looked puzzled.

"I didn't know they was mad at each other," said Bob E.'s mother.

Bette Wanda's eyes slewed round to her mother.

"Oh, honey," said Arletta, "course I knew they was cranky about something. But I didn't think anything about that. They was always at each other about something."

"You were too drunk to notice," said Bette Wanda evenly and rather cruelly.

"Oh, honey!"

"Well? It's true."

"Perhaps it was," said Miss Shaw, interrupting. "But you, Bette Wanda, obviously did notice something.

Reluctantly, the young woman nodded.

"Do you know what it was about?" asked Miss Shaw.

"No."

But it was far too smoothly said. Nor could anyone as experienced as Miss Shaw in the vagaries of the human condition have missed the sudden wariness in Bette Wanda's eyes. Moreover, out of the corner of her eye, Miss Shaw saw her ladyship's brow shoot up.

"Very well," said Miss Shaw as smoothly. "Perhaps you don't. Although I think we can tell you without compromising anything that we've already determined that it must have been about money."

"Really!" said Bette Wanda.

Miss Shaw, resisting a wholly commendable urge to slap her, merely nodded. "Yes. We gather there's been some trouble with money."

"Isn't there always?" said Bette Wanda.

"And there was some disagreement between you two about it, too."

Silence.

"Wasn't there?"

The Taylor women exchanged a quick—and frankly hostile—look.

231

"In fact," Miss Shaw continued, "there were words between you about Bob E. wanting to borrow money from you?"

Silence again.

"Well?" demanded Miss Shaw. "Did Bob E. apply to either of you for a loan?"

After a moment, Lady Fairgrief moved restively and barked out, "Answer the question, damn your eyes!"

Bette Wanda's eyes snapped around to glare at Lady Fairgrief, but—even though the answer was mumbled and definitely sullen—Arletta said, "Yes, he did."

"Mama!"

"Well, he did. And you were so grand and high and mighty 'bout me not giving it to him."

"You *didn't* give it to him?" said Miss Shaw.

Arletta shook her head.

"Why not?" asked Miss Shaw.

"'Cause I'd a never seen it again, that's why."

"How much did he want?"

"He asked me for ten thousand."

"That's a healthy amount of money."

"That's a lot of money," corrected Arletta. "Maybe it ain't as much as it used to be, but it's still a lot for me, and I wasn't gonna."

"Did he tell you what it was for?"

A surprisingly bitter laugh greeted this question.

"You don't think any of the Taylor men are gonna tell their womenfolk what they want money for, now, do you?" asked Arletta, spleen clearly getting the better of her wariness. "He just comes to me and tells me, 'Mama, I need ten thousand; when can you let me have it?' And I said, 'I can't.' And he gets real mean-mouthed, saying as to how Jimmy Bob was his daddy, too, and he deserves some of the insurance settlement. Yeah, Jimmy Bob sure was Bob E.'s father, and they's alike as two peas in a pod. No, Martha, he never told me what he wants my money for. As careful as he is with everyone else who give him money when he was just starting up that business of his, he treats me, yes, and you, too, Bette Wanda, like the dirt beneath his feet."

Miss Shaw merely eyed Bette Wanda, who commented bitterly, "She always raised him to think he was special just 'cause he was a man."

"Don't put it on me, Bette Wanda; that was your daddy's doing."

"Oh, and you had nothing to do with it?"

Miss Shaw tried to bring things back to the point. "Okay," she said. "So you didn't know what Bob E. suddenly wanted ten thousand dollars for. Was he desperate?"

"I think he wanted me to write a check for him right there and then," said Arletta.

This did not exactly surprise Miss Shaw. Experienced businesswoman that she was, she knew perfectly well that there are times anyone in business for himself may need a generous line of credit for brief periods now and again. The question, though, had still not been answered.

"Bette Wanda," she asked, "do you know what it was for?"

"No."

Good heavens! thought Miss Shaw; does the poor thing have no idea at all what a perfectly dreadful liar she is? She exchanged a silent glance with Lady Fairgrief, who left off her own amused contemplation of the younger woman and, looking to Miss Shaw, nodded once, a nod which Miss Shaw, in turn, had no trouble interpreting: Perhaps we had best leave this one to Matilda.

"I don't know," protested Bette Wanda, observing that glance and nod.

"Well, we'll have to take your word for it, now, won't we?" said Miss Shaw ambiguously. "So why don't we move on to Christmas Day?"

"Okay," said Bette Wanda.

Arletta nodded.

"First of all," said Miss Shaw, "I want to know: Had either of you been drinking before you got here?"

Arletta shook her head, but Bette Wanda said, "Yeah. I had a few before I left home."

"Hung over?" asked Lady Fairgrief.

"Oh Jesus!" said Arletta. "Was I!"

"How about you, Bette Wanda?" asked Miss Shaw.

"That's why I had a couple of Bloody Marys. They worked

pretty fast, too. I felt pretty good by the time we got here. But, apparently," she said ruefully, "I wasn't quite as on top of it as I thought." She added dryly, "I think I was feeling so good because I probably had so much adrenaline in my system after—well, after the night before."

Miss Shaw nodded. "Yes. You had been rather angry, hadn't you? On Christmas Eve, I mean."

"I thought we were going to move on . . ."

"Let me ask the questions, please," said Miss Shaw crisply. "You were angry," she repeated.

"Yes, I was."

"You were worried that you had lost a great deal of money."

Arletta was giving very serious contemplation to her folded hands. Her daughter's glance rested momentarily upon her and then, softly, said, "Yes, I was."

"You were angry and frightened."

"Yes."

"Are you going to be able to replace the money?"

"I don't know."

Bette Wanda shrugged, obviously irritated by the harping on what was clearly a very painful topic. Perhaps that was why she blurted, "But I knew I would be able to get it from my brother when . . ."

"When what?"

Nothing.

"When what, Bette Wanda?"

"I don't know. I guess maybe when Bob E. was sober."

"But how could you borrow it from Bob E. if he wanted to borrow money from your mother?"

"Bob E. didn't want to borrow money from Mother," said Bette Wanda almost with a snarl. "You heard her: He thought he had a right to some of Daddy's insurance money."

"I see."

"Look, it's true. Mama and I were the named beneficiaries on the policy. Bob E. didn't even enter into it."

"Okay," said Miss Shaw; "thank you."

Bette Wanda's curious ambivalence about her family was showing clearly. It was obvious that she was still more than a little distressed by her mother's irresponsible spending. She was also as obviously put out by Bob E.'s grabbiness—if that was, in fact, what it was. But overriding all irritations and all fugitive angers was also the determination—and quite a fine one—to remain loyal to her own at whatever the cost. It was too bad that in furthering the one aim she should have to traduce the other.

"Very well," said Miss Shaw. "Now let's get back to Christmas Day. You two were squeezing the oranges."

"Yes."

"Why did you volunteer to do that? You did volunteer, didn't you?"

Bette Wanda immediately grasped the implication of that question.

"There you go again," she protested, "making it seem like some horrible plot we cooked up."

"Well, did you?" asked Miss Shaw with a chuckle. Bette Wanda, however, was not laughing. With a sigh, Miss Shaw rephrased the question: "Was there any particular reason you volunteered for that particular chore?"

Frowning, Bette Wanda replied, "No. Not really," and looked with rather a bleak kind of affection on her mother, who was still studying her hands. "Actually, it was Mother . . ." she began and then stopped, appalled at the equally appalled expression on her mother's face as she looked up, her face alive with apprehension.

"Well, then perhaps," Lady Fairgrief interceded, "we should let your mother tell us."

"It wasn't nothing special," said Arletta reluctantly. "I just never worked one of those things before. I seen 'em on TV, but I never had nothing like that in my kitchen."

"Like what, Arletta?" asked Miss Shaw.

"That electric reamer." The woman actually blushed. "Anytime I wanted juice from a lemon or a orange, I had to work 'em on a glass reamer my own mama bought back during the Great Depression."

"Was that all it was?" asked her ladyship with rather a nasty inflection. "Curiosity? That's all it was?"

"What else could it be?"

"Why you might have wanted to put something in the juice when you were done."

"No, I didn't. I swear I didn't." The woman's voice rose in a fresh upsurge.

Immediately, too, Bette Wanda quite literally jumped to her feet and ordered, "You will stop this badgering of my mother at once!"

Simultaneously, Miss Shaw tried to soothe Arletta. The unfortunate effect of both women speaking together, however, was effectively for each to cancel the other out.

"But Larry said," Lady Fairgrief's voice rose triumphant over all, "that you were all set to pour rum into the eggnog when it was resting on the counter."

Miss Shaw glared angrily at her ladyship. That was almost sure to have been a major tactical blunder, and sure enough, Arletta saw the opening and went for it: "I wasn't thinking. That's all. I was pretty high by that time. But you just wait a minute here. Maybe it was Larry who poured something into the eggnog. He got rid of me fast enough. And let me tell you, he was still holding that bottle of rum, too."

"It wasn't rum in the nog, Arletta," said Miss Shaw, trying to regain some semblance of control. "But you did just answer another question: Both of you were drinking before dinner."

"Course we were," snapped Bette Wanda. "We were both drinking orange blossoms."

"Which are?"

"Orange juice and gin," said Arletta. "The juice just smelled so good," she said wistfully. "I thought it would go down real nice—what with my head and all."

"And did it?"

Both women looked more than a bit uncomfortable.

"Yes," they muttered together.

"You didn't—or someone else didn't—accidentally pour gin into the pitcher of juice?"

"No," said Arletta strongly. "You'd have tasted it. You can mix screwdrivers—with vodka—real strong if you like," she shared some of her dubious expertise; "but you can't do that with orange blossoms. They taste real nasty if you get 'em too strong."

"The fact remains," said Lady Fairgrief, "that the two of you got awfully tight very quickly indeed."

"Yes, that's true," said Arletta.

Bette Wanda nodded her accord.

"How do you suppose that happened?" asked Miss Shaw. "Did you have several drinks? Mrs. Anderson says you were making pretty free with the juice."

"We were," admitted Bette Wanda.

"But not that much, now that you mention it," said Arletta. "You know, I really hadn't thought about it."

"It didn't alarm you? When you got sloshed so quickly?"

"Not really," said Arletta. "I just thought I was reviving my"—she hesitated—"my drunk from the night before. Happens that way sometimes."

Bette Wanda had retreated inward and was wearing a puzzled frown on her face as she stared into the nether distance at nothing at all.

"Something bothering you, Bette Wanda?" asked Miss Shaw.

"Well, yes, there is. I was—I got"—she flushed—"as I'm quite sure you already know, pretty drunk before dinner. Very drunk. And now that I think of it, I can't figure out why. I mean, I was drinking. But not that much. And, while I wasn't exactly sober as a judge when I started, I wasn't more than a bit high."

"Maybe you were higher than you thought, honey," said her mother. "We didn't want you driving, remember."

"Maybe," said Bette Wanda. "But no, I don't think so." She looked up at Miss Shaw. "But, you know, I didn't taste anything funny in the orange juice."

"Neither did I," said Lady Fairgrief.

"Then what do you suppose it was?" said Arletta.

Her ladyship looked quite sharply at her. "What do you mean, Mrs. Taylor?"

"Just that. What was it? I mean, if it wasn't the orange juice and it wasn't the eggnog, what was it?"

"Indeed," responded her ladyship, frowning even more malignantly than before. "Well, I must say," she observed and caught herself on the brink of adding how surprised she was that it should be Arletta who had said it, "that you have rather hit the nail on the head, haven't you?" She turned and looked toward Miss Shaw, who nodded grim agreement. "This is really most perplexing. I really don't see how it could have been anything other than the orange juice. But then I'm afraid I can't see any more clearly how it could have *been* the orange juice."

CHAPTER 13

i

A short while later, Miss Shaw and Lady Fairgrief were rejoined in the library by Miss Worthing, who neither took any joy of their tidings nor was able to impart any herself. For a rather longish period of time, the three women sat there in the library, the perfect icon of disgruntlement, and contemplated their accumulating frustration.

Whereupon, as though fate wished to add fuel to an already blazing fire of irritation, who should almost literally erupt into the library but an extremely agitated Jessica Wu, pursued by a more than usually harried-looking Billy McClure, and Larry Worthing.

The three women turned almost in unison to glare at the interruption, which had the effect of bringing the other trio to an immediate halt just inside the door of the library.

It was Miss Worthing who recovered her presence of mind first.

"Yes, Jessica?" she asked mildly enough.

Mrs. Wu, however, put her left hand on her hip and, wildly wagging an extended index finger on her right, advanced upon Miss Worthing. "Don't give me any of that 'Yes, Jessica' stuff, Matilda, because it isn't going to work."

"I beg your pardon."

"You damned well better. Sibyl Anderson tried to palm me off with some nonsense and I'm not going to have it."

"Something eating you, Jessica?" asked Miss Worthing rather coldly. "All my inquiry meant was, what can I do for you?"

"You can tell me what's going on here."

"Going on?"

"Matilda!"

"Perhaps I can explain, Aunt Matilda," said Larry.

"Please do," said Miss Worthing.

"Mrs. Wu here apparently saw Arletta's reaction in the living room when Martha called for her and Bette Wanda."

Miss Worthing turned to lift a brow at Miss Shaw, who gestured her ignorance.

"Well, all right," said Miss Worthing. "I can imagine."

"Can you?" demanded Jessica. "Then perhaps you can tell me why some poor creature nearly faints from sheer terror just by having her name called."

Miss Worthing actually opened her mouth to reply but was immediately forestalled by Mrs. Wu.

"Oh, don't," she said. "Matilda, I'm not stupid. And neither is Dr. DeCastre. Both of us already thought something funny was going on here. And now I'm sure of it." She looked sternly round at those present. "Now I'm going to ask a question, and I want a straight answer. Was Henry deliberately poisoned? And if he was, by whom?"

"I should like nothing better than to answer your questions," said Miss Worthing.

In response to which Mrs. Wu gave a little scream of vexation. "That's what Sibyl's been trying to foist me off with."

"Then perhaps you should have listened!" Miss Worthing rose from her seat as though pulled up by puppet strings. "I can't answer your question because I don't know the answer."

"And if you did, you wouldn't tell me."

"I didn't say that."

"You don't have to. Matilda, this is outrageous."

"Do you think we don't know that?"

"What did you imagine you were doing? You can't keep something like this private and secret."

"Jessica, at this point I'm not sure any of us know what we're doing."

"Was Henry poisoned?" demanded Mrs. Wu.

And to Mrs. Wu's intense annoyance, Miss Worthing chuckled. Not a very mirthful chuckle, to be sure, but a chuckle nevertheless.

"I fail to see anything amusing, Matilda."

"Do you? Well, I can't say I find anything too hysterically funny myself. But still, I would have thought that it would be transparently obvious that Henry was poisoned."

"Don't you play semantic games with me, Matilda Worthing," warned Mrs. Wu. "In case you've forgotten, Rex and I have a legal as well as a moral right to know. Was he poisoned deliberately?"

And from the doorway came a voice: "Yes, Jessica, he was."

It was Mrs. Anderson.

"By whom?" said the nurse.

"We don't know," said Miss Worthing.

"But we're doing everything we can to find out," said Lady Fairgrief.

"Jessica," said Miss Worthing, reaching a decision, "sit down and get ahold of yourself. Who's with Henry?"

"Father Reggie," said Mrs. Anderson.

"Very well," said Miss Worthing and then addressed the others. "Okay, folks, show's over. Larry, Billy, Sibyl, get back into the living room. Now."

When they were gone, Miss Worthing gave a carefully edited explanation of the situation as it presently stood to Mrs. Wu. Not, however, of the results of their investigation, for the eminently practical reason that she was not entirely certain that there had been any results to speak of. She did, however, give a thorough exposition of the General's feelings in the matter.

"And so," she concluded, "that's where we are at the moment."

"Well, I can't say I like it, Matilda."

"Do you think we do?"

"No," said Mrs. Wu coolly, "you're in at least as invidious a position as Rex and me." She rose and pulled her uniform straight. "But I mustn't stay any longer. I have to check on Henry. And"—she frowned—"I have to think about this."

240

"Talk to Henry."

"Henry's slipping," said Mrs. Wu. "I don't know how much longer he can last. This business with the priest will use up a lot of what energy he has left. Henry," she said severely as she opened the door, "has made his peace with God. But we—you, me, Rex, everyone—we have to deal with the living. And I don't care how rich or powerful the Andersons may think themselves. This kind of thing is never a private matter. And I will not tolerate any more deceptions."

She, too, left.

ii

Whereupon Miss Worthing rose to her feet and passionately addressed the ceiling. "This is terrible!"

"It is that," said Lady Fairgrief with a chuckle. "And what do you propose to do about it?"

Miss Worthing eyed first her and then Miss Shaw. Finally, making a noise rather like a snort, she said, "Martha, take Aunt Eulalia back to the living room. And then," she added, "will you please tell Sibyl that I would rather like to speak with her?"

"What are you going to do?" asked Lady Fairgrief.

"I'm not altogether sure, but I have the ghost of an idea."

A scant ten minutes later, Mrs. Anderson sat staring downward at her hands folded in her lap.

"Why are you confiding in me, Matilda? Aren't I still a suspect?"

"Oh, leave be, Sibyl," said Miss Worthing. "You know perfectly well why I've had to include you in the catalog of suspects. I've just told you what I have because I need to know something: Do I go in there"—she gestured toward the living room—"and tell everyone, 'So sorry. There's been a mistake. Please go home now and pray for poor Henry's soul.'"

"You could do that?"

"No. Not easily. Not now."

"Why?"

"Because—though I still do not know how it was done—I have no doubt at all that this thing *was* deliberately done. But

241

since I have already been foolish enough to go along with you when I should have been calling the sheriff, I am now also going to leave this to you: Do I proceed? Or do we call it off right now and pretend that none of this ever happened?"

Mrs. Anderson blinked. "But I don't understand. If Henry was truly poisoned, deliberately, then of course you've got to find out who did it."

"Why?"

That took rather longer to answer.

"I don't know," said Mrs. Anderson presently. "I don't think it's for revenge. At least, I hope not. But I do want to know who did this thing to my husband. I have to. Do you think I could spend the rest of my life wondering if one of my children—or friends—murdered my husband? And I chose not to find out which of them it was?"

Miss Worthing sighed and rose from her chair. "I have to admit it didn't seem very likely that you would," she observed.

"Okay, Sibyl, we follow through. Now why don't you get back to the living room and, if you would be so kind, have Martha bring Bob E. to me. I might as well get this one over."

iii

There were times thereafter when Miss Worthing would candidly confess that, of all the interviews she had conducted in her time, few were as frustrating as the one she had that St. Stephen's Day with Bob E. Taylor. Several things, naturally enough, contributed to that feeling of uselessness and frustration. And by no means the least of it was that Bob E., in spite of a wholesale lack of anything even remotely resembling an education, was a very astute man with a more than serviceable intelligence. In addition to which, he was wary and fully prepared to parry even the subtlest of thrusts.

"Well, you sure waited long enough to see me, didn't ya?"

"Yes, I daresay we did."

"Didja get enough to pin it on me?"

"Mr. Taylor, we had that at the very beginning."

"Then why'dja go through all this BS?"

"Frankly, because it was too easy."

At that he frowned. And held his peace.

"Oh, come, Mr. Taylor. Does it surprise you that of everyone here you should be a very prime suspect indeed?"

"Hell no, it doesn't surprise me. Ever'body knew the General hated me."

"I rather gathered that the feeling was mutual."

"What if it was?"

"Then in that case, you can hardly call your little business with the orange juice unremarkable."

"You ain't gonna let that go, are ya?"

"Why should we?"

"I told you—I told *them*—I thought there was something wrong with the juice."

"No doubt there was," commented Miss Worthing dryly. "So why didn't you save even just a little bit to be analyzed?"

"Because I don't think of things like that. Normal people don't think of things like that."

"What were you doing before dinner?"

"Watching football. 'Cept when I had to go fetch the oranges from my house. Lost ten minutes of the game looking for wherever in hell Helen had stashed 'em the night before."

"But you found them."

"Yeah, eventually."

"And you were in a hurry."

"Damn skippy. I had fifty bucks riding on that game."

"That didn't prevent you from loitering in the dining room."

A genuinely blank look met this assertion.

"Cy told us he found you in the dining room eating the stuffed dates."

"Oh yeah. Sorry. Forgot 'bout that. So? What of it?"

"Nothing. However, let me ask you. What kind were you eating? What kind of stuffed dates were they?"

"What are you talking about?"

"There're usually two kinds. One is rolled in sugar, the other isn't."

"Never had none rolled in sugar. Sounds good, though."

"Oh?"

"No, these had almonds in 'em, and some kind of sweet cream Mama—Mrs. Anderson makes."

"You like them?"

He grinned. "I love 'em." And then, briefly, he frowned. "Trouble is, Helen hates 'em. She won't even make 'em for me. Says they're too fattening."

"They are," said Miss Worthing. "Very. Nothing at all slimming about dates." She leaned forward. "Tell me, Bob E., do you drink vodka?"

"Sure. I guess everybody does now and then."

"Were you drinking it on Christmas Day?"

He looked very levelly at her and she knew as plainly as if he had spoken aloud that he was thinking about the vodka in the eggnog.

"No," he said. "Bourbon. All day. I always drink bourbon if I can get it. I'd have been sick as a dog if I switched to vodka after that."

"You're sure."

"Trying to link me up to that vodka jug in the kitchen, ain'tcha?"

"Why, yes. That's precisely what I'm trying to do."

"Well, you can't, 'cause I wasn't drinking no vodka."

"You weren't having bourbon Christmas Eve?"

"No. No, I wasn't."

"You were drinking brandy, weren't you?"

"Yeah."

"You drank a lot."

"What of it? It was a party. It was Christmas Eve."

"But you were angry. Alienated."

"You mean with Ben?"

"No. Much earlier than with Ben."

"What do you mean?"

"I mean earlier. Before dinner. When you and General Anderson disappeared."

"Oh. Then. Yeah."

"And everyone has said that when you reappeared, both of you were manifestly angry with one another."

"So?"

"So why?"

There was no response.

"We already know it was about money, Bob E.," she prompted him.

"Yeah?"

"And we already know you've been trying to float a loan from your mother and sister."

"Yeah?"

"Why?"

"Why shouldn't I?"

"I beg your pardon."

"He was my father, too. I shoulda got some of that insurance money."

"But, Bob E."—again she leaned into it—"why should you care about a measly ten thousand dollars—that is what you asked for, wasn't it? I mean, you're supposed to be so well off, so prosperous. What on earth do you need money for?"

It was at that point, she would later realize, that the conversation effectively reached its conclusion.

Bob E. went completely still for a moment, his only motion a rapid blinking of his eyes. Which, for a moment, she thought a good sign—he was getting ready to lie and it would be a lie she could pick to shreds.

But then the blinking slowed and his tongue darted forth to wet dry lips.

"General Anderson tell you?" he finally asked.

"No. He wouldn't."

And the man went limp with relief.

"Then, if he ain't gonna tell you, I ain't gonna tell you."

"Just like that?"

"Just like that."

"Goddamn it, Bob E.," said Miss Worthing, in wrath revealed, "can't you see we're trying to help here?"

"Seems to me you're trying to fit my neck for a noose."

"Did you do it?"

"Did I do what?"

"Poison the General?"

"You expect me to answer that?"

"If you didn't do it, yes."

"Then you're a fool, lady."

"Get out of here!" She stood and, losing any last measure of patience, all but yelled at him. "Get out of my sight. Go on, get out."

Even Miss Shaw was taken aback by her fury.

"Mattie, calm down."

"Calm down, hell! I'm sick of the sight of the whole bloody lot of 'em. Go on, git," she repeated to Bob E. "Go back to your wife and stew in it together."

"Yeah," said Bob E. "My wife."

"Mattie, where are you going?" called Miss Shaw as Miss Worthing angrily strode past Bob E. to the door.

"A walk. And maybe even for a drive. And while I'm doing that I'll try to make some sense out of what may be the most irritating taradiddle I think I've ever experienced!"

CHAPTER 14

i

But twice around that very long block had no appreciable soothing effect on the roused wrath of Miss Worthing. None of it made any sense. And for one dismally simple reason. To be sure, all of 'em, every blasted one of the people involved had had clear and manifest opportunities and, God knows, there were motives galore.

But what about the damned means?

"We don't even know what the means were," she informed an importunate grackle which had hopped in a hopeful way toward her. When no Christmas crumbs were forthcoming, however, it hopped away, indifferent to the crisis, as it searched the pavement for likely morsels.

"And yet the fact remains," she continued, "it had to be the orange juice, and there had to have been alcohol in the orange juice."

The bird, deciding that this particular female primate was altogether too strange even for a member of that notoriously peculiar family, flew off.

Miss Worthing, trying to regain some measure of calm rationality, turned instead to the contemplation of the weather-vane on the south tower of the Elms. It had veered toward the west.

"Wonderful," she commented bitterly. "And now there's more bad weather on the way."

Whereupon, as is the curious way of the human mind, a datum floated up out of her unconscious. She looked at the tower again and frowned. It was not exactly the most helpful of data. But, at the moment, it represented the only glimmer of hope.

Quickly, she checked in her purse. Yes, she did have her car keys. She did not much like to drive, and Martha liked her doing it even less. But there were times . . .

And presently, she was pulling to the curb in front of Helen and Bob E. Taylor's home. She got out and spent a longish moment contemplating it, as she had done the Elms several minutes before.

"Could be," she muttered and approached.

It was, of course, locked. Or at least, she reminded herself, the front door was locked. It was not exactly unheard of for people to bolt and triple-lock a front door and then wander off leaving a window or auxiliary door open to the wide world.

Wherefore, she prowled . . .

. . . until, finally, after checking every window and every door, she had to admit defeat. There was no way in. The whole thing had probably been sheer foolishness anyway.

"Hey!" a voice rang out on the cold air. "What are you doing there? Who are you?"

From the house behind the Taylors', a man had emerged. He was clearly agitated and all but running to the fence separating the two properties.

Immediately, visions of a holiday weekend in the pokey, or at the least an embarrassing session with Sam Marshall, waltzed all too vividly through her mind when, as she too approached the back fence, she realized that she had had perhaps her first bit of real luck that day. She knew the man. Not well, to be sure, but she knew him. He was some kind of career military man, by no means overly bright, though hardly worthy of the ungracious epithet of "twit" with which he had been dubbed by Helen at the open house. For—by the manifest intercession of all the saints of heaven—he too had been at their open house on Christmas Day.

"Miss Worthing," he said as she approached. "I didn't recognize you at first."

"No reason you should, Colonel West."

"You trying to get in over there?"

"Yes, I was."

"They're all over to the Andersons' house."

"I know; I was just over there."

"How's the General? Tell him I said hello."

"The General's—very sick, Colonel West."

"Oh no! Not the same . . . ?"

She nodded, solemnly.

"Aw, that's a damn shame. Even if it was bound to happen sooner or later. They send you over here?"

She nodded, hoping that it would never occur to this earnest if rather dim individual to ask why she had not, then, been provided with a key.

"But the place is locked up tight as a drum," she said, wondering if she could by any stretch of morality enlist his aid in breaking in.

In the event, however, it was unnecessary.

"Yeah, I know. Bob E.'s real secretive about some project he's got going. Course," he laughed, "can't be too secret."

"What do you mean?"

"You wouldn't believe the smells coming out of there sometimes. I guess most of the neighbors have complained at one time or another."

"Smells? Chemicals?"

"No, it don't smell like that. Besides, he's doing that reconstruction of the Daimler. Got to expect smells now and again with that. No, it's more like"—again he laughed—"you're gonna think I'm nuts, but like overrripe apples mostly. Sometimes it's like somebody spilled a whole keg of beer. But mostly it's apples."

"Well, I guess I'd better go back and get the key," she said.

Whereupon, Lord have mercy, the man said, "Oh, I got a key," and fumbled a key ring out of his pocket.

"You have a key?" she asked faintly, not entirely crediting that such luck could be possible.

"Why, sure. We water their plants when they go away. Feed the fish. That kind of thing."

She took the key, thinking the while sour thoughts about Helen, who would use the man's neighborliness and then write him off so coldly.

She thanked him.

"Just bring it back when you go."

"I will, Colonel West," she promised and, momentarily, was letting herself in the back door.

It was a fitting tribute to Larry's and Ben's powers of description that she had no trouble whatever orienting herself. It took only seconds to locate first the dining room, then the living room, and finally the corridor leading to the master bedroom on the one end and the nursery on the other.

And, in between, the green-painted door.

It was locked. And, for a moment, she had that altogether too-familiar feeling of being thwarted before she had even properly begun. Presently, however, as she bent to peer closer at the lock, she chuckled happily. Finally, things were flowing in the right direction—and after heading pretty steadily downhill for far too long: The lock on the door was but an ordinary domestic interior door lock. Hardly the most insuperable of barriers.

Once more she opened her purse and, after burrowing about a while, withdrew therefrom an assortment of bits of wire and minute hooks that looked like nothing so much as an ultra-modern sculptor's rendition of a sea urchin. Bending down and getting to work with these unlikely implements, it was but a scant half minute before the door yielded to her manipulations and she turned the knob and went in.

ii

It quite took her breath away. Even though, she realized as she stood contemplating it, she should have been expecting it. But she would never have anticipated that it would be so beautiful, albeit in rather an austere fashion. It sat virtually by itself in one enormous room, and an immaculately clean one smelling of cold concrete and carbolic. Only the faintest hint of a fungal smell underlay it.

The furnace was a model of energy efficiency: small, compact, and, she had no doubt of it, powerful and thorough; when Bob E. was finished his ministrations there would be probably not much more than a small pile of potash to be disposed of.

But naturally enough, the truly impressive thing was the vast and shining copper boiler—that and leading from it the great twisting length of the coil. The latter was of glass, as were the towering cylinders, and she was more than a little shaken to think what it must have cost to have those giant things blown to order. Or, for that matter, what the price had been of the copper boiler and the copper solder that held the thing all together of a piece.

And that's not the greatest expense, she thought grimly as she stalked toward a small desk and office chair nestling in a corner of the vast room and utterly diminished by the imposing presence of the apparatus.

Soon, however, as she went drawer by drawer through the desk, she began to frown very seriously indeed.

"Hmmm," she muttered and once more approached the jungle of tubes and piping.

"Now this is very interesting," she said quite aloud as she finished once again tracing with her eye the full length of all that tubing.

Whereupon, to her extreme surprise, a voice behind her said, "I'm sure it is."

iii

It had not been, however, the simple unexpectedness of the voice which had caused Miss Worthing nearly to jump out of her skin. What caused that was the ominous and unmistakable sound of a rifle being cocked.

"Now turn around," Bob E. Taylor commanded. "Slowly."

Briefly, she wondered if she was supposed to put her hands up but decided that, really, there are, after all, limits. She did, however, turn. And very slowly.

He was standing just inside the door, the gun she had heard being cocked resting negligently in the crook of his left arm, his right hand wrapped around the trigger guard. She had not a doubt in the world that he would be able to bring the gun to bear immediately should he have a mind so to do.

"How did you get away?" she asked.

"It was easy. Your aunt got something going and while things were going crazy, I slipped out."

"How did you know I'd be here?"

"I didn't. I followed you."

"Why?"

"I wanted to keep you from finding this."

"Why bother? It isn't exactly the kind of thing you can keep a secret forever, you know."

"Yeah?"

"Yes, Mr. Taylor. Although"—she looked again at the array of tubing—"I can certainly see why you would want to."

"Goddamn you!" he snarled and stepped farther into the room. "Why'd you have to come snooping around here?"

"You know perfectly well why," she snapped back at him. And then, rather naturally curious, she asked, "And what do you intend to do about it?"

"I know what I'd like to do."

"You wouldn't get away with it, you know."

That he seemed to find rather amusing. "And I never expected to hear you singing that tired old song." Amusement, however, quickly passed. "What difference it make?" he barked. "After all, don't this make things look pretty bad for me?" He gestured at the apparatus behind Miss Worthing.

"Oh yes, she said, "very bad. All but for one very small detail."

"What's that?" he said suspiciously.

"There remains the simple fact that I still cannot imagine how this juice got into the General's juice."

"Easy."

"Well then, pray enlighten me."

"I had it in my coat pocket."

"In what?"

"A flask."

"What did you do with it?"

"I hid it."

"Where?"

"What difference does it make?" He stepped menacingly closer.

"It doesn't. We found the flask."

"Good," said Bob E. succinctly and swung the rifle around to point at her.

Not for the first time in her checkered career, Miss Worthing was more than a little chagrined at how very large the hole in the business end of a gun looks when it's pointing at you.

"What on earth do you think you're doing?" she asked, wondering if her voice was shaking as much as she suspected it was.

"I'm going to kill you," said Bob E. "The way I killed the General."

"A body is rather a difficult thing to get rid of," she pointed out.

"There won't be one." He looked meaningfully at the efficient furnace she had so admired earlier. "I got something going here that could make me the biggest thing in America. And in a few hours my wife is going to inherit five or six million dollars and I need that money and I'm not going to let you or anybody else—"

"And that, I think, will be quite far enough." This time it was Larry Worthing who spoke commandingly from the doorway where he stood shoulder to shoulder with Ben Anderson.

iv

Immediately, Bob E. swung the rifle around. Which set off a sequence of events, all of which happened in very rapid succession, so rapid, in fact, that, at the time, they seemed to happen simultaneously: First, the pistol Larry held in his hand went off, setting echoes to ring off the bare walls and the gleaming apparatus looming above them. This was followed a fraction of a second later by a loud, rather shrill, *ping* that set even further echoes scurrying, whereupon a loud shout of rage and pain escaped Bob E. and the rifle seemed almost to be wrenched out of his grip as he clutched at his right hand with his left and a flow of bright crimson welled between his fingers.

The wound, however, was pretty much ignored, even by Bob E. For the rifle, having been knocked out of his grasp by the expertly ricocheted bullet from Larry's pistol, described a great and graceful arc. It seemed to move with agonizing slowness, and even while it was still in the air, Miss Worthing knew exactly what was about to happen.

"Quick!" she shouted. "Get out of here!" Larry and Ben scuttled backward out the door while Miss Worthing grabbed the shocked and rather stupidly staring Bob E. and literally pulled him into the corridor, while behind them the rifle, having landed, went off and a shocking blast of noise ensued.

"No!" shouted Bob E. when, finally, he too realized what was happening, and, with the other three, he stood helpless and spellbound in the doorway and watched his dream undone.

The bullet struck a strut. It seems likely that it had not, perhaps, been soldered too securely, glass being notoriously difficult to work with. The sound of the bullet hitting the copper strut was surprisingly melodious and harmonized pleasantly with the hum of the great glass vessels already aquiver with sympathetic vibrations from all the previous noises.

And for a moment, it appeared that that might be the extent of the damage. Then, however, at first slowly and picking up speed as they fell, first the one and then the other of the two giant holding tanks began to bow their heads to one another. One fell slightly faster than the other, and while the second was still only a smidgen out of true, the other crashed into it. Like icebergs meeting in stormy arctic seas, both tubes shattered with a clash and a ring and a blaze of infinitely refracted light, while in the falling of all those countless shards of glass onto the floor below, the glass coil, too, was swept up in an overwhelming avalanche so that when, presently, it was all over in the chamber, only the copper boiler and the furnace remained, knee-deep, as it were, in shattered glass.

"You okay, Aunt Matilda?" said Larry shakily, when, once more, silence was restored, a silence broken only by the deep, ragged breathing of an equally shattered Bob E.

"Of course I'm all right," said Miss Worthing almost irritably. "Bob E., let's take a look at that hand."

The man was dead-white with shock and dismay and she had to repeat the order before he would obey.

"You'll be all right in a few days," she said. "It's just a flesh wound. And you're a lucky man, besides. With all the bones and tendons in the hand, anything could have happened. Either of you two have a clean handkerchief?"

"We seem fated to have fair damsels less than thrilled by our rescue attempts," said Ben aside to Larry before answering, "Yes, Miss Worthing, I do. Although, frankly, I don't know whether we shouldn't just let him bleed to death."

"First of all, you great ninny," said Miss Worthing severely, "he is in no danger whatever of doing anything so melodramatic. And secondly, whatever for?"

"What for?" bellowed Ben. "We just heard him admit to killing my father."

"And it really did sound like he was ready to plug you, Aunt Matilda."

She clucked. "You mustn't believe everything you hear, boys," she said. "Still and all, I guess you had better take him back to the Elms. I'll follow in my car."

"I can drive myself," growled Bob E., still ashen.

"Are you sure?" asked Miss Worthing.

"Yes."

"Very well, then."

"But you're not going to let him go alone!" protested Ben.

"Why ever not?" said Miss Worthing. "You'll go right back to the Elms, Bob E., won't you!"

Bob E. nodded.

"You see," she explained more than a little gnomically to Ben and Larry, "he rather has to, now." Again she asked Bob E., "You're sure you're all right to drive? Very well, then, let's move it."

CHAPTER 15

i

"You know who did it, Aunt Matilda?" said Larry in the car. She had asked him to drive her back and let Ben do his stewing alone in his car.

"Not to say 'know,' Larry, no."

"But you suspect."

"There are any number of possibilities."

"Even now?"

"Even now."

"But Bob E. . . ."

". . . may well have been the culprit. It certainly doesn't look good for him." Her mind inevitably went back to the large and expensive apparatus now lying shattered in the concrete room. "Indeed, it looks very bad. But the fact is that, other than that ridiculous confession, there's no hard proof. As well as"—she shrugged—"one or two other things."

And that was the last she would say till they pulled up in front of the Elms.

"What happened after I left?" she asked.

Larry snorted derisively. "Aunt Eulalia rather got on her high horse and announced that we should reenact the preparation for Christmas Dinner."

"Oh dear!"

Larry nodded. "In next to no time, things degenerated completely. Everybody was yelling, 'You didn't do that,' while everyone else yelled back, 'Yes, I did!' It was not until we had begun to assemble in the dining room that we realized that you had not returned and that Bob E. was missing."

"How did you know where to find him?"

"Someone had called to talk to Sibyl and said he had just seen you at the Taylors'."

Miss Worthing smiled and uttered a brief prayer of thanksgiving for the punctilio of the military mind.

She led the way indoors.

The return of the caravan from the Taylor house had caused a minor sensation, all the more sensational when Bob E.'s wound was observed. And commented upon. But of far more moment to Miss Worthing than any recrudescence of simple curiosity was the plain and immediately obvious fact that someone had managed to stir up the hornets' nest quite thoroughly. And she had no doubt who was responsible: Emotions had clearly run rather high during her aunt's little experiment in reconstruction.

"Well, Inspector Alleyn," Miss Worthing addressed Lady Fairgrief expansively, "I didn't realize that we had called in the Yard? Any luck finding the missing thread?"

Lady Fairgrief was looking extremely disgruntled. "Well, it seems you already know."

"Don't let it bother you, Aunt Eulalia. It always happens that way."

"Stuff," said her ladyship. "It would have worked if people had behaved themselves."

"But they never do."

"They did in my day."

"Perhaps," said Miss Worthing dubiously. "But we, I am afraid, are all rude moderns here."

Perhaps the most extraordinary comment on the prior proceedings came from Mrs. Anderson who, along with a quite pink-looking Miss Shaw, appeared to be cresting a wave of true mirth: "Oh, Matilda!" she said. "You should have been here. Even I couldn't help laughing—in spite of everything," which earned her a glare of the greatest possible malignance from Lady Fairgrief.

The others, for the most part, had found nothing whatever

257

to laugh about. Later, Miss Worthing would be told the details. And the upshot: How everyone in the piece had tried, more or less in good faith, to duplicate what he or she had done the day before—and almost immediately been challenged by someone else purporting to remember the sequence of events rather differently. In next to no time, tempers had flared and words had grown heated until each person was all but accusing some other person of having been the culprit and basing that accusation on little more than some (usually) minor disparity in the accused's role in the reenactment.

There was a piquancy to the picture which, perhaps one day, she would have the time fully to relish. There were, however, rather more pressing—and depressing—tasks at hand.

"Sibyl, do you have a magnifying glass?"

Mrs. Anderson looked quite taken aback by the question. "Well, yes, I believe I do. It's in the OED in the library. Oh, no. I forgot. That one got broken. Wait a minute." She went to a highboy and, after a moment's rummaging about in a drawer, held up a jeweler's loupe. "Will this do?" she asked dubiously.

"It will do splendidly," said Miss Worthing.

"Mother," said Ben, "what on earth—"

"It's useful for buying crystal," said his mother, handing the loupe to Miss Worthing.

"Thank you, Sibyl. Now, all of you. Wait here. And do you possess your soul in patience, Ben," she admonished, seeing him about to speak. "Martha, come along."

ii

They stopped in the kitchen just long enough to provide themselves with a pair of rubber gloves from under the sink and a bag in a lurid-yellow plastic on which was emblazoned in scarlet that Wing Wah sold only the freshest fish—the whole being repeated, it was to be presumed, in Chinese characters.

"Where are we going, Mattie?" asked Miss Shaw, who had been, as had everyone, more than a little piqued by Miss Worthing's obvious access of good cheer.

"All in good time, Martha; all in good time," she said and led the way out the kitchen door into the back garden.

The two women were enthusiastic gardeners. Their own personal preferences, however, distinctly ran to the exuberant, luxuriant, even wild, growth perhaps more characteristic of nineteenth-century tastes than twentieth. Not so the backyard of the Elms; indeed, it was a very monument to the suburban garden. Lush lawns as immaculate as those in front and as dotted about with elm trees spread out from a flagged patio (replete with brick barbecue and rough wooden picnic table) all the way to the bottom of the garden, where the kitchen garden, barren now, the ground covered with a mulch of straw and cornstalks, awaited a new season. At either side, flower beds ran down the fences and even clustered in little rings about the trunks of the elms. After a moment of gazing about, it was toward the back and the kitchen garden that Miss Worthing proceeded.

"What are you looking for?" demanded Miss Shaw.

"You'll see, dear," repeated Miss Worthing maddeningly and presently uttered a little cry of gladness and marched across the somewhat sodden mulch to a gleaming metal box.

It stood sandwiched between a small plantation of apricot and peach trees and the Concord grapevine covering the back wall, and for a moment both women regarded it with varying degrees of satisfaction and apprehension.

It was almost a paradigm of the scientific composter. A hinged lid, at about chest height, opened up into a bin into which sundry organic refuse might be tossed, while at the bottom was another hinged lip, which could be lowered and whence said refuse, mulched now to good fertile topsoil after the sundry actions of bacteria and bugs and worms within, could be shoveled.

"Here we are," said Miss Worthing with great satisfaction. "Hand me those gloves, would you?"

Miss Shaw handed them over and watched with scarce-concealed distaste as Miss Worthing proceeded to open the top flange of the composter.

Almost immediately and in spite of the chilly stillness of the day, a rich shout of rotting oranges emanated from within.

"Do be careful, Mattie!" said Miss Shaw, shying instinctively backward.

"Oh, fiddle, Martha," said Miss Worthing impatiently. "How can you be careful doing something like this? Lord, how *very* unpleasant. But do look. Henry certainly had it down cold. Layers of garbage and layers of soil. Perfect. We should be so tidy. Now, I'm quite sure we won't have to go far, thank God. Yes, I'm right. Here we are!"

A layer was revealed of orange-rind halves mixed all anyhow with the outer leaves of cauliflower, potato peelings, celery leaves, onion trimmings, and the end snips of green beans.

"I think it safe to assume that the top layer would be the most recent addition and the contents would indeed appear to be the detritus of a holiday meal."

Miss Shaw's answer was a muffled squeal through a tightly pursed mouth.

Miss Worthing then proceeded to hold the top open with her left hand while with her right she grubbed cheerfully about in the noisome debris, excavating reamed-out orange rind after reamed-out orange rind. Each of these she cast into a little pile atop the plastic bag at her feet until a goodly mound of them rose threatening to topple and engulf her shoes.

"That should do it," she said, after a glance downward.

"One would hope so," said Miss Shaw faintly, her nostrils decidedly pinched.

Miss Worthing slammed the top of the composter shut and, stooping down, hoisted the entire bag up to rest on the lid. One or two of the rinds fell off and rolled away.

"Martha, would you mind?" she said absently.

"Yes, I would," said Miss Shaw.

Miss Worthing looked up in some surprise.

"I'm not wearing rubber gloves," said Miss Shaw pointedly.

"Oh, very well," said Miss Worthing and recovered the peels.

She then proceeded to pore over the orange peels millimeter by millimeter, holding the peel under examination with her right hand, turning it first this way and then that, as she held the jeweler's loupe to the left lense of her glasses while she closed her right eye. Each one she held up in an attempt to catch what light there was coming through the cloud cover.

And evidently it was sufficient unto the day, for with the smallest grunt of satisfaction, she placed first one and then two and finally half a dozen of the juiced-out oranges into the yellow plastic bag. As for the rest, she kicked open the bottom tray of the composter and tossed them in, where they lay looking bright and immeasurably cheerful against the deep brown of the compost.

"Find what you were looking for?" asked Miss Shaw doubtfully.

"Rather more than that," said Miss Worthing, and then she was actually laughing out loud. "Oh Lord, I do love it when a hunch works out."

Almost immediately, however, she sobered, observing with austere disgust, "you know, it really took a sick mind to think of this one. Come along, Martha." And without more ado she led the way back to the house.

iii

"You knew all along," said Miss Worthing.

"No," said General Anderson weakly. "It wasn't until after you said 'Everclear.'"

"And you weren't going to help me!"

For a long time there was no response but the none-too-rhythmic breathing of the supine man. She was getting ready to repeat her half-accusatory statement when he spoke. "No. I wasn't. No more. I was—am—caught in a cleft stick, Mattie. No matter which way I go, I do something wrong."

"But the guilty party . . ."

"Is a guilty party." He sighed and after a moment added, "I am not without guilt in the matter myself, you know. I see that now. Not that"—she watched as a quick pain-filled frown flitted across his face—"it's of any concern to me now. As I need hardly remind you."

Miss Worthing's troubled eyes met the grim ones of Mrs. Wu across the bed.

"The guilt is of concern only to the guilty." It was a whisper, a soft murmur. The coda was even softer: "And the living."

The man was once again clearly fading into his twilight. This time, however, all present knew only too well that from it he might very well never emerge again.

"Henry!" said Mrs. Anderson, urgently bending over her husband. "Henry!"

iv

And below, in the living room, the others—yet again—waited. Though this time with a difference. Something was definitely afoot.

Perhaps, to most of them, the look of grim triumph on Miss Worthing's face would not have been as obvious as it was to Larry. What had stirred them was the efficient way in which Miss Worthing had managed to galvanize them into action. Clearly they were on to some kind of denouement.

"Sibyl? Have you a typewriter?"

"Of course. It's in the den."

"Fetch it, please. Martha, fill your pens and bring a fresh notebook. Aunt Eulalia, you're coming with us. No, Billy, you will wait here. With the others. No one else is to move out of the living room. No one. Do I make myself quite clear?"

"Quite clear" had indeed been the general consensus. It had nevertheless not prevented Ben from standing in the doorway eyeing the little procession up the stairs—Miss Worthing and Miss Shaw thumping Lady Fairgrief's chair up the stairs, while behind them came Mrs. Anderson bearing Miss Shaw's notebooks and pen in one hand and in the other a typewriter that had been considered portable somewhere around the time of the Korean War.

"Something's up," said Ben unnecessarily.

"Oh, very good, Ben," said Larry.

Ben turned sharply to look at his friend, but Larry's face was bland and noncommittal, his attention still fixed on the little band of elderly women as they disappeared around the landing of the stairs.

"I don't understand your aunt."

"Makes two of us," said Larry. He turned and gave Ben a slight half-smile.

"You worked with her on a case once, didn't you?"

Larry nodded. "I even found the clinching evidence. Even if," he added diffidently, "I didn't know it was the clinching evidence till days later."

Ben's face clouded. He gazed over the assembled, his glance coming to rest on his brother-in-law. Bob E. was sitting hunched over in a chair in front of the fireplace, a bottle of Jack Daniels at his feet and in his unbandaged hand a largish tumbler in which were at least five fingers of neat bourbon and from which he punctuated the passing minutes with considerable slugs.

Larry followed Ben's gaze and commented, "He's going to wind up a total alcoholic if he doesn't watch it."

"Goddamn it, Larry," Ben swore softly, "I would have taken a Bible oath that Bob E. . . ."

"So would we all, Ben," said Larry. He put a hand on his friend's shoulder. "But we'll just have to wait and see, won't we?"

Arletta, meanwhile, sat in her usual corner of the couch. No one ever knew precisely what she was thinking or, for that matter, if the processes of her mind could even be dignified with such an ordered concept as thinking. From the relative calm she had finally reached during her interview, she had, it appeared, reverted once more to a state of abiding fear—the bogeys of a lifetime having proved too strong and resumed their old habitual sway.

And once again in the embrasure of the window, Cy and Bette Wanda took what comfort they could of each other. But Bette Wanda had spent just enough time in the outer reaches of the legal professions to know that justice was such a very chancy thing. Particularly if you were poor and others involved happened to be rich. She had no faith in the impartiality of Miss Worthing. Impartiality had been to her so rare a thing that, in her personal pantheon, it was less a virtue than a myth, like Santa Claus or the Tooth Fairy. She had lived too long with the echoes of "white trash," "redneck," "dumb cracker," "Okie bitch," and the like in her ears to be at all sanguine now.

And Cy, too, young though he was, knew—rather more

than anyone should ever have to know—the force of unreasoned prejudice. He was, moreover, far too intelligent not to see the clear force of the considerable evidence against him.

Only Billy McClure stood placidly alert, watching the inhabitants of the room fretting, each in his own way, as the minutes passed by.

Mercifully for everyone, Mary Elizabeth was asleep, rocked in the cradle of her mother's arms. As usual, Helen's whole attention was rapt upon the child, though even she was not unaware of the general sense of waiting: Every now and then her head raised up from its besotted contemplation of her daughter as she glared about the room, her eyes finally coming to rest on the bowed head of her boozing husband before returning to her sleeping child.

And so silent had the room become but for the relentless ticking of the minutes by the clock and the crackling of the fire that when, in the corridor upstairs, there was the sound of murmuring voices, followed by a heavy thumping on the stairs which could only be Lady Fairgrief's chair, though no one moved or even changed position, yet the tension in the room was redoubled till it seemed like so many harp strings pulled suddenly taut to the breaking point.

And through the door came Lady Fairgrief, pushed by Mrs. Anderson, who parked the ancient crone, as she requested, near the fireplace before resuming her own accustomed place in the Sheraton chair. There—almost as though there were nothing in particular going on—she reached down and pulled a piece of crochet work into her lap and began rapidly plying the hook. Only the fact that her face was an expressionless mask and her eyes sedulously refused to meet those of anyone else showed to what an extent she was holding on to herself.

And then came Miss Shaw and Miss Worthing. The former proceeded without a word to a chair near the back of the living room where, still without a word, she flipped open her steno book, uncapped her fountain pen, and in a trice was as ready as ever to take notes.

"You needn't bother," said Miss Worthing.

Miss Shaw looked up and nodded. "I know. But I think I would rather be busy."

"Suit yourself," said Miss Worthing. And as she had done

the night before, she walked through the room to take up a place in front of the fireplace and turned to face the rest of them, backlit by the flicker of the flames.

In afteryears, to many of those present, the whole scene would take on a quality of the fantastic, as though the salamander of old had suddenly appeared to them in the burning heart of the fire in order to instruct them in the mechanics of murder.

CHAPTER 16

i

"Would you all please come a little closer," said Miss Worthing wearily. "I take no joy in shouting all this." She sighed. "This has been a painful experience to me, as no doubt it has been for all of us. But it's almost over now."

"Is Dad . . ." burst out Cy.

Mrs. Anderson looked up, though still her eyes did not meet those of her son. "He will be soon, Cy. Jessica said she would come for us so we can be with him. Go on, Matilda."

"Yes, Sibyl. I suppose I had better. I'm just wondering where I should begin."

In response to which Larry uttered a humorless little snort and then said, "Why not at the beginning? With all of us guilty till proven innocent."

"Don't be bitter, Larry," admonished Lady Fairgrief. "Sometimes it's the way one has to proceed. Matilda?"

"She's quite right, Larry," said Miss Worthing. "But the fact remains"—her eyes swept the room—"that every one of you did have at least some motive for wishing to remove poor Henry. All of you certainly had an opportunity, and God knows you all had access to the means.

"At least so it appeared."

"Goddamn it," Ben erupted. "Do we have to go over all this again? It's so bloody obvious that Bob E. did it that—"

"Will you keep your shirt on, young man," snapped Miss Worthing. "What do you expect me to do? Come right out with it and point a finger and announce that so-and-so did it? I should think that there have been quite enough of bald assertions unsupported by anything but hotheadedness and personal animosity."

"I don't—" began Ben.

". . . know what you're talking about," Miss Worthing cut him off. "So just pipe down. It wouldn't be fair to the innocent, much less to the guilty, not to provide them with some reasoning behind our discovery. Good God, Ben, your mother's a theologian; didn't you ever study logic or scientific method yourself?"

"Yes, I did."

"Good," said Miss Worthing. "Then perhaps I may continue. Rationally.

"As I was saying, each of you had means, motive, and opportunity. I won't trouble you with motives. Not here, as it were, in public. Each of you knows what your individual motives might have been.

"And so to opportunity. Again, it seems fairly obvious that any one of you could at one time or another have monkeyed with the juice. Each of you was in close proximity to the first, second, or third pitchers, or two of them, or even all three, long enough and alone enough to have poured something into it. In some instances," she admitted diffidently, "it would have required considerable daring to seize the moment and act. But," she added dryly, "when millions are at stake, I daresay most persons set on murder would seize any moment they could."

"But are you sure it was the orange juice?" said Arletta. "Why, I thought," she addressed Lady Fairgrief, "that you said you didn't see how it could be the juice."

"Process of elimination," barked her ladyship in reply.

"Just so," agreed Miss Worthing.

"But the eggnog."

"No," said Miss Worthing. "Too many people said that that

vodka jug was unopened and what was in the nog can only be vodka."

Suddenly Miss Worthing laughed—a genuine laugh of amusement. "We should count ourselves lucky that we have as many—" She hesitated; she had been about to say "heavy drinkers" but realized abruptly that it sounded altogether too depraved that way. ". . . sophisticated palates," she compromised. "The mind rather boggles at the thought of something like this happening at a temperance rally. Oh well"—she shrugged—"maybe it wouldn't be so difficult."

"You're dithering, Matilda," said Lady Fairgrief.

"So I am, Aunt Eulalia; so I am. Very well. Orange juice. Actually, Arletta, you bring us to a very good and indeed a very hard point."

"I do?"

"Yes, you do. Which is to say the means by which this thing was done. Simply put, what was it?"

"What do you mean, what was it?" demanded Ben. "It was the juice."

"No, Ben," said Miss Worthing, "the juice was merely the carrier, the conveyance. The means itself was some form of alcohol.

"Vodka—which certainly might have passed muster, though Henry assures me it would not have done so—was ruled out necessarily almost from the first."

"But the flask," said Cy excitedly.

"Patience, child," commanded Lady Fairgrief, irritated by the interruption.

"That left us with what each of you folks was drinking," Miss Worthing continued: "Bette Wanda and Arletta were drinking orange blossoms. Gin. However, gin, with its esters and juniper flavoring, is distinctive and sharp, and, in quantity in orange juice, enough to set the teeth on edge."

"It would have had to be a lot," observed Ben.

"Yes," agreed Miss Worthing. "A small amount of ethyl alcohol would have discomfited your father. But it wouldn't have killed him.

"So gin is ruled out. What now about Ben? Ben was absorbing Gibsons. Gin again. And what could be said about orange blossoms goes double for Gibsons, what with the vermouth and onion juice that go into the making of them. And all of you, much less Henry, would have certainly tasted that.

"Larry had Scotch in what Ben referred to as his repellent English fashion, which is to say a splash of soda and no ice. Again, a salty, rather acrid, drink which, if added to the juice, would have been immediately noticeable.

"Cy was drinking a kir—white wine and *crème de cassis,* or black-currant brandy. Apart from the fact that the alcohol content is virtually negligible, the brandy would have added a distinctive color to the juice and moreover would have floated, for the most part, on the surface of the juice, which, compared to a kir, has a much higher specific gravity.

"Sibyl had a beer. One beer. Now, first of all, that is hardly a quantity sufficient, and secondly, again we would have a most distinctive flavor.

"Helen sat in the living room the whole time of preparation, and as you all, intimately involved though certainly she was, and certainly she had a motive, she had, however, effectively no access to the juice.

"Bob E., too, had access to the juice. He was in the dining room eating dates when Cy brought in the first pitcher of the orange juice. Bob E., however, says that he was drinking bourbon."

"He was," said Ben.

"But—" began Cy.

Before the word was hardly out of his mouth, however, Miss Worthing cut him off. "Hold your tongue. We're getting to it," and in virtually the same breath continued her narration. "Finally, of those present, Billy and Lady Fairgrief had neither access to the juice nor any particular motive. Now have I left anyone out?"

No one said anything. Then, in a puzzled, wondering tone, Bette Wanda said, "But you've just eliminated everybody."

"So I did," said Miss Worthing.

"Then the alcohol *wasn't* in the juice?" said Arletta.

"Oh, it was."

"But how did it get there?"

In response to which Miss Worthing held up the bag of orange peels, from which she extracted one on the rind side of which a circle had been drawn in black grease pencil. "I would judge by means of an eighteen-gauge hypodermic syringe."

ii

"Once I realized that, my focus began to get rather a bit narrower. There are, given that, only two people who could have done this thing. Am I not right, Bob E.?"

All eyes in the room went to the man, who was staring in a none-too-focused way, looking dazed and rather sick.

"I suppose," continued Miss Worthing, "that someone of us should have seen it a great deal earlier. I mean, here is Bob E. Taylor, hotshot entrepreneur, and in the automobile-supply business. How long have you been experimenting with alternate fuels, Bob E.? A year? Two years? However long it took to eat up whatever capital you had and Helen's marriage portion as well."

"I thought it looked familiar," Larry suddenly shouted. "It was a still."

"Of course," said Miss Worthing. "But rather a special kind of still. All those enormous glass tubes means that Bob E. was in the habit of manufacturing—or trying to manufacture—quantities of pure anhydrous alcohol, the purest form of ethyl alcohol there is—and the only kind, incidentally, on which an internal combustion engine can run effectively.

"And furthermore," she went on relentlessly, "he was keeping it all a deep, dark secret. As indeed, who could blame him?

"I didn't find any licenses in your little stillroom, Bob E. Were you seriously going to try to get away with it?"

"The murder?" asked Cy, only to be silenced by a swift glance of irritation from Miss Worthing.

"That whole operation is completely illegal. There's not a government seal or lock anywhere on the thing, nor any sign of the book of licenses it requires.

"It must have looked like such a sure thing," she said, not unkindly. "But there you were, all your money gone and suddenly, unexpectedly, out of nowhere comes a new glut of cheap oil on the international market and you are left holding a very expensive baby.

"And so you needed money. Badly. You tried to get it. You tried to get some from your mother. She wouldn't. You tried to get the General to invest in your scheme. He wouldn't. But there was a way you could get some and get it fast. If you slipped some of that pure ethanol of your own manufacture into the General's orange juice and your wife inherited several million dollars, everything would be just hunky-dory again, right?

"No, don't answer—and don't you, either," she said severely to Ben, who was casting black looks upon his brother-in-law and had opened his mouth to speak. "Don't be so quick to condemn. You're hardly in the most creditable position yourself."

"But he . . ." protested Ben.

"Did he?" asked Miss Worthing. "Okay. Let us assume for a moment that the means of the General's murder was, in fact, the alcohol Bob E. was so busily brewing. How did it get into the oranges?"

"You said a syringe," said Larry.

"So I did, and so it seems. But syringes are not exactly easily come by in California. It is true one could hop into one's car and drive up to Oregon and stop at the first animal-husbandry-supply depot and buy some there; you don't need a prescription in Oregon. But let us not needlessly complicate this. It seems that someone essentially seized the moment, as we mentioned earlier, and, as far as I know, no one drove overnight to Klamath Falls and back.

"No, we must look at syringes. Access thereto. If this were fifty years ago, I would say let's rest with Bob E. Syringes filled with gasoline were not infrequently used to clear airlocks in a fuel line in those primitive days of the motor car."

Bob E., in spite of himself, looked up at her upon that utterance as though she had only recently come from the moon.

"Those days, however, are gone. But there is one of you who not all that long ago was accused of having deliberately hidden quite a number of syringes—and other medical paraphernalia."

Helen finally looked up from her child. A quick, calculating look that went immediately back to her child. She said, however, not a word.

"Where are they, Helen?" asked Miss Worthing.

Helen shrugged.

"Yes," she said. "I had them."

"Where are they?"

Again there came that shrug of utter indifference.

"I haven't seen them since we moved. Why don't you ask Bob E."

Her husband's head turned slowly, as though his neck were stiff, to look upon his wife, his face devoid of expression.

"All right, Bob E.," said Miss Worthing, "where were they?"

The man licked his lips as a look of perplexity flitted across his face.

Presently, very, very gently, Miss Worthing said, "Never mind, Bob E. You needn't bother answering. I know that you didn't know. . . now," she admitted candidly. "I really wasn't sure. I am now. But I did have to ask. Although, to be frank, I was already pretty certain."

iii

"And that was because of a piece of real stupidity. It is a mercy to all of us that people who have no compunction about doing these things all but invariably go that one step too far. In this case, someone, sometime during the night, tried very hard to bollix my investigation. It certainly did achieve the goal of confusing things. And people.

"But, first of all, it had to be someone who knew this house rather well. Where things were kept—the decanter of vodka in the library, for instance. And yet, at the same time, it had to be someone who had payed insufficient attention to what was going on yesterday so that two mistakes were made, one by one, and one relatively minor, though in the end quite significant.

"The big mistake was not being observant enough during dinner yesterday to notice that no one was drinking vodka. And so, when it came time to monkey about with things, whoever it was used up first the vodka in the study and then, in a piece of transcendent folly, opened a previously unopened jug of vodka.

"The small mistake was this." She produced the flask.

"But it's Bob E.'s!" protested Cy.

"Of course it is. And what were you two drinking out of it?" she asked Ben and Larry.

"Bourbon," said Ben. "It was bourbon. He shared it with us. At your open house."

"Yes. Bourbon. Bob E.'s tipple of choice. And today, this morning, we find it nestling behind the étagère in the dining room with vodka in it. No fingerprints on it, either. Cy," she asked with a wry grin, "what did you say Bob E. was engaged in when you brought in the OJ?"

"Eating stuffed dates."

Miss Worthing held up the polished silver thing. "I can't avoid leaving prints all over this thing while I'm handling it now. And I, I may point out, have been eating nothing near as sticky as dates."

"And furthermore," said Ben, as he and Larry exchanged a glance, "when the three of us finished that excellent bourbon at your house—"

"Bob E. took it and gave it to Helen before coming back to help us pour wine," Larry finished for him.

"And so, folks," Miss Worthing concluded, "it is, in the end, really rather easy. All of you, to be sure, had motives, and all of you, had the opportunity. But only two of you had access to the real means. And in the end, only one, Helen Anderson Taylor, had the complete access necessary—to the ethanol, the syringes, and to a box of oranges brought and left overnight in her home, to be brought back to the Elms to provide her father with orange juice during Christmas dinner.

"Only one thing puzzles me, Helen. Did you ask your mother to bring oranges to your Christmas Eve party because you were too lazy to go to the store? Or had you already, long before your father threatened to cut your adopted child out of his will, decided to kill him?"

EPILOGUE

Helen, meanwhile, continued blithely to dandle her child, still, by the mercy of God, asleep. Presently, however, the ensuing and ongoing silence must finally have penetrated whatever passed for her consciousness. She gave the babe one final bump and clasped her to her bosom. She reached to the floor and hauled the strap of her baby bag to her shoulder, settled it into place, and stood up. She cast only the briefest of glances at Miss Worthing, although, short as it was, it was replete with the most incalculable loathing. Then she spoke: "Come on, Bob E. It's time we went home. Mary Elizabeth should be getting ready for bed."

The others in the room could only gape blankly at the utter arrogance of the remark. All, that is, but Bob E. For a moment, his deep breathing was clearly audible as he drew breath after breath through flared and whitened nostrils. Then he got up, walked slowly to his wife and, with infinite tenderness, gently but firmly disengaged the child from its mother's arms. A spasm of hell-cat fury swept across the woman's face, to be instantly replaced by shocked disbelief as, loud and sharp in the palpable silence of the room, Bob E. slapped her across the face.

And from her chair, her mother, in a clipped and restrained voice, spoke. "You'd better go home now, Helen," she commanded. "And don't come back. Ever."

The expression which then replaced the shock on the woman's face was actually one of petulant indignation.

"Well, if you're all going to be that way about it," said she. She reached to retrieve her child and, receiving only a stony-faced shake of the head from her husband, turned and, quite literally, flounced out of the room.

A second or two later, they all heard the front door slam behind her.

"Is she sane?" asked Larry of no one in particular.

"Is anyone who commits murder quite sane?" asked Miss Worthing in reply.

"And you just let her walk out of here?" Cy was on his feet, his fair complexion mottled.

"What do you propose I do?" asked Miss Worthing.

"Call the police! Call the sheriff."

Miss Worthing shook her head.

"Aren't you going to do anything?"

"Nothing," said Miss Worthing.

"Nothing!"

"Nothing," said Cy's mother. "It's the way your father wanted it, Cy. I'm not sure I can agree with him. But we went up there and told him, you know. I still don't altogether know if he really understood what we were telling him."

Miss Worthing made an indeterminate sound and then added, "No, Sibyl, I think he did. He had already figured out the business with the oranges."

"He did?" said Ben.

"Oh yes," said Miss Worthing. "He, after all, knew about Bob E.'s still. So when I mentioned a certain bottle of Everclear"—she winked at Cy, who responded not at all—"he had already put the whole thing together. And, I must tell you, refused to tell me. The only thing I had to go on was a purely involuntary look of anguish that crossed his face when I mentioned it."

"Never mind that," said Cy in a strangled voice. "What about Helen?"

"Nothing," repeated his mother. And, rising from her chair, she went to him. "He said that when all is said and done she is his daughter and that she—and we—will have to live with what's been done. Just as he said of you, my poor long-suffering son, that he loved you and would love you—and pray for you—forever."

"'For the prayers of parents make firm the foundations of houses,'" for some unaccountable reason, Ben found himself quoting.

"Do they?" His mother looked at him. "One wonders sometimes. But never mind that now." She went to Bob E., who carefully handed her the baby. "I'm sorry, Bob E. I don't know what to say except that we'll help in any way we can." And then there was steel in her voice. "Only just do not ask me to see or speak to Helen ever again."

"I'm sorry, too, Mrs. Anderson," her son-in-law said. "I guess I loved her a whole lot more than she loved me."

"That," said Mrs. Anderson, "seems to have been true of rather a lot of us."

"Mr. Taylor?" It was Lady Fairgrief, who had remained most uncharacteristically silent through most of the proceedings. "I want to tell you that I think you must be a very good man. Right from the very first you tried to protect Helen, didn't you? All the way from pouring that juice down the drain to assaulting my niece."

Bob E. flushed and turned to Miss Worthing. "I'm sorry about all that."

"Don't think of it. I'm sorry we managed to destroy your still."

"I can build that up again. I—I suppose I should be thanking you, ma'am," he added. "But if you don't mind, right now, I can't."

He took back his sleeping daughter, and without another word he, too, left.

The front door had barely closed behind him when, in the doorway, Jessica Wu stood, her face an empty mask.

"Sibyl!" she called.

Mrs. Anderson turned. "Is it time, dear?"

"I think so."

"Cy, bring Lady Fairgrief. No, Eulalia, he would want you there. Ben, go on ahead."

Arletta Taylor rose from her couch. Miss Worthing thought that she and Bette Wanda would now beat a hasty retreat from the house in which they had been effectively kept prisoner for the last day and a half. Instead, Arletta went to Mrs. Anderson and said, "Sibyl, honey, you get on up there and now. Later on you'll thank the Lord for the last moments you had to spend with him. BW and I will clean up down here and rustle up something for the folks that are gonna be coming by. Folks liked the General. They'll be comin' and they'll want something to eat and drink."

For a moment, it almost looked as though this simple gesture of plain country sense would finally break through Sibyl Anderson's reserve. But as always she mastered herself, thanked Arletta formally, and was gone after her family out the door and up the stairs. Bette Wanda and Arletta, without a word, moved into the dining room and began to clear the unsightly detritus.

Miss Shaw, too, hauled herself upright and, briefly, she and Miss Worthing communed silently with one another. Finally, Miss Shaw jerked her head toward the dining room.

"Come on, Mattie," she said and set her notebook down. "Arletta's right. Let's get cracking."